Vampire Vic

Vampire Vic Trilogy, Book 1

Harris Gray

To Annie who pushed, guided, chided, and believed;
To Jen who agreed to get macho quirky;
To Peter who never met a sexy donut till now;
To DeAnna who probably should have tightened this too;
To Julie and Kathryn who are the only ones who know how to tell us apart;

For everyone we want to bite, but somehow resist.

ALSO BY HARRIS GRAY

Java Man

THETHERSON, AS NIGHT APPROACHES

I am a vampire. I am a vampire.

I am Vampire Vic. For two years they've been asking for it. Tonight, I will own it.

So thought Victor Thetherson, leaning forward so that he could just see the back of the head and shoulders of his employee, David Copperfield. Unfortunately not the magician.

Friday, 4:52 p.m., the close of a terrible week. Victor had caught hell for budget overruns on a big project, and now they were two weeks late on a report due to corporate. And yet his accounting staff had seen fit to knock off early for happy hour, leaving the office nearly deserted.

Conditions were perfect.

I can do this. I am a vampire. One bite and we'll both be changed, for the better. David needs it…

At the very least, David deserved it. He had been "putting the finishing touches" to the overdue report for the past two weeks. Victor had spent so many of those three hundred and thirty-six hours peering through his small office window, he saw David's framed, silhouetted bust when he closed his eyes.

David capped a series of chair stretches by limbering up his veiny neck like a boxer about to answer the bell. Victor practiced some vampire speak to amp himself up.

Insolent pup, do you think that extra layer of muscle will stop my razor-sharp fangs from plowing into your throat!? Go on, David Copperfield, stand in front of the gym mirror and grunt your way through another set of shoulder shrugs—your blood will spill no less easily! Your fit heart will only pump the blood all the quicker into the ravenous mouth of the vampire!

Victor gagged at the thought of a mouthful of warm blood and clamped his hand to his mouth in case retching progressed to hurling. Put his head to the desk and thought about assets equaling liabilities plus equity, and when that didn't work, bunnies wrestling kitties (bunnies victorious), until the spasm settled, leaving behind a sheen of sweat on his desktop and a bad taste in his mouth.

What is wrong with me?! Why do I suck so bad?

I don't suck, Victor reminded himself. *That's the problem.*

David mouse-clicked with a theatrical flourish and shut off his monitor, tidying his desk for the weekend. With a snarl Victor jumped to his feet. *I can do this!* Time to suck, in a good way.

Wincing on the pin pricks of an early-stage limb nap, he shook his leg until blood flow resumed and hobbled to yank open his office door. Like magic, David Copperfield was standing there.

"G'night," said David, gym bag slung over his shoulder, otherwise empty-handed. He leaned to the side to check his reflection in the window. "Whew!" His eyebrows elevated to theatrical heights. "What a week, huh?"

"David," Victor said as pleasantly as he could.

"Sir," David said with a hint of happy sarcasm.

Oh boy does he deserve it. Victor bolstered his resolve while noting that David had spritzed himself with another few bucks' worth of *Beckham*. Would there be time to wet-wipe his throat before the bite? "The Westchase report?"

"Got it right here." David hustled back to his desk, returning on a jog. He handed Victor a file folder.

It was suspiciously light. "The bulk of it is

electronic...?"

"You got a classic case of monitor strain going there." David air-traced the stress lines around Victor's eyes. "Your generation never evolved the ability to survive in the digital age." He nodded at the thin folder and stuck a piece of Juicy Fruit in his mouth. "So I kept it old school for you—that's the whole kit and caboodle, VV."

Two years ago, Victor Barton Thetherson was bitten by a vampire. At the time, Victor was forty-six, possessed of a balding comb-over and sixty extra pounds, with a disrespectful, underachieving staff of accountants, a disappointed ex-wife, and a daughter who would one day be someone else's underachieving, disrespectful, disappointed employee and spouse.

Upon entering the office the next morning, Victor's physical changes made it obvious he had become a vampire. He was met with fear, excitement and wonder. But when he didn't bite anybody, when he was overheard stuttering on the phone as his boss chewed his ass for missing another deadline, it was a return to business as usual. With the addition of his new nickname, Vampire Vic.

Victor showed just a smidge of one of his fangs. After tonight, the name would have a whole different vibe.

David's hands hovered over his perfect coif like a gypsy at her crystal ball, sensing static frizz. He nodded at the can of mousse on the far corner of Victor's desk. "May I?"

"You may not." Victor opened the Westchase folder. "David, Jeez..." He caught himself in time; his boss frowned on profanity. "...geez whiz. All you have here is a few bullet points."

"Did I forget the cover page?"

"No," Victor squawked, brandishing the folder's entire contents, bullet points in one hand and cover page in the other, for David's consideration.

"I know, right?" David joined Victor in his outrage. "That was a bitch of an assignment you gave me."

"A bitch of an assignment?" Victor chirped. "The audit was done in June. This was a task you were given three weeks to complete. Followed by two one-week extensions. I could have finished this audit report in three days."

"VV, surely you jest."

Victor couldn't prevent his head from slumping against his office door frame. If he bit David now, the report would be another week late. He couldn't afford to give his boss any more ammunition. He waggled the folder. "We have to finish this tonight."

David looked puzzled. "We? Tonight?"

"David, yes, WE. Our ass is on the line. Asses."

David was clearly upset. "Let's get another extension."

"No, David, no. Jay called three times today, looking for this Westchase report. I promised him he'd have it by the end of the day."

"Why would you promise that?"

"I promised it, because this morning when I asked you if the report was almost done, you said yes."

"To be fair, you asked if I was finished, and I was."

Victor growled softly. David looked uncomfortable, fidgeting and grimacing. Was he suddenly realizing the danger he was in? Regretting this day, and his whole wasted life? Petrified at the prospect of being held captive after hours in an empty office building, with the vampire?

"I don't know if this is jock itch, or something else, but I should spray it with some Tinactin or something." David stood on tiptoes to survey Victor's desk.

"No, I don't have anything for that." Victor was recalibrating his attack. They would pull a college-esque all nighter, standing over his computer together just before dawn, both of them bleary-eyed and celebrating the satisfying click of the Send button. He would bid David adieu, and then jump him at the door to his Mini Cooper, drink him dry and send his soul to Hell. "Let's see your audit workpapers."

"They are right there, my man," said David, pointing at his desk drawer. "Don't wait for me, I'll hit the ground running as soon as I get back from the drug store."

"You're not leaving," said Victor.

"Vic, I gotta," David whined, squirming like a poorly potty-trained toddler. "I got the itch, real bad."

"Fine. As long as you bring me back something. We'll eat in here while we work."

Victor found the Westchase audit materials in David's drawer, under a stack of fantasy baseball stat sheets and an impressive collection of more traditional fantasy mags. By 5:30 he had reorganized the paperwork to enable them to plow through in assembly line fashion. He marveled at his ingenuity and snacked on Little Debbies. Called David and left a voicemail.

After leaving his third voicemail and sending his sixth text message, Victor practiced his attack on the life-sized cardboard cutout of their CEO in a construction helmet. A speech balloon quoted their CEO on the cutout's right side—"Safety breeds quality, and quality breeds success!"—forcing Victor to go left. The maneuver was ungainly; he couldn't seem to get the angle right. He came at his CEO from behind, and felt much more comfortable.

Just after seven David strolled into the conference room and tossed his gym bag on the floor, whistling "She'll Be Comin' 'Round the Mountain". While helping himself to a Little Debbie he finally noticed Victor tapping his foot. "What?" he said innocently.

"What what, you've been gone two hours, that's what. I called, and I texted you several times."

With his mouth full of snack cake: "In all the excitement, I left my phone at my desk. The time thing, I'm fully prepared to say my bad, but our waitress was slow, dude. The place is nuts during happy hour, I know, but come on..."

A pointillist blotch of pink bloomed on Victor's pale

skin. "You went to happy hour?"

"They were expecting me. You know our department—band of brothers, if someone doesn't show, they get worried."

"And of course you left your phone here..."

"Imagine my frustration..."

"And you've been drinking, haven't you?"

"Just one. A two-for-one. And a couple jello shots with our waitress." David chuckled, recalling the scene. "You know how they stick the shot glass between their titties and bend their necks way forward..."

"I don't." He didn't. "I don't suppose you brought back any food for me?"

"Completely spaced it out. I was a little buzzed."

"Fine." Better hungry, Victor decided. His blood "craving" was more like a diabetic's sugar low, but his appetite for food could be frighteningly insatiable. For once it would work to his advantage. He opened his laptop and brought up the audit report template he was now extremely anxious to complete. "Let's just move on this project."

"Sounds good to me, boss." David scratched his crotch. "Forgot the Tinactin."

For forty minutes Victor typed, fleshing out David's skimpy bullet point list, tallying the testing results, asking follow-up questions—motioning for David to take out his iPod ear buds, and then asking again. David spent most of the time hovering over Victor's shoulder, providing motivating comments like *good job, nice work,* and *I did not see that.* Victor maintained two selves, one focusing on the business at hand, the other thrilling to what was about to finally happen.

And then they reached the end of David's contribution to the report. Victor's cellphone rang. He stared at David with Bela Lugosi eyes as he answered. "Yes? Oh, hi Barbara."

"Are you coming home soon?" said his ex-wife.

"Barb, I don't know, we've got a lot going on here.

Why?"

"I'm having company over."

"Who?"

"Who it is should be of no concern to you," Barbara said airily. "We are divorced."

These moments stung a little less each time, but still hurt. "I know, but it is my house. If I'm too nosey, you can move out anytime you like."

"With the money you give me? Where in the world would I go, Victor?"

Victor retreated to the window and lowered his voice. "I give you plenty of alimony."

Barbara gasped. "Which in turn I have to use for Amberly's education."

"Yes, that's right, God forbid we actually put her in a public school."

"Victor! Is that what you want? You want to stick our only child in a public high school? She's gifted, a child like ours belongs in a special, nurturing school."

Gifted, that's a good one, Victor thought. *She does one Sudoku puzzle when she's eight and forevermore she's gifted.* Amberly was almost seventeen now and barely pulled C's. She was in and out of detention, suspension, and the back of a squad car, twice. Also, she had not done a Sudoku puzzle in years.

"Shots, shots, shots!" David sang along to his iPod.

"Who's that?" Barbara asked.

"David. Speaking of which—"

"Oooo, say hi from me."

"In fact, Barbara," said Victor, fixing David with a gaze that would have compelled him to hop up on the table and bare his throat and tilt his head just so, had he bothered to look up, "I'm about to do something long overdue…"

"You'll break Amber's heart if you take her out of that school."

Victor sighed and turned back to the window. "I'm not saying we have to put Amberly in a public school. It's just that she goes to a *boarding* school five blocks from our house. I never see her, and it's putting me in the poor house. And let's be honest. You have never paid a cent of your alimony for her education."

"I bring her meals and take her shopping. Those are opportunity costs, Victor. Time that I could otherwise be spending at my job."

"I'm just saying, with the money I pay you, there are plenty of places you could live."

"Yes, yes there are, Vic," Barbara said condescendingly. "There are some fine apartments in the inner city, miles away from Amber. Do you want me out of the house, Victor? Out on the street somewhere in downtown Houston? Do you Victor?"

"No, it's not that."

"Who does your laundry?"

There was a long pause from Victor. "Uh, I do, Barb."

"Okay, who cooks your food?"

"Again me. I cook, clean, do my own laundry. I pretty much do everything in the house."

"It is your house, after all," Barbara countered. "And who's the one who has to feed Porky pug?"

"Porky pug is *your* dog, I didn't even want the dog. And, I'm the one who cleans up its, its...*shit*, in the backyard."

"You don't need to swear. I know Jay doesn't appreciate that, and neither do I." Barbara gave a sad little sigh, sounding hurt. "Victor, you have no grounds to complain. After all, I still welcome you in the bed."

"Some welcome," he muttered.

"There we go! Finally we get to what's bothering you. It's all about sex, isn't it? As if you're even capable. I'm sorry, that was uncalled for. Never mind. But we both know it's not my fault..." Barbara's voice quavered. "...for the way you bait me. We're supposed to maintain our civil boundaries, you know that very well. Our counselor made that super clear, didn't she? Wouldn't you say so? Civil boundaries, Victor?"

"Yes."

"I feel like I'm very good at respecting our boundaries. I'm trying to make the best of a difficult situation, Victor. You know that."

"I do. Listen Barbara—"

"'I do', 'I know'. That's all you ever have to say," Barbara stewed.

Victor eyeballed David, bobbing his head to his music and pointing at the laptop screen like a dance partner. "You need to know something, Barbara," he whispered. "I'm about to do it. I'm going to do it…"

"What? I can't hear you, Victor, speak up."

"I'm telling you I'm going to finally—"

"What? You're mumbling. It's those stupid teeth. Please speak clearly, for once."

"Never mind."

"Fine. Just tell me what time you'll be home tonight."

"I don't know. Eight, I guess."

"Can you make it ten?"

"I guess, I suppose I could."

"Good, I'll see you no earlier than ten."

David plucked out his ear buds as Victor hung up. "VV, the brain has been drained. Need to pop out for an energy drink."

Victor drew a deep, preparatory breath. "Good idea."

David did a double take. "Really? You're okay with that? Sweet. I'll be gone a half hour, tops. Hour at the most."

"Sounds good, David."

"Indeed it do," David marveled to himself and clapped his boss on the shoulder. "Don't finish without me, now."

Victor smiled. "David, before you go, could I get you to change out the ink cartridge for the copy machine?"

"No problemo. Ink cartridge, now where would that be?"

"In the supply closet."

"Supply closet…"

Victor remained calm. "Next to the copy machine."

"Right, where the Juicy Fruit is stored. I'm on it, VV."

David made his way to the supply closet.

David had mocked Victor Thetherson for the last time.

David opened the closet door and fumbled to find the light.

Victor walked on marshmallow feet to the closet, visualizing the attack he had perfected on the cardboard CEO.

David stretched on tiptoes to reach the ink cartridge box.

A fat thundercloud created premature dusk, a shadow rising up as if from the floor. Victor obsessed on David's neck. *Just another piece of meat, rare steak, steak on a stick, last one in stock, get it while it's hot, it's this or a salad...*

David Copperfield grabbed the ink cartridge box. Victor Thetherson bared his fangs, hopped nimbly to the right to better access David's jugular, tripped on the step ladder and grabbed David to stop his fall, one hand around his waist and the other clutching David's thigh.

David wheeled and pushed Victor away. "Yo VV! I'm not into you like that!"

"For God's sake, I wasn't coming on to you," Victor protested. "Don't you see, I was..."

David backed himself into the corner of the closet, clutching the ink cartridge. "Stay back, you gay maniac!"

Victor's thoughts cycled rapidly. *Apologize! Attack! Apologize! Attack!*

"David, I, I just wanted to, to ask you to pick me up an energy drink too. And to say, you can take your time...in fact, you don't need to come back tonight, I can get my own energy drink. I can finish up."

"Dude, you got that right." David thrust the ink cartridge box into Victor's chest and retrieved his gym bag from the conference room.

Victor fantasized flying after David as he stomped

toward the exit, pouncing on the young accountant with all his fury. But he remained rooted in the supply closet doorway. If instead of vampirism he had woke up one morning with Vulcan mind-control powers or time-travel abilities, he would have been just as reluctant, just as downright unable to use them.

Victor's father had been a high school math teacher who hadn't inspired, influenced or redirected the interests of one single student before botulism from the local café's undercooked duck ended him. His mother wrote thank-you cards to people who didn't attend her seventy-fifth birthday party, apologizing for the inconvenient scheduling. This personality they had given to their son, in nature and in nurture, in spades.

"Sweet boy," one of the scientists studying him had made note in his file when Victor was ten. Vampirism may have altered Victor Thetherson's features, but it hadn't touched his essence. "Not real comfortable in his own skin. But sweet."

"We both could have handled things a little differently," Victor called to David. "Going forward I'll try to provide you with better tips and strategies for finishing your tasks on time." He had to rush that last promise to get it to David before he disappeared through the floor's frosted glass doors.

THETHERSON, IN A DARK ALLEY

The confrontation with David drained Victor. Who drained who; for a vampire, Victor's flow was always moving in the wrong direction.

He had been gearing up for the bite for days, weaning himself off blood bank blood. Now he was at least four quarts low, ready to crash. He called Tripp, his blood source. "It's me, Vic. I should be there in three minutes."

"My man," Tripp replied. "Meet me in the alley by the malt shop dumpsters."

As quickly as promised, Victor stood waiting for Tripp in the alley. Twenty minutes later, Victor was still waiting when Tripp finally emerged from the back door of the Good Sisters blood bank.

Victor looked up and down the alley. "What the hell Tripp?" The day's stress boiled over and spilled out. "You leave me lurking out here? Do you know how many people have passed by, gawking at me?"

"You're a vampire," said Tripp. "You lurk. You're allowed."

"Don't, don't say that. Don't start. I've had a long day. You said you were available, and yet, and now, now, I am late to get home..." *To my trains.* "...to my wife."

"Whoa, calm down big guy, I had three people walk in just after you called. What was I supposed to say? Excuse me, hold your blood, I'll be back in a moment. I gotta go outside to give some blood to my buddy, the vampire." Tripp held his arms wide open, a Strawberry Shortcake backpack in one hand and a freshly lit cigar in the other. "Oh I get it, you wanted me to invite them into the alley. My blood isn't fresh enough for you."

Hearing Tripp refer to him as his buddy calmed Victor. They had known each other a long time—pre-bite, Victor gave blood for years at Good Sisters, and Tripp had been volunteering there since high school, continuing during college and now while in residency at the Rice University Longevity Laboratories, finishing his biochemistry degree.

Victor had been a regular at the Longevity Labs since he was an infant, a participant in a longitudinal study on aging. Tripp had been extremely nice to him, including taking a strong interest in Victor's challenges as a vampire. Victor always reminded himself it wasn't personal, that for someone like Tripp—young and good-looking if a touch bizarre, a bit wild but with a bright future—theirs was just an extended clinical relationship.

Now he felt sheepish. "I'm sorry. I know you don't have to do this for me."

"But I want to," said Tripp. "You donated more blood than any human alive, before. Before," he repeated, looking at Victor while taking a drag on his cigar. "Besides, I'm keeping track—when your withdrawals equal your deposits, we'll talk. And," Tripp became belatedly outraged, waving the cigar, "who cares if you're late for your wife? She's the devil incarnate. Come on." He jerked his head toward downtown Houston's enclave of bars, clubs and restaurants. "In half an hour I'll close up shop here and we can hit the town. Maybe you can bite someone for real this time."

Victor shook his head, uncomfortable. "Naw, I gotta run. I need to get to bed early. I have to be in the office early tomorrow."

"Tomorrow, what?" Tripp spluttered. "Isn't this..." He squinted at the sky while consulting his mental calendar. "Yes, it's *Friday*. Tomorrow is *Saturday*, which falls on the week-*end*. Again with the weekend work?"

Victor shrugged. "Big project that didn't get done."

"Vic, when oh when are you going to put the fear into your worthless employees and bite one of them?"

"I tried tonight, I really did. But I…I didn't." Victor stared at the pocked alley floor, feeling Tripp's eyes on him, feeling his disappointment. "But who's to say that's a bad thing?"

"I don't know if I told you, but I subscribed to a clipping service for vampire research," said Tripp. "Dr. Linciome saw me reading an abstract from a French lab looking for a cure. 'Why in the world would anyone want to cure the undead? They're a gold mine for us!'"

Victor chuckled. Tripp did a pretty good Dr. Linciome. "He's funny."

"This lab found that the rabies vaccine softens the traits of at least one strain of vampirism. I made a note in your file to keep you away from Saint Bernards. That's the last thing we need, is for you to become even less aggressive."

"Thank God you weren't bitten," Victor countered. "Everyone that looked at you wrong would either be dead or a vampire."

Tripp squinted at him with bemused affection. He eyeballed the broad expanse above Victor's eyebrows. "Why doesn't a burning cross appear on your forehead when you say 'God'?"

"I even dabbled my fingers in the bowl of holy water at church last Sunday, when no one was looking," said Victor. "Nothing."

Tripp gazed into the distance, briefly contemplating the universe. "Makes you wonder, man." He handed the backpack of blood to Victor, and was given cash folded to the size of a stick of gum. "Whoops," said Tripp, pushing the money-stick back at Victor. "I'm telling you, no one cares. This stuff is past its expiration date."

"I know," said Victor. "It's for your time. Buddy." The term of endearment came across clumsy.

"Both the blood and my time are on the house." Tripp

tucked the cash in Victor's shirt pocket and arched an eyebrow. "But if you ever start complaining about the freshness—"

"I know, you'll have to charge me."

"No," said Tripp, "I'd tell you to go bite someone!"

Victor nodded. "I just...I can't. I can't figure it out."

"Okay, let's break it down. I'd say you have to tilt your head to the side..." Tripp mimed the act. "Open your mouth real wide—I'm not sure how hard you have to come in..." He reached a finger toward Victor's mouth. "How sharp are those puppies?"

Victor batted his hand away. "I'm not talking about the mechanics. The...the why. Why me? And what would have happened if I had done it tonight...what if I had bit him?"

"Some screaming, a little gurgling. By the both of you, I'm guessing."

Victor hugged the Strawberry Shortcake backpack and gnawed on the top handle, relieving the constant, low-level teething pain. "I'm not sure I could live with myself if I cursed someone. How could I justify ruining someone's life like that?"

"They provoked a vampire, for crying out loud," said Tripp. "What do they expect? You mess with the bull, you get the horn."

That had a nice ring to it, Victor thought, chewing contentedly.

"You gotta stop worrying about consequences for the other guy," said Tripp. "That's the other guy's job. And as far as consequences go, I've seen worse than your vampirism." He brought the cigar in for a puff and nodded at the soggy backpack handle in Victor's mouth. "Stop that."

Victor lowered the backpack. "It's true, it hasn't affected me at all the way I thought. Like I said, I can still go to church."

"Curse me already, right?" said Tripp. "Guilt-free snoozing on Sunday morning—'lay off, Ma, I'm a vampire, for Christ's sake.'"

"Do you still live at home?"

Tripp frowned for an answer.

"And as far as I can tell," Victor continued his lament, "as far as you and the docs at the Lab can tell, I'm still aging." He held out the back of his hand, finding two new age spots and a budding wart. "There's so much I don't know. Shouldn't I figure it out first, so I could at least give my victim some idea what to expect? I don't want to be irresponsible."

"Heaven forbid."

"Yes, yes," said Victor, picturing the misty courtroom of Heaven, an angry, vengeful God presiding. "What if? Tripp, what if I'm being tested?"

"You let the Longer Labs do the testing, my friend," said Tripp, using his affectionate nickname for Rice's Longevity Labs. "Maybe we haven't seen the anti-aging effects in you that our theory predicted, but we've only just begun to plumb your deep dark depths."

Victor tried to coax Tripp's eyes heavenward. "You know the kind of test I'm talking about."

"I do, and that's the heavy, hand-of-fate shit we're supposed to be hashing out over a beer or ten," said Tripp. "Not here in the alley." He hooked a thumb at the back door of the blood bank. "I gotta get back inside. Sprung a leak in one of our pipes," he slipped into a Cockney accent, "and it's a bloody mess."

Victor smiled, showing a lot of fang. Tripp shook his head at the sight, and dropped the accent. "Vic, problem is, you still think of yourself as human."

"I am," Victor said weakly. "I'm the same person. With sharper teeth."

"You're not. You were done being human on that fateful night. You need to wrap yourself in that truth. Like a blanket. Wrap yourself in it and believe it. Own it, Victor." Tripp squeezed Victor's shoulder. "Viccy, babe, all I'm saying is, you were given a gift. Now use it. Stop letting your wife, your flunkies, and well, everybody step on you."

"Don't you think that if I was meant to use it, if it truly was a gift, that I wouldn't be queasy at the sight of blood? You call it that 'fateful night'..."

"I thought you'd like that," said Tripp.

"I actually thought of it that way," said Victor, "for a while. A short while, until I realized nothing really changed. How come I'm still so human? Where's my super strength? I can't fly, or turn into a bat. Absolutely no mind-control powers."

"You did say the sun bugs you."

"Bugs me—doesn't burn my flesh. I got the curse, with no benefits," said Victor, on a roll. "I'm the same ol' Vic. No faster, no stronger. No powers of seduction. And blood grosses me out. What kind of vampire gets grossed out by blood? I'd gladly own it, like, like a..."

"A blanket," said Tripp.

"Yeah, like a blanket. But I don't have a clue what that means."

"You need a mentor," said Tripp. "Don't new vampires always have a mentor to show them the ropes? Help them with their first sucking? Shouldn't that be the responsibility of the vampire who bit you? You got screwed."

"Just one more thing to blame on the Germans," said Victor.

"You really need to talk to your vamp," said Tripp. "Cruella deVil."

Victor nodded. "I should have gone back to the hotel the next day and confronted her, but I was too freaked out. But, did I tell you I'm heading to the home office in Dresden in September, for a big celebration?"

"Rock on," said Tripp. "Germany. Vampire chicks. *Big* glasses of beer. Rock *on*."

"I'm hoping to find some answers. I'm worried, though," Victor fretted. "You can't bring liquids on the plane, and I'm there for a whole week. Where am I going to find blood?"

"Blood is very accessible in Germany." Tripp tapped Victor's arm. "Inside Germans."

"Ha ha," said Victor. "Easy for you to joke."

"Vic, drop the pathos already. It's not like getting bit screwed everything up for you. You forget, my friend, I know how unhappy you were *before* the bite. Be a sunny vampire why don't you, and find the silver lining. Why couldn't this be a blessing?"

"A blessing from God," said Victor with heavy sarcasm.

"Maybe not from God. Maybe so." Tripp regarded him solemnly. "Figure it out, Vic. One way or the other, you deserve to be happy." He took one last drag on his cigar, put it out on the cinder block wall, gave Victor a salute and disappeared back into the blood bank.

Victor hurried down the alley in the ragged gait of the overweight middle-ager. He dropped into his Subaru, and laid the backpack gently on the passenger seat. "I am a vampire," he whispered as he started the car. "I *am* a vampire."

THETHERSON, BLOODY BLOODY

Victor pulled into the driveway, waiting for the garage door to rise, breathing a sigh of relief to see Barbara's empty stall.

He lugged his backpack of blood and bottle of vodka from garage to entryway to kitchen, calling out, "Hallooo...Amberly? Barb?" The house was deserted. Not quiet—Porky the pug dog was barking in the backyard, non-stop and rhythmic, sharp and urgent, maddening after forty seconds. It had been two years. Why their crotchety next-door neighbor hadn't shot or poisoned it by now was beyond Victor.

Into a pitcher went blood, vodka, tomato juice, assorted seasonings and a celery stalk. To mask the 'bloody' in the bloody Bloody Mary, Victor mixed the batch as spicy as he could muster, hold the garlic. After the first gulp, he belched and read aloud the note from Barbara.

Did you drink all the vodka again? Thanks a ton. Now we had to go out. Don't wait up.

Victor crumpled the note. At the hall closet he climbed up on the footstool and reached for the back corner of the top shelf, where Barbara insisted he store his conductor's cap. Donned it, and made choo-choo chugging sounds as he shuffled into the garage to work on his trains.

Last Saturday he had finished an intersection that reminded him of the one in his little hometown of Milford. Now he needed to make a railroad crossing sign, lest a tiny Milfordite drive unawares across the tracks and get t-boned by a fully-loaded freight train.

A few minutes past two a.m., Victor awoke slumped over the train track with the locomotive trying to tunnel through his head. Barbara's car was right next to him in the adjoining stall; he hadn't stirred when she came home, and she hadn't roused him.

He stumbled into the house to rinse the empty pitcher and take a fragrant leak. As was often the case during his mid-night bladder breaks, his mind turned to Wesley Snipes decapitating vampires in explosions of blood—this was just since the conversion—and then to his job, this time to replay and agonize over a week's worth of conversations gone awry.

Case in point was the exchange Tuesday with Larry, his fifty-year-old wisecracking team lead. Victor had intended to create a crisis management team—Larry—to ensure the Westchase audit was wrapped up and fully documented. Instead Victor found himself picking up the Maryhill medical center construction project so Larry could join an impromptu boar hunt in the Ozarks.

Digging in, Victor soon realized the Maryhill project was thirty percent over budget with no one the wiser. He had spent the rest of the week in damage control, identifying the cost overruns with the project manager and reluctantly informing and infuriating senior management, while every five minutes burning the picture of David's inert head and shoulders a bit more permanently into his retinas.

If only he could say what needed to be said. This inability was all the more frustrating for the fact that Victor Barton Thetherson had a phenomenal brain, a high-end organ equipped with massive storage space, a creative filing system, and lightning retrieval. Thirteen technical papers and a monthly column in the trade journal *Practical Principles* had made him a modern-day legend in the construction accounting world.

But real-time, at all the pivotal moments, his mind

raced in too many directions, ten trains of thought barreling at breakneck speed, confusing, uncoordinated, colliding. Or his brain simply locked up from the get-go, analysis paralysis by committee. If the perfect response ever came immediately to mind, his mouth bungled the job, and the moment would be gone. Timing was everything, and Victor had none.

One time, once, it had been different. For a short, memorable stretch his senior year in college, everything had clicked. For a brief, crucial period, the world had witnessed Victor Thetherson's true self. And the world, including the woman who was now his ex-wife, liked it.

Until then, and ever since, he had been encased, in fat, in bumbling lips, in a bundle of nerves. Give him time, after the fact, and he could put together one hell of a memo or e-mail. After the fact. After everyone had already made up their minds. After they had already gained their advantage.

He stood in their bedroom doorway and stared at Barbara's slumbering body. Funny how she could sleep so soundly, at perfect ease and in complete control, with a vampire in the house.

Upon waking up a vampire, after the standard why-me wailing, Victor had quickly warmed to the benefits of the world's sexiest curse. Famous examples inspired him—no tabloid was saleable without a pic of New York City hot dog vendor Sennett McGumphrey flashing his fangs while squiring a Hollywood hottie between the clubs and his apartment in Queens. Masters and Johnson came out of retirement to substantiate off-the-charts satisfaction levels of human-vampire interactions. The occasional reported death or conversion did put a damper on the public's fascination, but never for long.

More than anything, Victor had anticipated Barbara enthralled and enraptured. She had the most intense eyes he had ever seen, her eyelids with the slightest slant, hooding her eyes just so. He had wondered from the day they met what it would be like, to have her eyes turned full upon him. Wanting him. That vampirism's reputed gift of immortality meant he was destined to become his wife's caretaker in her twilight years, hadn't cooled Victor's passion at all. He had fantasized about Barbara asking to make her final exit in a fog of steamy lovemaking.

That was oh-so *then*. Barbara had long since given up on him, and Victor had long since given up on vampirism, as a ticket, as a gift, as an extreme makeover. Quinten, one of his employees, had been flabbergasted to learn that earning a black belt in karate hadn't made him lethal. Quinten was clumsy before, and after. Likewise, Victor realized vampirism could not work miracles.

Neither was it much of a curse. And so he didn't spend any time pining for a cure. Victor didn't like to think about the future, but when he did, he pictured it as various dioramas—still-life corporate offices, homey kitchens and doo-doo strewn backyards, all indistinguishable from his current setting. In these dioramas, Human Victor and Vampire Victor were interchangeable.

And yet...that didn't quite square with his feeling of *waiting for something*. Waiting for something to change. Victor was that close to accepting that the personality the world saw—the indecision, the compliance and the fat bumbling lips, was truly his essence. Forty-eight years and a membership revocation letter from Toastmasters was, after all, a great stack of evidence.

And yet, there had been that time, so many years ago. If it could happen once, then his real self had to be in there. That man had to exist. And so he waited, for a change.

Except of course the change had already occurred. Couldn't ask for a bigger one. And absolutely nothing had changed.

Victor circled to the far side of the bed and slipped

under the covers next to his ex-wife, wiggling into the position of spoonee. Tension coiled in his gut, twisting and drawing in the radiating nerves like so many tangled ropes around a spool. A single touch, he was convinced, an indication that she cared just enough to wish him a good night's sleep, would dissolve the spool and allow the bundle of nerves to unwind, stretched and frayed, but relaxed.

"Honey," he groaned, reaching back to take her forearm and guide her hand to his front. "Could I get you to—"

"Not on your life, buster," Barbara mumbled, flipping over, whapping him with her ponytail, and taking with her an unequal share of the covers.

With vampirism Victor did not get cold. A blanket, then, in a sense, and he would now wrap himself in it. *I still don't know what you meant, Tripp, but I'm betting this wasn't it.*

This wry thought was the next best thing to Barbara's hand on his stomach. Not quite to a smile, but Victor's face did relax, and he was soon asleep.

THETHERSON SPILLS BLOOD

Monday morning on the accounting floor. Victor leaned against his office doorframe, reading the latest budget-busting project status report from the Maryhill medical center construction team. The nonstop widespread chatter from his staff was an effective white noise concentration booster, for as long as he could ignore the fact that he was the boss.

He'd come to be standing in his doorway for fresh air. Nikki his admin was painting her toenails. By a quirk of the ventilation system the odor streamed into his office, and stayed there, so that the air around his desk was heavy with nail polish.

In so many ways vampirism hadn't changed him, but Victor did have a new olfactory system. Not enhanced— he wasn't closing his eyes and identifying people by their body odor, or sending back a bottle of wine with the whiff of a 2004 iron deficiency in the Tuscany soil, or smelling fear. Victor smelled things differently. Scents were identified, and occasionally had to be re-learned, by what he now thought of as their patterns, which sometimes filled his eyes more than his nose, as fanciful symbols. He had learned he now hated the sight of the smell of garlic, and lavender. Didn't mind the pattern of toenail polish, at least in moderation.

The place sounded like a phone bank of telemarketers, punctuated with an occasional shout and the demented fairy peal of Tessa's laughter. Time for a stroll of his domain. He glanced at Nikki, gave her a can-you-believe-this-racket expression.

"Go get 'em, Vic," said Nikki, then back to her toes. Last week Florence had complained about her walking around barefoot every Monday morning. Nikki had taken it to heart and worn flip-flops today. She would expect high marks for 'Shows Respect to Coworkers' on her upcoming performance evaluation.

Past David's empty desk to his first stop, Larry Cocachello, one of his two team leads. Larry was from Victor's home town of Milford. He carried on a torrid online relationship with a faux taxidermist who mounted tiny replica animal heads. Larry's "In" box always teeter-towered with work-in-progress, to clear desk space for his virtual sweetheart's micro mounts.

"...so we find him picking cactus barbs out of his nuts!" the fifty-year-old construction accountant drawled loudly into the phone, laughing and pounding the desk and falling into a fit of phlegmy coughing.

"We need to talk about Maryhill," said Victor. "And the Westchase audit..." He was stopped short by Larry's raised finger.

Larry and his thin résumé were hired as a favor to Victor's parents, who relished having Larry subordinate to their son after spending forty years listening to the Cocachellos tout Larry's accomplishments. And Larry had provided plenty, from the napkin holder he made in shop class, to the new computer he received in his previous accounting job at the Milford Grain Company, to the way his hunting dogs could fetch a duck.

Young Victor's successes were always overshadowed, oftentimes simply victim to poor timing. He had been unfortunate enough to win the state ping-pong championship the same week Larry almost bagged his first buck mule deer, and likewise was awarded a National Merit scholarship before the hoopla over Larry's purchase of an '82 Trans Am had died down.

As the botulism claimed him, Victor's father stewed less about his demise than that his death warrant had been made to order in the Cocachellos' café; he repeatedly awoke feverish and bug-eyed from the nightmare of wolfing down the duck in order to cut short Gail Cocachello's story of how Larry had heroically rid his lawn of chickweed. True to Thetherson form, one of his deathbed wishes was not that Victor take a blood oath to seek vengeance on the Cocachellos, but that he do his best to assign Larry a liberal amount of accounting grunt work.

Larry resumed regaling the person on the other end of the line. "The boar is crashing through the forest right toward us and Paul has his ball sack stretched to his knees—no-no-no, remember, the moron had already split open the crotch doing his pre-hunt yoga!"

Victor moved on, turning into the first full row of cubes. "Hi Florence," he greeted his other team lead. "Did you have a good weekend?" He gave a nod and a slow blink to Raj, Florence's aisle-mate.

Florence. Like the city in Italy. Lean and luminescent, raven black hair. Since he had first laid eyes upon her, Victor had been under a spell. He looked right past the dye job and the Texas tan, the tobacco stains, the bolo ties, the Copenhagen belt buckles and the hunch, forever destined to behold a vision of classic Mediterranean beauty.

"Perfect timing," Florence said in her gravelly twang, a hybrid of her native Texas and twenty years in New Zealand. She flicked the report in Victor's hand. "Raj here was just telling me how screwed up our monthly cost-gathering procedures are."

"No," Raj tried to interrupt.

"And how he'd do things a whole lot differently if he was in charge."

"Florence," Raj appealed. "That's not what I was saying. Please now." While Victor nagged everyone else—other than Florence—to elevate their dress code, Raj overdressed. Vendors and the occasional executive who walked onto the floor invariably introduced themselves to Raj first, even with Victor waving and hailing them from his office.

"Brainstorming new ways to do our job is a good thing," Victor told Florence.

"How about firing you?" said Florence. She nodded at Raj. "'Get rid of Vic', I believe is what you said."

"The assumption is that you would be promoted to a higher level," Raj explained, sticking a clove cigarette in the corner of his mouth and palming his gold-plated lighter from the desktop. "We'll get rid of you to Corporate in Chicago, huh my friend?" He rolled forward in his chair to lightly knuckle Victor in the forearm. "How is that old bastard Jay anyway?" he referred to Victor's boss, whom Raj had met once, briefly. "Up to his old tricks?" Raj thumbed his lighter open and flipped it shut, chuckling. "He's good shit, that guy."

"Missed you at Stacie's birthday party Friday night," said Larry, ambling up alongside Victor. "Of course for all I know, you showed up later. Hot damn did I get shit-faced. Again."

"A-gain," echoed Florence and a chorus of voices floating up from behind cube walls.

Quinten rolled into the aisle as far as his headset cord would permit. "I couldn't even have a good time," he whined, slumped in his chair in pouting formation, "because David said you were sitting here complaining about everyone leaving early."

"No," said Victor. "I was just wondering where everyone was. I didn't know there was a department party for...Stacie? Who's Stacie?"

Larry spread his arms and appealed to his coworkers. "Can you believe this guy? Never mind the fact we practically grew up together. Managers these days just don't take the time to get to know their employees." He crossed his arms and tapped his foot. "Stacie?" Victor was forced to deny knowledge of her a second time. "My brother's step-daughter's best friend? Anyway, I'm fairly certain I gave you an invite," said Larry. "Eight-and-a-

half by eleven, copy of a copy of a modified Ringling
Brothers and Barnum Bailey poster, talking about all
the thrills you can expect under Stacie's big top? No?
Shoot."

"Thrills under her big top," said Quinten, his giggles
staticky through too much saliva. "Her shirt, right? I
hadn't gotten it."

"Quinten, you poor dumb soul," said Florence. "How
do you get by, sugar?"

"I don't know," Quinten chortled, shaking his head.

"Okay everybody," Victor attempted to restore order.

Tessa appeared in the mouth of the cube across from
Quinten. "Speaking of David," she said, hoisting her
body from the chair like it weighed twice what it did.
She waddled into the aisle—the waddling made sense,
because she had very small feet. They reminded Victor
of hooves. "Where is he? Anyone heard from him?"

"The poor boy's probably exhausted." Florence pressed
the heels of her hands into her lower back in an attempt
to straighten her spine. There came a pop like the
snapping of a rotten tree branch that made everyone
wince. Life as a New Zealand sheep rancher's wife had
been hard, physically and otherwise. Her current
marriage to a Houston street sweeper hadn't been much
easier. "At the happy hour he told me VV was busting
his hump, making him come back here Friday night."

"If I'm not mistaken," said Tessa, "you can only bust
your own hump. Vic can't do that for us. No matter how
much he'd like to."

"There was no hump busting," said Victor, flustered.
"David and I had to finish the Westchase audit report,
because—"

"Which, by the way," said Larry, "I guess Jay was
asking about this morning."

"He didn't get it?!" said Victor. "I e-mailed it to him
Saturday!"

"Seems to me you're trying to change the subject,
Vic," said Florence, winking at Tessa. "Why won't you

tell us what happened to David?"

"Geez-lordy," said Larry, "Vic killed David. Can't blame you though, now that Jay is going to have your ass. David's death will be a good distraction." He tapped his head. "Savvy."

"Ohmygod Vic, did you have to kill David?" said Florence. "Couldn't you just suck a little here and a little there? I'd wager ten to make five that young man produced enough of every sort of fluid to keep his partner satisfied."

"Florence, you horny cowgirl," said Raj.

Quinten's gaze bobbed from speaker to speaker. He put two and two together, and his eyes widened. "Florence, no, he could be your grandson."

Victor watched Florence cinch up the Schlitz Malt Liquor clasp of her bolo tie and take a menacing step at Quinten, like a vengeful Italian starlet. "I'm forty-seven, you little shit. I'll bite you with a kitchen knife and bury your stupid ass."

Quinten's eyes bugged. He peeled off his headset, like a hat in his hands, a symbol of apology and a preparation to run. "I'm sorry, Florence. I didn't mean you're too old. I meant you're *like* a grandmother to us—"

"Hush now, Mr. Quinten," said Larry, taking the figurative shovel from his hands. "So where's the body, VV? I hope you had the good sense not to just throw the boy in the dumpster."

"Okay, okay…"

"All I know is, I'm not picking up the slack," said Tessa, stabbing her finger at the spot on the floor where she would take her stand. "God we are so swamped as it is. Then asking *us* to go audit this Westchase company. Don't we have an audit department for that?"

"Corporate better not expect us to absorb every employee you kill," Larry drawled.

"Please everyone," said Victor, sweat beading on the nape of his neck.

"Victor's not that kind of vampire, are you?" said Raj. "Vampire Vic doesn't like to bite people. Barbecue and ice cream bars, yes." Everyone's eyes went to Victor's large gut. "Not people. People make Victor nervous. Unless maybe David accidentally tripped and hit his head on a desk and died. Then maybe you'd quickly bite him and pretend it was you."

"Yeah, well..." Victor struggled for a witty response. "I'm sure he's just late..."

"Whenever I tell my friends my boss is a vampire," said Florence, "they're all impressed and horrified, and I just say, no, it ain't that way, Vic's a lamb. Lots of folks in this company have ten times the teeth our boss is packing."

"Okay, that's about enough of it." Victor tripped over the words, losing the intended forcefulness. He was surrounded. Larry stood slightly behind him, patting his shoulder, with Florence alongside, cackling in his airspace. Raj was crowding him low on the front right, his crossed legs extended past Victor's shin. Quinten now hung on the cube wall, leering, with Tessa walling off the other two-thirds of the aisle. "That's good. We're slow, we're slowly falling behind—"

"Vic?" came Nikki's voice. She wormed her skinny body into the gathering, forcing Florence to back off with a huff. "The temp's here. You should say hello." She plucked the cigarette from Raj's lips and tucked it along with a swath of stringy hair behind her ear. "Meet me outside in five," she told Raj. "Bring a couple more of these."

Raj opened his mouth in protest and received a kick in the shins. Nikki took Victor by the hand and led him through the newly widened aisle. "Busy man coming through." Out of the team's earshot, in the main aisle under the floor clock, Nikki turned on her boss. She carefully unsnagged her *Hot Enough For You?* shirt from her belly button stud and realigned the sequined devil horns across her chest. "Vic, what's the deal?

You're a great guy, the nicest guy I know."

Victor accepted the compliment like he had just been knighted. "Thank you."

"But you're a vampire, right? I mean, I know you are." Nikki cocked her head and blew a threadbare bubble with her Juicy Fruit. "Then why is everyone so comfortable around you? Shouldn't we be nervous?"

Victor relaxed the perpetual worry lines accenting his eyes and mouth and advanced on Nikki, using the hunch in his frame to loom over her, lips parting to reveal his fangs.

"Just kidding," said Victor, stepping back, too flustered to contemplate the way Nikki's eyes had gone to saucers and her mouth had fallen slack. He put the worry lines back in place. "I shouldn't joke in the office."

She took out her gum, used it to remove bubble remnants from her lips and big, imperfect front teeth. "Vic, you got these great fangs, and then..." She shook her head. "Bleh."

And Nikki had teeth that tainted her great body and perfectly groomed toes, so they were even, Victor decided petulantly. He was anxious to return to his office but had to pause to allow a woman to walk past. Nikki grabbed her arm. "Here's our temp now. This is Vic, our manager."

The temp accountant was plump and open-faced, hair in a ponytail. She hesitated before shaking Victor's hand, hers suddenly sweat-slicked. "Pleased to, to meet you."

Why was the temp taken aback? Victor's canines were long and sharp. His skin was pale to the edge of whiteness, capillaries faintly evident. His eyes were red-rimmed, even the pupils tinged red. Although he fingered and combed and hairsprayed his thin black hair across his crown many times a day, since the night he was bitten it habitually slumped forward into a widow's peak. Victor looked like a vampire.

"We're glad to have you on board," he said. "I

understand you spent some time at Farmar & Downs? They were a great company. Tough times in the industry, hm. I'll be interested to hear how we stack up. Don't hesitate to suggest any best practices that you liked at F&D."

"No, yes, I will sir. It's good—"

"Let me know if you need anything."

"—good to meet you. Yes. I will."

And why would it take the temp less than a week to lose her trepidation? Victor dressed in tight sport coats and slacks, not a tux-and-cape. He functioned fine in the daytime, and looked tired by evening. He was fat and balding, and he blushed. He had never bit anyone, and demonstrated no urge to do so.

Victor returned to his office. At his computer he clicked on the Sent Items e-mail folder—sure enough, there was the e-mail to Jay from Saturday night, with the audit report attached. "Nikki," he called out. "Could you call Vanessa and have her see what happened to the e-mail I sent Jay on Saturday? Larry said he didn't get it." He watched Nikki dial, watched her speaking to Jay's admin. After a few moments their conversation had clearly moved on to new, entertaining topics. Victor left his office to hover over Nikki.

"Okay honey, I got a visitor. Call me later." She hung up. "Vanessa says she sees the e-mail in Jay's Inbox, but that he hasn't opened it yet."

"Well...but...doesn't he—"

"She says he's traveling today."

"Larry," Victor called out. "Larry...?" Anxiety cramped his stance as he waited for Larry's head to appear. "When did you talk to Jay?"

"Didn't say I talked to him," Larry drawled. "I had a voicemail from him. He said he had expected to receive the report Friday from David."

"Why didn't he call me?"

"I suppose because David reports to me," said Larry.

"What time did he call?"

"Eight-thirty-ish," said Larry.

"Didn't you see it was Jay's number?" Victor's voice squeaked at the edges. "Why didn't you forward him to me?"

"I was gettin' coffee, Vic," said Larry with an impatient sigh. "I wouldn't pick it up anyway, though. He's your boss." His head disappeared back into his cube. "You manage him."

Victor wanted to charge Larry, bite him, strangle him...change form, spit blood, levitate, something to strike fear in the crusty bastard's heart. Anything to put him on his heels, to prompt his entire team to think twice before dismissing him. To make them pause before telling their boss what was what, to give him the chance to *think* and craft a powerful response and earn their respect....

When Victor had regained consciousness the morning after the company party two years ago—that fateful night, in Tripp's words—he wasn't the only employee sprawled out in the presidential suite of the downtown Houston Hilton, although most of the others were Germans from the Verrstagg home office in Dresden. Victor was unique in having lost blood, via two punctures in his throat.

Horrified and in a hurry to leave, dizzy from swapping two quarts of blood for a liter of vodka, he had tripped over Kurt Bleckmeier, Verrstagg's director of financial reporting and the biggest instigator of the "East German roulette" drinking game, and gone sprawling atop Agnes, the CEO's traveling secretary, a frighteningly wrinkled woman way past retirement age. With most of her body safely tucked under an end table, he had only landed on her legs, sparing Victor any guilt when word came that the old lady had died a day later.

On the drive home from the Hilton, dreading the hell he was going to catch from Barbara—they were only recently divorced at that time, and Victor took great pains not to create the impression he was eager to take advantage of his freedom—he had realized the inside of his upper lip was bleeding. When his tongue went to check out the situation, it got slashed too. *Oh my goodness, did I break a tooth?* Victor remembered wondering. The rearview mirror of his Subaru provided the first look at his fangs.

And the first sensation of what could only be called The Nagging (because it wasn't strong enough to call it The Craving; and if he called it The Thirst, he thought of drinking a big glass of blood, and retched).

Knowing what he did about East German humor, Victor had pulled over to remove what must be fake teeth. After all, they were a little too long, a little sharper than the classic I-vant-to-suck-your-blood! fangs. More like little Eddie's teeth from the Munsters. But they were very well affixed, and colored the same coffee shade as his other teeth....

At that moment his neck wound had started throbbing, and Victor's heart had sunk, so low that he began to cry. He thought of his widowed mother back home in Milford; of his plans to expand his model train set; and of someday being a grandpa for his daughter. His past had become foreshadowing to disaster, his future a phantasmagoria of blood, rats, and coffin upkeep.

Victor had locked himself in the basement guest bedroom, wailed at Barbara through the door to leave him alone, and finally drifted into snoring slumber, in the final coherent moments fully expecting to awaken at midnight, powerless to stop himself from sucking the blood of the two college girls living across the street.

Instead he had slept until his normal wake-up time, five a.m. The sun hadn't risen yet, but when it did, Victor was okay with it. Not delighted, but okay. Barb was definitely not okay with him, bawling while announcing that he had so upset her with his infantile behavior and the lipstick on his shirt collar, she would be calling her supervisor at Wal-Mart to tell him she wouldn't be able to make her ten-to-three shift that day, and probably the next. Victor had gone to work, early, again.

His neck wound had healed much quicker than he'd expected, but was still a perfect rendition of the classic vampire bite. Victor intended on holing up in his office with strict orders to be left alone, but Larry had intercepted him just past Nikki's admin station and launched into jealous needling.

"Well well, good to see we still have a boss. We all thought maybe you had left your wife"—Victor hadn't then, and still hadn't now, told anyone he was divorced; if his mother outlived him, she'd find out at the reading of his will—"to live with the German Cruella de Vil."

Victor had definitely been attracted to Giselda Munsch, Verrstagg's gorgeous, exotic director of capital allocation. He vaguely remembered spending a lot of time talking to her, repeatedly admiring the striking black streak in her white mane, composing a limerick ode to that black streak, and possibly accompanying her to her room.

"I have to admit," said Victor, "I got a little inebriated."

"You were shit-faced," said Larry. "And all I can say is, she must have been, too."

"You partied with the Germans?" Nikki exclaimed, pausing in painting her toenails. "Why wasn't I invited? I know, I know, only the bigwigs get the good stuff." She was basically correct—Victor's boss Jay had ordered him to restrict the soirée invite to his senior accountants, Larry and Florence. "Da-amn, I've heard the Germans know how to party. Couldn't you have slipped me in, told them I was an executive visiting from Chicago?"

That might have worked, Victor had thought, *except you look more like a vampire hooker than an exec. Of course*, he had noted, *so did Giselda, with a much higher billing rate....*

It had hit him—*it was Giselda who bit me!*—

simultaneous with Larry finally taking a good look at him. "Holy turdburger," Larry had exclaimed.

At the same time Nikki did a double-take and jumped up from her chair, capping her Turnip Twist polish and hurrying on her heels to join them.

"Jesus the good Lord Almighty," said Larry. He reached toward Victor's bite mark, and recoiled. "What the hell...?"

Victor lost sight of Nikki under his double chin as she fingered the marks, cooing. She measured the spacing with her pinkie and ring fingers and held them up to her own teeth to verify. "You've been bit!" Now her hand was covering her mouth to stifle a scream as she saw Victor's fangs. "You're a vampire!"

Cubes had emptied, everyone rushing to check out the commotion. If, instead of blushing and meekly trying to redirect attention to that day's accounting deadline, Victor had chosen that moment to lash out, maybe bite one of them—even to simply snarl at the fascinated, horrified, borderline-terrified accountants, turn on his heel with a flourish and stalk into his office, capping the performance with a dramatic door slam— things could have been different.

And in the following days, he tried. Tried to intimidate and frighten. But it was too late. They were already calling him VV. Vampire Vic.

Five-forty p.m. and Victor had been alone on the floor for an hour. He trudged to the break room, opened the refrigerator and removed a Tupperware container and a gallon baggie. Barbara had emphasized after the previous evening's dinner and again that morning that the two undercooked hamburgers and batch of French fries-in-blood was to be two days' lunch. But he was starving.

He popped both containers in the microwave and pressed the *30 sec* button. Soaked fries were one of the few ways he could stomach his necessary blood intake; but they couldn't be cold. And they still needed ketchup.

Back to his office. Victor was spent, but had no choice but to dive back into the Financial Accounting Standards Board's published literature on post-retirement benefits accounting. Raj had written a memo that caromed from a mystical tour of retiree medical afflictions to slanderous attacks on the members of the FASB working group; Victor had slid from dreams of making a few clarifying edits into the nightmare of rewriting the report. He had received two e-mails and then a phone call from their External Reporting division in Chicago, waiting on his group's fully-documented opinion. By the "end of the day", however loosely the term could be defined, that opinion would be overdue.

To Victor's dismay, Jay Hansen was sitting in his guest chair, drumming his fingers on the desk.

"Oh, Jay, are you supposed to be—I mean...I wasn't expecting you—hi, by the way." Victor hastily set his food down on his desk so that he could offer a handshake. "You know that e-mail I sent, on Saturday...well, we'll get to that. What, is it time for my quarterly review already?"

Jay, still casually drumming, nodded at the fry baggie. "It's leaking."

Victor overreacted to Jay's warning and knocked the blood-soaked fries to the floor. "Shit. Shitanski, I mean, I know you don't like cussing." Leaked blood pooled in the center crease of his Generally Accepted Accounting Principles sourcebook and ran across his desk. "Crap. Crapola." He ran out of Kleenex damming the flow and had to use the tissue mound to wipe clean the bottoms of various soiled items.

"Mousse?" said Jay, eyes moving dubiously from the can of hair-care product to Victor's limp remnants. "What, does it double as a screen cleaner?"

"I guess I could get rid of that," said Victor. He picked up the accounting textbook, desperate for someplace to dump the blood. For a moment he thought, *Might as well just drink it*, then thought better, and tipped the book over his wastebasket.

Jay carried himself as a fit, athletic man, although it was impossible to say whether he was slim-fit or stocky-fit under starch-billowed dress shirts and pleated slacks. His eyes behind wire-rimmed glasses were wide and joyless, forced by his habitually motionless head to gather data through constant, quick motion. "The cleaning people must hate you," he said.

Clear as a bell Victor heard *I hate you*. From the get-go upon arriving at Texahoma four years ago, Jay had been no fan of his accounting manager. When Victor became a vampire, distaste had ripened to disgust. If most of his coworkers had come to see his vampirism as a novelty, Jay increasingly saw it as a disease. "Just give me a second here..." Victor bustled out of his office and to the break room, tearing paper towels one after another from the dispenser, returning to mop up the mess.

Jay's eyes traveled from Victor's overwhelmed desk to the evidence of his overwhelmed antiperspirant—with a quick stop at the wastebasket, where a deep red driblet was coagulating on the inside rim. "How are things here, Vic?"

Victor glanced up, felt his faux widow's peak tickling his forehead, swiped at it with the back of his wrist, belatedly checking to make sure the wrist was blood-free. "Oh, you know...sorry, almost done." He got off his knees and hovered uncertainly over the Tupperware of meat, sitting in blood. Clutching the last unused paper towel, Victor finally decided to sweep the container into the wastebasket. "I'll have to take that to the dumpster myself."

Jay stared at him, an unbroken gaze while Victor three times met his eyes and looked away, making a small production out of sitting in his chair and arranging the papers immediately before him. "Life is difficult for you, isn't it?" said Jay.

Victor shook his head. "I don't like to complain."

"But it is, though," said Jay. "I was talking to Culvers earlier today," he referred to their Treasurer, "and he has a lot going on, he's just swamped, you know what I mean?"

"Sure, I suppose he—"

"But his challenges are nothing compared to yours." Jay again surveyed the clutter in front of him. "How much of this work should be sitting on your staff's desks right now?"

"Well, I guess…I'm not sure what you mean. Sorry."

"I mean, how much work should be delegated to your staff?"

"Well, I think actually that delegation is one of my strong suits."

"No it isn't," said Jay, with finality. "It doesn't count if you get the work back again, unfinished."

"They can't finish everything," said Victor. "Sometimes they need some guidance."

"No," said Jay, identical tone. "You're confusing guidance with covering for them. Where was the Westchase audit report that was supposed to be done two weeks ago?"

"If you remember, we asked for an extension."

"Vic, Vic, come on," said Jay. "You and I both know that report could have been done *three* weeks ago. But okay. Then why wasn't it done Friday?"

Victor's hands went clammy-cold while heat flushed up his neck. "I think you're right, I think that's a good point, I need to do a better job holding my team accountable. That's something I can work on, I'll have a sit-down—"

"Vic, don't—"

"—tomorrow with Larry and Florence, and then—"

"Vic," Jay silenced his word stream. "Come on." He scooted sideways to reach into his pants pocket and pull out his smart phone. He punched a few buttons and propped it against the nearest pile of papers. "Am I getting you upset? Is this making you tense?"

"Well, sure, yeah, I guess..."

"Does it make you mad at me?" Jay tugged down his buttoned-up shirt collar, exposing more neck. "Mad enough to want to take a bite out of me?"

"No, why are you—"

"Buh!" Jay lunged forward and Victor jerked away, banging his knee on the underside of his desk, the only thing preventing him from spilling over backward.

Jay retrieved his phone and punched a button. "I recorded that for my wife. She was afraid for me, coming here to have this talk with you. A vampire and all." He punched a couple more buttons, and Victor heard the tiny tinny replay of their conversation. "I wanted to have a little proof that I can send her, so she rests easy." He stopped the video replay and pocketed the phone. "That's the problem, Vic. You were a weak manager before you were bitten. Honestly, that's a fair evaluation. Hey, your technical skills are good, very good—again a fair evaluation, right? I figured you might be able to mold a couple accountants worthy of promotion and further development. But it hasn't worked out that way, has it?"

Victor had bit himself when his boss lunged at him. He didn't want Jay to see the blood, so he kept his mouth shut.

"It's gotten worse," said Jay. "I don't get it."

Victor shook his head in disagreement, without a clue what to say. He carefully parted and lifted layers of desk rubble in search of the pack of travel tissue buried beneath.

"Why did I know you would be here tonight," Jay challenged, "and all alone? Because you're too afraid to hold your staff accountable."

"Being...this way, it's hard," said Victor. "It's not easy. You don't know, you've never been..."

"A vampire?" Jay tilted his head to chuckle, the low sun beamed through Victor's porthole window and mirrored as orange flares in his glasses. "No, true. I wish, sometimes. But no. So anyway, I wanted to tell you before you made travel plans. I don't want you to go to Germany in September. Okay?"

Victor had found the tissues, held one to his mouth while shaking his head, *no.*

"Okay, well, I need to make some calls," said Jay, hopping to his feet. "Okay if I use one of your staff's phones?"

"Sure," Victor mumbled.

Jay considered him. "You have a good feel for Westchase's accounting department, right? What's your impression? Are they a well-run shop?"

Victor needed a moment to catch up to the change in topic. He nodded. "Looks like they do a good job. I wasn't on site, but I reviewed all the workpapers and didn't see any red flags. They have a nice system for allocating capital and expenses from their parent company, Oklarkana. Seems like a well-run department. I'd like to think they could learn a few things from me, or us, I should say."

Jay smirked. "Glad to hear they have such a great department, because we're not buying Westchase, we're merging with Oklarkana. We won't need two construction accounting departments, so we need to decide which one to keep. You've audited them, now they'll come in and evaluate you."

"Wow, I thought…"

"That's because that's what we told you," said Jay. "We're announcing the merger tomorrow."

"But then…" Victor's frown deepened. "Then Westchase will know it's a competition. They'll come in trying to find every problem they can."

Jay feigned surprise. "Come on, you just said you could teach them a few things. What are you worried about?" His expression degraded to disdainful sympathy. "We both really know it won't be that difficult for them to find problems, right?" This was stated as an obvious fact that Victor should readily acknowledge.

Victor tried to object but Jay talked over him. "Personnel problems, efficiency issues, insubordination, other stuff. Back when I was with Arthur Andersen, if we were auditing your department, right? We would have been all over this kind of dysfunction."

Jay's mention of Arthur Andersen, the now-defunct accounting firm, triggered a flash of recognition, a memory Victor couldn't quite access as he struggled to defend himself. "Well, we have some issues...I mean, of course, but, but if we had gone in *looking* for things like that at Westchase, I'm sure we would have found them."

"You didn't do a good job on the audit?" Jay challenged sharply.

"We did," Victor said quickly, too quickly, unable to think fast enough to keep up with Jay's attack. "But it wasn't the same. It's not a fair competition, if they know but we didn't."

"But I'm saying they would have to be terrible to lose to you, right? And that's clearly not what you found. Vic, come on, there's really not any doubt which department is going to win. You miss deadlines all the time. Your staff screws up regularly."

"No, they just—"

"Victor," Jay cut him off, frustrated and getting angry. "You constantly cover for them and do their work. Maybe you think it's admirable. It's not. I can't count how many times your staff has missed a key issue, misapplied an accounting pronouncement—or ignored it entirely—or screwed up the accounting for a construction project. What about the Maryhill project? This Westchase audit report is just one of many examples."

"We never send you shoddy work," said Victor defensively, throat tight and short of breath. "What I submit is well-researched and properly documented. I'll stand by our work product. Including the Westchase audit."

"That's because *you* correct it," said Jay. "You catch

your team's mistakes regularly. I see it, and so does Poorwig," he referred to the head of domestic External Reporting.

"That still counts."

"That's poor management, that's what that is. You're a terrible manager, Victor. I would say you could be a strong lead accountant in the Westchase accounting department, but..." Jay looked at Victor's mouth, at the smear of blood on his lip, and grimaced.

He rose to leave. "The Westchase controller is retiring, so it's already been decided that I'll get the nod. I'd love to tell you that this gives your team the inside track." Jay gave him a pitying squint. "But of course you understand that I need to be impartial, and retain the best accounting department for the new company."

Victor tried to sound confident. "We'll put our best foot forward. I'm positive my team will be up for the challenge."

"No, Victor," Jay snapped. "You do *not* tell your staff that it's a competition. I've seen what happens to morale in those circumstances. I need your people to be cooperative, so that the Westchase manager gets a clear picture of your operations. If I hear you told your staff, I'll can every damn one of them on the spot." He rapped on the office doorframe, two staccato knuckle strikes. "I need to head back to Chicago in the morning, but I'll be shuttling back and forth in the next few weeks, to keep tabs on this process."

He was gone for only a second before poking his head back in. "Don't stay too late. I know how vampires like to have their nights free."

THETHERSON, FAMILY NIGHT

Victor arrived home with his mind in test pattern, a screen of fuzzy white with the volume turned down to a dull buzz. He trudged into the house—and brightened to see his daughter stirring a diet protein drink at the kitchen counter.

"Amber, baby, welcome home! It's good to see you."

"Hi," said Amberly with a half glance in her father's direction. With her mother's hair, augmented with fluff and curls, a half glance was nowhere near sufficient to make eye contact.

Victor stopped in the middle of the kitchen and dropped the arms that had been rising for a hug. Porky pug was rhythmically barking in the backyard, rowlph...rowlph...rowlph.... "How was school today?"

"Good."

"Good is good." Victor shed his sport coat and unpacked his lunch cooler, including the empty dirty Tupperware he had retrieved from his wastebasket. "Anything fun or exciting or out of the ordinary?" He soapy-scrubbed the Tupperware—Barbara hated any sight of dried blood. So did he, actually. Or wet blood. One more opportunity for his staff to give him crap, when they caught him microwaving raw meat, just to take the edge off.

"Mm, no."

"So what's up tonight? It's so good to have you here. We're going to hang out tonight, just the three of us? I can rent a movie," Victor said hopefully, "or we could play Scrabble."

Amberly held up a finger until she finished swallowing the last of her drink. "I just needed a pair of shoes and more makeup. I'm in a hurry right now. I'm only back for a sec."

Victor had difficulty hearing the last of this because Porky pug had produced a rare double-rowlph and Amberly had spoken in a lackluster run-on with her back to him as she left the kitchen and headed upstairs.

"Why...what's going on tonight...what's on your agenda?" Victor kept rephrasing, louder each time, trailing Amberly but losing ground, enough space between them for her to reasonably claim not to have heard. He waited at the bottom of the stairs.

Barbara came out of their bedroom carrying a well-used and apparently full cardboard box. "What's all the yelling?" she asked in passing. In their early days she did a generic male impersonation they had affectionately come to know as her Old Jewish Guy. For a moment Victor thought she was doing Old Jewish Guy, perturbed that the world was too loud.

"Do you have to yell?" said Barbara, the irritation genuine, as she continued into the kitchen.

"Hi, no, just talking to Amber. Wow," said Victor, following her, "what a day today. Terrible, actually. I'll tell you all about it. How about here? How did your day go?"

"She's hurrying, she has a school function." Barbara stood at the door to the garage, waiting for him to open it. "My day, you don't want to know. Extremely busy. Lyle is an ass," she referred to her Wal-Mart supervisor. "You should have seen what he did today..."

While Barbara talked about "that asshole Lyle", Victor decided that for being such an asshole, Lyle was on Barbara's mind quite a bit, and the stories she told about him weren't all that unflattering. He had a feeling that asshole Lyle was sleeping with his ex-wife. *I really don't care*, Victor told himself. Whether he did or didn't care was in fact an open question, but that was what Victor told himself.

He propped the door while Barbara shoved the box under the storage rack's bottom shelf. "What's in there?"

"Pictures," said Barbara. "If there's a fire, we need to be able to get to our valuables."

"Good idea. So what's Amberly in such a hurry to get to?"

"Another mixer," said Barbara, brushing past him. "Faculty or college recruiters, maybe? I can't remember."

"Huh. Are you sure...? Seems like I was looking forward to tonight..." Victor went to his briefcase and began to flip through the pile of papers, looking for the McNulty Preparatory school calendar.

Amberly could be heard hurrying down the stairs. "Jasmine will be here any second," she called to them. "I'm going to wait outside."

"Have a great time, honey," Barbara called back. "I'm going to wash my hair in the sink," she told Victor, removing the rubber band that regulated her long brown hair, maintaining the ponytail with her hand. The only time her hair hung free was for its nightly brushing; when her head hit the pillow, the rubber band was back in place. "Grab me a towel?"

Victor found the calendar and ran his finger down to July twenty-fourth. "The Father-Daughter Dinner," he exclaimed. "That's tonight!"

"Vic, she's fine," said Barbara, but Victor was already heading for the front door. He made it outside to see Amberly getting into the back seat of a Lexus sedan.

"Amber!" he yelled, in hot pursuit but careful to navigate the broken brick from the second step and the sidewalk ridge caused by the uplift of the now-dead root of the oak tree they'd lost in a hurricane. Amberly closed the door and rolled down her window. A man got out of the driver's seat.

"Hi," he greeted Victor, rounding the front end of his car with hand extended. "Ho, yow," he blurted at the sight of Victor's vampirism, recovering with a smile but shoving his hand in his pocket. "Sorry. You're a, you got me, there. So—Amberly's dad?"

"Victor Thetherson."

Amberly hated her father's mouth when he said their last name. His fat tongue wiggled between his teeth, between the just-visible tips of his fangs. She watched him fidget and tuck his rumpled short-sleeve dress shirt past his jelly belly, while Jasmine's father, unexpectedly come face-to-face with a vampire, stood straight and still. He was short and V-cut, while her father was a big pear, a double pear, little pear on a big pear, both head and torso widening from top to bottom.

Victor gingerly pushed his forelock out of widow's peak formation. "Isn't this the Father-Daughter Dinner?"

Jasmine's father ran his hand through his black spiked hair. "It is."

Jasmine leaned past Amberly and poked her head out the window. "Tonight is really just an excuse to corner the parents and talk about fundraising."

"And Jasmine and I did our fundraising together," said Amberly, sharing window space, "so it makes sense for us to report them together. There'll be another parents' night soon, I'm sure."

"A real one," said Jasmine.

"You're getting off easy," said Jasmine's father.

"I guess..." Victor buried his hands in his pockets. "I don't know why they need to have fundraisers," he grumbled about the last thing he really cared about, "for as much as this place costs."

"I know, right?" Jasmine's father clapped Victor's shoulder. "At least we can save a little money by carpooling. The school's gone green, of course, so the girls will probably get extra credit for it."

"We're going to be late," Amberly complained, and rolled up the window.

"Okay, good to meet you." Jasmine's father was on the

move, skipping back around to the driver's side. "Just you and missus tonight, huh? That's a rare treat, am I right? What I wouldn't give to be home right now with the wife. Don't sweat it, though, I'm glad to do it for you. My pleasure. Have a good night." He threw a wave in the air and was in the car and accelerating away from the curb, laying down a thin squeal of rubber and leaving Victor fumbling for a protest.

He marched back inside the house, hollering to Barbara as soon as he cleared the threshold. "How come you didn't remind me? How can she go to the Father-Daughter Dinner with someone else's father?"

Barbara's backside was to him, her head in the sink, under the running faucet. She had a broad and flattened rear, but Victor had always like the shape. Early in their marriage Barbara had asked him to wash her hair, in the sink the way her mother always had. Her hair was strong, they had replaced the disposal three times in their twenty-two years in the house, the blades entangled, the motor burned out.

Victor used to worry her hair would become snagged while still connected to her head, the disposal through a terrible malfunction coming to life and dragging her down, tearing out great clumps of hair. Now he knew that the disposal would come out on the short end of such a battle, Barbara emerging unscathed and victorious, and he would simply have to replace the unit again.

Barbara turned off the water and groped the counter top, waving her arms blindly. "Vic! Towel!"

"Hang on." Victor motored to their master bath, feeding off the frustration over Amberly's betrayal. He grabbed a towel from the cubby shelving, yelled through the wall for Porky pug to shut up, and then paused coming back through their bedroom. The walls were bare, as were certain previously occupied, dust-free spots on the vanity and bed tables.

He laid the towel on the back of Barbara's neck.

"What happened to all the family pictures in our bedroom? They're all gone."

"You don't have much of a short-term memory, do you?" Barbara wrapped up her hair just so and came erect, dizzy, hand to the countertop for support. "You just watched me put them in the garage."

"I thought you were talking about our photo albums," said Victor.

"I bought some nice cowboy prints I'm going to hang in our bedroom," said Barbara.

Victor felt weak. "Amber went to the Father-Daughter Dinner without me."

"She's really good friends with Jasmine," said Barbara, collecting her shampoo, conditioner, brush, comb and ponytail band. "Don't worry about it."

"I'll worry about it, any time I want! She's my daughter, and I'm her father, and when she comes home, I'll tell her exactly that!"

Rowlph, rowlph.

Victor wheeled toward the back of the house and gripped his head. "Can't that dog shut up for once?"

"I don't know why Porky pug gets you so worked up," Barbara clucked as she left the room. "You're two of a kind, all bark and no bite. Except your bark is more of a whine."

Victor's shoulders sagged. He swabbed the hair out of the basin. "Amberly's embarrassed by me. This, this thing, this curse…it's ruined my life."

Barbara reappeared in the kitchen doorway. "Victor. It's not your vampirism. It's you. Look at you. What sixteen-year-old wants a vampire for a father that looks like you?" Her tone softened at the obvious damage to Victor's psyche. "You're just not the type. It's not your fault. Think of Ryan Tolbert," she referred to a friend of theirs, "he should have been bitten. Tall, dark, already mysterious and dangerous looking…"

"Ryan isn't mysterious or dangerous looking."

"Oh yes," said Barbara. "Oh yes. That's the way a

vampire should look. It's funny that you're a vampire. And if you're sixteen, you don't want funny." She patted his cheek and left the room a second time. "It's not your fault. You didn't ask to be bitten."

THETHERSON'S STAFF, SLAKING THE THIRST

At twelve-fifty p.m. the following day, the unmistakable pattern of purposeless motion caught Victor's eye. A growing number of his staff were assembling in front of Nikki's admin station. Everyone was holding or digging for a quarter.

"Flipping for Cokes already?" Victor called out to them.

"You want in? Hurry up then," said Tessa.

Quinten and Casey implored him to join them.

"No, I'm still good, got my soda from lunch." Victor held up the forty-eight ounce Big Slurpee Mountain Dew.

"Don't complain at one-thirty when you're thirsty," Florence warned. "Second flip isn't until three."

"You're flipping twice for soda now?" said Victor.

"Second time's for whiskey shots, when you're not around," said Florence for the group's benefit. "Sometimes when you are."

Victor pointed at the temp, a quarter on her thumb. "She gets paid by the hour, you know."

Larry came hustling around the corner. In retrospect Victor realized he had heard him huffing and puffing down the length of the hall. "Am I too late for the quarter flip?"

"Right on time," said Tessa.

"Where have you been?" said Victor. "I assumed you were out sick today."

"I was at the construction site," said Larry. "Doing my fieldwork."

A deep, fatigued frown settled into Victor's face. "Larry, I've told you I don't think visiting the construction sites is necessary to account for their activity. No one else does that."

"That's why it's my signature move," said Larry.

"But you're out of the office once or twice a week, for a half day each time."

"Go big or go home, that's my motto."

Florence practiced a quarter flip, the coin thunking audibly against the thinly cushioned bones in her hand. "I thought your signature move was online chatting with your taxidermist girlfriend."

"Your signature move is sleeping with your head erect and your eyes open."

"And your motto is 'Go home, early.'"

"And your motto is, 'Just because my monitor is asleep, doesn't mean I am.'"

"You scummy redneck, it's going to be a pleasure to have you buy me a Coke," said Florence. "Flip the damn quarters already."

"You're on," said Larry. "Borrow me a quarter."

Nikki tossed him her coin. "I gotta run to the lobby," she said, punching the call forward button on her phone and abandoning her post. "Put me down for a diet Rock Star."

"You gotta play to win," Larry dismissed her request.

"Flip," Quinten ordered, eager. Seven quarters launched. Tessa and Quinten botched their catches.

"Crap," said Tessa. "What is it?" she asked Quinten as he crawled after his quarter.

"Heads," he called out his own. He eyeballed Tessa's, lying by the temp's heel. "Tails."

Quarters were thrust into the group's middle for inspection, Casey's on her palm, everyone else's on the back of the hand.

"Heads."

"Tails."

"Heads."

"Tails."

"Heads."

Tessa held up her quarter to remind everyone. "Tails. I'm out."

"Me too," said Larry and the temp, the other two owners of the three minority Tails and therefore out of the competition to find the unlucky winner.

"What was it?" said Casey. "Heads or tails?"

"Four heads, three tails, so tails are out," said Larry. "You're still in, Casey," he told her when it still hadn't sunk in.

"Got-dammit, I hate playing with her," Florence griped about Casey. "You don't catch it and then just open your hand! You're supposed to slap it on the back of your hand! If you had finished that flip like you're supposed to, heads would be out!"

"I can't," said Casey. "My equilibrium's off." She pointed at the decade-old brain surgery scar visible in its arc across the part in her hair. She set the quarter on the back of her hand and watched it slide off and hit the floor. "See?"

"Flip the damn quarters," said Florence to the other three still at risk.

Flip-flip-flip-flip, Quinten swatted at his and sent it streaking across the office, sharply striking the conference room window. "Crud." He dashed after it.

Quarters were revealed.

"Tails," said Florence.

"Tails," said Raj.

"Tails," Quinten hollered from across the room.

"Got-*dammit*," said Florence, in the majority and so still in the running.

"Heads!" Casey exulted, triumphant, and shrinking under Florence's scowl.

"Me and the dummy and Fancy Pants," said Florence. She swatted a stiff stray swatch of hair from her face—

for Victor it might as well have been ruffled by a warm
Mediterranean breeze, along with the diaphanous toga
robes women like her often wore.

"I'm gonna puke if I lose to you two," said Florence,
"even though it is one-hundred percent luck."

Quinten grinned. "I'm gonna beat you, Florence, look
out."

Raj readied his quarter upon finger and thumb, the
other hand in his fancy pants pocket.

"Flip already," said Florence.

Quinten flipped his quarter in the air and made
another wild stab, this time successful.

Slap-slap-slap on the backs of their hands.

"Heads," said Quinten.

"Tails," Florence read Raj's quarter, which put her in
the majority regardless the outcome of her own flip.
"Got-dammit." She unveiled hers, heads.

Cheers, jeers and catcalls rained down on the two
finalists. Larry roughed Quinten's shoulders. "You got
this one, boy. Take Florence down."

Florence prepared to flip, glaring at Quinten. "If
David was in this position, he'd do the gentlemanly
thing and offer to buy."

Victor winced at David's name. This was the second
day the AWOL accountant had neither appeared nor
returned Victor's voicemails and text messages. If the
same held true tomorrow, he would have Nikki reach
out to David's emergency contacts.

Quinten deflated. "Sure, okay."

"That's a good boy," said Florence, dropping her hand.

"Quinten," Larry drawled, "just keep your lip zipped
and flip that quarter. Being a gentleman with Flo is a
one-sided transaction."

"I don't mind," said Quinten. "It's my turn anyway."

Tessa groaned. "If we took turns, we wouldn't have to
flip, and then we'd all be sitting at our desks working
right now. Duh."

"You know," said Victor, "that's probably a good idea.

Everyone that's lost already, you should head back to your desks. I'll send an e-mail announcing the loser."

"Just flip, Florence," said Tessa. "Best two out of three. Flip."

"You all suck," said Florence. She flipped and smartly caught her quarter.

Quinten's flip arced toward the temp, who yelped and hopped out of the way as Quinten lunged forward, stumbling and playing the quarter off Nikki's admin station wall.

"For crying out loud, if you drop one more, you lose," said Florence.

"I agree," said Larry. "That's embarrassing to watch."

Quinten held up his quarter. "Tails."

"Match," said Florence, indicating that she thought they would have the same result. She unveiled a heads. "Shhh..." Her jaw set and she cocked her arm to whip her quarter at Quinten, who flinched and fell out of his squat, bumping his head on the corner of Nikki's station. "I'm calling 'match' again, do you hear me?" she said, pointing at Quinten. "Your quarter better damn well match mine."

They flipped, and again unveiled one of each. "You little cheater," said Florence. "Fine."

"Okay everyone," said Victor. "With the merger announcement this morning, everyone needs to work double-time to clean up all their backlog."

"First," said Raj, smoothing his black inlaid-print tie against his caramel Brooks Brothers dress shirt, "we flip to see who has to take Florence's money down to the Pinch-A-Loaf for drinks."

"What?" Victor yelped. "No...when did you start flipping separately for that?"

"When we all realized how god-awful boring accounting is?" Tessa offered. "Come on, Vic, we need a diversion from time to time."

"Work hard, play hard," said Larry. "That's our credo."

"Hey Vic," said Nikki as she re-entered the

department. "The folks from Westchase are coming."

Victor went whiter than usual. He pictured Jay his boss, nodding and chuckling. "What time?"

"This time."

"What does that mean?"

"Now."

"Now? Nikki that's not...hi, welcome," said Victor, hurrying forward as three people rounded the cube wall. "Victor Thetherson, manager of this..." In his panic he couldn't remember the word 'department'. "...here."

Raj stepped slightly in front of Victor, aborting his attempted handshake with the woman leading the trio. "Raj Dajiv. Welcome to Texahoma. I've heard a lot about you and your team. Very impressive. We'll need to get together and talk about your philosophy, on marrying if you will the accounting area's task with your operations folks' goals. There's a fascinating McKinsey report on the topic I'm sure you're familiar with. I'd love to get your opinion."

"Great," said the woman. "Darla Kieler." Now she reached Victor. Her handshake was as stiff as the set of her mouth and the curve of her faded brown hair against her head. "I'm the manager of accounting for Westchase. This is Kirby Backer, my chief accountant," she introduced a frail man in a limp dress shirt and fluffy, irregular perm.

"Kirby." Raj stepped forward to shake his hand. "Raj Dajiv. Welcome."

Kirby fumbled the handshake and then waved at Victor. "Hello. Gosh what a nice department you have here. Huh," he said, noticing the teeth. He turned to Raj without taking his eyes off Victor's mouth. "You'll have to show me that report—was it McKinley? I've heard of him..."

"And this is Monique," Darla finished the introductions, "who reports to Kirby and handles special projects." Raj was fully occupied by Kirby, unable to do more than wave at Monique, who was reserved to the point of appearing angry, golden hair and peach skin, perhaps the most beautiful accountant in the world. She nodded to Victor and looked out the far window.

"Welcome, all three of you," said Victor. "I didn't know you'd be here so soon, we just announced the merger, and we were hoping to get things in order—which is fine, things *are* in order, and, well I guess, orderly. We just wanted to prepare a little for you. You know, dust off some desks, or, uh, prepare a list of good restaurants—"

"Jay Hansen said it would be okay," said Darla. She was doing all she could not to look at his mouth, while Kirby stared to beat the band. "And we live around here, so I don't think we'll need that restaurant list."

"Right, right. Well, luckily my team is basically all here, let me introduce—"

"Nice to see you again, Darla," said Larry, stepping forward to shake hands. "It's Larry. Your hospitality during the audit was top-notch. Hopefully we can match it. Kirby, hope your grandmother is feeling better."

"She battles..." Kirby gathered his thoughts and smacked his lips. "She battles gastric distress. It's just something she needs to live with."

Darla cut Kirby short on what appeared to have the makings of a more extensive explanation. "We're very glad to have the opportunity to review your operations." She scanned the remaining faces. "Where's David? Is he out today?"

"He is," said Victor.

Florence hissed and made a bite motion with thumb and two curved fingers. Monique leaned around Darla to get a better look at Victor. "Ooh, that sounds bad," said Kirby. "Snake bite? You know, I've *heard*, but thankfully haven't had the good fortune—or rather the misfortune...I've *heard* that rattlers can—"

"Where should we set up?" said Darla, hiking the strap of her satchel higher up on the shoulder of her dowdy gray business suit. "We won't waste any more of your time."

Quinten produced his quarter. Victor shook his head and frowned. But quarters started appearing on multiple cocked thumbs.

"We have quite a list of documents we need to see," said Darla. "And we'd like to spend some time interviewing each of you. Victor, maybe you and I could talk this afternoon. Right away?"

"Sure."

"You want in on the flip?" Quinten asked Monique and Kirby. "We flip every afternoon for drinks."

"Good idea," said Florence. "Let's do this over."

"Guys," said Victor, "just...just one this afternoon."

"Kirby and Monique, go get set up," said Darla, declining Quinten's invite on their behalf. "Nikki, can you show them where they'll be sitting?"

"Right this way," said Nikki, skipping into the heart of cube country.

"Don't worry," Quinten told Kirby and Monique. "We'll be having another flip at three."

The afternoon was awful for Victor. Darla, his counterpart at Westchase, knew her stuff. She asked all the right questions, forcing him to highlight the processes he had yet to implement, the procedures he had been planning to formalize in a policy manual, the latest accounting pronouncements his team didn't yet have a handle on.

He would have suspected Jay of planting the questions, if Darla didn't seem so able to smell incompetence all by herself.

By five-oh-five, four people remained in the department: Victor and the Westchase team. His staff were truly oblivious to what was transpiring. Darla informed him they would be working late to copy and organize all the materials they had collected, then spend the next day or two back at their office before returning Thursday or Friday to "hit it full speed".

Victor worked until they finally left around six-thirty,

then drove numbly home, prepared a pitcher of bloody Bloody Marys, and retired to the garage to run his trains, full speed, and to wonder...nothing. He kept trying to ignite a spark of self-pity, but not a single thought, nor the emotion to stimulate one, came to his head. Not anger, not sadness, not hopefulness. Victor Thetherson was empty.

YOUNG VICTOR THETHERSON

Coming off three months of Legionnaire's disease, a ravaging bug that had dulled his senses such that he saw no color, heard no highs or lows and felt little beyond innate pulls to the apartment's refrigerator, toilet and bed, twenty-two year old Victor Thetherson awoke from a lifelong ignorance to the wonders of mousse.

His benefactor was his roommate's older brother, in town for the regional NCAA basketball tournament. God bless this stocky hippie jock for leaving his crap everywhere, disemboweled backpack on the living room floor, gym shoes on the kitchen counter, and can of Suave Extra-Firm Hold atop the toilet tank.

Without the forty pounds shed by the Disease, Victor never would have experimented. Exiting the shower, toweling off his longish flat mop, he saw for the first time in memory a *tapering* of his torso from chest to pelvis, vertical shadows in the absence of gut fat that framed hillocks of abdominal muscle before converging and disappearing into his pubes.

Somewhat attributable to an optical illusion or at least an optimal confluence of the vanity's missing light bulb, water droplets in his eyelashes, and the overhanging cowl of the towel, the attractive vision led to posing, and dabbling with the mousse.

"About time, you princess," Lester his roommate greeted him when he emerged from the bathroom. "Come on, they're waiting for us, Bert wanted to get there before—what did you do to your hair? Gimme that..."

Young Victor fought like a starving wolverine over a mink carcass, largely avoiding damage to his updated 'do.

At the basketball game he watched for reactions to his new look. Years of being fat made Victor an expert in derision recognition. He saw none. For a change, people looked at his eyes instead of his stomach, his hair and his clothes, which were also a prop of sorts—Lester's brother had insisted Victor borrow a University of Northern Arizona sweatshirt. Men and women alike seemed to take him in as a whole, seemed to be curious as to his nature, seemed to like what they saw. Out of respect for Lester's brother he tried not to enjoy himself too much, because Michigan was trouncing UNA.

Monday was his first day back at school, in weeks. Tuesday, Wednesday, each day he allowed Mousse to put a little more lift in his hair. On Wednesday he asked a question in class—this was his senior year at the University of Houston, and it was the first time since fourth grade that his nerves hadn't squelched the attempt.

At the accounting banquet Thursday night Victor stood and re-tucked his dress shirt into his drooping pants for the fourth time and nodded at Annie Poykins, a cute freckly redhead. Annie disengaged from the small group parked at the warm end of the appetizer bar and crossed to Victor's table. She had another girl in tow.

"Hey, you made it," Annie greeted him. "I wasn't sure."

"I'm feeling much better now," said young Victor.

Annie cocked her head, unsure what to make of that. "I want you to meet my roommate, Kathy. I drug her here, and now she's regretting it. She's ready to kill me, and then herself."

Kathy stepped forward and shook Victor's hand. Acne reddened her cheeks but didn't stand a chance against her smile and her eyes. The girl was beautiful. Short like Annie, but with a waist, softer here and firmer there, and everything alive. Not fidgety like Annie; vibrant.

"You don't look like an accountant," said Kathy. "Who drug *you* here? This guy?" She pointed at twenty-five year old, seventh-year accounting student Larry Cocachello, head down over his plate, consuming appetizers.

"Followed me here, like a puppy," said Larry. He popped a pizza bite in his mouth and clamped his hand on the back of Victor's neck. "Mary had a little lamb, but everywhere Larry went, little Victor Thetherson followed him."

For the first time Victor could remember, dating even further back than the fourth grade, his blood pressure did not elevate, his ears did not ring, his mind did not stumble all over itself to construct a face-saving response. It was Mousse, and more: the Disease was gone but in retreat had left behind the trenches of its neural warfare, a wholesale disruption of communication links that unexpectedly served as a mental defense shield, so that Victor didn't need to raise his own.

"We're from the same hometown, three years apart," Victor told the girls. "I heard Larry hated accounting, so I thought, that's something I'll probably like. And I do." He winked at Kathy. "Sorry, but I am one."

"I would say that *being* an accountant but not *looking* like one," said Kathy, glancing at Larry, "is the perfect combination."

Victor had looked like an accountant his whole life. Frown of consternation since birth. Shirts buttoned all the way to the top. Buster Browns. Ordinarily he would have corrected Kathy, explained how he had recently, unnaturally lost a sixth of his body weight, and found mousse. But his synapses were still a disease-broadened gulf across which messages of insecurity could not travel. Instead he said what he wanted to. "Would you like to join us?"

Kathy waited until Larry scooted two chairs down, then sat next to Victor. Annie fulfilled her minimum obligation as wing-woman, five minutes hearing about Larry's dorm room taxidermy business before excusing herself.

"So I have to tell you." Kathy rested her fingertips on Victor's forearm while she talked, with a soft Texas twang. "Annie told me there was a good-looking new student in her Accounting Theory class. Since she's practically married, she wanted me to meet you."

"I've been in accounting classes with Annie for three years," said Victor.

"You have?" Kathy laughed, an effervescent patter that tickled Victor's ears. "Annie's such an airhead. She won't even *see* guys that have me drooling. It's because she thinks she's found her man. She and her boyfriend stay home Friday nights to watch movies, in their pj's. I don't even think they fool around anymore."

Victor tsk-tsked.

"How long are you planning on being here?" said Kathy.

"I graduate next month."

Kathy laughed as she pressed the heel of her palm into the confluence of Victor's shoulder and chest—by no means a bundle of muscle, but no longer swollen with fat. "I meant this banquet."

The conversation and the laughing and the light contact continued through dinner, the awards presentation, and the motivational speaker. When pressed to explain his choice of the accounting profession, Victor rhapsodized on the satisfaction of focusing a wide stream of noisy information overload into a single coherent journal entry. When he brought Kathy back to the lobby of her deluxe upper-classmen dorm, he was kissed goodnight. Like his hair, Victor was lifted like never before.

This was the beginning of a short stretch of desirability. Throughout, Victor was too flu-dulled to get excited, floating above the events with out-of-body detachment, marveling at his good fortune.

Less than a month later, and to the present day, Victor was cherishing the fact that he never saw Kathy again, and talked to her but once more, forever leaving her with the wrong impression of him.

Two days after kissing her, Victor and most every other graduating senior attended the accounting department's Interview Day at the campus armory. They had been measured by their instructors for four years; and most had just sat for and received their pass/fail mark on the CPA exam. And yet the tight-lipped smiles, shrill laughter and moist handshakes suggested everyone was starting from scratch, even-steven in the competition for a coveted spot with one of the eight major accounting firms.

Next to the armory's circa-1950's scoreboard hung a modern electronic board, columns of red LED 2-digit numbers, each assigned to one of the interviewees and paired with a dollar amount currently ranging from a little under $20,000 to just over $30,000. Eyes were drawn to this board like weather-threatened travelers watching an airport's departure schedule as an electronic wave swept top to bottom, updating the dollar amounts.

Larry stood with Victor, studying the board. "No stinkin' way. I dropped another three hundred bucks! Seven years at this school, and nineteen grand is the best they can do for me? What brainchild came up with this God-awful system?" He threw his Franklin Planner to the floor, stomped on it, picked it up and brushed it off, and turned to Victor. "Am I right?" He hoisted Victor's hand to check out his coat-check chit and then found the corresponding number on the Big Board. "Thirty thousand? Victor Thetherson broke thirty? That proves it. This is a terrible system."

"My last interview went well." As in the six prior interviews, Victor had calmly, articulately lauded the Auditor's recent and rapid evolution from financial reporting cop to trusted business consultant. "They seemed to like me."

Over the preceding months, long before falling into his sick bed, Victor had agonized over this day, wishing prospective employers would rely solely on grade point average.

Now, thanks to the lingering effects of the bug, Victor's reflexes and autonomic nerves were running way behind his IQ. With his thoughts unaccompanied by blushing, sweating, and stammering—a fair nutshell of his personality for the first twenty-two years of his life— his lips and vocal chords did a great job conveying them.

"Remember Mr. Schlabbin's favorite saying?" Victor referred to the Milford science teacher. "'Make sure the brain is engaged before putting the mouth in gear.' I think I finally figured out what that means."

"Schlabbin's a sensei now?" Larry exclaimed. "The world's gettin' screwier by the second."

"So how does this work?" A girl stood beside Victor, looking from the Big Board to his numbered chit, and back.

Victor had never laid eyes on her. She had a severe face and killer eyes, pouf-bangs, and a luxurious two- foot long mullet. A pert auburn lock curled around her waist, had to be tickling her stomach where it was laid bare by her abbreviated top.

"For me," said Victor, skipping the detailed explanation his mouth had wanted to give, "very well."

"Because it's a system designed by morons," said Larry.

The girl faced Victor. She hooked her thumbs in the belt loops of her Jordache designer jeans, drawing Victor's eyes to a muscled abdominal wall. "I overheard one of you accountants describe it as a cross between the stock market and an auction," she said.

Marshall Bell, big chin and sharp tongue and one of the architects of this bidding system, had joined them. Jay Leno was a caricature of Marshall. "I would call it an intrinsic valuation system," he said. "Every prospective graduate starts with a market value based on a combination of their grade point average, whether they passed the CPA exam, any awards or internships, that sort of thing."

"Extra credit for wearing a belt *and* suspenders," said Victor, slightly detached from his body, enjoying the mellow, lucid sensation.

"He's not usually this funny," Larry told the girl. He gave Victor a quick shake of the head, asking him to stop it.

"Everything you described is in the past," said the girl to Marshall. She put her hand on Victor's shoulder and pointed at the Big Board. "So why did this guy's number just go up?"

Sure enough it had, $30,000 become $32,500.

"One of the accounting firms must have just upped their bid for him," said Marshall, as incredulous as Larry, squinting at Victor, clearly wondering if he was somehow gaming the system.

Larry flung his chit across the floor. "Screw this. I got a damn fine job offer waiting for me back home. Vic, I have no doubt I can get you in at the grain elevator too, if you're as sick of this dog and pony show as I am."

"Thanks Larry," said Victor. "I'm fine here."

Larry nodded. "You betcha." He drifted away, toward the door.

The long-haired girl couldn't take her eyes off The Board. "That's what you would make? Your starting salary?"

Victor looked down into her face. He forgot to worry about his bad breath, his tendency to spit-spatter his interlocutor. "Are you regretting your major now?"

"Not at all," she replied. "I'm an artist. Accountants bring home the bacon, and artists make the world a more beautiful place."

Young Victor smiled. He didn't have the nicest teeth, but at this stage of his life, they were still white. "So what brings an artist into the world of accounting?"

"Art show tomorrow," said the girl. "I'm in charge of setting up. This was supposed to be over by now."

"I wish we had a grand finale to entertain you with," said Victor. "But this is as exciting as it gets."

"What the hell is that?" said Marshall, facing the armory's rear entrance. The three of them joined most everyone in the room in picking out who, or what, Marshall was looking at. "That's the first one I've seen," Marshall spoke out of the corner of his mouth, eyes not leaving the vampire as he moved past Larry, frozen in place, and joined the Arthur Andersen table.

"I saw one at the Galleria, shopping for shoes," whispered the girl. "Her taste was impeccable." She moved closer to Victor, against him, so she could point with her thin tapered chin, minimizing movement so as not to draw the vampire's attention. "Her teeth weren't that long."

The vampire couldn't quite close his mouth, for the size of his fangs. He began a one-way banter with the two other Andersen representatives—a smooth-skinned man in a full-cut crisp-starched dress shirt who had been striking a confident slouching pose while surveying the room, now ramrod-straight and shrinking in the vampire's presence, and a woman in her thirties with coiffed short red hair and pale skin that glowed pink alongside the vampire's white.

They competed for their associate's approval, a contest of boisterous laughter and echoing affirmation, until the vampire tapped the placemat-sized dot-matrix printout on the table in front of him. "Who's next?" His words carried across the subdued hall.

The starched, shrinking man leaned forward to read the list. "Victor Thetherson."

In seconds most everyone in the armory had located

Victor. Now he strode forward.

Again, vibrant cognition ensconced in neutered emotions encouraged Victor to stop, to slow the moment and turn around, to find the girl with the sculpted abs. He retraced three steps. "After my interview with this vampire, would you like to go get something to eat?"

"That would be wonderful," she said. "I'm Barb, by the way."

Victor nodded. He saw Larry shaking his head, and Marshall stroking his chin, trying to bring his wit back online. Beyond and around them, more eyes were on Victor at this one time than in total during his entire college career. He inclined his head at the bid grid on the wall. "Keep your eye on the board, Barbara."

The only one uninterested in Victor's identity was the vampire, and to a lesser degree the woman beside him, throwing occasional glances at Victor to gauge how much time she had to score points with her associate. She pressed a curved, jewel-spruced fingernail into the back of the vampire's hand and leaned in to speak in his ear.

The vampire didn't react. He watched Victor approach and stand before their table. "Let us move to the next room, shall we?" said the vampire.

The third wheel on the Andersen team was to his feet and leading the way, into one of fifteen temporary offices created by frame-and-canvas cubicle walls. They took folding chair seats around a square table. The vampire's associates deferred to him, waiting as he opened a blue Andersen folder and extracted Victor's transcript, résumé and a fat fountain pen. He brought his fingertip to his mouth and flicked his tongue, using the moistened digit to uncover a fresh page in his notebook.

"So." The vampire settled back in his chair. "Student. I won't imagine that every three-nine-five grade average is equivalent. Occasionally it's an indication of issue-resolution skills. Often it's nothing more than a sterile academic execution of study-and-regurgitate. For these interviews however we're assuming every three-nine-five we see has the desired skillset."

The vampire spoke in rapid bursts, separated by long pauses. Almost as if he were receiving the script via earphone from a remote de Bergerac, one sentence at a time.

"Which leads us to ask: Why you? Why should we choose *this* three-nine-five?"

The vampire was low-centered, with thick legs and a torso that tapered from waist up to shoulders, to pin head; cursed with close-set eyes pinching the bridge of a hook nose, above fleshy lips; and perfectly at ease with his homeliness.

He was also at least ten years younger than the woman, who from her age—in a rigidly hierarchical industry where each year you were either promoted or pushed out—had to be a partner. Judging by her deference, the vampire was also a partner, and a more senior one to boot.

Or he was powerful enough to be breaking all the rules.

The easy answer, the one Victor had given seven times already that day, was queued up: I have a desire to learn. I have the ability to solve problems. I have fabulous communication skills.... "You choose me," said Victor, "because every other person you've talked to today is ready to follow the rules and rise according to the schedule. I'm interested in running a business."

The vampire's eyes narrowed. Feeding off him, the other two stiffened and frowned. The vampire brought his hands together, slowly clapping. "Cheers."

He had been about to say "Bravo", Victor was sure. The vampire's careful sentence construction, Victor realized, was to avoid impaling his lips on a double-lipped consonant.

"Auditors are guilty of thinking that we exist to further the fortunes of our clients," said the vampire. "You have hit the nail on the head. We in fact exist to further our own fortunes. We are not a service."

The vampire turned his piercing gaze—the power of which Victor had now come to see (see, not fall spell to, thanks again to the insulating sac surrounding his mind)—upon the woman.

"We are a business," she was compelled to utter.

"Do we like young Victor?" the vampire asked his colleagues.

"Yes, definitely," said the other man. "Just a few more questions—"

"Bullshit!" The vampire's temper flared too quickly to avoid the big "B", drawing two beads of blood to his lower lip. "If we are, as Cheryl says—" He cued her with a long yellow-nailed finger.

"A business."

"—then why would we waste time on...on..."

"Protocol," Victor assisted him.

"...when we already know what we want?" the vampire finished.

"I don't—"

"Choose a life of service if you wish," the vampire bellowed, cowing his associate. "Don't choose it for our firm. Don't choose it for me. Don't you dare choose it for young Victor."

In the vampire's grip the metal frame of their table groaned; a fracture line spread across the Formica.

"Agree," said the other man, sweat stain sapping the stiffness out of a growing swatch of his white shirt as he made a shaky entry on Victor's score sheet.

The vampire let go of the table. The woman patted his hand, soothing him, leaving her hand there when his face relaxed to a smile.

"Thank you for taking the time to talk with me," said Victor, rising. As he shook each hand, his knees were wobbly. The vampire had gotten to him after all. "Very informative."

"A treat," said the vampire.

Barbara watched Victor's market price hit forty grand

before she backed out of dinner, blaming the three hours of art show set-up still ahead of her. However, Victor was informed, she and a friend would be out later that night at Bayou Mama's.

…and so he had just downed a shot with Lester his roommate when he caught sight of Barbara on the Bayou's dance floor, arms in the air, hair swishing past the small of her back, stomach bare and working it to Tears For Fears' latest number.

Victor fought through the bar huggers to ditch his shot glass, then grabbed Lester's arm. "There she is." They met Barbara and her dance partner as they were leaving the floor.

"If it isn't the vampire slayer," Barbara greeted him, loudly over the dj's pulsing techno-stutter transition into *White Wedding*.

Victor stared, struck nearly mute by the woman at Barbara's side. "Hey there."

Barbara paused, voice sharpening. "You know each other?"

"Hi, I'm Gail," said the tall raven-haired beauty, Grecian features, immense dark eyes, olive skin, slow toothy smile.

"Yes. No. We haven't met." Victor had only gazed upon this woman from afar, in the dorm complex cafeteria his freshman year, in Principles of Accounting his sophomore year, and by chance sightings then and thereafter, infatuated and in fantasy love for all four years at the university. Always he saw her glowing from within, doubly separated from the crowd by heavenly light beamed down upon her face.

Now he pictured her in a toga, stomping grapes and clapping along to a Mediterranean tune, atop a cloud. "Victor."

"And Les." His roomie asked for and received a high-five from both. "What are you drinking?"

"Campari and soda," said Gail.

"Pepsi," said Barbara. "I'm a cheap date, huh?" she

said to Gail.

"Only in that sense," said Gail. "High maintenance," she pretended to share for the boys' ears only. Barbara tried to pinch her nipple.

"That's unfortunate," said Les. "Vic and I are poor in every sense of the word. Okay you three, don't hesitate to hit the floor without me. I'll be right back with the goods."

Les earned a big smile from Gail, lost on the back of his retreating head. Gail crossed her arms and turned to Victor, making him blink in disbelief, that he was actually talking to his goddess. "So Barbie tells me you kicked a little butt in the Accounting world today. Faced off with a vampire. Lived to tell about it."

"So far so good," said Victor, at a loss for anything better to say.

"I saw a *60 Minutes* the other night," Gail continued. "They said vampires have always been out there, but something has changed. Maybe a genetic mutation, they weren't sure. But now some of them are going mainstream. I can't imagine working with a vampire." She directed this final comment to Victor, and shivered on his behalf, not without some pleasure.

Victor planned on accepting a job offer from one of the other firms, even though it was four thousand dollars less than Arthur Andersen's bid. Simply opening the envelope from Andersen had dropped his body temperature and brought his heart pounding into his throat. Seems his autonomic fight-or-flight responses hadn't been missing, just buried, and now exhumed by the vampire.

Gail wielded similar powers. "Why don't you two go ahead without us?" she said, when Victor's response time lagged. "I'll wait for Lester."

Victor nodded grimly and offered Barbara his hand. In conservative fashion they transitioned from Billy Idol to Adam Ant, surrounded by what seemed to be an audition for the stage production of *Footloose*. Sedate, pensive, Victor was sweating less when the song ended than when he had taken the floor.

Barbara thanked him for the dance and excused herself to the bathroom. Gail wasted no time doing likewise when Victor joined her and Les beside the out-of-service mechanical bull.

"How'd it go?" Les asked with a smile that suggested he had made good progress.

"Fine." Victor sought a glimpse of Gail wending her way through the crowd. "I've been lusting after her for four years. Now with my best chance, my only chance, I came across as a dufus."

"You're talking Gail?"

Victor nodded. "Can you believe it? Can you believe she's Barbara's friend?"

"There is something attractive about her," said Les.

Victor's eyes bugged out. "She's Aphrodite and Helen of Troy and Susanna Hoffs all rolled into one. She's untouchable, a goddess—I mean, look at her face. Could you even imagine being able to kiss her?"

"I might not even waste time on her face. Did you see those legs? Hey." Les was suddenly angry, backhanding Victor's chest. "Why are you talking about her? You're already lined up with Barbie. Don't mess with the system."

"I don't know if I can…"

"And what's with your hair again?" Les demanded. He came after Victor's moussed 'do with both hands, and they tussled.

A bouncer separated them. "Stop doing that," said Victor, tousled.

"Just stick to the plan," said Les, straightening the collar of his interior polo shirt. "Which is, me screwing your dream girl."

Victor spotted the girls at the bar. Barbara caught his eye, smiled and waved. A dude standing in front of her raised his beer to reclaim her attention, saying something to make her laugh. Gail nudged Barbara and turned away from their hopeful suitors to speak in her ear. They glanced at Victor and Les, and laughed, not uncharitably.

"I'm going to wave them over," said Victor. "You go get them another drink. Put some alcohol in Barbara's Pepsi this time."

"Incorrect," said Les. "It's time to play some pool."

"Good idea. I'll ask them to join us."

Les's tone was sharp. "Have you never played hard to get? Now's the time."

"That only works for women."

"Let me ask you this," said Les, getting in Victor's personal space. "How confident are you in your ability to go head-to-head with those two guys?"

One in a blue open-necked silk shirt, the other in a green cashmere sweater, both garments tucked into tight blue jeans, both men chewing gum, smoking cigs, swigging beer and holding court.

Victor pictured his moussed hair and hint of an abdominal muscle in the steamy bathroom mirror. "Fifty-fifty."

"Wrong. You forget." Les put his arm around Victor and leaned in even closer. "You already won the battle. This chick wants *you*, not vice-versa. You're a graduating senior with a great job. She wants to marry you. Officer and a Townie, Gere and Winger. You don't want that, not in a million years, but what matters is that she does."

For a moment Victor was able to evaluate Barbara without comparison to Gail. "Don't you think she's pretty?"

"That's irrelevant. But yes…that hair, oh baby. Vic, you've just come into money. You're holding an asset, for the first time in your life. Now you're putting that asset up for sale. You don't take the first bid." Les waved his hand like shooing flies. "We're getting ahead of ourselves. Right now just trust me. Walk up to the bar, a few feet away from them, and buy four beers. Nod politely to her in passing—wink if that's in your repertoire—and then join me at the pool tables."

Les clapped him on the back and headed for the back of the club. Victor did as told, ad libbing as he passed behind the two club professionals, using what turned out to be one of the last trickles of flu-spawned composure left in his tank, pausing to force a gap between the playboys and tell Barbara that "It was nice to meet you." He successfully fought the urge to hedge his bets, ignoring Gail and looking only at Barbara before moving on.

The pool tables were occupied. "There's no time to wait," said Les. They pumped fifty cents in the dart machine and picked through the basket until they found three plastic darts with serviceable tips.

They had completed one round when Barbara and Gail joined them.

"What, are you two antisocial?" Gail challenged.

"We did what had to be done on the dance floor," said Les, zipping a dart through the air to embed in the board with a solid *thunk*. Double two. "It was time to display our broad array of skills."

"All you're going to get is your ass kicked," said Gail. "Are those beers for us?"

"No, but..."

Gail drank from one bottle, handed the other to Barbara, and held out her hand. "Gimme."

"Wait your turn."

"No—"

"Hey Miss Grabby Pants..."

Les grappled with his second opponent of the night. Triumphant, Gail toed the line and made a show of readying her frame and form, drying out Victor's eyeballs.

Barbara put her hand over his eyes. He heard the *clack* of dart hitting the board's frame, sideways. "Ooh," he said, blindly wincing.

"Keep your eyes on the board," Barbara advised him.

"That's good advice for Gail," said Victor.

"That's actually not her name," said Barbara. "Gale is short for Nightingale, because she wants to be a nurse. Just so you get the name on our trophy right, it's Florence."

"Last place doesn't get a trophy," said Les as he picked up both her darts from the floor. "Maybe another beer."

"I'm just getting warmed up," said Florence. "But speaking of which, these beers aren't going to last forever..."

"This date just got more expensive," said Les.

"You have no idea," said Barbara, looking straight at Victor.

At that point a tall bearded man in a small cowboy hat marched into the pool room and called out, "Me Sheila!"

Florence squealed and ran to him, jumping into his arms, feet free of the sticky pool room floor for a full French kiss.

"Who the hell is that?" Les asked Barbara.

"That's Morley, the New Zealand sheep rancher," Barbara replied, romance dripping from her words and putting tears in her eyes. "I can't believe he's here. How did he find her? They haven't seen each other in six years."

Victor calculated. "Six years.... How old is Gail?"

"Florence. Twenty-one."

The three of them watched Morley the sheep rancher whisper in Florence's ear, hands on her waist, keeping their hips locked together.

"Flo," Les barked. "It's your turn!" He jammed the dart in the waistband of his parachute pants and pointed.

Florence waved him off without so much as a glance, gazing smitten up into Morley's face. "Don't wait for me."

Good for Les that he didn't, as he never saw Florence

again.

Victor and Barbara saw each other non-stop. Later that night back at the apartment, his bedside phone rang, it was gorgeous acne-cheeked Kathy from the accounting banquet, wondering what he was doing and whether he had any interest in coming over to her place. Victor looked down at naked Barbara kissing his chest, and declined. The click of Kathy hanging up was the sound of the hypnotist snapping his fingers, awakening Victor from his hipness.

They were married six months later. The next time either of them saw Florence was when she showed up at Victor's office, forty-two years old and looking to start a new life ("Wrap things up" were Florence's sour words). Victor hired her on the spot, smitten by her heavenly glow, the intervening one-fifth of a century like the needle skipping across a dj's turntable.

To be fair, Victor largely saw Barbara the same way, shorn of the years' accretions.

Two women who constantly wondered why they had gone wrong; and Victor, who even during that period of confident lucidity couldn't have imagined any other destination, his tepid vampirism notwithstanding. They had in common an unconscious and mistaken assumption that whether it had occurred at birth or at the Bayou, their fate had long been sealed.

THETHERSON, BACK WHERE WE LEFT HIM

Victor had put a tremendous hurt on the pitcher of blood and assorted masking agents when his cellphone rang. He stared at the derailment that had occurred at sector three; a tiny dairy cow was trapped under an anhydrous ammonia tanker, only its back legs and udder showing, and Victor was too listless to care. He answered without checking the number.

"Vic! I'm glad I caught you," came a vaguely familiar woman's voice. "What're you up to?"

"Six-one and about two-fifty. Sorry, that's a joke. It's accurate, but...it's just something I like to do. Nothing. Engineering."

"What? Vic," the girl was yelling over a lot of background noise, "where are you?"

"Who is this?"

"Nikki! Your secretary!"

"Nikki," Victor said, both statement and question.

"Come get me, Vic. I need a ride. I'm hammered!"

"What?" said Vic. "What...where are you?"

"The Opposite-Striped Zebra. Do you know where that's at?"

"No...no, Nikki, I can't. I've been drinking."

"Vic, you bad boy. How many have you had?"

"Two."

"Well I've had six, or something. So I'm a lot drunker than you are."

"I suppose."

"So you have to come get me, Vic. Please. Come get me."

Victor wasn't familiar with the Village district north of the Rice campus, trendy shopping, warehouses redeveloped into condos, art houses and clubs. In the course of his searching he dead-ended three times in the vast parking lot of a deserted tire factory. He drove by the *OSZ* sign more than twice before realizing it was an acronym.

And so it was nearly an hour after they spoke that Victor found Nikki. She was dancing with Tripp.

"Vic!" Nikki squealed, throwing her arms around him.

Victor, uncomfortable, started to return the hug as Nikki broke it off. "Hey, wow, so…Tripp, hi. I didn't know you two knew each other."

"That would have been true two hours ago, man," said Tripp, dressed like an urban cowboy and sounding like Neil Diamond. "I like to come here after an evening shift at the Longer Labs. I've actually had my eye on this little gal for a long time." Tripp patted Nikki's butt, making her skirt's fringe of tiny metal longhorn skulls tinkle, receiving a quick kiss on the cheek. "Tonight was the first time we talked. We've been dancing all night. When she told me where she worked, we had a small-world moment and decided we needed to get you down here pronto. What took you so long?"

"The directions were awful," Victor complained to Nikki, who was watching her own bare feet as she danced.

"I'm glad you came, brother. Hold down the fort, I'll be right back with another round."

Tripp had a clear path to the bar through a sparse population of glum goths shuffling to the Bee-Gees. "That was nice of you to get drunk in the house of the un-dead," Victor said to Nikki. "I guess I should feel right at home here."

"Disco night brings in a different crowd," said Nikki. "They're poseurs, Vic." She gave him a long look that suggested her comment was heavy with meaning.

A roar went up from the bar. Tripp seemed to have just lost an arm-wrestling match with the bartender, who thrust one victorious hand in the air while the other poured Tripp a shot. Dressed in fitted black mesh with sliver sequins for sleeves, the bartender was either old, bald Duane "The Rock" Johnson back from the future, a member of the Village People unwilling to leave the past, or a vampire.

Tripp tossed back the shot and turned down the bartender's offer of a rematch.

"Why didn't you tell me you had such a hot friend?" said Nikki, resuming her slow soft-sole gyrations.

"Yeah, well..." Victor said no more until Tripp returned, with shots and martinis. Victor tried to share one or the other with Nikki, obliviously back in her own dancing world. Tripp frowned and shook his head, silently indicating she'd had plenty. They saluted each other, they saluted the bartender at Tripp's urging, and they polished off the shots.

Victor grimaced and then asked hoarsely, "Do you have a few bags on you, by any chance?"

"Oh, man." Tripp theatrically slapped his forehead, sloshing his martini and knocking off his cowboy hat. "I forgot to carry a couple bags of blood with me, just in case. Sorry bud. Looks like you're going to have to get it the old-fashioned way. You're going to have to *earn* it." He tipped his head at Nikki as she retrieved and donned his hat, way too big, hiding all but her pimpled chin and limp stringy curls.

"Will you be at the Bank tomorrow?" Victor asked, suddenly feeling on the verge of a blood deficient stupor.

"Nope." Tripp took Nikki's hand and led her through a slow twirl. He reversed her direction and stopped her halfway. From behind Tripp removed her hat, tilted her head and put his mouth to Nikki's neck. She gave a little squeal and kept gyrating, eyes closed. Tripp looked at Victor. "See?"

Nikki looked up at Tripp. "Are you a vampire too? God that's so sexy."

Victor gulped martini and looked away, shamed by his conscience's accusation that he had been fantasizing about what might happen with Nikki. The alcohol, the Nagging bloodthirst, and the frustration, ingredients to a potent cocktail of emotional chemicals roiling inside Victor Thetherson's brain.

Tripp turned Nikki loose and moved nearer to Victor. "Tough day, mi amigo? You look a little frazzled."

"Well, now that you ask. Did I ever tell you that I'm divorced but still living with my ex?"

"What!?" Tripp doubled over like he'd been punched. "You and Barbara are divorced?"

"For two years," said Victor. "Here's another one," he said while Tripp gaped at him. "Last night my daughter attended her school's Father-Daughter Dinner. With another father."

Tripp went from incredulous to apoplectic, gurgling, slapping his blue jean thigh.

"And, my boss showed up out of the blue and told me I'm a failure. Because of which, I won't be going to Germany next month for the company's hundredth anniversary celebration."

"No—aw, really?" Tripp lost the histrionics and gave Victor a sober look of consolation. "That son of a soulless witch. How could he?"

"We're merging with a competitor, and he pretty much promised that me and my incompetent staff will be looking for work soon," said Victor. "But I think I'm more unhappy about Germany. I didn't know how much I was counting on that trip. Until he took it away."

"Aw, Vic, that's a raw deal. Geez…and I have to admit, I was kind of considering the possibility of joining you. A trip to Germany, the beer, the confrontation with that vampire hottie…aw man." Tripp was now feeling equally bad for himself.

"So, anyway…" Victor raised the martini glass to his

lips, then lowered it. "I'm guessing you can give Nikki a ride home. You're good with Tripp?" he checked with Nikki.

She stopped dancing. "You're leaving? We're just getting going. Come on, Vic, stay."

"Here, have a half a drink on me." Victor handed the martini to Nikki and winked at Tripp in a tepid attempt to be lascivious. "I'm gonna hit the lavatory on the way out. See you both later."

On his way to the bathroom Victor hyperventilated and had to open his mouth to breathe, like a gazelle on the run, drawing wide-eyed looks. In the long hallway to the bathroom he paid it forward, ogling three couples demonstrating assorted selections from the Fully-Clothed Kama Sutra. They were less self-conscious about their dry humping than he was his vampirism.

His mood cycling quickly, Victor was now outraged that Nikki had lured him here and then rejected him in favor of Tripp. He was going to have a hard time facing her at work the next day.

He wouldn't have to wait that long. When he emerged from the bathroom, Nikki was waiting. "What do you want?" Victor growled.

"What do you think I want?" Nikki seemed poised to move closer, then settled back on her heels. "What do you want, Vic?"

Victor moved toward her, and Nikki took a step back. Three more strides and they were in the shadowed alcove leading to the alley door. Nikki took Victor's hand and pulled him to her. She had been breathing hard from the dancing, and now was positively gasping. She closed her eyes and tilted her head back ever so slightly.

Victor leaned in, his own breath ragged, his heart pounding. Her throat was long and skinny, finely muscled. His mouth was on her, eliciting a moan from Nikki, inspiring movement in Victor's long dormant pants. His arms encircled her thin frame and Nikki struggled without resolve. Victor slid his lips up her throat to kiss her jaw, one hand rising to her chest.

Nikki knocked his hand away. "No! What are you doing? Do you think...God, Vic, what's your problem?"

"What's your problem?!" Victor countered, his face pulsing with embarrassment. "You came on to me, you...never mind!" He banged through the back door into the alley, fuming, digging in his pocket for his car keys, stumbling over a drain pipe and cursing loudly. His head hurt, his libido was back, and he hungered for blood, a stifling mass of confusion that had him picturing a cow's neck with the skin peeled back to reveal raw hamburger.

Nikki burst into the alley and stormed after him. "How dare you try to put the make on me," she yelled. "I'm your secretary! You're so pathetic, you can't even—"

Victor wheeled and charged her. He lifted Nikki in a bear hug and carried and stumbled with her until they slammed into the brick wall. "Is this what you want?! Is this what you want?!" Victor wrenched Nikki's head back and dove at her throat. One fang gashed her thin skin, her blood smearing across his lips, hot and salty and filled with a palette of scents and flavors he had never experienced.

Nikki screamed, and Victor sank his fangs into her throat. Her scream died out as he drank.

The door opened and Tripp stepped into the alley, noticing the two locked in embrace. "Hey now you two..."

Victor jerked his head back and stared at Tripp. Blood covered his mouth and chin; blood pulsed from the wounds in Nikki's throat, burgundy on pale yellow in the exit sign light.

"Oh my God," said Tripp. He lurched to his right, knees buckling before he found the wall for support. "Oh boy. Oh, my."

Victor started to cough, half-dropping Nikki to the grimy pavement. He just stood there, unable to articulate what had happened.

Tripp crawled to Nikki's side, grasping her hand as her head lolled. "Vic, holy shit. How much did you..." A rumbling came from Tripp's stomach. He was on the verge of puking.

"I don't know," Victor whispered. He was moving backward, wiping his mouth with his bare arm, turning and striding quickly for the parking lot at the end of the alley, wrenching his keys from his tight slacks pocket.

Street construction meant the alley was the only way out. Victor drove slowly, riveting his attention on the encroaching trash bins in the tight confines, letting his eyes wander just once and getting a clear view of Tripp's anguish as he cradled Nikki.

"What have I done?" Victor screamed as he drove, making wrong turn after wrong turn. He looked in the mirror as a streetlight swept across his face, smeared in blood. "No!" He pounded the steering wheel and the seat beside him, and braked just in time to avoid running a stop sign at a deserted intersection. Finally he chanced upon the main drag that would take him to his neighborhood. As he approached his street, forty minutes after fleeing the scene, he expected the police to be waiting for him.

But he knew nothing the law could do to him was sufficient punishment for the crime he had committed on his secretary. In one impulsive act he had cursed Nikki, doomed her to an eternity of suffering and damnation.

Victor Thetherson pulled into his empty driveway, into his garage, and cried, the wracking sobs taking every last bit of his energy and angst, leaving him as listless and drained as he had left Nikki.

THETHERSON, THE MORNING AFTER

Victor didn't sleep that night. Every waking moment was misery. Even the tried-and-true solace of running his trains didn't help. He walked like a zombie into his office, at six-thirty the next morning.

Somebody had been in his office. All the papers and files, his computer and keyboard and can of mousse, everything had been pushed to the edges of his desk. Even his desktop protector had been tossed the floor, to draw full attention to the wooden stake, centered in this clearing.

No one else was on the floor, to Victor's knowledge. He went to Nikki's workstation, but it didn't appear she had been in.

The stake was actually a lath or landscape marker, shaped like a mini picket fence post, lightweight and nearly flat, whittled to form a sharper point. Victor paced the floor, agitated. The stake had no markings. It was cracked at the base—hardly meaning to, Victor split it in two, and then snapped each piece over his knee, more because he could than out of any anger.

Who put it there? It could have been any of his employees. Jay, maybe. That janitor—make one innocent comment about there not being enough toilet paper and forever be on the janitor's bad side. Maybe Nikki had a brother, who wanted to send a message for what Victor had done to his sister. Maybe it was Nikki, cowering in a dark closet, slobbering with bloodlust, waiting till Victor's normal arrival time to call him on her cell and beg him to come drive the stake through her heart.

With the arrival of Larry, Florence, Tessa, everyone (except David) in a three-minute window either side of eight o'clock, Victor was struck by another level of self-loathing for what he had done. He had ruined a life. All Nikki had wanted was to come to work, do her job however poorly, and go home to her Swinging Office Workers Online community or the season premier of *How I Met Your Mother*. It didn't matter how much she had begged for it, didn't matter how drunk she was, how naïve. He had had no right to bite her.

At eight-forty-five, Florence and Raj grabbed Larry for the morning smoke. They paused at David's empty desk, and stopped in front of Nikki's vacant workstation.

"Geez Vic," Larry called into his office, "first David and now Nikki? Gawd man, who's next?"

Raj struck a thinker's pose. "Hm, is there a pattern?"

"Let's see," said Florence, "good-looking men, heroin-addicted girls..." She slapped Larry's shoulder. "I got it. Vic's a lazy vampire. It's whoever sits closest to his office. Heads up, Vampire Vic's gonna get you next."

Victor couldn't even look at them. He was sweating so hard it trickled from his armpit down his side. He wanted to throw up.

A squeal from behind made Victor jump and twist in his chair. The window washer peered in through the porthole window, waved, and made another pass with the squeegee.

"Whoa, take it easy, Vic," said Larry with a grin. "I always wondered what vampires were scared of, besides garlic. And Jesus. Never would have guessed window washers."

"Lets in more sunlight when they're clean," Florence speculated.

"Victor has plenty of sunscreen with him, don't you worry," said Raj. "I've seen him applying SPF one hundred before we go out for lunch. In the winter."

"Sorry I'm late," said Nikki, hustling to her admin station. "Did I miss the smoke break?"

Victor jumped to his feet, and froze. Everyone stared as she slung her duffel bag under her desk.

"I left my last pack of cigs at the bar last night," Nikki explained. "I woke up so late this morning, I didn't have time to stop on the way here. Raj, you packing? I could use something with a little extra sizzle."

"Honey." Florence moved closer and reached tentatively for the square white bandage covering the left side of Nikki's throat. She started peeling at the top corner. "What hap—oh my." Florence recoiled and crossed herself.

Nikki peeled off the bandage, displaying her bite, inflamed and glistening, oozing blood, open and angry. Victor couldn't help but compare his handiwork unfavorably to movie bites, so clean and well-spaced, almost art-like. This looked like it was done by a rabid beaver.

A sharp chirp escaped Raj's lips before he covered his mouth to stifle the rest of the scream. Larry lost color, staring at the mark, his lips working without sound.

Everyone's eyes turned to Victor as he slowly emerged from his office, studying Nikki. She smiled at him—no fangs.

"What?" said Quinten, hurrying over, ignoring Tessa's request to wait up. "What's going on?"

Victor took Nikki by the hand and marched her to the conference room while his staff stared, stricken dumb. Victor shut the door and held Nikki in the near corner, mostly out of sight.

"You're okay?" he asked.

"Groovy, actually," said Nikki.

"You haven't, you know...changed?" It was hard to tell, she normally resembled a vampire anyway, pale skin and bulging eyes, scary teeth, creepy cackling laughter. "You're okay? Anything?"

"I'm grade A," said Nikki with a Cheshire Cat smile. "Maybe a little infection where you bit me. Hurts."

"Show me your teeth," Victor ordered, sticking a finger between her lips before she could comply.

Nikki giggled, exposing crooked, fangless teeth. She kept smiling. "You bit me." She popped him, both hands to his chest. "You *bit* me." Nikki popped him harder, and screeched it, "You bit me!" She spun around and skipped elatedly toward the window, stumbled a few steps at an increasingly acute angle to the floor, and smacked headfirst into the metal window frame.

"Awk," Victor blurted, rushing to where she lay dazed, a vertical cut on her forehead. "Oh Nikki, ohmygosh, this is all my fault." He hung his head and said, "Fuck. Fuckarooni, I mean." Jay hated swearing.

Nikki propped herself on her elbows and looked up at Victor with puppy dog eyes, the puppy drunk, happy, sedated and under a spell. "Am I yours now? Is that how it works?" She ran a finger across her chest. "Property of Vampire Vic."

"No, no, you're not my property."

The blood that trickled into her bushy eyebrow elicited a mixed reaction inside Victor, gyrating stomach and giddy sparkles behind the eyes. "Hang on," he said, bustling out of the conference room and through the crowd that had formed. "I need a band-aid. I need lots of them."

The temp took one step inside the conference room and saw Nikki and screamed.

"Boss, what have you done?" Tessa demanded.

"Nothing," said Victor, searching the supply closet, finding the first aid kit and a box of tissue. "She fell." He hurried back to the conference room. "She fell all by herself and hit the window frame."

"I was dizzy from last night's blood loss," said Nikki as Victor wiped her face and blotted blood oozing from her cut. She could not stop smiling.

Victor realized everyone was silent and gaping. He

turned to look at his staff. "Yes, I bit Nikki. Last night. Yes."

Minor chaos and low-level pandemonium ensued. Two exceptions: Larry turned around and walked like a zombie back toward his desk, and Florence pressed against the conference room window, transfixed on Nikki's throat. The rest of his staff babbled at each other and wrung their hands and hollered out rhetorical commands, until Victor could take it no longer.

He strode toward the door. "That's enough," he snapped at them. "Back to your desks."

Eyes widened, mouths were shut, and everyone backpedaled and cleared the area. Victor returned to Nikki and finished a poor job fixing her up, four band-aids side-by-side up her forehead.

"You okay?"

"Never better."

"I'm, I just lost control, I shouldn't have. I didn't think…. I'm so sorry."

"Don't be." Nikki flashed her eyes. "I broke your blood-letting cherry, didn't I?"

Victor blushed. "It wasn't awful?"

"That was the wildest thing that's ever happened to me."

"What happened after I left?"

"I don't know," said Nikki, daubing a tissue at the blood trickling into her eye. "I woke up this morning in Tripp's bed."

"He didn't…"

Nikki ran her hands up and down her body. "Not as far as I know."

"The police, I mean, he didn't call the police?"

"Same answer," said Nikki. She thought about it. "Why would he?"

Victor stuttered. "Because, because-because I bit you. I bit you. Nikki…God help me, I drank your blood."

"You're a vampire," said Nikki. "That's how you dooze it."

"But..."

"Let the cops come, I'll never press charges." She sat up and two of her band-aids slid down to her eyebrow. "It was the most incredible experience of my life."

Victor stared at her while a third band-aid tilted like a hanging sign with one broken hinge. "And you're not, you're not hungry? For blood? You're not...changed?"

"Not as far as I know. How long did it take you?"

"It was instantaneous. I woke up a vampire."

Nikki got glum. "Really? Maybe it works differently for different people." She brightened and slapped his chest. "Maybe it takes three."

Victor gave her a wad of tissue. "I hate to say this, but I think we need to take you to the clinic for stitches for your forehead."

"Don't let them touch my neck."

"Deal," said Victor, shaking his head in amazement.

They stopped at Nikki's desk so she could grab her duffel bag. His staff stood near the copier, some distance away. Victor was ushering Nikki down the aisle when Larry appeared, blocking their way.

"What is it?" Victor demanded as Larry screwed up his mouth and shook his head, trying to dislodge the right words.

"God dammit anyway," Larry blurted, eyes darting to Nikki's throat. He lost color in his cheeks and grunted, "Nothing," and retreated down the row of cubes, before turning around and pointing. "You know what? I'm going to call your mother."

Victor shook his head and hurried Nikki to the exit.

Nikki didn't have a doctor, and Victor didn't know where else to go—he thought about and ruled out calling Barbara for advice—so by default they wound up at the clinic he and his family went to. Victor held the door for her.

"Oh my," said the receptionist as Nikki approached the front counter. "Honey, what happened to you?"

"I tripped and fell," said Nikki.

"No," said the receptionist.

"Honestly," said Nikki.

"No, I believe you, honey, I was just saying...ouch." She started filling out a patient input form. "Have you been here before?"

"No, but he goes here," said Nikki, pointing at Victor, who was choosing a magazine to bury his face into.

The receptionist saw Victor and made a face. "Did the accident happen at work?"

Victor blanched at the prospect of getting Human Resources' attention for a workers' compensation injury. "No," he called out.

"I wasn't working at the time," said Nikki.

"Were you at work?"

"No, I was not *at* work," said Nikki. "It always takes me a bit to get going in the morning."

"If it happened at *work*," said the receptionist, "then we'll need to file this as a workers' compensation claim."

"No thanks," Victor called over.

"It wasn't an offer," said the receptionist. "Did this happen at work?"

"I would have to say no," said Victor. "We'd rather it didn't."

The receptionist stared pointedly at Nikki. "Did this happen at work? Yes or no?"

"I'm going to say no," said Nikki.

"Just say the truth," said the receptionist, exhibiting frustration.

"Vic, what would you say?" said Nikki.

"I'll go with no," said Victor.

The receptionist shook her head and made a note in Nikki's file. "Have a seat. The doctor will be with you shortly." She waited until Nikki walked away before scooting on her roller chair to whisper to the medical records clerk and nod ever-so-slightly at Victor.

"They got Cosmo?" Nikki asked Victor.

"I don't know," said Victor.

A nurse opened the door into the waiting room.

"Ms...Hathaway?"

Nikki jumped up and hurried forward. "Close enough." She waved at Victor before disappearing inside.

An hour and twenty minutes later, Victor's doctor appeared at the door. "Vic?" He beckoned Victor to join him, and then directed him into the first empty exam room and shut the door. "How are you, Vic?"

"Good, thanks Dr. Choose." It was pronounced "Shoes", but Victor never remembered until after he screwed it up. "Choose. Sorry."

"No problem. No issues with the...teeth, and all?"

"Nope."

"Thought about losing any weight?"

"Sure..."

"I think it would really help," Dr. Choose continued. "Not the...you know. I mean in general."

"No, I know," said Victor.

"Speaking of which," said the doctor, "we have a young woman in the other room with a pretty big wound. You're acquainted with her?"

"I suppose you're talking about my secretary, Nikki. She fell, not at working, so I brought her right in."

"What do you mean, 'not at working'?"

"It's not work-related."

"Work comp is pretty broad," said the doctor. "If it happened at work, regardless whether she was actually working at the time, we'd have to treat it as work comp."

"It did not happen while *at* working."

"Fine," said Dr. Choose. "And the neck? Did that happen *at* working?"

"No. What did Nikki say?"

"This is why I interview you separately," said Dr. Choose, showing some irritation. "So that I can compare your answers. But she said it happened last night. Were you with her?"

"Just for a bit."

"As we counsel teenagers who come in here, that's all

the longer it takes." Dr. Choose stared sternly and then stepped closer, producing a pen light and indicating Victor should open his mouth. He lifted Victor's top lip and peered inside. "I can see you've used these recently."

"You can tell?"

"No. That was a bluff." Dr. Choose stepped back and pocketed the pen light. "I ran a blood test on your secretary. Are you interested in the result?"

Victor slumped forward and buried his face in his hands. "Yes," came his muffled response.

"It's just a preliminary result. We're going to run a full panel that'll take a couple days. But do you remember when you came in to see me after you'd been bit? It was obvious right away."

Victor nodded.

"I don't see any of that in her," said the doctor. "I don't see any of the things in her that were obvious in you." He studied Victor. "Are you surprised?"

Victor uncovered his face. "That's great news."

Dr. Choose crossed his arms and gave Victor a cross look. "Are you going to start biting people now, Vic?"

"No," said Victor, sullen like a fourth-grader scolded by his teacher.

"Okay then." The doctor made like he was going to pat Victor on the back, thought better of it. "The flesh around the bite mark is slightly infected. I'm going to give her an antibiotic prescription. Nikki doesn't seem to bear you any ill will. But I suggest you pay for it."

"Okay," said Victor as Dr. Choose left the room. "Thank you, doctor."

The Houston air was already more water than gas, but the wide open spaces above his head cleared Victor's mind as he inflated his lungs. He donned his sunglasses and pulled the travel tube of Banana Boat spf 75 from his sport coat pocket and rubbed a glob on the wide open spaces on top of his head, slicking his hair to the side in a more traditional comb-over. Nikki exited the clinic a few minutes later.

Victor inspected her stitches. Tears welled up in Nikki's eyes. "It's so awful," she sobbed, moving into his arms for a hug. The shock had worn off, and Nikki was finally succumbing to the horror.

Now he wanted to cry too. One rash act, and everything had changed. The doctor had no right to give assurances—ask Tripp, science was still in the Dark Ages on vampirism. At the very least his job was in jeopardy. This was why he was timid. He couldn't handle bold. "Nikki. I'm so sorry."

"Couldn't you have caught me? You knew I was a quart low. Do you think it'll scar?"

"The cut, you mean? You're worried about the forehead?" Without his reading glasses Victor had to hold her at arms' length to see her forehead clearly. "I don't know, looks like they did a good job. No, no, I think it'll heal okay."

"Good." She wiped away the tears, and instantly perked up. "So you wanna get some breakfast? I didn't have time this morning."

"Yeah, sure, okay." They got in his Subaru. "We'll fill your prescription, and get some breakfast. Both on me. Doctor's orders."

"Sounds like a plan, man." Nikki rolled down her window and stuck her foot out. Looked at Victor and slapped his arm. "Cheer up, Vic." She rearranged limp locks over her stitches, flipping down her visor to aid the cover-up, immediately distracted by the bandage on her neck. She sat up taller in the seat and peeled back the bandage to get a better look. "I was actually planning on getting a vamp mark tattoo. I hope this doesn't heal too quickly."

EUGENE

When Eugene Foreman's neighbors approached his third floor apartment, they held their noses, picked up their step and hurried past his closed door as quickly as they could. The smell was too much to bear.

Eugene understood their revulsion, and accepted it as his cross to bear. No one truly understood the danger. The danger they were in. How much worse the world would be without the vampire hunters, and in particular how lucky these people at the Shining Gate Apartments were—with not one but now two voracious vampires in the neighborhood—to have a vampire hunter for a neighbor.

Eugene S. Foreman, Vampire Hunter. Make that Vampire Slayer. "S" for Slayer. Eugene had been fixated on vampires forever. On killing them. When he was little the other children knew not to dress as vampires for Halloween, because Eugene Foreman would kill them. Fake kill them, but painfully.

Not long ago on Ancestry.com, Eugene had learned that he was descended from a long line of vampire slayers. He traced his lineage back to a slayer named Corsecreu in the thirteenth century town of Tirgu Mures, in the heart of Transylvania.

Rarely in this life does one discover that he is fated to be exactly what he has longed for. Eugene's family mocked and shunned the proud heritage he brought to their attention, and the t-shirts emblazoned with the family crest he had designed. How could they resist the calling? Inexplicable to Eugene, who had sobbed tears of joy while filling out a positive customer experience feedback form on the Ancestry.com site.

The top Slayer sites recommended "milieu immersion" as essential preparation for battle with the loathsome bloodsuckers. And so Eugene adorned his Houston apartment with hundreds of garlic necklaces and crosses of many sizes and colors. He cooked with garlic and accented with garlic sauces. He disinfected with bleach and holy water. He stashed terrible, terrible weapons for the coming clash with the un-dead. With his recently uncovered nemesis.

Vampires were about as common as movie stars, sports heroes and rock'n'roll gods, and likewise had historically created quite a stir when the populace found them in their midst. For that reason most maintained a defensive perimeter—instead of limousines and gated mansions, they relied on makeup, contacts and false teeth.

Eugene was born and raised in New Orleans, lived there with his family until moving to Houston eight months ago. Vampires in New Orleans were revered rather than scorned for the infection upon this earth that they were. This made Eugene want to puke up his garlic-pasted saltines. Plus, the local slaying competition was intense.

Eugene was therefore extremely disappointed to discover that Houston—every city, he suspected—had adopted a decidedly Big Easy attitude toward the bloodsuckers. The whole planet had gone vampire gaga. This made vampires more difficult to kill, but easier to track. A new vampire had recently popped bright and blinking on his radar screen, right there in his neighborhood.

The timing was perfect, because Eugene had recently completed the honing of his skills. All that was left was to sew his costume, and to print and post the flyers reminding his fellow tenants that their building had been vampire-free for eight months *and so would they please stop calling the police because of the stench?*

THETHERSON, DARKLY DRESSED

By Friday Nikki was clearly not a vampire. Her teeth remained offensive but non-threatening. She brought a bag of day-old garlic bagels to the staff meeting Thursday—during which Quinten's nose suddenly began to bleed, without any reaction from Nikki beyond starting a debate on whether Quinten had a brain tumor.

Neither had Quinten's nose blood done anything for Victor, but he didn't consider his disinterest to be any measure—if Nikki were a vampire, nose blood was exactly the type that would get her going. Nikki was freaky like that.

She tapped on his office doorframe at eleven-thirty. "Master, we're all running to lunch."

"Master? Nikki, come on now."

"It's what you are, so..."

"No, I'm not. I'm not your master."

"Vic, that's the way it works."

"No it doesn't."

Nikki brushed aside his protest with a wink. "I just wanted to let you know the Westchase folks will be out of your hair for the next hour."

"You're going to lunch with the Westchase people?" Victor shook his head, and tried yet again to convey their dire situation, without disobeying Jay's order. "You know, they're auditing us. It's not supposed to be a love-fest."

Larry walked past his door with dandelion-head

Kirby from Westchase. Kirby said something and Larry punched Kirby good-naturedly in the arm. Kirby poked Larry in the ribs, and Larry tousled Kirby's puffy hair, and then they were beyond Victor's field of vision.

"Can we bring you back something?" said Nikki.

"No, Barb packed me a lunch." This was half true, she had told him at the prior night's dinner table that they (she) had overdrawn their checking account and so his lunch Friday would be whatever he managed to keep from eating at dinner. So Victor had a small container of blood grits and two fatty spare ribs awaiting him in the refrigerator.

"What are you doing tonight?" said Nikki.

Assuming he could finish the regulatory report and prepare all the month-end reconciliation templates for his staff, and then make a big dent on the pension accounting research project Jay had assigned him, Victor was going to browse the hobby store and then head home to play with his trains. "Just hanging with the family."

"You're divorced though," said Nikki.

"Oh. You heard me tell Tripp."

"But you still live together?"

"Yes, it's easier that way."

"Are you allowed to date?"

"Well, I don't know," Victor stammered, immediately heading down the wrong road. "I mean, we should probably, intra-office relationships—"

"I have a friend who would love to go out with you."

"Oh. Wow. Okay, sure, yeah...wow. Yes. I can date." Victor giggled. "How should I get her number, or talk to her, do you think? I don't know exactly when I'll be done here, so hopefully she'd be okay with something a little later."

Larry had walked past Victor's office, and then again, now on the third pass stopping shy of the threshold and reaching out to knock on the open door. "Sorry to interrupt." His eyes swiveled to Nikki's stitched-up forehead and then down to her throat, two scabs ringed by intersecting orange bruise-blotches.

"Did you look down my shirt, you perv?" said Nikki, not upset in the least.

"No I did not," said Larry, a quaver to his drawl. "Victor..." He was unable to make eye contact; unwilling to look in Nikki's direction; addressed Victor's hardhat paperweight. "I just wanted to make sure you were okay with me providing project accounting spreadsheets to Kirby and the Westchase folks."

"We need to give them whatever they ask for," said Victor. "But remember, this is an audit. Make sure everything is in good shape before you give it to them. We want to look good, right? I mean, what if, say, just for argument's sake, Westchase was acquiring us?"

Larry scoffed with a snort and a raspberry lip-buzz. "In their dreams."

"Or pretend we're merging," said Victor, "and this audit is how the executives are going to measure which one of us has the better department. We'd want to look good, right? We'd want to look our best."

"Victor," Larry was earnest, "you know we are all committed to looking our best."

Now it was Nikki's turn to snort. Victor sighed. "I'm just saying, it wouldn't hurt to clean things up before you give it to them," he told Larry. "Make sure everything looks okay and is fully documented."

"Certain sure on that count," said Larry. He shot Nikki a dirty look and stepped closer to Victor's desk. "I also wanted you to know...well first of all, I didn't call your mother."

"Oh. Okay. I appreciate that." Victor hid his sigh of relief behind a flutter of hand waving. "I, uh, I hope your folks are well."

With this courtesy from Victor, Larry was suddenly at ease. He hooked his thumbs in his belt loops and settled into his bowlegged stance. "We were just talking about your folks. Kirby," he welcomed the loitering Westchase accountant into Victor's office. "You should hear this. Give you a little insight to your new department. Vic's daddy died of botulism. Caught it in my family's café."

"Ooh, I'm very sorry to hear that," Kirby said to Victor, soft eyes wet with quick tears.

"Long time ago," said Larry. "Point is, it was June. My parents were floored someone would be foolish enough to order duck out of season. And with the botulism scare we had a couple years before."

"Honest mistake," Victor said in a rush. "Your folks shouldn't have, uh...well, I hope they haven't had to deal with any more outbreaks."

The worst feeling, uttering that line. He might as well have added, "And I hope they find time here and there to drive out to the cemetery and spit on my father's grave." Victor pictured his father's restless spirit squirming in discomfort, in his Laz-y-Boy recliner, watching his son's shameful display on the Limbo-lounge's black and white nineteen-inch television screen.

Larry harrumphed loudly, belatedly covering his mouth. "So anyway, I wanted to tell you I went ahead and prepped the reconciliation templates for my group."

"You did?" *It's okay to be surprised*, Victor counseled himself. *Just not pleasantly.* But his lips, his posture, his tone, all betrayed his gratitude. "I was going to do that, but...thank you."

"Don't get yourself accustomed to it," said Larry, his Texas twang ringing cleanly once again. "I remember a whole bunch of us watching you get your hopes up when Ginger Gallegos picked you as her dance partner at the pep rally. Remember that? You were smiling like true love had just bloomed."

"Everyone's ready," said Kirby, trying to direct Larry's attention to Nikki's admin station, where the great majority of the two companies' accounting departments had gathered, staging for lunch.

Larry continued squinting at Victor, seemingly the only safe way for him to view his boss. "Ginger didn't become a steady thing, now did it? Most likely this was a one-time deal, too." He winked at Nikki. "Coming?"

"Give me a second, you old perv," said Nikki, pinching Larry's butt.

"Nikki." Victor couldn't put his heart into chastising her, he was reliving his tongue-tied attempt to ask Ginger out, on the bottom steps of the fire escape after the pep rally.

"So we were thinking a double date with Tripp and me," said Nikki.

Victor tried to enjoy crossing the reconciliation templates off his to-do list. "Okay. I can probably get out of here by six."

"Work as late as you need to," said Nikki. "I'm making Tripp a private meal at my apartment. We can meet for drinks at nine."

She joined the others and they left in a babbling, cackling bunch. Victor retrieved his lunch from the break room fridge and returned to his desk. He had just started to eat when the Westchase accounting manager appeared in his doorway.

"Oh, I'm sorry," said Darla. "I didn't know you were eating."

"No-no," said Victor through a mouthful of lukewarm undercooked sparerib. He put the rib back in its container and wiped his hands on a paper towel. "I'll take any excuse not to eat that. Please come in."

"Thanks," said Darla, taking a seat. "You're not a fan of leftovers?"

"It depends, I guess," said Victor, hiding the blood grits behind the framed picture of Amberly. "Did you eat already? If you'd like to go somewhere…"

"I'm fine. I actually get sick of leftovers too. When I'm out of the office like this, I convince myself it's okay to eat out. I end up looking forward to it all morning. I already went and got a burger," she confessed.

Darla had a girlishness to her voice, a sweet contrast to her pursed lips and tired eyes. Victor assumed she was about his age; and from the little bit she had divulged during their previous conversations, concluded that she worked at least as many hours as he did.

"You know we've met before, right?" she said. "At the industry conference in Topeka three years ago. You gave a talk on maximizing the allocation of indirect expenses for tax purposes."

"That was a good one," said Victor, recalling it fondly.

Darla smiled at him. "You probably don't remember me, because I was just one more admirer swept up in the rush to the stage when you finished your presentation. The last time I felt that way was at a Loverboy concert in eighty-four. I remember the reporter from *Practical Principles* shouting out questions, but he couldn't get your attention for all the accounting managers wanting to shake your hand. Me included. You were a construction accounting rock star."

If he couldn't place Darla amongst the throng crowding the speaker's platform in the Topeka Holiday Inn conference center, Victor saw her now, through a sort of psychic tunnel that had formed across his desk, connecting the two of them and growing shorter by the second. He pinched the inside of his thigh as a reminder to focus on what he could see of her, which was drab, and her purpose, which was dark, ensuring there was no room in his thoughts for peer bonding. "Good times. So tell me what I can do for you now."

"Well..." Darla's smile faded. "I just wanted to bring you up to date on how our review is going."

"Your audit, you mean."

"I guess that's what they're calling it. Your team is being very helpful."

"That's because they don't understand what's going on."

"I'm sorry about that." Darla's brown and bloodshot eyes softened. "It's not how we would have preferred it. It's coming from your side."

"I know," said Victor curtly.

"I want you to know we're going to be very fair," said Darla. "As fair as we can be."

"Fine," said Victor.

Darla looked pained. "We're not coming in here trying to find things, honestly. We just want to document what you do, and compare it to how we do things."

"And point out which one is best."

"I have to be honest, we're already seeing some things that I think should be done differently," said Darla. "We do need to make recommendations. You had the same opportunity," she rushed to add.

"We didn't approach our audit the same way," said Victor. He heard the defensive self-pity in his voice, and ordered himself to stop. "It doesn't matter."

"It does matter," said Darla, leaning forward. "I've already gotten a good idea for the challenges you're facing. I think we're very much alike—"

Victor nodded at the yellow notepad Darla had set on his desk, flipped open to a sheet with six questions spaced down the page. "I see you have some questions. Let's get to them."

Darla sucked in her lips, temporarily smoothing the skin around her mouth. "Okay. So. I noticed that your reconciliations often aren't completed until the following month, or sometimes even later...."

Victor's date couldn't look at him. The disappointment had been obvious when Nikki introduced them, and every time thereafter when they looked at each other. Downright disgusted, this Melanie had been, when he asked her whether she had any chapstick. So Victor was relieved when she fixed her gaze upon the writhing masses on the Opposite-Striped Zebra's dance floor, and didn't look back.

Tripp nudged him, nodded at Melanie, angled his head toward the dance floor.

Victor shook his head. He nodded at Tripp and subtly tipped his head in Melanie's direction.

Tripp gave a quick head shake, and pointed with his head toward Nikki, who was in a grind sandwich between two slick bar boys. "Jealous."

"She's dancing with someone else," Victor shouted over the deep irregular techno pulse from the overhead speakers. "Someones," he corrected. "It's only fair."

"Doesn't work that way," said Tripp, in a high-register monotone that rode easily and audibly above the bass beating they were taking. "I'm okay with double standards. So, nice threads, man."

Victor held up his arm for a self-appraisal of the maroon windbreaker. Underneath he wore a thick black sweater. His pants were black, corduroy. "Nikki told me to dress dark," he shouted.

"Which would have been perfect," said Tripp.

Victor fit together the two components of the windbreaker's zipper. "Should I zip it up?"

"No," said Tripp.

"Halfway?"

"Nope."

"Just that there's a *stain* on the bottom of my *sweater*," Victor emphasized every few words to avoid a full-out shout. "I *forgot* I had spilled some *Clamato....* I haven't *worn* it for awhile."

"Since you moved down from Canada?"

"The *nights* can get *chilly*, you know that!" he shouted into a pause in the music. "Shut up. So how's the blood bank? Good week?"

This turned Melanie's head. Tripp gave her a smarmy smile as the song took off again—on behalf of Victor, Tripp was not a Melanie fan. He turned away from her. "Not bad," he told Victor. "Landed two new AB positive donors. That always cheers everyone up. You've never had AB positive, have you? I'll have to see if I can get you a recently expired bag or two." He became a French chef. "I have 'eard it is mag-ni-fique!"

Victor nodded as he took a toothpick after some bar cracker gunk wedged against a fang that his tongue dared not go after. "So I'm really *sorry* about last *week*end." He was slow to pick up on Tripp's dancehall communication technique. "I left you a couple *voice*mails, not sure if you *got* them or not."

"Yeah, got them, no problem," said Tripp.

"I just wanted to say *thank you* for not *telling* anyone. I *saw* how it *affected* you—"

"I said no problem, man," said Tripp. "No problem means I don't want to talk about it."

"Not *every* time," said Victor. "*Some*times when you *say* that—"

"Vic," Tripp cut him off. "As far as that topic goes, you're going to come in Monday, and I'll set you up, and everything will be cool. I've been setting aside a bag here and there, should be plenty to last you awhile."

Victor nodded, wanting to say more. "Thanks." He fell silent. After a few minutes spent tapping his foot to the industrial thrash music, he tapped Melanie's elbow and leaned in close enough to speak within a few decibels of his normal range. "So, how do you and Nikki know each other?"

Melanie leaned toward his ear. "We're friends."

"Oh, ah, that's nice. That's a good deal. So, you're originally from Chattanooga, Nikki tells me."

"Yeah. I'm thinking of moving back there," said Melanie, only her lips pointed at Victor, like an inconsiderate smoker redirecting her secondhand fumes, her eyes remaining locked on the dance floor.

"I've heard a lot of good things about Chattanooga."

Melanie was in her mid-thirties. In her modestly high heels she was an inch taller than Victor. Under an ornamental sweater she wore a form-fitting satiny red dress trimmed with hieroglyphic stitching, complementing her platinum blonde Cleopatra hair. "Really," she said.

"I'm, uh, I'm really into trains."

She glanced at him. "You mean jumping box cars, hoboing from town to town, things like that?"

Victor considered this. "Exactly."

Melanie contemplated Victor's body, and sighed. Victor was sure she was picturing him struggling to climb into a boxcar, calling for a boost. She drank her Disaronno on the rocks.

At eleven-thirty she and Nikki returned from a twenty-minute session on the dance floor. Nikki daubed at the pus beads on her forehead and throat as they gulped their drinks.

"You two should hook up IV bags, so you can just stay on the floor," said Tripp. "I can set you up." Thirty minutes earlier he had moved them a few tables further from the speakers, where normal conversational volume was almost possible. Since then neither he nor Victor had said more than ten words. He rubbed his eyes. "I'm getting to be done for the night."

Melanie stepped in front of Victor, striking the hyper stance of a kid at the crotchety old man's front door, ready to ding-dong ditch. "So you bit Nikki? I don't believe it. Are those even real?" She pushed up Victor's lip and hesitantly touched a fang.

"Come on honey," said Tripp, steering Melanie away from Victor. "Why don't you start working the floor for someone a little more your speed."

Melanie yanked her arm away and spilled some Disaronno on a big sweaty gent. He had been holding forth on the copious hordes of money to be made trading oil futures during a crisis while his entourage steadily expanded their holdings in the club's increasingly tight real estate market.

He wheeled, with Victor the first person he laid eyes on.

"What'd you spill on me?" the soggy trader demanded.

"I don't know," said Victor, with the left side of his dry lip still stuck up on his gums. "Melanie, what are you drinking?"

The trader recoiled and backed into two members of his entourage, raising a chorus of exuberant protests and a minor outbreak of shoving. The trader compelled his buddy to stop groping one of the women long enough to point out Victor, who had now replaced his lip, carefully, because dry lips were prone to getting poked. A few jokes were exchanged and comments hurled his way, before Victor was forgotten.

Nikki dug a finger into Tripp's stomach. "We don't know each other well enough for you to be such a grump. Snap out of it, son."

"Just not my night," said Tripp. "My dancing shoes are too tight."

"You're wearing moccasins," Nikki pointed out.

"To match my buffalo hide vest, duh," said Tripp, petting the garment's coarse fur. "The ballet slippers are underneath."

"We need to get back to your apartment and free your toes," said Nikki. "Fast."

"The lady has spoken," said Tripp. "Shall we call this one?"

"Guys," Melanie complained. "Really? The night is young, and the music is *good*." She looked at Victor. "Where do you stand on the issue, Mr. V?"

"I could stick around for one more drink," said Victor. "I should make sure you get back to your car safely."

Tripp inserted himself between Victor and the girls, and said as quietly as conditions would permit, "What are you doing? Come on, man, this isn't your scene."

"You want me to go home and play with my trains?"

"No, Vic—"

"You've been on me forever to cut loose, and now you're telling me to go home."

Tripp put his hand on Victor's chest, and lowered his voice further. "You're not going to bite her, are you?"

Victor made a sour face. "She can't stand the sight of me. As soon as you leave, I'm sure she'll be all over the oil trader. I just want to stay out a little later, okay?"

Tripp patted his chest affectionately. "Okay, be that way. But be good. And watch those guys," he referred to the oil traders. "Couple more drinks and one of them starts thinking he's van Helsing."

"I can take care of myself," said Victor.

Tripp grimaced. "Couple drinks under your belt and you think you're Dracula. Okay," he said, turning back to the girls, "behave yourselves. We're off to free my toes."

"Bye master," said Nikki.

Victor shook his head at her.

Melanie gave him a look as she called after Tripp and Nikki, "Go get married and settle down and plant a garden why don't you." She polished off her dregs and waved her glass at Victor. "Another?" Without waiting for confirmation she fished a twenty from her purse and attracted the bartender's attention. He whipped out the drinks and slapped down her change, then put his hand to his mouth, two fingers extended like fangs, and hissed.

Melanie handed Victor his drink and clinked her glass against his. "Here's to a night with a vampire." She chuckled, and leaned in closer than she had been all night. "It's funny, I was so intrigued when Nikki told me about you. You get all caught up in the stories, the books, the tabloids. But you're just a guy, right? You have a corporate job, you drive a minivan."

"It's an SUV. Well, a Subaru. Sort of a cross between—"

"Yeah you bit Nikki," Melanie continued, "but really, you get your blood from a blood bank, right? It's pretty obvious. These guys," she opened her stance and pulled the oil trader forward, "they see me with a *vampire*, right? And they're like, whatever. They don't even feel the need to rescue me."

The oil trader slid his arm around Melanie's waist. "When darkness falls, we're all after the same thing, am I right, bud?" He stuck his nose in Melanie's hair. "Damn, Cleopatra, you smell good."

"Must be the more I dance, the better I smell," said

Melanie.

"Then let's get you out there, honey." The trader picked her up and carried her to the dance floor, to Melanie's delight.

When they returned, a few minutes after midnight, Melanie's forehead and throat were glistening with sweat. She slipped off her flimsy sweater, revealing soft arms and rounded shoulders. "Can you hold this for me?" she asked Victor, fanning herself, draining half her drink. The trader patted her butt and thanked her for the dance and turned back to his group, then turned around and again buried his face in her neck.

"Yep, it's true," he said. "Even better."

Melanie laughed and pushed him away. She took the sweater from Victor. "So, what do you do for a living again? Do you enjoy it?"

Victor pushed through a wave of melancholy in order to answer. "Sure. It's a good company. My staff is pretty—"

"Isn't that so true?" said Melanie. "I've worked for some just *horseshit* companies, and a couple great ones, and it makes all the difference."

"Oh, so what do you do?"

"I'm a graphic designer, working on layouts for clients who are interested in breaking new ground. We don't care, we'll handle any industry. Because marketing isn't industry specific, it all comes down to psychology..." Melanie talked, and Victor listened. He finally excused himself to go to the bathroom, and when he came back, announced he was going home.

"Really?" said Melanie. "Now?" She fidgeted with her purse, and shook out her sweater. "I mean, we're having a good time talking, and it's not even one yet."

The trader had been listening. He put his arm around Melanie's shoulders. "You've cooled down, Cleo. Let's go rectify that situation."

"I'll be going," said Victor. "Thank you." He put his head down and moved quickly through the crowd, jostling, apologizing, keeping his face to the floor, exiting the club's front door with a great exhalation of relief.

"Hey." Melanie had followed him, and hurried to pull alongside as he walked across the street. "I decided you're right. It's late. And we had a date, right? I'm an honorable gal. We gotta leave together."

Victor's forbid himself from reading too much into Melanie's action. Even though he hadn't witnessed it at the time, he could vividly see seventeen-year-old Larry Cocachello's face now, sitting in the bleachers with his buddies, pointing at Victor dancing on the gym floor with Ginger Gallegos, laughing. "Where's your car?"

"Just down the block." This side of the Village entertainment district was dark, the boutiques and specialty shops long since closed for the day. "You know I'm sorry if we gave you a hard time tonight."

"Really? No, I didn't see it that way," said Victor. "It's fine." They walked past his Subaru.

"It's probably compensating, you know," said Melanie. "For being nervous."

"You're nervous? Around me?"

"Well yeah, you know. I mean, as a woman, you can't help but wonder—I mean, God," she glanced at him. "It would be so awful, getting, you know, the whole thing. Getting bitten. I mean, it's not like a normal bite, it's—you know, your teeth are so sharp, and they just...kind of *pierce* the skin, on my throat..."

Melanie ran a finger along the window of a beauty salon and made a hard right down the adjoining tight alley.

"You're down here?" said Victor skeptically.

"This is a shortcut."

The buildings eclipsed the streetlight. When Melanie kept shivering, Victor struggled to shed his windbreaker.

"No, you don't have to," said Melanie.

"It's okay, I have a sweater on underneath."

"It's not cold..."

"The humidity can go right through you."

"I'm just..."

Victor slung the windbreaker around Melanie's shoulders, clumsily, forcing her to slow down and then stop. "Here, this should help. Wow, you're trembling..."

Melanie's eyes were saucer-sized. "What are you going to do to me?"

Victor's breath snagged in his chest. She wanted him to bite her. He looked to the right, where the alley continued into darkness, and to the left, where no life was visible in the rectangle of light. "I'm going to..." He searched the classics for the right line. "I'm having the need for you." With an arm around her shoulder he leaned in, pushing her hair away with a clammy hand.

"You need me," Melanie paraphrased in a hoarse whisper.

The chemicals rising off her body flooded Victor's nose and mouth, registering in his swirling senses as musical notes and Lucky Charm symbols. He was wildly aroused, arms around her, one at her waist, pulling their bodies tight together.

"No, no, no," Melanie was moaning. Victor wrenched his thoughts away from the rest of her, willed himself to think of her throat skin. The windbreaker collar was in the way—he nuzzled it aside and got a mouthful of her hair instead, a wig, the taste of dye replacing the scent of music with visions of flattened, threaded petro-globules.

"Bleh," said Victor. Melanie struggled, trying to escape. She stumbled backward and Victor hung on, rode her to the ground. She groaned in pain—and so did he, his hand pinned beneath her, his wrist afire.

"Are you okay?" he asked.

"Vampire!" came a shout, and a man in a Zorro costume ran at them from the mouth of the alley. "Prepare for your final slumber!"

Before he could untangle from Melanie, Zorro was upon them. Victor bellowed at a sharp pain in the middle of his back and rolled away, tumbling into a basement window well.

Zorro howled, looking at his hand, which seemed to have a piece of wood glued to it. Victor clambered out of the well without using his damaged left hand as Zorro yowled and worked at the lath—the same whittled garden stake Victor had found on his office desk, now affixed to Zorro's hand with splinters.

Victor winced as he reached for where the lath had struck him, right on the spine, cushioned by his thick sweater. "You tried to stab me," he said to Zorro. "Are you insane?"

"Ow-ow-ow," said Zorro, Eugene Foreman, Vampire Slayer. He finally dislodged the stake, so flimsy it almost floated to the alley floor, bouncing with the softest of clatters. Eugene sprang forward to pick it up, with his good hand, and pointed it at Victor. In his hand o' slivers he brandished the ropes of garlic slung around his neck like the leis of a Hawaiian newbie. "Stay back!"

They both rushed forward to protect Melanie, bouncing back just before collision as if from a forcefield, circling each other. Melanie crabwalked out of the center of their conflict, taking refuge against the nearest wall. Eugene thrust the stake at Victor, who swatted it and sent it floating down the alley.

Eugene ran for the stake, keeping an eye on Victor. Both eyes. The bottom of a hanging ladder solidly affixed to the beauty salon caught him flush on the temple. With a soft "oof" the vampire slayer laid down in the alley for a couple hours of shut-eye.

The ladder's vibrations tickled Victor's tummy. He hurried over to Melanie and held out his good hand. She reached tentatively to him, and was pulled to her feet.

"Oh my God," said Melanie. "Who was that?"

"I have no idea," said Victor, checking to make sure Zorro was still horizontal. "I hope you're okay."

Melanie cowered in his arms. "What are you going to do to me?"

"Don't worry," Victor reassured her, feeling pity for her. "It's over. I'm not going to do anything to you."

"Please," she whimpered. "Please."

"Melanie, it's okay."

Her head lolled to the side, exposing her throat, stretching out her small wrinkle folds. "Please...be gentle."

"Oh for crying out loud," Victor mumbled, and bit her.

THETHERSON ON THE SLIPPERY SLOPE

Tripp called him at the office Tuesday afternoon. "Hey buddy, what's up? I missed you at the Bank yesterday. I went on break around seven-thirty—knowing you, you hardworking sonofagun, that's when you got off work and showed up."

"I didn't go," said Victor.

"Why?" said Tripp. "Man, you must be starving."

"I'm okay."

"You're okay? Are you stepping out on me?" said Tripp. "Are you going to the Bonfils on the north end?"

Victor covered the mouthpiece to talk to Florence, who stood in his doorway like a temple statue, with the foot-thick, year-to-date general ledger printout. "Give me five minutes and I'll stop by." He resumed his conversation with Tripp. "Did Nikki say anything about Friday night?"

"She hasn't spoken to me since Saturday morning, other than to call and chew my ass for giving her toe fungus."

"It's inside her tongue piercing," said Victor. "It really looks awful."

"Those moccasins just don't breathe, dude," Tripp lamented. "It was like a sweat lodge in there."

"So she didn't tell you about Melanie, I take it."

"Please don't tell me it turned out she wasn't looking for a long-term commitment with a good man. I swear I'll lose my faith in humanity." Then the sarcasm left Tripp's voice. "Whoa, Vic, no. You didn't do that. Tell me you didn't bite that girl."

"She's hardly a girl, Tripp."

"Vic!"

"Tripp," said Victor, swiveling toward the outside window, taking in the porthole view of an expansive oil field, filthy with prairie dogs. He lowered his voice. "She was practically begging for it. I didn't want to."

"How much did you drink?" Tripp demanded.

"I wasn't even drunk," said Victor.

"I mean *blood*, Vic. You drank so much you're full, three days later? You don't need more from me? God help you man, is she okay?"

"Nikki says she's fine," said Victor. "I guess it took her a couple days to recuperate, but she's back at work today. Get this," Victor started to giggle, having a hard time believing it himself. "I have another date tonight. Nikki set it up, with a friend of Melanie's."

"I don't think 'date' is the right word."

Victor reveled in how Tripp was carrying on. He had never had a buddy giving him crap about his romantic exploits. "Girls can't date vampires?"

"It's more like rape," Tripp retorted.

"Melanie wanted it, Tripp. You should have seen it—"

"Doesn't matter what you think they want—or even what *they* think they want."

"That's a little sexist, don't you think?" Victor baited him.

"Better that than an exploiter."

"I don't know why you're complaining, I'm probably drumming up business for you," Victor joked. "Either they'll need transfusions, or they'll realize giving blood isn't so bad. Speaking of which, it turns out blood isn't bad tasting after all. It's runnier than I thought—the stuff you give me is always a little thick."

"Gosh, all apologies."

"And the temperature is just right," Victor continued. "And I like the concept that it's lifeblood I'm drinking."

"That's stupid to call it lifeblood," said Tripp,

irritated. "It's blood. It's what lifeblood was named after."

"Blood of life, then. So are you up for another double date? Or whatever the right word is—but remember, a rose by any other name..."

"I've decided to hang up on you now."

"May I suggest a set of vampire falsies? I think Nikki would really groove on you playing a vampire..."

Tripp disconnected. Victor sat back in his chair, chuckling. He hadn't even had the chance to tell Tripp about the crazy dude who had tried to put a stake in his heart. It was the kind of story guys like Tripp loved, the kind of story Victor never got to tell. He realized he hadn't felt this good for...a while now.

Florence was back at his door, toting the hefty general ledger volume and speaking too fast to pop her gum. "Victor, I'm sorry to interrupt, I just wanted you to know there's been a problem with the month-end cut-off, but we're working on it."

"Oh great." Victor's contentment had lasted all of thirty seconds. "Have the Westchase people caught wind of it?"

"What do they care?" said Florence. "Do you want me to let them know?"

"No," Victor snapped. "Don't you have any idea..." He stopped mid-sentence, surprised to see Florence taken aback. She was actually concerned by what was about to come out of his mouth.

His pleasure at her reaction was brief. The last thing Victor wanted to do was upset Florence, make her feel unappreciated. He thanked her ancient Olympian gods every day for bringing her back into his life. And he had almost divulged the Westchase team's secret motive. "Okay. I'll get on the phone with the general ledger people in Chicago—"

"Already did," said Florence. "They're gonna wait to close the books until we have it fixed. Tessa suggested preparing manual entries in case the automatic ones don't post, she and Quinten are doing it now."

"Really? You all took care of it." Victor set the phone back in its cradle. "That's wonderful."

To his look of surprise Florence said airily, "Victor, that's our job. I also wanted to let you know, Raj asked permission to spend a little time reviewing the Maryhill cost data and site logs. He wants to see if he can understand where the job went off track and over budget..." She paused. "That okay by you? You look upset."

"No, no, I'm just..." *Floored.* "...pleasantly surprised. Raj thought of that all by himself?" Victor marveled. "Yes, sure, of course I'm okay with that."

"Okay, good." Florence mulled something over, glanced over her shoulder and then shuffled into his office, to the near corner of his desk. "I know you don't have to tell me..."

"I'll tell you whatever you want to know, Florence." Victor immediately began studying his monitor that had gone to blank sleep, to turn his words into a throwaway line.

Unnecessary, because Florence was using one and only one of her senses, visually exploring Victor's mouth. Undressing it, if lips were clothing. "What did you do to David?"

Victor looked up, something odd in her voice, another octave, a keening track laid floating above her normal throaty rasp. Florence's eyes lifted to his. "I wish I could tell you more," he said. He had received an e-mail the day before from Human Resources, that they would be contacting him soon to discuss "the David Copperfield situation". "I haven't heard from him either, but I'll let you know as soon as I do."

"Of course I'm just wondering on behalf of everyone else." Under the weight of the ledger Florence was curved like a question mark and wheezing like a sleeping Porky pug. Victor decided that's what he had heard.

"You know you shouldn't be carting that thing around."

"I wanted to have it ready in case you needed to see proof."

"I trust your explanation, Florence." With hands and arms Victor pulled stacks of paper like claiming a monster poker pot, clearing space on his desk. "Just leave it here, I'll take it back to the file drawer."

"Phsht, this thing weighs less than a lamb. And it doesn't kick me in the cooch. It's a regular pleasure to carry." Florence lugged the ledger back to her cube.

Victor heard Raj's voice, calling to the temp. They stopped in perfect frame, like a vignette staged for his office doorway, the snazzy accountant giving instruction, the light dawning on the temp's face, the two of them crisply continuing in their separate directions, intent on their assigned tasks.

Victor pondered the change he was seeing in his staff. They didn't seem to have a clue that their jobs were on the line—but there had to be comprehension at some subconscious level, an intuitive understanding that was stoking their energy and commitment. He poked his head out of his office door. There was chatter, but it didn't involve a quarter-flipping game or weekend party planning. The airwaves carried appropriate business content, numbers, news and data entries.

It was also quite possible he was finally reaching them. After the exchange with Florence, he actually felt like—he had a hard time saying it, even in his head—a manager.

Victor walked lightly down the aisle to the small conference room where Darla and the Westchase crew had taken up residency.

Darla was alone, just snapping her cellphone shut. For a moment she didn't seem to be registering his arrival.

"Knock-knock," said Victor. "Just wanted to check in, see how things were going."

"Oh, sure. Sorry. Yes." Darla pushed her cellphone away from her, but it continued to hold her gaze.

"I can come back," said Victor.

"No. Sorry." As if electrically prodded, Darla's body snapped back into work mode, spine straightening and hands springing to life, shifting paper to bring the desired stack in front of her. Her face was slower to recover, the skin slack below her eyes. "Sorry I'm a little disorganized here, I don't want to hold you up, I know you're busy. Please have a seat."

Victor pulled out a chair and sat.

"I do have a few questions for you," said Darla. "Things my team is finding that I wanted you to be aware of." Her shoulders drew up and fell back down in a poor attempt at a deep breath. "Wow, I'm just a little overwhelmed. This merger is going to be a huge deal. I really don't know how I'm going to get through it, to be honest."

Victor watched her hand go to her brow, before quickly dropping back to the papers in front of her. A brief moment of defenselessness.

"I wish you and I were together..." Darla smoothed papers that were already wrinkle-free. "I mean, I wish there was some way we could work together on this. I know that's not how we've been set up."

"I know you have to do what you have to do."

"Yeah, well..." Darla's eyes darkened, perhaps on the verge of tears. "I've been wondering a lot more lately whether just doing what I'm told is always the right thing to do. You know?" She turned away, dropping below the table to dig in her purse. "I'm sorry," she said, still out of sight and rummaging. "Maybe you should give me a couple minutes. This isn't appropriate. I'll come find you, if that's okay."

"Sure," said Victor, rising. "Take your time." He saw her thaw at this slightest show of compassion. "If there are things you need to take care of first, that's fine." And now she melted, the icy mask of corporate skepticism gone from her face.

Victor was drawn back to the oblong conference table. "Uh, are uh…" At light speed he saw a vignette play out where Darla requested a reduced role in the merged company due to personal considerations, leaving him the surviving manager by default. "Are things okay?"

She shook her head, then corrected it with a quick nod. "I just got off the phone with my son.…" She shook her head again. "I guess it shook me up a little more than I thought."

Victor nodded, listening.

"You're divorced too, right?" said Darla. "Nikki told me that you were. And I apologize if that was in confidence, it just kind of came up when we were talking."

"It's okay."

"Do you have kids?" Darla asked.

The thought of exploiting an advantage was already foreign enough for Victor to be wispy and hard to maintain. Now a crashing wave of self-pity scattered it to incoherent bits. "A daughter."

"Me too. And a son." Darla sighed. "Who is having a few problems, to say the least. I just got a call from the rehab facility he was checked into." She dabbed at her eyes with a tissue. "I think it just hit me, how quickly things have changed. How he used to be such a sweet young kid. Not that he isn't still sweet.… Sorry." Darla wiped away tears in earnest. "I know everyone has troubles. I just wish my ex would take a little more interest into what's going on, just to share some of the burden with me. It's selfish."

"No, I understand," said Victor. "My daughter—"

"Hi there," said Kirby, startling Victor, hustling into the room and unloading an armful of ledgers and reconciliation books onto the table. "I was just going over your month-end process with Casey. I'm not sure she understands everything completely, although she could, it's very possible that I just didn't spend enough time with her to really get a feel for what she knows, because we did spend a lot of time talking about our cats. She has a calico, I don't know if you knew. I always think of that poem about the calico cat. I can't remember the name—I'm sure you know the one I'm talking about, if I recited a couple lines. It has gingham in it. So anyway I was hoping, unless you'd prefer that I go back to Casey, that maybe I could get you to walk me through your month-end process."

"Darla has a few questions I'm answering," said Victor. "As soon as we're done—"

"Mine can wait," said Darla, by now composed and engaged in the workpapers before her. She nodded at Kirby. "Go ahead."

"Great," said Kirby. "Give me a second here, and I'll be ready in a jiffy...."

Victor sat at the far end of the table with Kirby, answering all the questions that Casey could not, and correcting the answers Casey had given. Kirby jotted down everything he said, content to take dictation with little follow-up. But Darla was listening, Victor knew, and so he gave intricately detailed explanations, forcing Kirby to take page after page of notes, trying to paint a picture of the department he wished he was running.

Victor and his date had agreed to meet at one of Houston's many open-air cantinas along the busy south-end strip. Like a father fretting over his daughter's first date, Nikki had made him promise to call her if anything went wrong. Victor had scoffed at the time, feeling his oats, but as the minutes spent alone at his table accumulated, he began to wish she was there, to guide him through the opening moves.

The sun was setting when he was approached by an auburn-haired woman. She was average height and amply proportioned, in a brief lightweight sundress, her bare shoulders, arms and calves muscled to the point of sturdiness.

"Hi. Are you Vic?" she asked.

"You must be Karina," said Victor. She had been in the cantina for twenty minutes; he realized she had been surveilling him, debating whether to approach.

"I am. Pleased to meet you." She looked at the door and wrapped her arms around her well-designed bosom. "You know, I apologize, but after Melanie suggested that we, that we go out, I actually got back together with my boyfriend. It just happened, late yesterday." She saw Victor deflate. "I'm so sorry. I just can't..."

"It's okay. I understand. I know I'm not much to look at."

"No, no, it's not that. I honestly just reconciled with, with him," it took Karina a second to come up with her boyfriend's name, "with Peter, and I *never* thought we would, or else I never would have agreed to let Melanie set this up. Honestly."

Victor nodded, and smiled in resignation, showing a hint of long, pointed canines. "Can I at least buy you another margarita? And one more tequila shot?"

Karina blushed. "You've been watching me."

"That's what we do." The sentence had just kind of tumbled out, unintentionally very vampire of him.

Karina nodded through a brief decision-making process, and sat down. She pointed at his bandaged wrist. "Is that from Friday night? Melanie told me about that guy."

"Vampire hunter. Yeah. Sprained it during the attack." Victor held up the hand, wiggled his fingers, saw that it was making an impression on Karina, and winced. "A lot of pain. Comes with the territory. So how do you know Melanie?"

"We work together at the design studio."

"I heard a lot about it Friday night," said Victor. "It sounded like a great job." Their drinks arrived, and he continued to engage her in small talk. There were extended awkward silences, but there was also a second round of drinks.

"How about the Astros, huh?" said Victor, watching the nearest elevated television. "Maybe they have a chance this year."

"Yeah," said Karina. "I know. I know. You know, it's getting late."

"I know," said Victor.

"And I don't really.... I mean I'm not sure what I'm doing, and my boyfriend is no doubt waiting, so..."

"Do you want to take a walk?"

"Sure. That would be good. Get some fresh air." A nice breeze wafted through the cantina. "Fresher air, I guess. A break from all the racket."

Victor offered his hand, and together they exited through the rear patio door.

A cobblestone path led them to a bike lane that ran roughly parallel to the road. "It's a dark night," Victor commented on the unlit path, while clouds crossed the crescent sliver of a moon. He hadn't made a trip to the restroom during their ninety minutes in the cantina, and had to pee, urgently.

"With so many city lights," said Karina, "it's never really dark."

"Just enough light to find each other." *I will hold it,* Victor laid down the law for his bladder. "When we're close together."

"Seems like there's always someone nearby," Karina's voice quavered, "who sees what you're doing."

Victor reached for her hand, snagged her forearm, and stopped her in front of a stretch of pungent eucalyptus trees. Karina looked wide-eyed into his face; her chest heaved the way he had been imagining it might. "I've found," he said, "that everyone is so busy in this city, you can be hidden in plain sight. Shoot..." Even though he was aroused, he was suddenly worried he could still pee his pants at the moment of truth. "Excuse me a moment. I'll be right back."

Victor pushed through the waxy leaves, too intent on his mission to care about the branches scratching his face or see the ditch until it was too late, feet skidding out from under him. He landed on his hip and slid down the embankment, one heel ramming a concrete curb, wrenching his ankle, partially arresting his slide. "Oh mama," Victor moaned, still with enough momentum to complete the fall into the drainage trough. "Yuck." Shoes soaked, he gingerly ascended the trough, then turned around and peed in it.

"Hey, are you down there?" Karina was calling. "Hey...I'm getting freaked out.... I think I'm going to head back."

Victor wrapped it up prematurely and crawled like a bear with two bad paws, up the rough dirt slope, cacti stabbing one of his good paws, his breathing ragged by the time he reached the top. He fought through the tree belt and limped onto the bike path.

Karina was there. Victor lurched toward her like Quasimodo and grabbed her with both hands, ignoring shooting pain from each. "I'm back," he announced. He squelched his panting. "It's time I tasted your blood."

Karina's eyes boggled. Victor bent forward and Karina bent backward. He grabbed the back of her neck, but Karina was strong; he pulled, and she planted a hand in his chest and pushed. With his cacti paw he grabbed her hand and now they were arm-wrestling in the tight space between them.

Victor grunted and turned it on, full force; Karina held, and then slowly pushed his hand down. "Stop resisting!" he ordered, lunging forward.

"No!" said Karina, and kneed Victor in the groin. He collapsed to the bike path, groaning.

Karina put her hand to her mouth. "I'm sorry. I'm so sorry."

"Nikki," Victor called out feebly.

Karina bent down. "What?"

"Nothing."

She patted Victor's shoulder while he squirmed and rocked. "I'm so sorry. I just got a little panicked. And my range of motion is so good in this sundress. Are you okay?"

Victor squeezed his eyes shut, trying to block the ghastly mental image of a ruptured testicle. "I think so."

"Just take your time." Karina helped him to sit up, a little prematurely. He shook his head when she tried to pull him to his feet.

She paced back and forth, crouched in front of him. "Victor, listen, I'm sorry. I shouldn't have done that. I could uh...you know, I better go. I'll just be on my way," she said, rising and turning, stumbling—"Oh!" Karina went down in a controlled tumble, winding up on her back, the back of her hand to her forehead, eyes fluttering. "Uhhh, I'm so weak...like I'm under some kind of spell. I feel so helpless..."

Victor regarded her, sagging further. *Pity bite.* "I'm good, thanks."

Karina sighed and got to her feet. "Okay. Well, it was nice meeting you. I'm just going to go then."

Victor nodded. Karina walked smartly down the bike lane, threw a last glance over her shoulder at the cobblestone path, and was gone.

When his groin recovered to the point his other assorted injuries began throbbing, Victor limped back to the Subaru, ignoring curious looks from cantina patrons.

He was home a little after eleven. The house was dark, but a lamp clicked on as he shuffled through the living room. Barbara sat curled on the end of the couch, staring at him.

"Hi."

"What the hell happened to you?"

"Fell."

"You fell. Again." Barbara crossed the room to inspect him from a distance of a couple feet. "Where?"

"At a bar. Again."

"A bar..." She tugged at his torn black sweater and shook her head in disdain. "Victor, are you club fighting? Is that what's happening?"

"Do you mean fight club?"

"Yes."

"If I was, then I couldn't talk about it, right?" Victor continued, slowly, toward the bedroom, plucking cactus spines from his palm. "And as it turns out, I'm not going to talk about it, because it was a woman."

Barbara looked at him sideways. "Well, you have never been the type to assert yourself. If you're trying to be a fifty-year-old Casanova, you're bound to get your ass kicked."

She followed him into the bathroom and watched as he undressed to take a shower. Hands on hips, Barbara stared at his bruised and naked body with a frown. "Victor, have you lost weight?"

He waited for the dig. "I don't know. Doesn't seem like it." He climbed into the steamy shower and checked out his waist. Looked the same to him. Had there been less huffing and puffing on the flight of stairs to the Accounting floor that morning? He looked down at his gut again, shrugged.

"Okay, fine," said Barbara. Victor realized he had been ignoring her. "I'm going to bed. You should too," she said, leaving the bathroom, "but I suppose you'll wile away the hours playing with your trains..."

Victor finished his shower, covered his aching body with pajamas, and hobbled out to the kitchen, where he fished the newspaper out of the recycling basket, planning to lose himself in current events while finishing an old bag of blood he had found in the back of the fridge, with a box of saltines. He sucked down the blood and mowed through the Metro section, comprehending nothing, picturing Karina's disappointed face on every page.

In the garage he stared blankly at his train set for awhile before turning to the storage rack to retrieve his favorite, an 1875 Baldwin steam locomotive. Victor squirted smoke oil into the reservoir, and struggled to couple the engine and its tender box to the railcars waiting on the track. Only after fumbling and grumbling for nearly a minute did he realize he was trying to bring two incompatible eras together—the sleek anhydrous ammonia tank car had no ability to grasp the wood burner's advances.

Victor stood up on his damaged ankle and limped out of the garage, lacking the energy to even return the treasured antique engine to the shelf.

He eased into bed, careful not to wake Barbara—she always had a devil of a time falling back asleep, and then her effort at Wal-Mart would suffer. After some minutes, the mental and physical discomfort mounted, and Victor ever-so-carefully tossed and turned.

Melancholy over disappointing Karina was a domino triggering the depressing recognition of how he had let his staff down as well. Jay was right; he had let them slide for too long, and now they were at Westchase's mercy. And with everything Darla's team was digging up, there was no doubt their days were numbered.

The day had started out so promising, but had ended like usual. He fell asleep without noticing that Barbara had inched closer to him.

THETHERSON, AWAKE

When Victor awoke, he noticed changes.

First of all, Barbara was gone. He called her name twice on the way to the can, then remembered Wednesday was her workout morning with her personal trainer. Another two hundred bucks, another ripple on her stomach. Barbara was freakishly gifted with abdominals, and so that was all she liked to work. She had gone from a six-pack to an eight-pack two years ago. Last month Victor surprised her coming out of the shower and thought he caught sight of cans nine and ten under her low-slung boobs.

Second, he had difficulty peeing, but for good (the only good) reason. He had a morning missile on his hands. He stared at it, dumbly, like answering the phone to a beautiful voice from the nearly forgotten past (acne-cheeked Kathy, for instance). He backed away from the toilet and yanked open the medicine cabinet. Laid eyes upon that beautiful blue jar of Noxzema—and then was made instantly nauseous by some sort of jangling behind his eyes, like an implanted joy buzzer going off. Victor incorrectly wrote it off to the emergency klaxon of an overloaded bladder.

The erection would not be coaxed into a curtain call. Victor wasn't upset, this was the fourth morning in a row it had made an appearance. Odds were good the big fella would be back.

Four straight mornings, after months—years, if he was honest—of deep hibernation. There could be only one explanation. Biting Nikki and Melanie had changed him.

Of course the simple physical contact with women ten to twenty years his junior was a powerful aphrodisiac. The awakening of his long-dormant libido didn't necessarily have anything to do with the biting.

Except Victor also noticed that his body barely hurt. All the parts that should have taken weeks to heal, the wrist, the ankle—the gonads—all of them felt just fine. The bruising that had colored his wrist and should have been hideously present on his ankle—and probably his groin—was all but nonexistent. Not even the magical aura of the younger woman should have been able to accomplish that kind of healing.

And he wanted blood. Being nagged by it, needing it, that was one thing; this was a *wanting*. He pictured blood spilling and pooling, and wanted it all the more. Blood spurting, blood congealing—

Victor's stomach twisted and sent a blob of bile halfway up his esophagus. Maybe not congealing, he decided.

The feeling, the *wanting*, was strange, unsettling, exhilarating. He found himself looking forward to the day. Within minutes of waking his mind was ordinarily seized by all the urgent work issues that needed to be addressed, launching him into low-level panic as he ate breakfast and drove to the office. And this morning was no different, the lengthy To-Do list demanded his attention.

But as he mentally flipped through the day's tasks, each was magically recast as a steppingstone to get what he wanted, which was: A date lined up by Nikki, a date which could very well lead to blood. He couldn't wait to get to the office and get started.

Coffee brewed while he cleaned up Porky pug's vomit—in its two years of wretched existence the dog had consumed light bulbs and many cubic feet of pillow stuffing without incident, but couldn't seem to keep tampons down—and put him outside. After hurrying through his bathroom routine, he sat down at the breakfast table with a cup of coffee, two slices of toast, and Porky's barking.

He read an article about the West Nile Virus outbreak and imagined himself as a mosquito, sinking his proboscis into warm flesh. He reached for the Skippy jar in front of him, then decided he'd rather have jam. Grape or marmalade? Neither, he was picturing something redder, and runnier. Marmalade would be okay, he decided, mixed with blood.

"That's it," said Victor. He left Porky barking and his toast unfinished and was shortly in the car and on his cellphone.

"Yello," Tripp answered.

"I need blood."

"Victor, good morning to you too," Tripp said sleepily. "This is a pleasant surprise. I'm assuming it means your date didn't work out the way you planned?"

"Dates don't always go as planned," said Victor, hand gripping the wheel a little tighter.

"Maybe you're not cut out for that kind of dating," said Tripp. "That would be okay, you know."

"I'm heading to the Bank now," said Victor. "Can you meet me ASAP? Unless, you have some blood at your apartment?"

Tripp groaned. "No, Victor, I don't have blood at the apartment." Some sighing, some additional groaning. "I was late at the Longer Labs last night." One more sigh. "And then later with Nikki. Have you ever talked to her, Vic? For more than a few minutes?"

"Can't say I have," said Victor, uninterested in any topic other than his reason for calling.

"A lot of strange things going on in there, man. A lot."

"Um, yep."

"Alright," said Tripp, irritated, "give me a half hour or so and I'll meet you at the Bank."

A half hour? Or so? Victor's blood urge surged. "You're

always making me wait, Tripp."

"Don't abuse *all* the virtues, Vic. You're smacking a couple of them around pretty good these days. Let's keep patience unscathed."

Thursday night Victor arrived home from work to find Barbara standing in the kitchen, arms crossed. "Have you lost your mind?" she demanded.

"What's wrong?"

"What did you do? How could you?"

Victor sagged. Why had he thought he could get away with this? You don't just bite people, or even attempt it, without repercussions. Melanie must have turned, and after a brief struggle, an extremely fortunate neighbor had managed to barricade her in the basement, slavering and red-eyed and desperate for human blood, and no doubt screaming his name. Or, Karina had pressed charges. "It just happened…"

"These kinds of things don't just happen," Barbara snapped at him. "How much did it cost?"

Could he stick to the hard dollars, or would she demand a broader reckoning, accounting for the cost of human suffering, lost productivity, the potential hush money…. Victor decided to start small. "It was just a couple drinks."

"A drink?" Barbara squeaked. "Is that the hip new accounting term for five hundred dollars? 'Just a couple drinks, Jay, that's all my new computer system is going to cost.' Well we aren't a multi-million dollar company, Victor. A couple drinks means everything to us."

"What are you talking about, Barb?"

"The weight machine."

Victor brightened. "My Bowflex came already? Oooh." He rubbed his palms together, heading for the front room.

"If that's your way of telling me I'm getting fat, then that's despicable, buster."

"It's for me, Barb," said Victor, standing in the open

convergence of living and dining rooms, arms spread wide.

Barbara frowned, unable to get her head around the idea. "Seriously?"

"Is that so hard to imagine?"

She frowned some more.

"Whatever," said Victor, on-the-spot upgrading his goal, from being able to out-wrestle an average-strength woman, to looking good in a Speedo. "Where is it?"

"I had the UPS man put it in the attic."

Victor deflated. "Barb," he whined. "Now instead of feeling like I got something new, it's going to feel like I'm getting something old out of storage."

"You're not getting anything out. We don't have the room. That's where it stays."

"I can't work out in the attic," Victor complained. "It's filthy, and the ceilings are five feet high."

"Listen to you, 'work out'," Barbara mocked. "In all the years we were married, the only time I heard you use that term was for your ping-pong 'work-outs'. You remember them?"

"No." Victor headed for the stairs. "And I'm not keeping it in the attic."

"You'd stand in the garden and swat butterflies."

"I wasn't *swatting* butterflies, because you don't *swat* the ball." Victor mimed his forehand as he climbed the stairs. "You *redirect* it."

"And yes you are keeping it up there," Barbara called after him. "Unless you want to put it in the garage. But of course that's already taken by your precious toy trains."

Victor paused at the top of the stairs. "Fine," he said, and twisted the tiny latch on the small attic door.

Unpacking the box in the garage, Victor swore the Bowflex smelled like mouse droppings and mildewed cardboard.

Such was the fate awaiting his trains, now boxed and

stored behind that small attic door.

Setting up the Bowflex was his first workout, although the exertion was more mental than physical, and his exhaustion was better attributed to the emotional energy spent packing up his trains. But to never again make a mockery of another woman's vampire fantasy—and to make Barbara eat her words—the psychic pain was worth it.

Victor followed the Bowflex manual's recommended Day One routine. He completed the first round and started a second, but the muscles at his joints burned white hot, stretched like taffy. Desperate to call it a night, he called up the memory of being out of breath after climbing the short slope to rejoin Karina, and was inspired to run in place, until his stomach heaved and his head spun and his knees would no longer rise.

Victor drug himself inside the house and downed a glass of lemonade, exacerbating the exercise-induced nausea, hoping Barbara might catch him puking in the sink. Instead he set the glass down feeling pretty good, his heavy panting already improved to a light wheeze, his vision back to normal. He flexed his arms—the muscles were tired, but the searing pain was gone, taffy improved to rubber.

On the table was a letter from the Good Sisters blood bank. Were they finally deciding to bill him for all the blood Tripp had given him? More likely this was the official notice that he was cut off, Tripp's punishment for doing exactly what Tripp had been begging him to do.

Instead, the Bank was inviting him to come be feted Saturday, as one of their top donors the past ten years.

No sooner had he tossed the letter in the garbage than the phone rang—Tripp, asking whether he'd received the invite.

"Pretty good humor," said Victor. "A vampire as the blood bank's best customer. Sorry if I'm out of breath, by the way." He manufactured panting. "I was just working out."

"Good for you. Vic, the invite is serious. They know you're a vampire. It's great publicity for the Bank, man."

"No it's not."

"Au contraire, mon frère. If a vampire can give blood, how can anyone else complain? 'I can't donate, I *need* my blood.' 'Yeah? Well, this here vampire needs his blood, and your blood, and your mother's blood, and *he's* down here, every damn week!' We have a newspaper reporter coming—you'll probably get an interview."

"But that's the point, I'm not a donor anymore," said Victor.

"Only because we don't let you," said Tripp. "You probably would if you could, you generous SOB. If push comes to shove, we play it straight and show you downing a bag: 'Keep vampires off the streets and out of your bedroom. Give blood.'"

"That's stupid. I can't."

"You're coming. You have to come—I have a gift for you. You're going to love it."

EUGENE

Eugene Foreman's head hurt for days. He didn't know what had hit him. From the shape of the indentation in his skull, from the force with which the blow had been delivered, Eugene was guessing lead pipe. The Vampire had lured him into an ingenious trap, likely a pressure-triggered counter-balanced trip-wire, of the sort one would find in a fifteenth-century Transylvanian castle. Or, he had a partner, a henchman, a stout, hideously deformed and muscle-bound Renfield, hiding in the shadows and swinging with all his might when Eugene had unwittingly crossed his path.

The concussion-induced vomiting was occurring less frequently. This consoled Eugene as he clawed the lid off his latté and retched into the half-full cup. "This Vamp is cunning," Eugene announced by way of explanation to his wide-eyed fellow Starbucks patrons.

Eugene was currently signed into the Experts Only room of SuckThis.com, one of the internet's premier vampire slayer chat forums. Eugene typed a question to the group.

I am faced with a Level 7 Vampire. The usual method of killing such a Vampire has been met with no positive results. Please provide suggestions.

There came a flurry of responses.

Level 7? said HalYesImAHunter.

Holy shit, I have never been close to a level 7, said Once-Bitten-Now-Im-Freakin-Blade.

Have you tried Holy Water? said U-Luv-Maggie-Moo-

2.

What about my patented anti-Vampire chant? said vKillah4Hire. *Guaranteed success. Starts with: "Go down to 34 and vine, look at your palm and make a magic sign, you can make it up right there in your sink, smells like turpentine, looks like Indian ink..."* $9.95 *gets you the rest.*

That's lyrics from Love Potion Number Nine, said Colin-Case-Theres-Trouble. *It's free on lyrics.com.*

I swear I didn't know, said vKillah4Hire.

I have heard it works, though, replied Colin-Case-Theres-Trouble.

What about a Silver Bullet? someone else said. The suggestions continued to fill the screen.

Rusty chainsaw?

Pentagrams?

Gold tipped arrows?

Eugene paused in his furious note-taking just long enough to type, *Please don't insult me with such obvious weapons.*

The chatter fell silent. Then, *Is this Eugene Foreman?*

Eugene smiled to himself. *My reputation betrays me*, he typed.

The cursor blinked like a weak pulse. Once-Bitten-Now-Im-Freakin-Blade and Colin-Case-Theres-Trouble left the chat room.

Don't be intimidated, I'm sure only half of what you've heard is true, Eugene typed. *Two-thirds at the most.*

No responses. The chat participants were obviously eager to hear his story.

Eugene obliged them. *I'm in the Houston metropolitan area—I won't divulge any more details on my location, for your own protection. I have learned the folly of challenging the Vamp on his hunting grounds, and so I am stalking the Vamp relentlessly, infiltrating his daily life. Before long he will have nowhere left to hide.*

Eugene hit enter and realized his connection had been severed.

"Vamps!" he exclaimed and pounded the table, making his latté cup and the surrounding patrons jump. "How did they know I was here...?" Fifteen pairs of eyes were upon him. Moving with cobra-coiled-control, Eugene closed the laptop as he stood, studying each customer and every employee. Not a friendly face in the bunch. He was surrounded.

Which suddenly made sense—he remembered reading that Starbucks had been picketed in San Francisco for welcoming vampires. Or was it handguns? Something dangerous. He walked backwards along the counter and into the kitchen, then turned and burst out the back door. The security alarm was went blaring as Eugene ran down the alley, this time staying safely down the middle.

THETHERSON, BROKEN

Seventeen months and four days since he had last set foot inside the Good Sisters blood bank, Victor opened the door and hesitated.

"Come in," said Perry Farrish, Bank manager, one of thirty-one people staring at Victor.

"Oh jeez, it's true," blurted Tanner Gillicuddy, like Victor a member of the Ten Gallon club, designated by his maroon cowboy hat pin. "You do have to invite them in."

Victor bowed his head and stepped inside, cursing Tripp under his breath.

Perry rubbed his fine-boned hands together as he bobbed forward to greet Victor. His palms were slicked with too much sweat to be frictioned dry, so he was forced to wipe them conspicuously on his trousers. "Hi, hello Victor," he said in his soft squeaky voice. "It's been too long." He smiled at Tripp, who joined them and handed Victor a glass of red wine. "We're grateful you could come on short notice."

Victor was nodding at various attendees, keeping his lips pressed together. "Thanks for having me, Perry." He raised the wine glass to his mouth and looked sideways at Tripp. "I was right. This was a stupid idea." He sipped, and felt the familiar coating on the back of his throat. "You spiked my wine."

"That's just to whet your appetite, big man," said Tripp with a mischievous grin.

"So Victor," said Tanner, moseying over to join them,

bringing along Nurse Collette, the Bank's head RN. "How long's it been since we shared a chair and a sleeve of Fig Newtons?"

Victor mentally tried out a couple replies, looking for one with minimal lip action. "Few months."

Tanner flexed his knees to get a low-angle view of Victor's teeth. "Those are sweet," he said in his low-key manner. "Gotta come in handy around the house."

"They'd be great for perforating important papers so you can file them in a ring binder," Perry suggested.

Nurse Collette shook her head. She was buxom and boisterous. "I'm sorry but that's lame, Perry. You would be a really boring vampire, honestly."

"I was thinking can-piercing for shotgunning beers," said Tanner.

Perry nodded. "And snipping thread if you don't have any scissors handy."

"It's no good," said Victor, warming to the conversation. "They don't match up with my bottom teeth."

"Sounds like a Martha Stewart roundtable for vampires over here," said a woman as she joined their klatch. She held her wine glass like a pro and had hawk-bright eyes.

"One hundred fun and practical uses for your fangs," said Tripp. "Vic's going to sell the book to Martha, demonstrate a couple of his favorites on her show, and make a mint. Huh buddy?"

"Nurse Collette," called an aide tending to a donor in a chair against the wall.

Tanner nudged Nurse Collette. "You're wanted."

She threw a half-glance at the aide and donor and then resumed ignoring them. "So," she said to Victor, "what blood type are you again?"

"Oh, I don't know…"

"Which is it, O, or you don't know?" Nurse Collette doubled herself over in laughter.

"Now they really need you over there," said Tanner,

directing Nurse Collette's attention to the aide putting pressure on the donor's blood-smeared arm. The donor cast terrified glances at Victor while the aide strained for a bandage just out of reach on the other side of the chair.

Nurse Collette rolled her eyes. "That's how they learn to handle these things. But alright." She touched Victor's arm. "It was nice to see you again, Victor."

"What did I tell you," said Tripp, for Victor's ear only. "You're the belle at the ball."

Victor frowned at him, smiling on the inside.

"It's Victor?" the hawk-eyed woman confirmed. "I heard you were one of the Bank's biggest donors." She transferred her wine glass and put her arm around Perry in one deft, practiced move. "I think that's so admirable. I've known Perry and have been coming here to donate for, how long has it been, thirteen years?"

"Fourteen in September," said Perry.

"It's such a good thing to do," said the woman. "I'm Clancy." She extended her hand to Victor. "I'm surprised we never bumped into each other. At least I don't think so. I'm sure you would have stood out."

"I've only been a vampire for two years," said Victor.

"Your hand is nowhere near as cold as I would have guessed," said Clancy with a warm smile.

"Victor," he was greeted heartily by Father Crist his elfin priest, wading into the group, swapping Clancy's hand for his own. "Good to see you *inside* the Bank for a change. Perry tells me most of your transactions take place in the alley these days."

"Oooh," Clancy cooed. "Giving blood to the vampire in the alley. Sounds dangerous."

"As long as I'm punctual," said Tripp, "no one gets hurt."

"Vampires and their 'cravings'," said Clancy, adding both the open and closed quotes with one hand.

Half the room was now gathered around Victor, with a number of the newcomers' heads subtly angled to catch a glimpse of his teeth. "You still attend church?" marveled a white- and bun-haired lady.

"Unless the Texans are the early game," said Victor. He grinned, to a round of twitters and gasps, followed closely by sighs and chuckles.

"God's a Texans fan too," said Father Crist. "That's why he invented Saturday evening services just for Catholics."

"We Episcopalians have them too," said Perry.

Father Crist ignored him and squeezed Victor's shoulder. "Victor's a regular in church. And at confessional. That's all we can ask. Although," he did a squeaky-voiced Groucho Marx, "I'm just waiting for the day he confesses to biting Traci Mitchell in the rectory."

"She has a sweet rectory, huh?" said Tripp. The laughter turned to boos. "Sorry. But seriously, to prevent just such an occurrence, we went ahead and got Vic a little gift."

"Excuse me, more wine for anyone?" A gangly young man with grease-flat brown hair weaved his way into their midst, bearing a bottle of red and a bottle of white.

"Most of you haven't met our newest volunteer," said Perry. "This is Eugene. He just moved here from New Orleans."

Eugene Foreman had a number of glasses extended to him, Clancy's the most salient. He was refilling her chardonnay and preparing to answer her question about the aftermath of Hurricane Katrina when he noticed Victor for the first time. His spasm clanked the bottle against Clancy's glass, knocking it from her hand. She caught it a foot off the floor, and sucked the few drops of spilled wine from her wrist.

"Great catch," said Tanner.

"I love my chard," said Clancy, responding to the applause with a curtsy. "I'm not letting any go to waste."

Making sounds like a bubbling magma pit, Eugene Foreman barged out of the throng, jostling patrons, spilling their wine.

"It's okay, honey," Clancy called after him. "No harm done."

Perry pulled a limp creased handkerchief from his pocket and offered it around, with no takers. "He's a little high strung. Sorry everyone. Tripp, maybe now's a good time for you to bring out the gift?"

"Be right back." Tripp left the room, returning in seconds carrying a stiff body over his shoulder. He moved to the center of the group, which was now everyone in attendance, and laid the fully-clothed female dummy at Victor's feet.

Victor looked at Perry and he looked at Tripp. He looked uncertainly from face to face.

"Meet your next victim," said Tripp.

Victor blushed and swiped his widow's peak to the side. "I don't get it."

"Go ahead and bite her," said Perry. He giggled, titillated. "Try her out."

"That's a paramedic training dummy," said Nurse Collette, rejoining them.

"And her name is Jenny," said Tripp. "EMTs use Jenny to learn how to stop a wound from bleeding." He beckoned to Victor and lifted Jenny's shirt. "Put your hand on her heart." When Victor hesitated, Tripp hiked it to her chin, took Victor's hand, and placed it firmly above the dummy's left breast. "Feel it?"

The dummy was warm…with a heartbeat. "Oh wow," said Victor.

Quickly there were many hands on Dummy Jenny's chest. "Her skin is so soft," said Clancy, "and life-like."

"Help me," said Jenny, making Clancy jump, spilling a lot of chard.

"Was that the doll?" said Tanner, nudging Jenny's head with his foot.

"She knows there's a vampire nearby," said Tripp with a gleam in his eye.

"Ooo," said Clancy, elbowing Victor, "she's scared."

Father Crist knelt to raise Jenny's arm and

manipulate her hand to make the sign of the cross.

"Pretend she's what's-her-name and bite her in the rectory," Tanner encouraged Victor.

"I'd recommend the carotid instead," said Tripp. "Closer to the heart. Better blood flow."

"Come on, Tripp," said Victor, extremely uncomfortable. "No."

"*Bite her, bite her,*" a few of the guests started chanting and stomping their feet.

"You're not serious?" said Clancy. "Are you?"

Perry pushed his tinted glasses up to the bridge of his nose and then clasped his hands at his waist. "Tripp replaced Jenny's standard fluid with something nearer and dearer to Victor's heart."

"Blood?" said Clancy, more excited than grossed out. "You didn't. Did you?"

"I also installed a little heater back here," said Tripp, rotating Jenny, again pulling up her pretty pink blouse and tapping on the outline of a compartment in the small of her back. "Keeps her life fluid at ninety-eight point six."

"Well she's hot blooded," sang Tanner, "check it and see..."

The front door banged open, and all eyes turned to the masked, caped man standing silhouetted by the *Big Sale!* sign in the display window of the department store across the street. He thumped the floor with the butt end of a gold-tipped spear.

"For Pete's sake," said Victor. "Not you again."

"Stand back!" Eugene Foreman motioned everyone to back away. "Vampire! By the power of the Holy Good Book..." He dug with his free hand inside the flap of his dark blue overcoat. A soft-bound Bible fell to the floor, causing Eugene to drop the spear while trying to retrieve it.

Tripp stepped forward while everyone else stood and stared, some grinning and chirping excitedly, possibly believing they were about to enjoy a unique version of the singing telegram. "Whoa big boy," said Tripp.

Eugene abandoned the Book, clutched the spear, and drew his arm back.

"Yike," said Tripp, reversing direction and covering his head while women screamed and people scattered and Eugene flung the spear.

The whittled closet dowel was off-kilter from the moment it left Eugene's hand. The gold-painted tip veered down and stabbed the floor, snapping the dowel, the butt end continuing forward and striking Victor in the mouth.

"Aw!" Victor staggered and dropped to his knees, blood trickling from his lip. "My teeth! Fuck...arooni!"

"Oh no," said Clancy. She hurried to Victor's side, carefully setting her wine down and scowling at Eugene. "Why would you do that? Are you supposed to be a Zorro? Perry, call the police."

Eugene hopped back and forth, gripped by uncertainty, wrestling to extricate an unruly garden stake from his belt. When he made a move toward Victor, a handful of Bank patrons shuffled forward, as a group debating the wisdom of challenging him.

Eugene reluctantly abandoned the idea of finishing Victor off. "You haven't seen the last of me," he said before bolting out the door and taking off down the sidewalk.

"My tooth," Victor moaned, hand covering his mouth.

"Oh honey," said Clancy. "Let me see."

"He broke my tooth..."

A collective pitying moan came from the assembled. "Oh my son," Father Crist consoled him.

Clancy guided Victor's hand away from his face and gently pulled his lip back. "It's okay, it's one of the two front teeth," she reported, and now everyone could see the broken incisor. "His fangs are fine."

There was a collective expression of relief. "Well thank goodness," said Nurse Collette.

"You dodged a bullet, mister," said Tanner, finger

pointed like a gun.

Crouched beside Victor, Tripp tousled Jenny's wiry hair. "I spent a lot of time modifying this gal. If you were going to tell me that now you can't properly bite her, I'd throw a tantrum." He looked toward the front door. "That dude was a trip."

"That was a gag, right?" said Clancy. She stood and polished off her wine and slipped into the party ambiance that had re-started around them. "A gag that went bad."

Victor had been staring blankly at the door. Now he glared at Jenny. "I'm not biting your damn doll," he said through lips that were fattening from the blow.

"Check it out," said Tripp. "Her skin is made of that same polymer that lets those Goodyear tires seal themselves—you know the commercial, where the tire gets jabbed by that nail and then *gloop*, all better."

"I'm not biting it," Victor repeated, getting to his feet with assistance from multiple hands.

Tripp knelt and slipped an arm under Jenny's back, stretching out her latex throat. "What better way to get your blood, *and* that real vampire feeling."

"I *am* a vampire," Victor retorted. "Excuse me everyone. Thank you for the party. I'm going to the dentist now." He practically galloped out the door, pursued by well wishes and applause that grew from a smattering to a full round as he hit the sidewalk and speed-dialed his dentist.

Dentist Mulvane clucked as he poked at Victor's broken tooth. "That guy did a number on your incisor. Vampire hunter, you say?"

Victor shrugged. He was feeling very low. "Guess so."

"Cut your lip pretty good," said Dentist Mulvane, both hands engaged in Victor's mouth, swabbing and rinsing and probing. "The impact drove your lip up into your left fang. But the fang itself is just fine. For as slender and pointed as it is, it's remarkably strong. Is that a fang trait?"

"Not sure," said Victor, being careful not to bite his dentist.

"Good news is, there's enough tooth left to save the incisor," said Dentist Mulvane. "No pulling necessary. We can cap it with some shiny rapper's metal, or take a little extra time to craft a color-appropriate composite, that should bond pretty well."

Victor pictured himself sporting a gold tooth, Flavor Flav with fangs. "Composite."

"Good choice." Dentist Mulvane sucked in his breath. "Mama. Just poked myself on your fang."

"Sorry."

Dentist Mulvane checked the back of his finger. "Got a little blood going here. I need to fix it up before we can continue. Of course that's dentistry standards, but especially prudent when working on a vampire, am I right?" He smiled, tapped Victor's fang with an instrument. "Those things are really sharp. You want me to file them down a little?"

"That's okay." Back when they had first appeared, Victor had tried filing, with no luck. Like moussing his widow's peak to the side, like snapping off a lizard's tail, the fangs just grew back.

"Round them off, just a tad?" said Dentist Mulvane. "They'd still look cool."

"No, thanks."

"Your call," said Dentist Mulvane. "I'll just have to be more careful. Sit tight, and we'll get you fixed up in a jiffy."

THETHERSON, INTO HIS LAIR

"Master, I have the lady from HR," Nikki called into his office.

"I told you to stop calling me that," said Victor. "Seriously."

Nikki stared at him, eyebrows raised.

"Okay, patch her through."

"I have her, physically," said Nikki. "I just buzzed her onto the floor."

"No," said Victor.

"Oh yeah," said Nikki.

Raj was sitting across from Victor. Their exchange before Nikki's interruption still hung in the thick nail polish vapors:

"Victor, you know I've been wrapped up in the Maryhill variance analysis project—Florence told you about it, right?"

"Yes."

"I'm very sorry I didn't get the revised inventory valuation factors pushed down to the business units before quarter end. I didn't know about it until late last week."

"Florence said the two of you discussed it two months ago."

"I mean, I didn't know it was going to get you this upset until last week."

"I'm really torn over what to do about this."

"No-no-no, I'm going to make it right, pronto. I'll send out an explanatory memo and the revised numbers as soon as possible."

Now Raj looked at the door. "Sounds like you have company. I should go, right?"

Victor nodded at the door.

Raj jumped to his feet. "I'll keep you posted on my Maryhill project. And I'll cc you on the memo to the business units."

"I want to approve the draft," said Victor.

A woman with a wheelie suitcase in tow appeared in the doorway. "Hi, Sally Bornel from HR. Victor?"

Raj dismissed himself, leaving the introduction to Victor. He shook the HR lady's hand—while she was smelling the nail polish and circumspectly checking his fingernails—and motioned to his guest chair. "So I didn't know you were coming all the way from Chicago for this."

Sally parked her suitcase and took a seat. She adjusted the jacket of her business suit and crossed her legs, reaching down to pull an electronic notepad from her briefcase, flipping her straight hair back. "The allegations by Mr. Copperfield are serious. As one of our managers and long-term employees, we're committed to ensuring you're not unfairly treated during this process."

"That's good to hear," said Victor.

"Far outweighing this is our concern about what this kind of lawsuit could cost us."

"Crap," said Victor.

Sally received her first glimpse of his fangs. "Wow, if you'll forgive me. It's true." She fingered the arc of the necklace in the opening of her midnight blue blouse. "I don't know what I was expecting. But wow."

Nikki knocked on the door jam. "Can I get you two anything?"

"This is Nikki, our admin," said Victor.

"The stories I could tell you," said Nikki, clucking at Victor.

"We'll get our own coffee, thanks Nikki," said Victor.

"Sure thing, m—"

"Uh-uh-uh," Victor cut her off with the m-word on her lips.

"My boss," Nikki finished and left.

Sally touched her own throat where she had spotted Nikki's two scabs. "Did you bite her?"

Victor nodded. His panic at the HR woman's arrival was in the process of being replaced with indignation at her intrusion. "I did. Not during working hours, so, I really don't think it's your concern."

"Not during working hours," Sally echoed, typing into the e-pad. "Employment law's still a bit fuzzy on vampires. But I think it's safe to say the 'after-hours' defense won't work."

"Fine, I won't bite any more," said Victor. "Employees."

This addendum had an impact on Sally. Her fingers hovered motionless over the notepad. She cleared her throat, and wiped away the dampness that had sprung to her forehead, disguising the act as a finger-combing of her hair. Finally she typed a quick note. "Well let's talk about why I'm here." She rose to close the door, then took her seat again. "David Copperfield hasn't been to work since Friday, July twenty-first, correct?"

"That's right. I was helping him finish a report that was three weeks overdue. He went to get an energy drink and never came back. I've had Nikki call, because we were concerned. The last time she tried, she couldn't even leave him a message. His number was disconnected."

"David changed his phone number, and moved."

Victor shook his head dumbly. "Why?"

"So you can't find him. David's alleging you tried to sexually assault him."

Victor's eyebrows flew up and he gripped the arms of his chair.

"In a closet," Sally continued. "Which he said was ironic. That instead of coming out of the closet, you lured him into it."

The arms of Victor's chair creaked in protest. "That's not what happened," he exclaimed.

"Did you send him into the closet for an ink cartridge?"

"Because that's where we keep them," Victor retorted.

"And then you joined him in the closet?" said Sally. "To quote Mr. Copperfield, 'He snuck up on me from behind,'" she read from her e-pad.

"Well, yes, but that's because..." Victor pressed his fingers to his forehead, felt the widow's peak and combed it to the side. "He was really making me angry, and we had to finish the Westchase report, and I just felt like there was all this pressure—"

"Slow down," said Sally. "Are you married, Victor?"

"Yes—well, no. We just live together."

"You live with your ex-wife?"

Victor confirmed this with a nod, and then at Sally's judgmental expression, real or imagined, blurted, "It's for cost-saving reasons!"

Sally held up her hand, requesting patience. "This is just fact-finding. I'm not the enemy, Victor. I just need to know how a jury might view this, should we decide to fight it. Cost savings are important these days, I'm sure everyone understands."

And that's why we still sleep together, too, Victor pictured himself testifying on the witness stand. *One bed is so much cheaper than two.* He stared at his desktop, brooding.

"Would you show me where the incident with David took place?"

"You know a lot of couples live in a loveless relationship," said Victor, "so at least we had the courage to make it official, and just as soon as our daughter graduates from the private school Barbara thought was best, which is very expensive but does an excellent job I'm sure, and Barb gets a promotion at Wal-Mart—"

Sally cut him off. "The closet, Victor."

Victor's breath came shallow through constricting lungs. She was the female Jay Hansen, smug and all knowing, judging him. His heart revved to a rapid fight-or-flight beat as he led her out of his office and past the conference room.

"We were working in there. Well *I* was working. Well, David was a good worker, he just wasn't always focused." He stopped and would have chewed his lip if it wasn't a guaranteed wound. It had been a hard habit to break. "He was actually a terrible employee." Saying this was instantly liberating, like a confession years in the making. "Now I don't know why I didn't fire him a year ago."

"But he stayed late on a Friday night," said Sally. "That sounds dedicated."

Victor darkened. He bit his lip on purpose. "You know what, you want to see the scene of the incident, why don't I show you David's desk, where he never did any work. And the service elevator where I found him..." Victor struggled to find the business-appropriate term. "...making whoopee with a girl from the Tax department. And Florence's desk where David liked to stretch his quads."

"All that might be relevant," said Sally, "but let's stick to the attack."

"Sure, fine," said Victor, getting worked up. "So Jay has been waiting three weeks for this report—it's the audit report, the audit of Westchase, which turns out to have all our careers in the balance, and Jay's been waiting and waiting for it to be done, and finally very late on a Friday David hands me this incomplete, terrible draft, and now we have to stay late and David goes to happy hour and does shots on their breasts and I'm doing all the work here late on a Friday night—"

"It's okay," Sally soothed. "Slow down."

Victor didn't. "And now he's feeling *sluggish* and decides he needs to go get an energy drink and I tell him before he goes he needs to replace the printer ink cartridge, and he's worked here for over three years and he doesn't even know where we *keep* it..."

Victor marched to the walk-in closet, Sally following close behind. He opened the double doors and took the human resources representative by the arm and steered her into place. "David was standing there, looking clueless, and I came up behind him—"

"David said he had the ink cartridge," Sally interrupted, with an investigator's tone, backing Victor off a step with a hand to his chest. "Where are they kept? I want to get a good picture of both your positions."

Blood pumped red in the soft creased flesh around Victor's eyes, setting off the relative whiteness of his orbs, in turn creating a glowing effect. He was back in the moment, regretting the favorable performance appraisals he had approved for David, seeing his mocking smirk and hearing him say, slightly embellished, *I would have had this report done if you weren't such a terrible manager. VV.*

He stuck his foot under the ten-pound step stool stashed in the corner and flipped it up to his hand. He slammed it down in front of the closet shelf, put his hands under Sally's ribcage, and set her on top of the stool, eyes locked on hers, inches apart.

"David's about that tall." Victor forcefully rotated her so that her back was to him. "He was reaching for the ink cartridge up there..." He stretched Sally's hand toward the upper shelf. "And I was coming up behind him, and his throat was right here, and I knew it, knew it was right, something in me was screaming to just *bite* him—"

"*Vic,*" said Florence, taking in the scene with Larry. "I think she gets the point." She moved in and slapped Victor's hand with the blank expression of a lion tamer, hyper-aware of her surroundings and deaf to her instincts, backing him off.

Larry, mumbling and grumbling, helped Sally off the step stool. The HR rep's lips were pressed together as she readjusted her blouse under the suit jacket, nodded her thanks and hurried down the hall.

"That's a no-no, Vic," said Florence, arms crossed, a smile nearly unpuckering her lips. "You were about to bite that woman, weren't you? That HR girl, isn't that so?"

Larry was head down and pacing. "What the hell's gotten into you?" he said in a low hiss, arms flapping. "Are you looking to get fired? You don't like this job? You don't like feeding your family?"

Victor tucked in his dress shirt and walked to burn off his agitation, gravitating to the closet, hyperventilating through his nose, throat knotted and walling off his voice box.

Florence was drawn to him. "I'd say maybe it's time our boss started doing a little biting."

Larry turned on Florence, face elongated and taut from his rising blood pressure. "Speak for yourself. We don't need corporate coming in here and taking over. You think things will stay the same if Jay…" At the sight of Raj, Tessa and Casey hovering beside Nikki's admin station, Larry clamped a hand over his mouth and physically peeled the rest of the sentence off his lips, along with a bit of white goo. He stuck his chin out at Victor. "They'll can you, Vic. They will can you in a heartbeat."

Dewitt from the Tax department on the other side of the floor came around the corner, accompanied by a florid-faced man. "VV," Dewitt hailed him. "Do you have a second? There's someone I'd like you to meet."

Larry stomped his foot. "Come and gawk at the vampire, is that it Dewitt?"

Dewitt drifted to a stop, head rotating side-to-side on his pencil neck. "Justin here is new to the department, and I thought—"

"Gawl-dammit," Larry cut him off. "Doesn't anyone do

any work around here? Don't you think we have things to do? Do you have any idea what kind of pressure we're under?"

The opening flashed like a lighthouse beacon across Victor's eyes. "You're right, Larry's right, with the merg...er, the, uh, whatdoyoucallit, the uh, acquirement of Westchase—"

"That's a non-event," said Larry disdainfully, owning all the momentum, pushing Victor back on his figurative heels. "I'm talking about you screwing up left and right, pissing off Jay, putting us all in the gawd-damned hotseat."

"I haven't been...I mean," Victor stammered, "it's been all of us..."

"All of us?" Larry pressed forward. "You're pretending to think about the rest of us? If you cared about *us*, you'd be back at your desk, getting that HR lady off our back and getting our work done."

"I'm sorry sir," said Justin the new tax department employee, beet red and fairly kowtowing to Larry. "I meant no disrespect, and will now return to my desk and learn my job to its utmost."

"He's not the vampire," said Dewitt. He pointed at Victor. "It's him."

Victor grimaced and lifted one side of his lip for confirmation. "Welcome to Texahoma."

Casey let out a warbling cry, "My brain!" and crumpled to the floor, head thumping to rest atop Raj's foot.

"Sweet Jesus, I think she's hemorrhaging," Tessa exclaimed.

Victor closed the gap, snapping his fingers at Dewitt. "Call 911. Casey, stay with us," he implored, dropping to his knees beside her. "Get me a pillow," he redirected Nikki as she hurried toward them.

Raj stared down at Casey, horror on his face. "I can see her brain," he said, and then collapsed to the floor beside her like a forgotten marionette.

Victor eased Casey's head off Raj's twitching foot and gingerly examined her. "There's no wound. He must have seen the ribbon in her hair," he assured everyone who was still conscious. "Nikki, call Casey's sister and let her know she'll be taken to Methodist. Don't get her upset, keep it as low-key as possible."

Casey peeked out of one eye and broke into a big grin. "See, Larry," she said. "VV loves us. He isn't going to do anything to hurt us." She sat up and pecked Victor on the cheek, and jumped to her feet.

"You crazy headcase," said Nikki, hanging up the phone with a grin. "You got us."

Florence advanced on Casey, jaw set and sparks shooting from her eyes. "Are you out of your lobotomized mind?"

"It's okay, I practice my falls all the time," said Casey, beaming, mostly protected in Tessa's arms amidst a steadily-growing group of coworkers and Westchase accountants.

"Looks like you can cancel that order," said Dewitt, on his cellphone with the 911 operator. "Unless...?" He pointed at Raj, on his back with his limp arms spread wide, mouth lolling open, eyes rolled back in his head.

"Nope," said Florence, scowling down upon the sharp-dressed junior accountant, finding an outlet for her irritation. "A bucket of water for him."

Victor had gradually retreated, relieved to reach his office without anyone but Nikki noticing. He was easing the door shut when he heard Casey's childlike voice. "Don't worry so much," she soothed Larry, who stood apart from the group, sulking. "Victor's a good vampire."

At four-fifty-five that afternoon, Sally knocked and opened Victor's door. "Just wanted to say goodnight."

Victor was flustered, all day stewing about the incident, expecting every e-mail to be from Jay, telling him he was fired. "I didn't know you were still here."

"I used an open office on the Sales floor."

"I'm very, very sorry about this morning, I didn't

think about what I was doing. How that must have been for you."

"It's fine," said Sally. "I asked you to show me what happened, right? Your staff shouldn't have been so worried. They must not know that you promised not to bite any more employees. Or was that just local employees?" Her eyes danced. "I guess I should be clear on the rule."

"Well, no, I mean, it's not a rule…"

"Say." Sally pulled her wheelie suitcase into view. "I'm at the Hilton tonight, before I fly out tomorrow morning. Do you know the one, close to the airport?"

"Sure."

"Great. So I'll be working late in the room, finishing my report for our legal team. At which point I'm going to need a drink. It's just my thing—the booze guarantees that when my head hits the pillow, work issues are the furthest thing from my mind. This report will probably take me until midnight to finish."

Sally paused. But the day's frustration left Victor slow to recognize the opening.

"So…what do you think, is the Hilton bar open after midnight?"

"Until one, I suppose," said Victor.

"Good to know." Sally leaned over his desk to shake his hand. "It's been a pleasure. I sincerely hope to bump into you again. Soon, alright?"

Distracting, entertaining Tripp wasn't at the Longevity Labs for Victor's monthly battery of tests. Instead a distracted, disinterested lab tech put him through the paces, testing his vision, hearing and reflexes, running him twenty minutes on the treadmill, taking his blood and urine. As a result Victor arrived home just as edgy and unsettled as when he had left the office.

Barbara was bringing Amberly to the house for the evening to plan her wardrobe for the new school year. In his prickly mood, Victor was apt to wonder aloud why Amberly needed a thousand dollar budget to accessorize her school uniform. He didn't want to be that way. He poured a bloody orange juice, to soothe his nerves.

When Barbara and Amberly drove into the garage, they found Victor, eyes glued to the screen of a seventeen-inch tube TV sitting on the floor, sweating through a set of wide-grip lat pulls on the Bowflex. Victor had just stepped up to a beefier rod, and his grunts had increased commensurately.

"No way," said Amberly. "Dad's working out?"

"I told you," said Barbara.

"Seeing is believing," said Amberly. "What's the deal?"

"Sweetie, it is so good to see you." Victor crossed the garage to embrace his daughter.

Amberly recoiled. "Ugh, you're all sweaty. I've never seen you sweaty. Not from exercise, anyway. It's gross."

Barbara cocked an ear toward the television. "What are you watching?" She checked her watch. "It's seven-thirty. That doesn't sound like *Glee* music."

"It's P90X," said Victor. "First day is Chest and Back. It's killer."

They both stared at Victor's bare arm. "What's that?" said Barbara, pointing.

"I think it's a bicep," said Amberly. With a dainty two-finger pinch grip she lifted her father's t-shirt. "I suppose you have a six-pack under there..." Victor's hairy belly rose and fell with his labored breathing. "Nope. Ew." She looked for somewhere to wipe her fingers.

"I haven't done the Ab Ripper yet," said Victor.

"I don't know who he's trying to impress," Barbara told her daughter as they entered the house. "If it's not his trains, it's that bow-thing. That's all your father's interested in. Or he's out at bars getting into fisticuffs."

Amberly turned in the doorway. "What's gotten into you?" she asked, sounding far too mature to Victor.

"Got a vampire hunter on my trail," Victor said,

striving for nonchalance.

"Really," said Amberly, staring at her father seemingly against her will.

Porky pug ran up to them, snorting and gasping and looking for attention. Victor bent down to tousle its ears, and Porky's bladder released on the entryway floor.

"Porky!" said Victor, and the pug crawled off, belly to the floor and trailing pee like slug slime. Victor looked up at Amberly, who was pinned against the door to avoid the puddle. "That's the third time he's done that lately. Does he pee for you too?"

Amberly shook her head, disgusted. "No."

"Well just to prepare you, Porky may not be with us much longer. That could be a sign of cancer."

"That would be okay," said Amberly.

"Alright, Daddy has some more iron-pumping to do. Get some paper towel or a wet vac and clean that up."

"No way."

"Tell your mother then," said Victor. He took Tony Horton and his band of merry exercise fiends back a few frames and hit play, hurrying into position for dive bomber pushups. "And have her set up a vet check-up for Porky."

Amberly fidgeted at the doorway. "Dad…I met a boy."

Victor threw a glance her way as taskmaster Tony counted out the reps. She was glowing like a switch had been thrown. "That's nice. I'd like to meet him some time."

"You're in luck. We're having him over for dinner tonight."

"Oh great." Victor used the muscle strain to manufacture a scowl, fighting the urge to smile. He was always envisioning boys jumping the school walls for an illicit midnight rendezvous with Amberly. To see her excited over the prospect of a traditional date soothed his soul.

The rest of the workout was a joy. He tore down his pecs and biceps until they screamed white hot and passed out from exhaustion, and then got cleaned up, eager to spend quality time with his family, and meet Amberly's date. This would be his first chance to play the role of stern, intimidating father, and Victor couldn't wait.

The house was filled with the promise of dinner and the doorbell was ringing when he exited the bedroom after his shower. Victor and Amberly met at the front entryway. She gave him a nervous smile and opened the door.

Eugene Foreman stood on their stoop, in black, wearing calf-high goose-steppers and a Trotskyite cap. He held forth a dozen red roses.

"Hi," said Amberly shyly.

"You," said Victor, cocking his head to access his memory bank.

"Dad," Amberly scolded.

"Eugene Foreman," the vampire slayer introduced himself. "I met you at the blood bank. Officially, that is."

Victor now pictured the tall scrawny youngster in his Zorro costume. "Good grief. It was you. You're nuts."

"I believe what you mean is, I'm the last guy in the world you wanted to see standing on your doorstep," said Eugene.

"No, no," said Victor, "I'm glad you're here. Now you can tell me why you're doing it."

"What's going on here?" Amberly demanded, looking troubled.

"Dinner's ready," Barbara's voice carried to them.

"Your father knew this day would come," said Eugene. "He's just wishing it hadn't been so soon."

"It's just a date, Dad," said Amberly.

"No, I know," said Victor genially. "It's fine. We can talk over dinner. What's your mom cooking? Stir fry? My sense of smell is a little off any more," he explained to Eugene.

"Come on," said Amberly, taking Eugene's hand. "Come in."

Eugene didn't budge. "I believe the rule states that your father has to invite me in."

"I think you have it backward," said Victor.

"Pretty sure I'm right," said Eugene.

"The rule is set up to keep *vampires out*," said Victor, irritated. "I'm already in."

"Do not fear," said Eugene, "you have my word. Tonight is for social pleasure and no more. A temporary cease-fire in our game of cat and mouse, our winner-take-all dance—"

"For crying out loud," said Victor, turning and heading for the kitchen, "just come in already."

"Thank you," said Eugene. He took a deep breath and stepped into the house. Amberly quickly shut the door behind him and towed him toward the kitchen, where Barbara beamed as she greeted Eugene, admired the roses and welcomed him to the table. They passed around the bowl of ravioli, and passed their plates to Barbara for a ladle of meat sauce from the pot.

"Dad thought this was stir fry," said Amberly with a suffering sigh.

"Maybe it's the heavy garlic smell coming from your young gentleman friend," said Barbara, smiling at Eugene, who received this with a grave nod.

"Not too much," said Victor as Barbara prepared to fill his plate.

"I suppose your tastes run to something runnier and uncooked," said Eugene, staring at him.

"I just got done working out," said Victor. "Stomach still hasn't settled."

"So what do you do, Eugene?" Barbara asked.

"He works at the blood bank," Victor informed.

"But my passion lies elsewhere," said Eugene, casting an arch look at Victor. "Bounty hunting."

"Does that pay well?" said Barbara.

"It all depends on the value you place on ridding your community of the type of vermin I hunt," said Eugene. "Unfortunately, with the economy and all, the city's budget is tight. Looks like the first one will have to be on the house."

"Avocation versus vocation," said Barbara. "I can relate. I'm an artist, but the market is tight right now, so I make ends meet working at Wal-Mart."

"Let me guess," said Eugene. He finished slicing and arranging his ravioli and set down his knife and fork. "You work the night shift, so you two can sleep together during the day and then work all night."

"I'm an accounting manager," said Victor. "That's a day job."

"Interesting," said Eugene. He pulled out a pen and a small spiral-bound tablet and made note, mouthing *works in daylight.*

"How did you two meet?" Barbara asked.

"Eugene was always driving by the school during lunch hour," said Amberly while Eugene scribbled. "He would drive by real slowly and stare at me." Eugene glanced up for a second to nod and smile. "Finally I slipped across the street when the monitor wasn't looking. I did that thing where you pull up your skirt to show some thigh. Eugene pulled over, and one thing led to another."

Victor's fork clattered to his plate, freeing both hands to rub his temples.

"Honey," said Barbara, "that's not a charming story. If you two end up getting serious, you'll need to make up something more tasteful."

Eugene leaned over to put his arm around Amberly. "I assure you, Mrs. Thetherson, my intentions with your daughter are completely honorable." He snapped his fingers at Victor. "Now as far as your husband is concerned..."

"We're not married," said Barbara.

"How old are you, Eugene?" said Victor.

"Twenty-two."

Victor pushed away from the table. "That's too old. You're forbidden from dating Amberly."

"Dad!"

"I've struck too close to home, haven't I?" said Eugene. "I've penetrated deeper into your lair than anyone has ever achieved."

"No," said Victor, "you're just too old. I want to punch your face when I think of you with my daughter."

Eugene held up his plate for Victor's inspection. He had arranged his ravioli in the shape of a cross. The crenellated edges all faced outward, giving the cross a Celtic touch. "Punch me? Or drink my blood, so that I can join your soulless legions?"

"I'm old enough to date anyone I want!" said Amberly.

"Honey, your father's right," said Barbara. "Give it a year apart. If you're still serious about each other, you'll have our blessing."

Amberly bowed her head, fuming. "That is just so unfair! I care about Eugene. It's what's inside that counts, you always told me that, Mom. Age shouldn't matter."

Eugene gulped down milk and held the glass poised before his lips, staring at Victor over the rim. He groped blindly for Amberly's hand. "Age has nothing to do with it, does it, Victor Thetherson?" Eugene's voice echoed into the glass. "Beautiful Amberly, someday soon you'll understand the deadly game that raged around you, while you were innocently caught in the crossfire. The conflict your father refers to is timeless, something that can't be measured in human years."

"Yes it can," said Victor. "You're exactly five years too old."

"More like two," said Barbara.

"I'm tired of listening to this!" said Amberly. "Eugene, take me back to school, right now!" She swung out of her chair and stalked out of the kitchen.

"I would be honored to escort your daughter back to school," said Eugene. He wiped milk from his lip. "Solely as a friend. You have my word."

"What a gentleman," Barbara admired, rising with

Eugene. "I'm disappointed we won't have the chance to see you for a year."

"Oh, I'll be around, Mrs. Thetherson."

"I go by my maiden name," said Barbara. "Klein. But please call me Barb."

"Barbara." Eugene paused to kiss her hand. "It has been a pleasure. And to the master of this castle," he addressed Victor, who had remained seated. "Until we meet again." He clicked his heels and executed a bow like a bowler's delivery, driving his jackbooted heel through the plasterboard of the wall behind him.

"Mm-hmm," said Victor. "Bye Eugene. Drive careful. Bye honey," he called out, receiving no response from Amberly.

After they had left, Barbara returned to the table. "What a nice young man. He seems smitten with Amber. I have a feeling we'll be seeing more of him."

"He's a vampire hunter," said Victor.

"Who?"

"Eugene."

"No," said Barbara.

"He's stalking me. He's already tried to kill me twice."

"Victor," Barbara scolded.

"You think I'm exaggerating? It comes with the territory."

"Listen to you. You're so feisty lately. I think you're overcompensating for Jay telling you that you can't go to Germany."

"Barb, that is ridiculous." Victor pushed his plate away and pouted. "I can't eat that. I don't know what you did to it."

"That, that was delicious," Barbara spluttered. "Don't you dare take your work anxieties out on me! You're not *forceful*, Victor. You're just not, and it drives Jay crazy. That's just the way it is."

"I'm not forceful?" Victor's voice raised. "You don't think so?"

"No."

"You haven't seen me lately at work, with everyone stumbling over each other to please me."

"To please Jay, I'm sure."

"*Me*, Barbara! They want to do a good job for *me*."

"Please."

"I've been biting people, Barbara!" This erupted with such force that Victor felt the need to twist his face away lest the words themselves do her damage. He seethed over the array of nearly full plates.

Barbara stopped gaping, and stated, "No you did not."

Victor stood quickly, rocking the table and knocking over his chair. These were the times when his temperature elevated, blowing mental circuits and taking his personality offline. When he would stammer and Barbara would press her attack and, these days almost distractedly, prove him wrong.

Not this day. A cool breeze seemed to pick up just behind his eyes. His body temperature, he could actually feel it drop a couple degrees, slowing his heart, slowing time along with it. Victor stabbed a piece of ricotta-filled pasta from the center of Eugene's ravioli cross, and popped into his mouth. "Oh yes I did."

Victor put on his pajamas and climbed into bed at nine-thirty. He planned to be asleep, fast asleep by midnight, when Sally would be heading to the hotel bar.

She was beautiful. Her face was weathered and her hair was flat with sprecks of gray. But she was beautiful. And she had seemed to want him.

Victor Thetherson had never, ever seen *wanting*. He had seen contented resignation when he asked Barbara to marry him. She wanted to *marry* him, but that wasn't the same.

He might have *heard* wanting, over the phone from cute, acne-cheeked Kathy as he laid with Barbara. Could Sally be attracted to him? For one thing, Victor reminded himself, she had been sure he was gay. For another, no. He didn't spend much time looking in the mirror, but he had a clear measure of the physical gulf between them. He was no longer young, thin, and moussed.

So...did Sally want to be bit? Victor blushed for contemplating it. This wasn't Nikki and her wild set. Sally was a professional woman.

He fell asleep thinking such thoughts.

In his dream Sally was Fay Wray tied with vines to a palisade wall. She was waiting with a smile as something came crashing toward her through the surrounding jungle, when the bedside phone woke Victor, just a bit after eleven.

"Vic, VV, baby!"

"Nikki?"

"You're getting better at recognizing my bar voice."

"What's going on? I was asleep."

"I'm at the scene of the crime, VV! You remember the Opposite-Spotted Zebra?"

"Striped?"

"Huh?"

"Opposite-Striped, you mean?"

Nikki cackled. "Yeah, what'd I say?" She was drunk. "Striped?"

"Spotted."

"Huh?"

"Nikki, why are you calling?"

He heard rustling. She was covering her mouth to shield her words. "I've got a job for you. A dirty deed. Done *real* cheap."

"What are you talking about?"

"I've got a friend here who can't stop talking about you."

"Sally?"

"What? The HR woman? No! That cold fish? Eeu. The Ice-Pick Princess, that's what we were all calling her today. She has eyes like a husky, Vic! She asked me a lot of questions today, by the way. Stay away from her, Vic. She's HR, for crying out loud. They don't exist to help us. Besides, you're not even a *human* resource, so she should just leave you alone."

"Okay, okay."

"I'm talking about my friend, Rebecca. I told her you're a vampire, and how you bit me and Melanie and Karina."

"I didn't bite Karina," Victor set the record straight, while Nikki kept talking.

"She's flipping out about it. She keeps asking what it's like...yes you do," Nikki said to her friend Rebecca. Victor heard friendly arguing and wild laughter, for some seconds. "Sorry," Nikki came back on. "So, I don't know..." More insistent arguing and nervous laughter. "You wanna come wait for us in the alley?"

"Nikki, no, you don't have to do this."

"Uh, yeah, I do, VV. Ding-dong hello? I'm your property now, remember."

"No you're not."

"That's the way it works. I serve you."

"*I swervoo,*" Victor heard Rebecca making fun of Nikki's drunken lips. There seemed to be a skirmish, and then the connection was severed.

Victor lay there for some time.

Barbara entered the bedroom as he was getting out of bed. "You don't have to leave," she said. "I'm just coming in to get my book. I can't sleep," she said accusingly.

"Me neither. You can read in here. I'm going out."

"Uh-uh mister," said Barbara. "No. You get your oils all over the upholstery. Unless you want me to put the plastic back on, you do not sleep on the couch."

"Out out, Barb." Victor pointed into the distance. "I'll be back later."

Barbara looked like she'd bit a cherry pit. "Who was that on the phone?"

"It's not your business."

"Yes it is," she barked. "We are living under the same roof, don't you forget."

"If we were married, I'd tell you," said Victor,

removing the tags from the recently purchased black turtleneck.

"Victor, that's disrespectful! Don't you use our divorce as a weapon."

"It's not a weapon, Barbara." Victor checked the mirror to ensure the turtleneck hadn't disrupted his combed-forward widow's peak. "It's the truth."

Barbara stared, shaking her head while he pulled on his black cords. "I saw those hanging in your closet. Those are thirty-eights. You bought the wrong size." Victor buttoned and zipped them as she spoke, and pulled on his black tennies. Barbara crossed her arms. "You lost more weight," she said accusingly.

"Blood is low carb," said Victor, leaving the bedroom.

Barbara followed him. "Where are you going?"

"Why do you care?"

"Because you're only doing this to hurt me! I *don't* care! Except it hurts, because you're trying to *hurt* me."

Victor plucked the keys from the holder beside the garage entry door. "Rest assured, that's not what's driving me. I've never tried to hurt you." He reached to squeeze her arm, but Barbara turned away with a whimper. "I'll see you later. Probably shouldn't wait up."

Victor got lost again. He hadn't been born with a good sense of direction, and vampirism hadn't worked any magic. But he found the Zebra quicker this time, the type of small victory that the spatially-impaired celebrate. He parked on the street, and as the Zebra's front door opened and a group of college-aged kids spilled out, slipped into the alley.

Briskly passing the spot where he had bitten Nikki, Victor continued to the edge of the small parking lot, nearly full. There he waited, and then retraced his steps, past the door and to within a stride of the sidewalk; and repeat. Looking for hiding places and losing the antsy urgency in his legs, until he was strolling. Finally he settled against the opposite wall, twenty yards from the door.

Victor watched Nikki and her friend Rebecca exit the Zebra through the alley door. He was too far away to make out their words, but close enough to get the gist:

"We should go."

"Are you scared?"

"No. Yes!"

"If you wanna go, you can."

"No, let's walk this way."

The women's exchange was accompanied by constant shrieking and hugging and playful wrestling, until they were walking toward him, clutching each other, giggling and whispering.

Victor had chosen well, in the shadow cast by the overhead fire escape. Nikki and Rebecca—blond and tall with thin shoulders and outsized hips, a little chinless in profile thanks to a full fleshy neck—walked right past him. Victor had rehearsed. He stepped out of the shadow, now behind them, and said, "Good evening, ladies."

They both screamed. For an instant they fell into each other in a delightfully frightened embrace. Then Nikki gave her friend a separating shove.

Rebecca protested and reached for her while backpedaling, her momentum widening the space between them. Into the gap Victor glided.

"I, uh..." His prepared script was short. "How was your time there, in there?"

Rebecca could only giggle and shake her head, backpedaling and grinning with wild eyes darting to Nikki and back to Victor. "You're old, kinda." Her gum fell out of her mouth.

"I'm..." Victor had intense second thoughts, feeling suddenly ridiculous. He could see his pot belly in his lower peripheral vision. "I'm sorry." He stopped and turned to Nikki. "I just, after you called, I mean, we don't have to..."

Nikki shook her head vehemently, and then jerked it

in Rebecca's direction. She widened her eyes and mouthed, *Do it.*

Victor turned back to Rebecca. She was bent forward, contorted by booze and nerves, her butt still in retreat. Victor calmed his brain and said, "Rebecca." It came out a croak, but she stopped. She froze. He resisted the urge to stumble forward, it could only be a stumble, because his legs were weak from stagefright.

He held out his hand. Rebecca stared at it, then at his face. Victor nodded and stared at her intently, the way he thought he should. "Come to me. Rebecca. Come to me." He heard Count Chocula's voice.

And yet Rebecca obeyed, still bent forward, faltering but ever approaching, eyes so round as to nearly be taller than they were wide, blinking with eyelashes mascara'd into sunburst-surprise.

From the corner of his eye or senses Victor saw Nikki covering her mouth and dancing tight circles, chirping in a drunken emotional overload, as Rebecca placed her hand in his. He moved in, and now Rebecca leaned back, lengthening her arm to full extension, resisting minimally as he pulled her forward. She was against his hips and gut and chest, her skin so delicate and sweet-smelling and her eyes so big and tall.

"Who are you?" was all she wanted to know.

"Victor Thetherson," he said. "I love you."

"What?" said Nikki.

Victor squeezed his eyes shut, without a clue why he had said that. He reached up and pushed Rebecca's chin back, and sank his skinny fangs into her throat.

Rebecca screamed. "Shoot," said Victor, muffled against her skin. He had taken too small of a bite, only getting fatty tissue. He unhooked his fangs and wrapped one arm tightly around her, preventing her attempted escape, feeling her back bend as it yielded to his strength. He opened his mouth wider and thrust his mouth fast and hard against her throat. This time his fangs sunk and punctured a blood-carrying vessel.

Victor's mouth filled, fast. He drank, fast, but couldn't keep up. His throat closed to prevent drowning and blood shot up his sinuses and came spilling out his nose. He dropped Rebecca and staggered back, coughing and choking. "Gaa! Agg!"

Nikki rushed to him. "What happened—eww, ehh, yuck." She opened her purse and rummaged and finally pulled out a feminine pad, peeling off the backing and shoving it in Victor's hand. He coughed into the pad, continuing to gurgle and retch. Pressing one nostril closed, he blew a boogery bloody stream out the other.

"Vic, baby, stop it," said Nikki, blanching and turning away to assist Rebecca, who sat in her stretch skirt on the grimy pavement, blood sprinkling her pale green blouse and trickling down her neck. Nikki unwrapped another pad and pressed it to Rebecca's neck.

"I've got some wet wipes in my purse," said Rebecca in a flat monotone. She unslung the purse from her shoulder, rooted inside and pulled out a travel pack of the moistened towelettes. Glassy-eyed, she offered it to Victor, who plucked a few and finished his clean-up.

"So that was wild," said Nikki. "I've never seen anything like that. It was blooood-dee."

"Did I lose a lot of blood?" said Rebecca, dully.

"It came out really fast," said Victor. He fluttered his fingers in front of his face. "Went up my nose."

"I've got a strong heart, huh?" Rebecca gave them a weak smile.

Victor dug in his pocket and pulled out a tube of Neosporin. He handed it to Rebecca, nodding at her throat. "Keep the area from getting infected."

"That's very thoughtful," said Rebecca.

"I'm sure she can buy her own disinfectant, VV," said Nikki disapprovingly. "I think it's time for you to be going. We need to get you rehydrated," she told Rebecca. "Back inside for screwdrivers."

"Sounds good," said Rebecca, with Nikki helping her to stand. "Will you join us?" she asked Victor.

"That's not happening," said Nikki. "One's all you get."

"I do have a prior commitment," said Victor. He hesitated, then reached out his hand. "It was nice to meet you."

Nikki slapped it away. "Stay in character, Vic." She slipped an arm around Rebecca's waist and ushered her toward the Zebra door. "Help!" she yelled. "Somebody! We've been attacked..." She cast a look at Victor. "Better get out of here." They continued slow progress up the alley. "My friend was attacked by someone! By some...*thing*!"

Victor took off in the opposite direction, through the little parking lot to the side street, taking the long way around to where his Subaru sat across from the Zebra. A small crowd had gathered around the women at the mouth of the alley, inspecting Rebecca's neck, chattering excitedly. As Victor pulled away from the curb, a group of men marched into the alley, while Rebecca and Nikki regaled a newly arrived cluster of Zebra patrons, Nikki gesturing, Rebecca beaming.

Victor tried various side doors before resorting to entering the Hilton through the front entrance. Memories flooded back...drinking wine with Cruella and a few others beside the baby grand in the lounge that occupied the far half of the main floor; trying to negotiate a discount with the desk clerk on a room he hoped to share with Cruella; stumbling and sprawling into the sunken seating area under the large chandelier as he made for the exit the next morning, bitten.

Of their own accord his fingers touched his throat. Victor stuffed them in his pocket, irritated like a poker player at a habitual tell...but not before having another flash of a dredged-up memory, of rough sex—had he been screaming?—in a hotel room.

"Can I help you, sir?"

Victor had slowed opposite the front desk, lost in

thought. "Sorry," he said to the female desk clerk. "I'm meeting someone. In the lounge."

"It's straight ahead. Have a nice night, sir." She returned to her busywork.

Victor started forward, got as far as the broad entrance to the lounge, and hesitated. Shuffled left to survey a stretch of the bar and saw Sally on a high chair, talking to no one, her back to him. Imagining Nikki's guidance, he moved quickly down the hall, toward the guest rooms.

The hallway turned ninety degrees, became a spacious foyer outside the Sam Houston and Sam Bowie meeting rooms, then resumed as a hallway to the elevator banks.

At a noise from the direction of the lounge, Victor slipped into the darkness of the Sam Houston room, blocking the door's attempt to close with his foot, providing a narrow gap through which he could stake out Sally's approach, and somehow assess her mood and decide whether and how to approach her.

As he waited, Victor's spirits sagged. On the drive to the Hilton he had been high from the encounter with Rebecca, boldly believing Sally would be just as eager to be his victim. Now his bloodlust seemed to be fairly well slaked, and any scenario where Sally welcomed his advance farfetched. Larry had been outraged after his boss's near-attack on Sally in the office; Victor could only imagine how betrayed his staff would feel upon hearing he was being fired for accosting their HR rep at her hotel.

"Waiting for me?"

That was a man's voice, and right behind him. Victor discarded the idea of escaping into the hall; fleeing was not how he wanted to encounter Sally. He let the door shut, took two quick sideways steps that he hoped would take him off the man's radar screen, and speed-walked toward the other side of the room with a low hand sweeping for obstacles.

"Where you going?" said the man. "Turn around!"

Victor complied and was blinded by a flashlight beam. He recoiled and appeared to snarl.

"Yah!" the man yelled in revulsion. "You're one of them!" The beam dipped and Victor was caught off-balance, unprepared for the tackle. He staggered backward, body accelerating faster than his feet, landing hard under the man's considerable bulk.

Now Victor was hauled to his feet. "You picked the wrong hotel to visit twice," boomed what had to be a mountain of a man. Victor was shoved backward, slammed into a wall, a flexible wall, a room divider that absorbed enough of the violence that Victor was able to keep his feet. He stumbled and banged along the divider, heading for a patch of light, a partially open door on the other side of the room.

Tie went to the bigger man. Victor was tossed against the wall, this time of the load-bearing variety. He slumped to a knee as the overhead lights snapped on. The man had one hand on the switch and the other on the door, pulling it closed.

He was as big as Victor had sensed, a hotel security guard with shaved head and clenched fist. "I can*not* believe you came back." The man's voice quavered with wild emotions barely in check. "Every, what, year and a half? Two years? Is that the cycle?" He advanced as he spoke and caught Victor with a backhand fist, sending him face down on the tight carpet. "I suppose you figure no one would remember, is that it?" The man's voice cracked into the upper ranges and he kicked Victor in the stomach.

Victor rasped for oxygen as he rolled feebly away in a loose fetal position.

"Can you see it?" the security guard demanded, stretching his neck and jabbing a finger at his throat.

Victor shook his head, unable to look, face screwed up in pain.

"She bit me," the guard spat. "Not she. *It*. You aren't

human. One of your *females* bit me, drank so much blood I nearly died. Got a God-damned infection and nearly died!"

"Me too, she bit me too—"

"Shut up!" The guard raised his foot and stomped. With both hands Victor deflected the soft-soled shoe from his face, his body absorbing so much impact that his shirt ripped across his back.

Enraged to have been denied, the guard dove on him, screaming expletives and nonsense. He threw a quick series of short punches before grabbing Victor's throat and squeezing, tilting forward and bearing down. "You want the throat, huh? That's what you want? That's what you're looking for? I'll break your frigging throat!" Victor was turning purple. "You're not so tough when I'm ready for you!" the man screamed at him. "Slinking around in the shadows—who were you going to bite? Me? Me again?!"

Victor bucked and the guard had to let go to catch himself, using Victor's face as a brace. Victor bit him.

The guard screeched and gaped in horror at his hand. He tried to recover, but Victor had taken his first good breath in some moments and thrashed with enough conviction to prevent the guard from getting a good grip. The bitten hand now felt weaker on his throat.

Continuing to twist and buck, he got hold of the guard's shirt and yanked, for a second bringing the guard's face close to his. "Stop it!" Victor squeaked through dented vocal apparatus, and he saw the guard's rage give way to fear.

After a brief struggle, Victor was now firmly on top. The guard's violent babbles turned to a scream which a second later gurgled to pleading. And Victor realized that with his newfound strength from just a few sessions with Tony and the Bowflex, coupled with the guard's debilitating fear, the throat was his for the taking.

The thought of his mouth on the man's ruddy

whiskered folds caused Victor's diaphragm to spasm and drive bile up his esophagus, like the very recent old days when blood made him nauseous. With an open-mouthed snarl he wrenched out of the guard's feeble defensive grasp and backed away, unwilling to fully straighten up through the pain in his side where the guard had kicked him. Hearing voices approaching the near door, Victor beelined along a row of folding chairs, back to the hallway entrance.

He tore open the door and burst through, tripped by a wire strung across the opening, hurtling headfirst to the floor, the sight of the onrushing carpet abruptly replaced with a silent, violent explosion of light.

Victor awoke staring at a hotel room ceiling, triggering a memory-image of a terrible fanged face above him. The nightmarish vision mercifully resolved into the life-lined but by no means horrible face of Sally from HR.

She was holding a bulky washcloth, which she now placed on his temple.

"Owie," said Victor.

"You got quite a goose egg forming already," said Sally, flipping her long limp locks off her cheek.

Thanks to the ice-packed washcloth, Victor only had use of an eye-and-a-half, generating two Sallys. "What happened?"

She pulled away the washcloth and there were still two Sallys, prompting him to squeeze his eyes shut, until he couldn't take the feeling of the room spinning. "I was coming down the hall from the bar," said Sally, "and I see a man crouched outside the ballroom door. He's got a mask on, like Zorro. He's got a cape like Zorro too, come to think of it."

Victor liked the guttural grumble deep in Sally's throat. "That's my vampire hunter. Eugene."

"Really." Sally stared at him with cool bemusement, and then pressed the icepack against his sore head again. "I get closer and I see this spike-thingy sticking up from the floor. He had a stake anchored into this metal base, so that it sat on the floor and stuck straight up."

Victor whistled. "He's creative."

"I guess so. I keep walking closer, a little freaked out, but a little intrigued too, because I figure it's some kind of reality game or whatever. Then all of a sudden you burst out of the ballroom and go flying headfirst, and Mr. Zorro goes airborne too—I think he was holding the wire that tripped you and got yanked off his feet. You two collided and he landed on the stake."

"Wow."

"You whacked your head on the base of a luggage cart that I'm assuming Zorro…"

"Eugene."

"…that Eugene used to transport his stake contraption." Sally sat back and set the washcloth on the nightstand. "Eugene was screaming. I think it impaled him here." She straightened and stretched a little further yet, raising her shirt to indicate a spot on her shapely stomach just under the ribcage. "He'll probably live. Unfortunately for you, right?"

Victor shrugged.

"People came running from all over," said Sally. "A lot of commotion. You were pretty much out cold, and sort of moaning. Any time your mouth started to open, I put my hand on your face like I was soothing you." Sally demonstrated. "I told them you were my husband. We loaded you on the luggage cart and brought you up to my room."

"Eugene didn't say anything?" said Victor. "'Vampire, vampire! Evil bloodsucker. Undead demon.' That sort of thing?"

"By this time he was already in shock." Sally shivered at the memory. "The point of the stake was sticking out his back. I could see the bulge in his cape."

"Is that a stake in your cape or are you just glad to

see me?" said Victor with a weak grin.

Sally giggled, which caused Victor to chortle, which made him wince in a couple places. "Was there a big security guard there?"

Sally shook her head as she thought. "Not that I remember."

"He jumped me in that ballroom. Caught me by surprise while I was waiting..." Victor wondered how this would sound. "I was waiting for you."

"So the guard was trying to protect me? What did he think you were going to do to me?" She fiddled with the icepack washcloth as she asked, working to be casually conversational, possibly shifting a hair closer on the bed.

"I can't blame him for being suspicious. Then when he saw I was a vampire, he freaked out."

"Some people do, I suppose." Sally demonstrated that she was not a member of this club, leaning closer to inspect his bruised temple.

"He was bitten before," said Victor. "I think he was bit the same night I was."

"Where?"

"Right here. I was at a work party here at the hotel."

Sally's eyes widened. "When?"

"Two years ago. By one of the Germans from home office."

Sally was making memory connections. "Not the visit where Hofmeister's traveling secretary died? That party?"

"You heard about it?"

Sally chuckled ruefully. "That party caused us so many problems. We had a monster bill from all the damage to the hotel. The Hilton threatened to sue, and we settled for a big, big figure. We also had to implement a company policy that anybody traveling to Houston is required to stay here. Everyone but the Germans." She slapped the bed in a muted a-ha moment. "I didn't know you were there. And that you got bit..." She squeezed his leg. "Who? Who was it?"

"Giselda Munsch."

Sally nodded, still incredulous. "I've met her." She tapped one of her canines. "I didn't notice the teeth, but, yeah. Unbelievable. And she bit this guard too? Unbelievable..." Her eyes intensified. "How many times did she bite you?"

"Just once," said Victor.

"Then if the guard was bitten too...why isn't he a vampire?"

Victor sat there. He opened his mouth, assuming an answer would come out. Deep puzzlement settled in quickly. "I don't know. I don't know."

Sally rose at a sharp rap at the door and crossed the room. "Hotel staff wanting to make sure you're still alive, I'll bet."

Victor bolted upright, regretting the abrupt motion. "They must have found out I'm a vampire," he hissed. "Don't..." He clammed up as he heard Sally open the door.

"Is my husband here?" came a voice that was far enough out of its normal register that Victor couldn't place it until Barbara marched into view. "Victor! Ohh!" This was a grunted roar of displeasure. "How could you? We have one little fight, and that gives you the excuse to do this?"

Victor was on his feet, eager to reverse the shock and shame darkening Sally's eyes. "Like I told you today, we're not married."

"We live together, Victor," Barbara retorted. "Are you so modern now that that doesn't mean anything? You can just, you can just *trash* it, trash the commitment that implies? Am I just a roomie, like a college dorm buddy?"

"Sort of," said Victor, wavering on his feet, vision sparkling from a rush of blood to his head.

"Were you going to come home tonight and crawl in bed with me and tell me about how you got *laid* tonight?"

"Excuse me," said Sally icily.

"Excuse *me*," Barbara countered, shooting Sally a contemptuous look. "Excuse *me*, for making assumptions about a woman who would invite a man into her hotel room. Onto her bed!"

Victor resisted the urge to speculate how many men Barbara had brought home to their bed, or their couch, without the plastic on. "Honestly Barb, I came to bite her." He brushed past her. "But I ended up in her bed, and it was nice." As Barbara squealed her outrage, he turned at the door and added, "Because she was nice to me. Thank you," he said to Sally, who received it with a nod, arms crossed and staring at the floor. "Come, Barbara," Victor commanded.

She stomped her feet and motored past him, out the door and down the hall, braided ponytail swishing. Victor paused, exchanged one more glance with Sally, and then retreated so that the door could swing closed.

Certain the police would be marshaling in the lobby, Victor headed in the opposite direction, to the stairwell and the exit door at the far end of the Hilton.

THETHERSON, TRADEMARKED

Victor stayed home the next day. Barbara sniped that *she* had planned on staying home, but was not about to spend one more second under the same roof with him (today), and so now because of his selfishness had no choice but to go to work.

In the darkened bedroom Victor lay, dozing, listless, feeling the house heat up and the sheets underneath become damp and sticky along with the Houston summer day. He finally realized that Barbara must have shut off the central air. Still it required a great mental whipping for Victor to heave himself to his feet and sluggishly don tanktop and coach's shorts, abandoning the hot house for the cooler garage, the Bowflex, and Tony Horton's massive guns.

Why was he a vampire, and the security guard was not? Same for Nikki and the other women he had bitten. Other than when Tony challenged him to "bring it" through a few more repetitions, that question would not leave him.

The next morning he reached the office later than usual, pushing eight o'clock. His team was already at their desks, every single one of them. His supervisors' odd behavior continued when he stopped by to check in—Florence seemingly unable to take her eyes off him, Larry unwilling to meet his gaze. But both of them had clearly been working when he arrived, along with the rest of his staff, glancing up from their computers only long enough to bid Victor good morning as he passed by.

In his office Victor engaged the blinds over his porthole, eyes bruised by the circle of morning glare off the bleached prairie dog field. After skimming through the twelve e-mails already received from his team, he sat back and marveled. He was accustomed to seeing long-running chains of fragmented exchanges, an initial thrust followed by endless parrying from his team of defensive artists, virtual multi-player fencing matches that finally petered out from the original inquisitor's exhausted confusion. At which point Victor would need to come to the rescue and provide the answer.

These e-mails had depth. Evidence that his staff had actually been intent on providing solutions, not just that morning but over the prior days as well. They had showed…Victor searched for the foreign word…initiative.

At eight-thirty Nikki bustled into the office. Before long a crowd gathered and buzzed around her desk. "You've worn inappropriate clothing before," Victor heard Larry crack derisively, "but this takes the cake."

He reluctantly left his desk. Could her attire actually be worse than the bra-less midriff-baring white tubetop from earlier that summer? Or the Santa shorts worn on five separate occasions over three holiday seasons, with mistletoe hung like tassels from the back pockets? Or the "Are you gay? Not for long!" t-shirt she had unveiled the day after the company launched its diversity initiative?

Not coincidentally Florence was the first to see Victor appear at his office door. Larry tracked her gaze, saw his boss, and colored. To Victor's knowledge this was a first. Also the first time he had contemplated the blood beneath someone's blush.

"It ain't right, that's all," Larry grumbled as Victor approached. "You're all making out like it's some kind of game."

Tessa and Casey separated, creating a visual alley to Nikki, who posed at her desk, chest thrust forward to display the red screenprint on her shirt.

Team VV.

"Shameful," said Larry, encouraging everyone to concur.

"Huh," said Victor. Given that the *V*s weren't designed to direct attention to her nipples, he would classify it as tasteful for Nikki.

"Don't you get it?" said Nikki. "I'm on your team."

"Ahhh," said Victor, without comprehension.

"Where did you get it?" Quinten asked. "I want one of those."

"What other teams are there?" said Victor.

"None, as far as we're concerned," said Tessa.

"I had a friend make it for me," said Nikki. "My design." She tucked her chin to check it out, poking the pointed tips of the Vs, prompting Victor to give a second thanks for their relatively innocuous placement. "I wasn't sure whether to put blood droplets here."

"It's savvy," said Raj. "That's the only word I can think of to describe what you've achieved, Nikki. I'm impressed. Collegiate u-rah-rah connotations overlaying a darker theme of vampire indentured servitude."

"Savvy," intoned Casey, nodding.

"We all need to get one," said the temp. "T-shirts and hats. This should be our official department logo."

"You'd think I'd be a hat girl," said Casey, bending over and fingering her brain surgery scar. "But I'm always afraid a seam is going to snag my scar and rip a chunk of my scalp off!"

"T-shirt for you," said Nikki.

"Unless they're soft seams. Do the hats have soft seams?"

"I don't know, Casey," said Nikki.

"I'd like it on a coffee mug," said Quinten. "It'd be like I'm drinking blood."

"Do you think that's funny?" Larry challenged.

"Think about it," said Quinten, chuckling. "Blood."

"There's something you should all be aware of," said

Larry, edgy and throwing a sidelong glance at Victor. "Something our boss doesn't want you to know."

Victor's early life flashed before his eyes, a montage of embarrassing moments growing up in Milford. Which one was Larry going to dredge up? "We shouldn't, uh, deviate, we need to stick to what's relevant, to our jobs."

"Oh it is, little Thethy."

Victor shook his head, a quick terrier death-snap. A competition was raging inside, a lifetime of accumulated inferiority demanding that Victor show everyone how sorry he was and how hard he was working to make things right...matched against something, something new in his head, that couldn't care less.

"Mess with the vampire at your own peril," said Florence. "Lil' Lawrence."

"If you care about your job, you'll *mess* with him too," Larry shot back. "You know the vampire who bit him?"

Everyone in unison, "Cruella."

"Her real name is Giselda Munsch," said Larry.

Victor pictured Giselda in a Morticia Adams spider web dress, black hair electrified with the white stripe glowing. Fangs glinting behind blood red lips. The old bite site on his throat throbbed.

"And she's on her way out," said Larry. "They're forcing Giselda out, because of what she's become. Because she's a gawd-damned vampire."

Florence soured and stepped toward Larry in challenge. "How in the hell do you claim to know that?"

"Because I got someone high up in the home office who comes over here every year to grouse hunt on my land. Got the inside scoop."

"Come on, Larry, this is VV we're talking about," said Tessa. "He's got our backs."

"Larry you sexy old codger," said Nikki. She touched the underside of her chin. "Your giblet tightens right up when you get feisty."

Florence wasn't playful. "You'd do anything to protect your job, wouldn't you?" she spat the words, arms cocked at her sides, the long strip of gristled biceps twitching to smack the heel of her calloused palm alongside Larry's noggin.

"And why the hell don't *you*?" Larry spoke aggressively while subtly assuming the classic defensive posture of a batter afraid of a wild, flame-throwing pitcher. "You all should be. It ain't fair what happened to David..." Now he retreated formally, while making quick intense eye contact with everyone but Victor. "And one way or the other, thanks to *him...*" Larry jabbed a finger at his boss while glaring at Florence. "...it's going to happen to the rest of us."

There was a pause, everyone checking the carpet and ceiling tiles and fingernails. Everyone but Florence, who stared after Larry until he was a few seconds gone from sight. Then she turned, and the mood reverted, attention back on Nikki's t-shirt, eager eyes on their boss. Florence crossed her arms and gave Victor (eyes and mouth) an intrigued look. "So we missed you yesterday, boss," she said.

"I was a little under the weather," said Victor.

Tessa gave him a sly grin. "Recuperating from your alley encounter Monday night, no doubt."

"That was between you and me," Nikki scolded Tessa, although it was clear Nikki had already made the rounds to everyone in the department. She gave Tessa a playful slap on the shoulder, which Tessa returned. By Victor's recollection, this was another first—Tessa playful.

He was flattered to be the subject of such intense interest, but determined not to let on. "What did Nikki tell you?" he feigned annoyance. Victor had never been good at playing stern—a happy staff had always been his primary managerial goal, and so he had no skill at conveying disapproval. Now he came across as threatening.

"Nothing," Tessa assured him, echoed by a few others. "She just said you had a good time. That you met a friend of hers—what was her name?" she strove to deflect Victor's attention to Nikki.

"Rebecca," Nikki said with a wicked grin. "Vic bit her." She made a wide mouth and feigned a big bite with her bad teeth. "Bit her real good."

"Ooh, let's hear it," said the temp. "Dish."

"Dish it to us, VV," said Quinten. "Dish us a great big helping, of dish."

"Yes, Victor," said Florence, eyes alight. "The cat's already clawed its way out of the bag. You need to give us all the gory details."

They crowded him, bodies radiating heat, waves of carbon dioxide pouring from their mouths. Shuffling closer, leaning in, as if they were each intent on maximizing the distance from their desks. He had been wrong about their initiative, Victor realized, belatedly seeing this "Team VV" chatter for what it was, just another of his staff's ploys to shirk their work. Another quarter flip for sodas; another black mark for him in Jay Hansen's eyes. All of a sudden Victor wasn't faking his displeasure.

He spoke quietly, but his words struck the surrounding ears like a bomb blast. "Can we just once put in a full day of work?"

Tessa was the only one to visibly flinch, but everyone moved, bodies propelled in a slow-motion shockwave away from Nikki's admin station.

In the seconds following, Victor came that close to apologizing. What if his pointed rebuke stayed with them, the stinger burrowing ever deeper, disintegrating their self-esteem and reducing their sense of well being? What right did he have to cause that kind of permanent damage? In the past, this possibility had always necessitated that he quickly find a way to make things right.

This time, he of the red-rimmed gaze shut his fanged mouth and stalked back to his office.

At the very least, Florence's psyche would be fine.

Before Victor slammed his door, she could be heard whispering to Nikki, "Get me one of those shirts, girl."

EUGENE

Eugene Foreman was somewhat lucid when the shadowy figure approached his bed. He had been laying there for...how long had it been, since the *incident* at the Hilton? Dry blood caked his sheets; wet blood still soaked them. The impaling stake stood next to his bed, stained red. Eugene was running a fever. He was sure he was going to die.

"Damn, that vampire is cagey," Eugene thought to himself, looking up bleary-eyed at the imposing figure looming over his bed. Eugene was sure Victor had tracked him down at his apartment. "Go ahead and finish me," Eugene croaked. "Do it you damn vampire, I will be avenged."

The man began to talk to him. The man sounded like an old confederate soldier.

"Boy, you are a mess." The man motioned to someone behind him. A middle-aged woman in Gestapo garb stepped from the shadows with a big medical bag, and sat beside Eugene. As she prepped her wares the man toured Eugene's dank, rank, dreary apartment..

Eugene regarded the woman fearfully. "Who are you guys? Did Victor send you? Why am I surprised, he knows I'm close to finishing him off."

The gentleman, dressed in a heavy all-gray suit, shook his head and chuckled. "Son, the only thing you are doing, is getting in the way. You are going to kill yourself well before you manage to harm anyone else."

Eugene suppressed his tears and almost incoherently

asked, "So, what are you doing here, come to finish me off, alright. Doing the vamp's dirty work?"

The woman was deep into the medical bag, most of her equipment now arrayed on Eugene's nightstand. Almost in a whisper, the woman responded, "We are here to save your life." She pulled out a needle meant for a horse.

Eugene passed out and the woman went to work.

When Eugene woke he looked around. Again, he had no clue how long he had been out. A week? Two? A month? He didn't see any of his garlic or crucifixes which had adorned his abode. And it smelled like? Like? Mint? "What did they do to my apartment?" he asked himself.

There was the man, in the corner in a rocking chair, rocking slowly with a Mint Julep in his hand. Eugene tried unsuccessfully to prop himself up. "Uh, sir, where's my stuff? What happened to my place?"

The man stopped abruptly in mid-rock. "He lives," he toasted Eugene. "You mean your crap? Between the rancid garlic and your sticky blood, I had to have your place basically fumigated. We had to pay the cops not to come in here and condemn the place. You like?"

Eugene was starting to collect himself. "No, I don't *like*. Without my stuff, I am susceptible, anyone could come in here at destroy me."

"Anybody can destroy you. At any time."

"That's it, I thank you good sir for taking care of me, but your abuse I will not stand."

The man stood up. Slowly, deliberately. Stayed there for a moment and sized up Eugene. Took a sip of his drink. "Fair enough. I'll be on my way."

Eugene felt compelled to apologize, and stammered, "I am sorry. Sir, don't go. Please tell me, why you have come and what you want?"

The gentleman took off his hat. Looked deep into the middle of the hat and spoke quietly. "I want to teach you. Teach you what you are doing and why you are doing it."

"I know what I am doing. I come from a long line of Vampire Hunters—make that Slayers—and that is what I am called to do."

"You are huh?" the man said, still looking deep into his hat.

"Yes, and I mean to inflict pain upon the vamps and make my family name something to be proud of again."

"You need answers," said the man, "answers that lay in Germany. The old East Germany."

Eugene swung his legs off the bed, his toes barely touching the floor. "East Germany? My family is from Tirgu Mures in Transylvania."

"Your family is older than you know, and Tirgu Mures is only one of the many places they are from."

Eugene squinted at the man. "So?"

"So, that's where you're going to go."

Eugene, thoroughly confused, "What, where?"

"To the old East Germany. Dresden to be exact."

"Why, what for, when?"

The man moved a bit closer to Eugene without taking his eyes off of his hat. "Because, you need to know more about yourself, your family and your duty. Class begins soon and you leave tomorrow night."

"I don't understand?"

The man sat next to Eugene on the bed. Seemed ready to give him a look inside the hat, didn't. "You will, not everything now, but in time."

"I can't go, I can't afford it."

"I took care of it already. The plane, the place to stay, and your objectives."

This was happening too fast for Eugene. "I can't go, I have a job."

"You were fired. Now listen, you need to be aware of a few things before you leave."

Eugene shook his head, the man edged closer and started to talk to Eugene in earnest.

After a bit Eugene stopped shaking his head and slowly started to nod.

THETHERSON, FOUR-LEGGED BEAST

It was August twenty-first, ten days before the effective date of Texahoma's merger with Oklarkana, and sixteen days before a select group of the newly-combined company's employees would travel overseas to celebrate with the Germans at the home office in Dresden.

To build camaraderie for the integration and the coming pursuit of cost-savings in the weeks to come, Oklarkana's Westchase Construction and Texahoma's construction division scheduled a joint company picnic, families included. To avoid the oppression of a Houston summer day, the picnic began at five p.m.

Victor waited longer, for the sun's angle to lessen. He was irritable, and a certain wavelength of sunlight only made things worse, a wavelength removed by the atmosphere by this particular time of the day, at this particular point in the season. He was irritable, because in the six days since the last two "dates" Nikki had arranged for him—a dental hygienist who insisted he don a cape first and a Realtor who might have been a vampire herself, cold, clammy and verging on bloodless—all he'd had to drink was Tripp's poor substitute.

He was irritable and late, because he and Barbara had come home, separately but at the same time, to find Porky pug not barking, because he was decapitated. His little body lay centered on one of the backyard paving stones leading to the glider swing under the magnolia tree. They had checked the obvious places where Eugene might have hidden the head, in the bed or a pot on the stove. Barbara was distraught, still searching when Victor had left for the picnic. Amberly was no doubt going to be devastated.

Temperature and humidity were both ninety-two when he arrived at the Bane Park recreation center. The two companies' employees and their families were mingling in the rec center and spread out over the surrounding lawn, the nearby playground, and the ball fields down the hill beside the lake, two hundred-plus in attendance. Still he picked Darla out immediately.

She waved and headed for him, disengaging from a teenage girl who appeared miserably wilted, even in the air-conditioned center.

"Welcome to hell."

"That is an ominous greeting," said Victor. "Tell me what I missed." He was pleased to have reclaimed the deeper, cleaner timber of his voice from twenty years ago. Dissolved these days was the slimy crud that had over the years accreted layer by layer in his throat. Taking his time when he spoke, enunciating clearly, avoiding contractions—it made speaking a pleasure. Victor now liked the sound of his own voice.

"Oh nothing," said Darla. "Probably my own mood biasing my opinion. I'm glad you're here. I've run out of engaging conversation to entertain my daughter. And our staffs."

Now recognizable faces stood out in the crowd—Nikki, Florence and her chain-smoking street sweeper husband Buddy, Tessa and her best friend Jeff, Quinten and Raj, Kirby and Monique from Westchase, architects and project engineers Victor had long worked with, folks from the other finance areas in their building.

Victor nodded in greeting as various pairs of eyes sought his. "Tell me what is bothering you," he said to Darla. "If you can."

"You already know, basically." Darla's brow was

knotted at the center. She opened the sizeable purse under her armpit and pulled out a stapled report. "I finished the audit report yesterday." She stared down at it, rubbed at the type with her thumb. "It's going to be difficult reading for you."

"That is really no surprise." What could she have written that Jay—and Barbara—hadn't said many times before? At least Darla liked him. Scratch that. Darla was *drawn* to him. There was a difference, Victor had come to realize, to accept, and even to enjoy.

"And it's more than that." She sighed. "I'll tell you later. Like you want to listen to *my* troubles."

"I am all ears."

"Thank you," said Darla, softening. "It's just that—"

"VV!" Nikki flew at them and ran into her boss, a collision hug. "It's about time you got here!"

"Nikki." Darla's tone was stern. She straightened her frumpy blouse and rolled the audit report into a tube, passing the time until she had Nikki's full attention. "There's a pretty clear line that identifies inappropriate behavior." She spoke with affection, with unmistakable authority. "You don't address your boss with a nickname. Especially not in public. Probably not ever."

"VV is okay," Victor assured Darla. "In fact, over the past month, I have grown to love it. I own it now, you could say."

"Good," said Nikki, impatient for him to finish. She peeled off a terrycloth tunic to reveal her Team VV shirt beneath, along with a few seconds of her stomach, ribcage, DemonLover tattoo and lack of bra, until the t-shirt was properly adjusted. "I'd hate to think we wasted our money."

On cue the rest of the Texahoma construction accounting department shed, unbuttoned or unzipped layers to reveal their allegiance to Team VV. Their concerted action created a buzz, until most everyone's attention rested on Victor.

Just two weeks ago he might have been embarrassed,

if flattered. Now, he bared his fangs and elicited a squall of gasps, fist-pumping, delighted squeals and some applause. Victor tipped his virtual hat to his staff and turned back to Darla. "VV is a term of endearment. Please do not worry, or hold it against them."

Nikki looked at them, back and forth, her jaw slowly dropping. "What's going on? How can she hold it against us? VV, are you getting the axe?"

To Victor's mind, this represented his staff's first-ever display of intuition, or even rudimentary awareness.

Darla pooched her lips to *shh* configuration. "It's a long process we're going through. Nothing's been decided."

"You better not." Nikki threaded her arm through her boss's. "Without VV, this place falls apart." She disengaged and rejoined the gaggle of accountants, pausing to thrust a fist in the air. "Team VV! Whoo!"

Entering the rec center under cover of the echoing hooting, looking mussed and fussed, was Larry. His normally flat gray-brown hair stood up at the part. His standard-issue tan chamois shirt was high side/low side, misbuttoned. He had a black eye. He was followed closely by his mother Gail, just as wild-eyed and disheveled. Growing up, Victor had never seen Mrs. Cocachello with a hair out of place, her pantsuits anything but immaculate, and looking at her now would have suspected dementia, except that mother and son appeared to have just suffered through some sort of trial together.

Gail Cocachello found him, as she trailed Larry wending through the crowd; for an instant her plucked and painted eyebrows ran halfway up her forehead, before settling down to cap the sour pucker Victor remembered too well. Mrs. Cocachello's perm may have come undone, but the same forbidding mind waited beneath. Victor kept his crowd-pleasing snarl in place, denying his thoughts the permission to time-travel to his adolescence.

Darla was still reacting over Nikki's display. "I have no doubt she's right." She never looked so overwhelmed as when she smiled. "I do have to be honest, though," she continued, smile fading as she unfurled the audit report. "The comparison between our two staffs is pretty cut and dried. Their workload, and the amount of work they get done…there's no comparison."

"You should know that they have really improved over the past month." Without his asking, Florence had her team draft the accounting entries that would recognize the consolidation of the two companies' construction operations. A step-by-step action plan for integrating their respective accounting systems was already on Victor's desk, courtesy Larry's team. And Victor couldn't remember the last quarter flip. "An audit of the past is not indicative of their current abilities."

"Of course they're performing better," said Darla. "They're fighting for their lives."

Tessa's fairy godmother laughter lilted above the crowd buzz. She was tickling Quinten, who stumbled into Florence, who sloshed her beer and staggered, one two three-four steps sideways and down, a modern day Helen of Troy too intoxicated on nectar of the gods to recover her equilibrium. Her husband Buddy shook his head and took a deep drag from his Swisher Sweet before helping Florence stand. He apologized on her behalf to the red-shirted Westchase employee with beer in his topsider.

"I was forbidden from telling them this is a competition," Victor reminded Darla. "And clearly they haven't figured it out by themselves. The improvements are independent of that."

"Then what's causing it?"

"Pride," said Victor, fully believing it. "Finally, some pride. And inspiration. I've changed, and my team has grown with me."

"It's probably the kind of hubris that'll come back to bite me," said Darla, "but I think we have that in common. We have the ability to get the most out of our staffs. We have a lot in common, don't you think?" She faced him, head tilted up, the first time he'd seen it on other than an even plane. "We're very much the same, the two of us. I just think that maybe I was given a little more to work with." Darla's fingertips rested lightly on his sternum. "I don't think you've gotten a fair shake, and I told Jay that."

Much the same way Darla employed the long pause to gain the upper hand over her staff, Victor had been using the long gaze, on nearly every woman he encountered. It was obviously working on Darla. He pressed her hand to his chest for a couple heartbeats. "Thank you, Darla Kieler."

"Even so..." She gave him a sad lip. "I'm sorry, but Jay asked me to go to the meeting in Germany. I tried to turn it down—it's the last thing I want to do. I can't keep up with the work that hits my desk as it is. A week out of the office is going to kill me. I told Jay you should go. But he doesn't feel that way. I'm sorry." She squeezed his forearm and worried over his reaction as he squinted into the distance. "Maybe we should get away somewhere and talk about this."

Victor was less than surprised to learn Jay was likely working to squeeze him out at the earliest opportunity. And days, maybe weeks had passed since he last mourned losing the trip to Germany. The urgency to get there, to confront Cruella and learn the full story of his vampirism, had faded.

Instead his thoughts were focused on the next few minutes. He was gazing through the floor-to-ceiling windows at the soccer field and the reed-ringed lake. Even the low-angled and indirect evening light was sufficiently harsh on Victor's eyes, forcing him to squint, to zero in on a walking path that extended past the lake and into a copse of trees that appeared thick enough to cast enveloping shadows. Darla might enjoy being bitten in there. "A walk sounds like just the thing."

"I'm going to run to the ladies' room," said Darla. Her shoulders rose and fell through a deep breath that didn't seem to relieve any of her tension. She handed him the report. "I'd like to talk through the main points before you read it, but I'll understand if you can't wait."

"Hey there." Sally from Human Resources was at his elbow, arms crossed, blatantly checking him out from top to bottom. "Honest to God, Victor, I didn't even recognize you."

"I have lost a few pounds."

"It's a lot more than that." Sally took a step back and re-started the appraisal process. "What, merger stress and battles for supremacy bring out the best in you? Everyone else at corporate, and in this room, look like they've got migraines." She turned to look at Darla. "Hi. Sally Bornel from HR."

"Darla Kieler, migraine sufferer. If you'll excuse me." She gave Victor a look and moved away, drifting until spotting the restroom sign.

"Let me guess," said Sally. "Your counterpart. Just a first impression, but not exactly a power personality. Although I have heard Westchase has a great accounting department."

"That glowing assessment was probably courtesy of my team's audit," said Victor. "One more reason why I should have bitten David when I had the chance."

Sally's eyes glinted devilishly. "I have his address. It's never too late." She tossed her hair back with a practiced twitch. "Although now it would be purely for pleasure. That's what brings me back by the way. The lawsuit. And this great picnic," she said sarcastically. "What are they thinking, right? You've got two companies barely civil to each other during business hours. So throw 'em together on a hot Saturday afternoon with a few kegs of beer, and tell them to unwind and have fun. I've only been here a few minutes, but it's like the Sharks and Jets squaring off."

"Except for my staff." Victor watched Quinten and

Casey yukking it up with two Westchase accountants. "They are truly clueless."

"She's right," said Florence, materializing next to him, in an inebriated cant, feet at a respectable distance, her head inches from his. "Sally thinks you're different. I agree. You're not the same person, Victor. You're something else now."

"I believe our entire team has grown," said Victor. "I was just telling Darla the same thing."

Florence was listening to something other than Victor's words. "When I moved back from New Zealand, I looked you up because I heard you were managing a department, and I knew you'd hire me." She seemed to think she was whispering. Florence wavered on her feet, but her eyes were fixed on his. "Now I think it was fate. I want to grow too, Victor."

Her husband Buddy cleared his throat with a crackling mutter. He was smoking his thin cigar to the consternation of those around him, observing Florence, just within earshot. She gave him a surly glance. "There's something else I should tell you. I really didn't see the need to say anything…" She made it clear it was Buddy who did. "But no doubt *someone* will flap their gums…" Now she glared at Nikki, who fidgeted a few feet in the other direction, seemingly wrestling with her own conscience and debating whether to approach.

"Sure," said Victor, although he would have preferred to continue on the topic of fate.

"I was at your house today," said Florence, flinching when Buddy objected with a staccato grunt. "I was *in* your house," she clarified. "I came over to say hi. To say hi to your wife.…"

Nikki marched over. "Are you confessing to breaking into Master's house?"

Florence was for the moment tongue- and fit-to-be-tied, while Sally, bemused and ever more impressed with Victor, mouthed, "Master?"

"Barb and I went to school together." Florence was

miffed having to justify her actions. "It's been way too long since I've seen her. Years."

"You wait all that time, and then you can't wait another hour or two until they get home?" Nikki needled her.

"I thought I heard a *come in*. Turns out it must have been that dog." Florence set her jaw like she'd been deliberately tricked.

"You saw Porky pug?" Victor confirmed. "Moving? What time was that?" he inquired, detective for the moment.

"Noonish," said Florence. "Slobbered all over me."

"Okay fine, you were there for a visit," said Nikki, arms crossed and swaying smugly side to side. "Then why were you wearing a negligee?"

"That's a got-damned sun dress," Florence snapped.

"From Frederic's of Hollywood," said Buddy, stepping in close enough to join the conversation. "I wondered why she had a raincoat on when she left the house." Whether Buddy had truly possessed such curiosity at the time was debatable; there was none on his face now. He was just saying.

Florence took a long swig of beer. She visibly abandoned her defenses and rested her case with an air of fatalism. "Because it was sunny with a chance of thunderstorms."

"You wanted to be bit," said Nikki, too titillated to make it an accusation.

Florence's eyes darted to Buddy, who didn't react. Instead he claimed Nikki's attention by jabbing his cigar at the two slanted *V*s on her chest. "What were *you* doing there?"

Nikki popped her gum. "To work on Victor's dating schedule. It's been so busy at work, I figured we should do it after hours."

Sally backhanded Victor's arm. "You date so much, you need your secretary to manage your calendar?"

"In a manner of speaking," said Victor, as a booming

voice plowed through the rec center chatter, summoning the two companies' management teams. He traced the voice to the bald dome and mournful eyes of Mel Parish, Texahoma's chief construction engineer, that much taller than most everyone else in the room.

Sally took her leave with a touch to Victor's arm, while Florence stepped forward and motioned Nikki closer, pausing for Victor to lean in as well and create a small huddle. "Dating schedule?" she confirmed with Nikki. "Then why," said Florence, "were you wearing a blood-stained shirt?"

"Well," said Nikki, struggling for an answer. A pout formed on her lips as she shuffled in tight to Victor. "Because I'm way overdue for my second bite, master. I woke up this morning and decided to take the initiative. I drank a quart of orange juice, put on my lucky shirt from our first bite, and went to your place. I thought maybe you'd be working out, all pumped up and thirsty…"

"Speaking of which," Florence purred, "nice beefcake poster hanging in your garage."

"It's Tony Horton," said Victor, seeing no need for further explanation.

"I would have been there waiting for you," said Nikki, "if Larry and his folks hadn't shown up."

"Larry was there too?" Victor exclaimed. "And his parents…?"

"Bite me tonight," Nikki whined. "Surprise me, master. I set up all these great dates for you, without you even asking. You never do anything spontaneous for me."

Gail Cocachello, so certain in her every action, was en route. Larry trailed, looking uncomfortable to go along with his dishevelment. Gail tapped Buddy on the shoulder in passing and gave a curt admonishment while pointing to the No Smoking sign above the door.

"These aren't cigarettes," said Buddy, but Gail had already moved on, leaving him to weigh the consequences of disobedience.

She stood before Victor, hands on her hips. "Larry told me you finally lost some weight. You've struggled so long, I'm happy for you. But you'll find out that if you're destined to be a heavy person, it's almost impossible to keep it off. Ask Oprah."

"Well, my destiny, it's possible that it's changing, but I'm not sure..."

Florence picked up Victor's fumble. "Victor's change looks permanent to me."

"His mother's overweight," Gail invalidated Florence's opinion. "But if you're talking about being a vampire..." She moved no closer but Victor felt claustrophobic in her scrutiny. Gail nodded to her son, who hovered a step outside the conversation circle. "I told you when he got bit that he wouldn't be able to handle it. Back in Milford—that's where we're from," she filled in the backstory for the outsiders. "Honestly, it was sad how everyone laughed when they heard Victor Thetherson had become a vampire. I'm so glad your father can't see you now."

"Maybe they *should* see him now," said Florence sharply. She looked to Victor, waiting for him to say something to prove it. Perhaps put on a short demonstration.

But Victor was stammering, ten years old again. The memories didn't flood back—he didn't recall the time he got so winded on the ever-so-slight incline on the walk to school, so that he had to bend over and grab his knees to catch his breath, right in front of the Cocachello house, to the delight of Larry's mother, pausing from watering her flowers to mimic his panting. But the accompanying shame blanketed him the same.

"If one doesn't already possess a strong personality, one becomes a weak vampire who causes misery for everyone around him," said Gail, as if quoting from the manual.

"You should see VV in action," said Nikki. "For his

last date, I disguised myself as a league bowler and followed the two of them out behind the lanes, where VV did his thing. I'm sorry master, I didn't tell you, but I just had to see one."

"Did you know Victor lisped in high school?" Gail wondered.

Florence ignored her, slurring to Nikki, "You've got to give me the details," eyes alight and oblivious to her husband's grumbling objection.

Gail Cocachello was not easy to ignore. Certainly not for Victor, stomach roiling, resisting the maddening urge to ask solicitously about their café. "Girls," she said, and with the age-based honorific Florence too was now in thrall, only briefly, but sufficient to throw her off-stride and allow Gail to recapture the floor. "A woman's strength in the workplace comes from making good decisions. Visiting the house of your married boss reflects poorly upon all of us."

"I'm not married," said Victor in a numb, flat monotone.

Gail clucked. "Your mother used to worry about you so. She would ask us to watch out for you, you know. And now you repay us by shirking your responsibility to watch out for my son. It's shameful."

The retaliatory vigor lacking in Victor was being absorbed by Florence and Nikki, their blood pressures mounting. They found a release valve in Larry.

"Where's your Team VV t-shirt?" Nikki demanded, getting her hands on his chamois shirt, undoing one button before Larry could fend her off.

"His mama wouldn't let him wear it," said Florence.

"You know I had my opinion on that already," said Larry angrily, forced to unbutton all the way down and then back up again to correct the misalignment. "And I'm the only one doing anything about it." He jabbed a thumb over his shoulder at the confab of executives near the door. "Take a look around why don't you? You're making fools of yourselves in front of the wrong folks."

On cue: "Can I have everyone's attention?" Mel Parish stood at the door leading to the recreation area. He had a rumbling, rough-hewn voice. Over his barrel torso the yellow Texahoma Construction Division polo shirt was stretched thin, the collar reduced to dog ears on either side of his bull neck. "We're starting the four-legged race in five minutes, down on the soccer field. Before you say 'no thanks', let me tell you it's mandatory."

How to describe the mighty row occurring in Victor's skull, evident to those who chose to watch him over the Texahoma executive? The innate, embedded Thetherson alarm system was spreading its panic, demanding that every neuron drop what it was doing and circle the wagons, to prepare for Gail Cocachello's continued onslaught and limit any further damage.

While simultaneously a dark master strode those neural halls, cracking his whip, orienting all eyes to him, in the harshest terms reminding everyone of their new goal, their new reason to be: to build The Wall. External inputs were irrelevant and to be repelled, this new overlord decreed; Victor Thetherson would now be inner-directed.

Until medical science determined the physiology behind Victor's transformation, metaphors like this would have to suffice.

"What happened to my dog, Larry?"

Nikki squawked and got in Larry's face. "Did you hurt the master's hellhound?"

Larry pointed at her with a nodding finger. "Me and Ma decided to wait in the backyard. We come around the corner of the house, and here comes that dog, on me lickety-split. I swear, in the milli-second I had to react, that's exactly what went through my mind: *hellhound*. Ma was right behind me—I didn't want her turned, Vic."

Victor glanced at Gail, hands clasped at her navel and eyes turned heavenward, the picture of a thousand good works yet to come.

"It was all happening in a split second like I said,"

Larry continued, faster, making it hard for his drawl to keep up, "and I guess my instincts kicked in. I pulled out my boar knife and cut that dog from ear to ear. He fell kerplunk, dead on the spot."

A goodly number in the room caught the end of Larry's story, thanks to Mel Parish's attention. "Bub, it's lucky for you we already lined up the teams," Parish called to Larry. "Otherwise, you'd be the last kid picked on the playground." He took a second, long look at Victor, perhaps for the first time seeing the vampire as out of place in the corporate gathering. He again addressed the assemblage. "Can't think of a better segue to the spectacle that is about to occur. Let's head on down to the soccer field, and we'll get this over with."

Led by Parish, the rec center emptied out the lake-facing double doors, flowing around Victor's little group, held captive by his darkening mood. Then Florence was sprung by her husband, a somewhat reluctant jailbreak into the fading light of day. Darla had been approaching but now thought better of it, waving to Victor and joining the flow, as did Nikki, summoned by Parish's admin.

Gail stayed put. "I don't know why anyone would want one of those damnable pugs anyway. I'll tell you what your daughter would *really* like. A Morkie. We know a breeder who—"

"I would like Porky's head returned," said Victor. He had witnessed Raj and Quentin modeling their *Team VV* t-shirts to Dewitt from the Tax department, and the sight had triggered a physical change to Victor's eyes—they had gone raw, like a protective membrane had been peeled off. Now viewed unfiltered, Gail Cocachello was suddenly just another crabby-looking lady, and he left her.

Larry caught up to him at the tail of the exodus. "About that head..." As he spoke, Larry's eyes were drawn to the audit report in Victor's hand, adding an extra furrow to his brow. "Dad thought the dog might be rabid. He insisted we mail it to the state lab in Austin for testing."

"It was the least we could do," said Gail, and Victor couldn't say why he knew she was lying, or what reason she had to do so.

"Just the head," said Victor.

"That's all they need to run the test," said Larry, his eyes again finding the audit report. Victor rolled it back into a tube and stuffed it in his pocket. "Cheaper than mailing the whole thing. Don't worry about the postage, it's on us."

"That dog was all skull and teeth," said Gail. "Like cutting the head off a piranha."

"We should have the test results back in a week or so," said Larry.

Sally was waiting outside. She took Victor's arm, and in a few strides they caught and fell in step with Tessa and her doe-eyed friend Jeff, making slow progress down the hill, Tessa selecting each landing spot on the patchy hillside for her shoed hooves.

"So you had a Cujo moment this morning?" Sally asked Gail. "You and I have something in common." She included Victor and Larry in the same wink. "We were both saved from a ravenous animal by your son."

Tessa tugged on Sally's sleeve, bringing the group to a near standstill. "So you're HR, right?" she said. "Do you really think it's a good idea to make us do this?"

"There's no other way to get down to the field, sweetie," said Sally.

"I mean the four-legged race."

"They're creating a potential liability, you know," said her tall friend Jeff, bobbing as he walked, so that his words arrived with a Doppler effect.

"Not everybody is going to be comfortable with this," said Tessa. "I would think HR would be worried about discrimination lawsuits."

"Come on, chubbies!" Quinten hollered from below. "Pick up the pace!"

"Honestly honey," said Sally to Tessa. "I wouldn't know where to start."

Beyond Quinten, two young and burly construction foremen threw Dewitt from Tax kicking and screaming into the lake. Watching from the edge of the soccer field, Mel Parish shook his head with a chuckle and resumed the conversation with his Westchase counterpart while Dewitt thrashed about in the reeds.

"I'd say something about this race," said Sally, "but I don't want to end up in the lake. Trying to get the construction industry in step with the times is a losing battle. Believe it or not, they're still more concerned about a building collapsing and killing a couple hundred people than they are about one of their employees not enjoying a game.

"However," Sally continued before Tessa could retort, "I'd like to see any company match our executives' willingness to take a stand against gay harassment." Victor received another wink. "Under no circumstances will they tolerate a gay employee harassing a straight one. Speaking of which, there's something I need to discuss with your boss."

She forced Victor to veer left and pick up the pace, creating separation from the other four. "I wanted to bring you up to date. There's been a change of heart at corporate. Thanks to me," she said, pleased with herself.

From the near end of the soccer field where everyone was gathering, Victor's name drifted to them. "They're calling for you," said Sally. "I can tell you later."

Victor stopped her at the bottom of the hill, at the anchor wall of a zip line. Children were queued for twenty yards atop the hill to take their turn. A young boy in a University of Houston baseball jersey descended the line with a delighted yodel and thumped into the heavily padded barrier behind them, dropping happily into the sand pit. "Everyone can wait," said Victor, eyes locked on Sally's. "I want to hear what you have to say."

In a low-level trance, Sally brought her arm up for inspection. "Goosebumps. Like I said, you've changed."

"Vic!" Casey called to him from the top of the hill. "Watch this!"

Casey had donned her bike helmet, which Victor knew from experience was a bad sign. Last time was during World Cup when Raj was teaching everyone soccer basics; Casey had strapped on her helmet and attempted a bicycle kick, shattering the glass conference room wall. Raj had everyone sign a red penalty card as a get-well memento while Casey convalesced after the hip replacement surgery.

Now she wrested the T-bar from the boy before he could hand it to the next child in line, and sat on it. Her butt immediately hit the ground and spun her, so that she zipped down the hill backwards. Ten yards from the barrier her backside caught turf again and yanked her off the seat, sending her tumbling into the sand, helmet flying free and bouncing off toward the lake.

They helped Casey to her feet and dusted her off. "Unfortunately, the part of her brain that would warn her away from dangerous acts like this is the very part they had to remove," Victor explained to Sally.

Casey pointed at the scar and shook her head with a pained smile. "Can you believe the luck?"

"Then you better buy a better-fitting helmet," Sally told her.

Casey stared longingly at the T-bar as a youngster retrieved it and started back up the hill. "I'm going to try that again later."

She found her helmet and limped toward the soccer field, briefly engaged by Nikki, who was marching their way.

"We're going to fight David's harassment charge," said Sally. "I made a strong case to my boss and our employment lawyer, to throw everything we have behind you. They're willing. It won't be easy, though. They sent me back down here to help you gather documentation on David's work performance."

She opened her pocketbook and showed Victor her room key, as if it was just part of the briefing. "The Marriott this time. The Hilton's had enough of us." Sally took the opportunity to apply lipstick, making seemingly idle chit-chit. "It's the Marriott near the airport. I made sure the bar is open after midnight."

"Whether or not David wins will have no impact on me," said Victor. "Jay wants me out, and he has the ammunition." He brandished the tightly-wound paper tube in his fist. "Westchase's audit findings."

"So she's playing nice to your face," said Sally with some venom, "and nailing you in her report."

"Darla is a good manager, and a good person," said Victor. "But she has to do her job." He strengthened his tone. "You will treat her with respect."

"Fine," said Sally, enjoying the reprimand. "I'll be good. But have you considered biting her? I think you'd be amazed what kind of effect that might have."

A pre-teen girl screamed as she bailed off the zip line, landing hard in the sand pit, gasping and laughing. Nikki reached them now. "VV, it's time. I'm one of the organizers. You have to participate."

Eighty or so employees of the two construction entities were snaked across the near end of the soccer field, beer cups in hand or set unstably on the artificial turf behind them. A smattering of family members spread out along the sideline, adults mostly, the children either at the zip line or on the adjoining playground. Fifty yards downfield a woman in a red polo shirt and a woman in a yellow one stood thirty yards apart, the finish line.

Mel Parish's admin Mary directed Victor to join a twosome—one of the Texahoma foremen who had tossed Dewitt in the lake, and a man with a red Westchase polo shirt.

"We get the vampire!" the foreman crowed. He pumped his fist at his buddy, who flipped him off from his threesome further down the row.

"Go VV," said Casey, helmet back on and trying to jump in cheerleader style with her leg tied to a Westchase employee.

"No fair," said a chubby graybeard with burnt gray cheeks, at the left end of the nearest threesome. "We want our own bloodsucker. Is anyone from the Law division here?"

"Alright listen up, everybody," Mel Parish growled over the laughter. "You bright people have no doubt already figured out that there's at least one Westchase and one Texahoma person in each team. By 'bright people' I'm referring to everyone in the back office staff groups. I don't expect anyone in construction to have figured that out."

Victor's foreman took a great gulp from his keg cup, waiting for the boos and catcalls to die down before saying into the relative quiet, "If we got paid to think, we'd all look like Dewitt and be building doll houses."

Dewitt was the anchor between Graybeard and Monique from Westchase's accounting department. He responded by peeling off his black-and-orange rugby jersey, flinging the soggy garment to the turf, and flexing his muscles Charles Atlas style.

"That just earned you another swim," said the foreman. Dewitt ignored him, now doing the Hulk Hogan.

"Dewitt," Parish barked, "you don't see us trying to recite Dungeons and Dragons gaming code. Put your shirt back on." Monique curtly seconded that order while trying not to make contact with the pale, hairy, sunken-chest tax accountant.

"Here honey." Mary had finished tying Victor's left leg to the foreman and his right to the slender Westchase employee. She bustled over to a box of yellow polo shirts and dug through it, bringing one back for Dewitt. "Sorry, we didn't order any smalls."

"Now if I can finish this little spiel," said Parish, "and

we can get this carnage underway. About these pairings. What you may not have noticed, even the smart finance folks who somehow figured a way for us to make money even in this economy, is that the folks on each team are from three different areas. Areas that need to be able to talk to each other."

He ambled over to Victor's group. "I'll give you an example. Here we have Teddy from the construction side."

Foreman Teddy hoisted his cup and gave himself a rousing cheer.

"And here we have...what's your name?"

"I am also Teddy," said the slender man, with an accent that Victor guessed was Polish. Pole Teddy was nervous, sweating and trying to move away from Victor, made difficult by the bandana about their ankles.

"Teddy One and Teddy Too," said Parish. "Teddy Too is an architect. Teddy Too needs to be able to communicate with our man in the middle here, Mr. Victor Thetherson, to give Victor and his accounting team an idea what a new construction should cost. And Vic needs to be able to talk to this knucklehead," Parish pointed at Foreman Teddy, "to find out why he just blew right through that budget."

"Because architects don't have a clue what goes on in the real world," Teddy One exclaimed. This was met with vocal agreement from Texahoma and Westchase construction workers up and down the line. "Vic, you need to double whatever Teddy Junior there tells you. Or just come to me in the first place."

"And spend five times what you otherwise would," a woman far down the line hollered. Victor recognized the distinctive voice of Shari Stone, a Texahoma architect. "And end up with an overbuilt monstrosity with half the usable space!"

"Save it," Parish barked at Teddy One, who was preparing a belligerent retort. "You think this little race will be difficult, just keep wasting time levering your traps until you have to do it in the dark."

A wave of laughter started at the far end and swept toward Victor. He leaned out to see Quinten lying on the turf. In slow progression his tethered teammates lost their balance and fell on him.

"Heaven help us," said Parish. He waited a few moments for Quinten and his team to regain their feet. "One more thing. Quiet down everyone.... I think it's only fair to tell you that there's a little bit more to this competition. Then you can decide how seriously you think you need to take it," he said ominously. "I want you to see that this team here is a mirror image of Mr. Victor's team."

He had stopped in front of Darla's threesome.

"We have Darla Kieler, Mr. Victor's counterpart at Westchase. Shari from the Texahoma architectural department. And a Westchase foreman..."

"Barry."

"Barry," Parish echoed. "This is not a coincidence. We've been told by our Human Resources experts that this game was designed and has proven to be a good indicator of the ability to coordinate communication in a corporate environment. Which means that you're competing with all the other teams, but more importantly, you're competing with your mirror-image team."

Victor made eye contact with Darla. She gave him an apologetic smile.

"This comparison isn't end-all be-all," Parish wrapped up his speech. "But we will be watching."

"Okay everybody," said Mary, joining her boss in front of the broad starting line. "I hope you have a good strategy in place, because this can be a little tricky."

Victor watched Darla quietly leading a discussion with her teammates on the best motive technique for their four-legged configuration.

"Ready?" Mary called out. "Go!"

Between "ready" and "go", Quinten sprawled forward

again, followed again in short order by his teammates. Teddy One laughed and cupped his hands to his mouth to holler at them over the explosion of cheering and yelling as the teams lurched forward. Darla had her team moving forward in slow steady coordination.

"Maybe we should get moving," Victor suggested. They were the only team remaining on the starting line, Quinten's team being somewhat of an exception.

"Any time," said Teddy One, while Teddy Too seemed more intent on lateral movement away from Victor. "You're the boss." Then without waiting for Victor's lead he hopped forward, bringing Victor's left leg with him. Victor stepped with his right, carrying along Teddy Too's left foot, compelling him to quickly step forward with his right.

Teddy One only briefly paused for this chain reaction to occur, stepping forward left-right, and again, and again, until they had a locomotive, Teddy One, and a caboose, Teddy Too, with Victor shuffling madly in between, groin stretching a little further with each shuffle as their train lengthened.

"Whoa," said Victor, "this isn't working." Ignored, he grabbed Teddy One's forearm. "Stop. We need a different system."

"Hands off," said Teddy One, yanking his arm away. "It's enough we gotta have our legs together. We ain't gonna be holding hands too. C'mon then, hurry it up."

With some struggle, Victor and Teddy Too hobbled forward to bring the three of them even again. "Watch them." Victor pointed to Darla's team, a good ten yards ahead. "First the two of you step forward with your right leg. Then your left. I'll be doing the opposite. Two steps instead of four. Small steps right away, until we get the coordination. Go."

The Teddies took an ill-timed stride with their right legs. Teddy One immediately stepped with his outside leg and then tried to bring his left leg forward, but Victor was ready, holding fast until Teddy Too was ready.

"And again."

In halting ungainly fashion they made headway, three cycles, four, and in the midst of the fifth when Teddy One caught his breath and stopped.

"Ow, oh, jeez, ahhh...nuts. Pulled a muscle. I don't think I can...ow!" he exclaimed upon trying another step. "Nope. Sorry boys, that's it for me."

"Blessed Virgin Mary," said Teddy Too. "Thank God." He bent to untie his leg from Victor's.

Victor watched Darla's team making progress in sweet synchronicity. *People never do what they're supposed to!* a voice inside him raged. *But they do what they're told.*

He saw himself spotlighted on a stage, house lights extinguished, black all around. A chaotic rush of his past failures took flight in the inky periphery, screaming panicked harpies fluttering and calling for withdrawal. Finding himself calm inside his newly-constructed mental fortress, that steadily rising and thickening Wall, Victor decided he was not going to lose this race.

In the footlights of his peripheral vision Teddy Too was dimly visible. Victor grabbed his collar and brought him upright. "We go." With collar in hand he took a long step forward, forcing Teddy Too to match him. Against great resistance he brought his other leg even.

"Nope, sorry dude," said Teddy One. He winced and clutched their shared leg, ensuring any onlookers knew his pain. "Can't do it."

"I must not have communicated clearly," said Victor. He grabbed Teddy One by the back of the neck. "We're finishing."

"Hey!" Teddy One protested, twisting to knock Victor's hand away.

Victor didn't allow it. He squeezed harder and stepped forward, left-right, an iron grip on each of his wingmen, compelling them to follow suit.

"Yo!" Teddy One complained more shrilly. Victor responded with more force and a longer stride, staying in a deep lunge as he moved, forcing his companions to do likewise, chugging forward in piston-like strides, punctuated with locomotive breathing, his eyes burning hot-coal red.

Darla's team finished ahead of them, but Victor and the Teddies passed five groups in the final fifteen yards, their relative speed enough to make the sideline audience gawk. They were three strides beyond the finish line before Victor willed his hands to let go. Teddy One cursed under his breath, joining Teddy Too in trying to undo knots that had been drawn into tight nuggets.

Parish and a handful of the two companies' executive management team joined them while members of Victor's staff cheered and called to him from where they sat untying their bonds. Nikki ran out of patience, kicking off her shoe and slipping her skin-and-bone foot out of the linkage in order to race to her boss, skidding into a hug.

"I thought you three were out of the running," said Parish. "And then you took off."

"Teddy had a cramp," said Victor. He was alive with a power he had never experienced, basking in the exertion from hauling the Teddies across the finish line, and the aura he saw reflected in the faces around him. He patted Teddy One on the head. "We talked about the problem—we communicated—and decided to change our approach."

A "V, V" chant grew, led by Nikki and spreading to the onlookers making their way to join their family members at the finish line. A corpulent Westchase executive put out his paw for a handshake. "That's the kind of collaborative problem-solving we're looking for. We're going to be needing that in spades over the next few months."

"I hope to be able to contribute to the effort," said Victor with a smile, as Teddy Too called for a pocketknife.

"Hum-Jesus, look at those teeth," said the jowly

Westchase exec. "They just for show, or do you put 'em to good use?"

Victor turned his gaze to the only woman on the executive team, tall with a multi-hinged torso, dressed in a business suit despite the informal occasion. "When the opportunity presents itself."

"Huh…" Parish drew closer to examine Victor's face, throwing comparative glances at the others around him. He looked over his shoulder to find the setting sun and leaned to the side, allowing the rays to again strike the vampire's cheek.

The portly Westchase exec saw what Parish saw. "Son," he said to Victor. "Are you sparkling?"

"Something like that," said Victor.

"No, they mean your face," said Nikki, getting up in his grill, huffing on his cheek and rubbing it like smudged spectacles. "You got sparkly skin."

"Dad!"

Victor stopped Nikki from pulling up his shirt to check his belly skin, turning to see his daughter jogging across the field toward him. Adrenaline abruptly abandoned his system, leaving him defenseless, fueling the tears that filled his eyes.

Amberly hurried to her father. Her hug was uncertain and awkward, but felt wonderful to Victor. "You didn't tell me this was a family deal," she said.

Victor jabbed a fang into his lip and made the blood conspicuous. "Bit myself," he said as explanation for the tears he wiped away.

"Careful son," said the Westchase exec.

"Good thing it's not someone else bleeding," said Parish. "Vic'd be all over 'em."

The growing crowd around them laughed. Tessa and Raj kept it going, relaying how the hemophiliac down the hall made their boss sign a no-bite pledge. Victor focused on Amberly. "How did you find out about this?"

"We had a school outing to the commuter airport a little ways away," said Amberly, while her friend stood a couple feet away, eyeing Victor in awe. "Maddy's dad works at Westerfield."

"Westchase," Maddy corrected.

"Her mom brought us over." Amberly frowned. "Dad, is your skin..." As she rose on tiptoes for a closer look, the sun winked below the horizon. "Huh. Never mind."

"It was nice to meet you, son," said the Westchase exec, interrupting to shake Victor's hand. "I'm Don Chleber, by the way. We're gonna go huddle with our HR experts and compare notes on the race results. I'm looking forward to talking to you some more."

"Likewise," said Victor. Parish slapped him on the arm, and the female exec gave him a wink.

Darla moved in as the bigwigs moved on. "Darla is from Westchase," Victor introduced her. "This is my daughter, Amberly."

"Hi Amberly. Very nice to meet you." Darla's daughter slipped in beside her. "This is my daughter Kim."

"Is that short for Kimberly?" Victor asked.

"It is," said Darla.

"You two have that in common," Victor told his daughter. "-mberly."

"Dad," said Amberly, irritated with a touch of affection. "So did you win? With all the cheering, I figured you must have."

"No, that would be Darla's team," said Victor.

"Your dad would have beat us," said Darla, "but he had a handicap. He had to drag two sleds down the field."

They all looked down on Teddy One and Teddy Too, sitting on the ground and trying to undo their knots.

Teddy One looked up in heartbreaking fashion. "I can't get free."

Teddy Too was frantically digging at the scarf knot. "If I was more flexible," he mumbled, "I'd chew my leg off."

That reminded Victor. "Honey, I have bad news about Porky."

"I know, Mom told me," said Amberly. "Our dog died," she told Kimberly.

"What was it?"

"Pug."

Kimberly made a face. "Maybe you can get something cuter next time."

"In fact, Larry's mom knows a Morkie breeder..."

"Yes!" Amberly lit up. "I want one of those!"

"I think you skipped a couple of the grieving stages," said Darla. "Why don't you girls walk up to the rec center and get some ice cream. Victor and I will be right up."

Amberly and Kimberly looked at each other. They looked *like* each other, Victor decided. They agreed to this course of action and with Amberly's friend Maddy crossed the field toward the hill.

Darla and Victor watched them go. "Maybe a walk along the lake before we head up there?" said Darla. "We can talk about the audit report...or not."

Victor looked down at the Teddies. "You two up for a stroll through the woods with us?"

Mary came to the rescue with scissors and severed their knots. Victor and Darla started for the walking path and the little grove. "Where is the report?" Darla asked, scanning Victor's person.

Victor physically did the same. "I had it in my back pocket. I don't know.... I must have dropped it."

They looked back at the soccer field just as Larry tore out the report's staple on the far sideline, flung the curled sheets in the air, and took a swing at Kirby.

Victor and Darla ran with very different forms at the same speed. They reached their lead accountants just after Larry's mom and diminutive Mary drug Larry and Kirby respectively across the turf. Larry jumped to his feet and retrieved his beer, spewing a stream of rhythmically punctuated curse words. Kirby sat sulking with his head drooped between his knees.

"What's going on?" Victor's question was echoed by

those employees who hadn't yet left the field or made it all the way up the hill, now converging on the sideline.

"That's a great question for her," Larry muttered, glaring at Darla, who was retrieving the strewn-about report.

"This is just a draft," said Darla, chasing the last sheet as a stray breeze rolled the curled paper up against Florence's feet.

Florence pinned the sheet with her foot. Darla squatted and paused, expecting resistance. Florence removed her foot but said, "Let me see that."

"It's still in draft form," Darla repeated. She was unable to adequately reassemble the permanently curled and crimped papers, finally jamming and cramming them into her purse. "And quite frankly, the intended audience isn't this department. It will be up to senior management to share whatever they deem appropriate."

"That's bunk," said Florence.

"Bunk," her husband Buddy echoed, midway through a long drag on his thin cigar.

"First of all," said Tessa, loud and sharp enough to settle everyone back on their heels and seal their lips, affording the agitated accountants a pause to either reconsider or refuel. "Kirby, are you okay?"

"Well the punch didn't hurt me," said Kirby. He worriedly, gingerly pulled up his shirt, twisting and trying to get a look at his back. "But I think I got a turf burn from the dragging."

"I might've got carried away," Mary apologized to him.

"It almost pulled my pants off, too," said Kirby.

"You need to cinch your belt a little tighter," Casey advised. "I've thought that since the first time I saw you."

"The trouble is," said Kirby, "is that my hips are very tender. I don't know whether it's genetic, or whether it represents a deeper issue, but my belt really aggravates my midsection, right across here." He indicated a broad swath of his waist.

"Makes sense," said Casey.

Tessa was staring up into the sky, waiting to continue. "Then the next question is, what does that report say? Larry?"

"What d'you think it says?" Larry snapped. "They're getting rid of us." This made Gail Cocachello whimper. "That was the whole point of this little visit from our Westchase 'friends'," Larry said derisively. "Kirby here wrote down everything I told him about the things we needed to do differently."

Kirby paused in his effort to get a look at his turf-burned back. "That was my express order from management."

"What I told you was in the spirit of collaboration," said Larry, taking a step toward Kirby, looking ready to take another swing. "I thought you wanted to know how we *did* things so we could merge our departments! You weren't supposed to be looking for how we did things *wrong!*"

"I'm sorry," said Kirby, seemingly on the verge of offering up his chin again.

"I'm gonna love to see what Raj told you," said Florence. She glared at the junior accountant. "I'm sure you gave them all kinds of examples of how we royally screw up the books, didn't you?"

"Florence," Raj appealed, hair disheveled from the four-legged race, the tail of his polo shirt untucked from his linen shorts. "Mergers are the best time to take a step back and reexamine everything you do. Isn't that right, Vic?"

"How would Vic know?" Larry said bitterly. "All he cares about is playing vampire."

"He's playing games with every one of your lives," said Gail.

"What did I tell you?" Larry demanded of his coworkers. "I told you to quit egging him on. This wouldn't have happened if Vic was his old self."

"Victor Thetherson," said Gail, putting her foot down with nary a sound on the thick grass, cutting off Nikki's attempted protest nonetheless. "It's time for you to stop this ridiculous *vampire* nonsense. You had a terrible childhood, we all understand that. But it's time for you to grow up, and take responsibility for all these wonderful people who are counting on you."

"Who's she?" said Casey.

"A consultant, I'm pretty sure," said Quentin.

Deeply ingrained in Victor Thetherson's psyche was the image of Life as a train hurtling forward while he clung to the side, buffeted and struggling to hang on. As both his staff's productivity and his Nikki-managed nocturnal activity had ramped up, Victor had settled in, content to let the wheels turn.

Today he had found the conductor's seat unoccupied and the train pulling into the figurative switchyard, open to a change of direction.

"The examination is over," said Victor, rising above the gathering by taking a few steps up the slope. "But the grading is just beginning." His voice carried as if amplified. "Trust that we are looking after your best interests." He picked out each of his staff, sweeping up a couple of Darla's as well, calming them with his gaze and the languid pace of his speech. "I want you to trust in me."

The gathering stood in silence, divided in their willingness to look at Victor. He flexed his hands, working out the last tension from the exertion at the napes of the Teddies' necks.

Sally had been observing from a few yards uphill. "Translated," she said, descending and tearing her eyes away from Victor, "that means we all need to simply do our jobs as we strive for an optimal role in the combined company. You," she said to Kirby, "we're going to have a doctor give you a check-up to make sure you're okay. And you," she scolded Larry, "will have a report filed with my Employee Relations department."

Gail Cocachello startled to find Victor standing beside her, just a little bit behind her. He put his arm around her and felt her stiffen. "We know where Larry gets his fire," said Victor, "don't we."

"Everyone." Sally pointed up the hill at the rec center. "Up there for some ice cream." She gave them the scoot signal.

Victor saw that the girls had taken it all in from halfway up the hillside. Amberly waved at him, and smiled. Victor nodded. He watched Darla walk up the hill toward them, and tried to think of ice cream instead of blood.

An hour later Victor crouched within the copse of trees bordering the playing fields. After the altercation, the gathering had sobered up and wound down, most taking their ice cream and leaving, including Amberly, who had invited Kimberly to accompany her and Maddy's family to dinner.

Some attendees had parked beyond this short stretch of forest, in a lot shared with the adjoining baseball complex. From his hiding place Victor had watched several pass by, in twos, threes, and groups. Now a solitary woman entered the dark grove and walked quickly along the path. Victor stepped out.

"Good evening."

"Oh my gosh you scared me," said the woman. She put her hand to her chest and took a deep breath.

"I apologize," said Victor, closing the few feet of compacted dirt between them. "It was the only way we could come together away from the crowd."

A London-style streetlamp clicked on directly overhead. Victor's face was illuminated, the tips of his fangs glistening through parted lips.

The woman's eyes widened and she backed up a step.

"I'm sorry," said Victor. "I thought you were someone else," he lied to the woman. "But I recognize you from the gathering. Payroll, is it?"

"I'm a..." The woman struggled for composure. "I'm a sales associate...the Westchase hospitality construction division."

"Ah," said Victor. She was short and flat-faced, the lower half of her hair permed into twisting waves that reached the top of her red Westchase polo shirt. With the back of his hand he moved her hair out of the way. "Do you know who I am?"

She nodded.

"Do you know *what* I am?"

Now she shook her head, eyes on his fangs. "What do you want..."

"What I want from you," said Victor, heart beating faster and faster, "I *need* from you. Do you understand?"

"I'm scared," the woman said, her voice rising in pitch and volume. "I can't, please..."

"What I need, you can freely give, you can replenish—"

Victor had more to say, but the woman's panic was rising, outpaced only by the acceleration of his thirst. He swept her up to her tiptoes and buried his mouth upon her throat, stifling her scream. Immediately he relaxed, and so did she, and Victor took his two pints in controlled fashion, experiencing a euphoria that the planned bites hadn't provided.

THETHERSON RISING

Victor rose from his seat on the Bowflex bench, took the DVD player off "pause", and disconnected the call with Tripp, but not before reluctantly agreeing to another round of tests at the Longevity Labs the following afternoon. Victor had called Tripp, to announce that he was done with the tests. He absolutely hated parting with his blood now, and had lost interest in further delving into the mysteries of his vampirism.

Receiving the first of a month-long series of rabies shots earlier that day hadn't helped his aversion to the needle. Larry had been extremely sorry to report that Porky's head had gone missing, lost in transit. The dog had slobbered prodigiously ; at the department of health's order, the three Thethersons along with Nikki, Florence, Larry, his mother and maybe twenty neighbors were all receiving the vaccination series as a precaution. The shots were no longer in the stomach as they had all feared; Victor was still fed up with getting stuck.

On the call, Tripp had been persuasive, and after a couple minutes of light argument Victor agreed, as a favor to his friend. Unspoken, but surely recognized by Tripp, was that this would be the last time.

It had been at least a week since they had spoken. Tripp had regaled Victor with the Longer Labs' latest personality clashes, fueled by the increasingly strident pressure for results from their investors. Victor had brought Tripp up to date on the merger, including the anxious atmosphere after Darla's report had come to light. He didn't mention his unsolicited attack on the Westchase employee. Tripp would be unable to share his excitement.

Barbara stood in the raised doorway to the house. "Good workout?" she wondered.

Intense exercise was one of Victor's techniques for staying home at night. If he burned enough energy in the garage—and lately out on the streets for a hard three-mile run—he had a good chance at falling asleep before the urge became too great.

Barbara had figured out the pattern, to the point where she would now recommend a workout if the evening wore on and he hadn't yet gone to the garage. Those times were rare. Victor was becoming addicted to the results—and maybe more so to the feeling. He was thrilled to find that at the point of muscle failure and oxygen depletion, his body still had more to give.

Of course the depth of this reservoir of strength seemed to be dependent on his natural blood intake. "Natural" as opposed to the blood bags supplied by Tripp and the Bank, which by Victor's gauge didn't have the same energy-stimulating effect. And so a late-evening workout could backfire—if his performance was less than gratifying, Victor's thoughts turned to the women of Houston's nightlife.

"I used it today," said Barbara. "The PX-90."

"P90X," Victor corrected her.

"When I got home from work," Barbara continued. "Instead of shopping. Which means I didn't get the chance to pick you up another bottle of Bloody Mary mix."

"Save your money," said Victor. "Alcohol is too hard on my stomach." He reached back and grabbed his foot, mimicking the beautiful people on screen stretching their quads. "And I no longer have need for mixers."

"That's good to know," said Barbara. She pulled out the ponytail bracket.

"Washing your hair tonight?" Victor asked without taking his eyes off the screen, familiar with the *whump* of her hair falling down her back.

"No," said Barbara. She bent over to shake out her hair, then straightened and tossed her head back. Her hair swept around her shoulders. "I've actually been using your machine quite a bit, you know."

"Really?"

"It's fun," said Barbara, pulling her sleeve back and extending her arm to reveal relatively tight flesh. "I can tell in my arms already." She lifted her shirt, and there were those washboard abs. "That video has a few great exercises for the stomach, too." Then she stretched her neck and ran her fingers down her throat. "I think I lost some weight here, too."

Victor had begun a set of shoulder shrugs. "Good to hear," he grunted.

Barbara watched him. "I'm going to head in to the bedroom now. But I'm not going to fall asleep. So, come on in, whenever you're ready."

"Will do," said Victor, dropping the dumbbells and moving into a headstand, encouraging the muscles in his lower back to relax, hating the feeling of his upside-down stomach overlapping his ribcage.

After a protein-rich recovery drink and a bag of blood, Victor entered the bedroom, removing his shirt and using it to wipe off his torso. The paunch remained but his man boobs were gone, the pectorals' curvature apparent through the thinning layer of fat.

Barbara patted the bed. The action pooched her satin nightgown, revealing more of her chest. "Come lie down with me."

Victor stood and stared. The scenario was so unfamiliar, he had no ability to respond. "I'm sweaty. I should shower before I touch the sheets."

"Towel dry is fine," said Barbara. She scooted back and opened the covers wider. "You can leave your shorts on if you'd like."

Victor tossed his shirt at the hamper and got into bed. Barbara brushed at his chest hair—"You had a fuzzy"— and then left her hand there. Victor lay still and breathed, the back of his hand in light contact with Barbara's hip.

"Who were you talking to on the phone while you were working out?"

"Tripp. He wants me to come in for more tests tomorrow."

"You're going to do it, right?" Barbara finger-combed her hair, redirecting a swath of her locks to rest upon Victor's shoulder. She spread the light brown hair into an even covering that meshed with his chest hair. "I like how Tripp looks out for you. He's a good friend," she purred.

Victor's brow furrowed, widow's peak elongated. "I've never heard you say anything remotely charitable about Tripp."

"Well, I've had a chance to get to know him a little better, when he brings the blood by for you." Barbara stroked his shoulder through her hair. "So, Amberly said she enjoyed your company picnic Saturday."

"Seeing her there…" A lump formed in Victor's throat, a composite of the love he had for his daughter and his self-pity for the state of their relationship. "It was great. I didn't even invite her, because…. I just didn't think she'd want to."

"She said you were great in some kind of team race. She said everybody was cheering you. Was Jay there?"

Thanks to the new personality that vampirism had built for him—rather, a fortress wall around his personality, repelling the vast majority of the never-ending horde of demands, giving him time to breathe, to be selective in his responses—when Victor left the office these days, he didn't think about work. Couldn't, with all due respect to free will, not even about the merger and all its negative implications for him and his staff.

With his beautiful barrier so easily breached by the

onrush of emotion for Amberly, he thought about his staff now. "It's been a month since Jay's been to Houston. I've left him voicemails and sent him e-mails telling him I need to talk to him about my staff, but I haven't heard from him."

"Jay will keep you," said Barbara. "I have no doubt about that." Her fingers trailed down past the ends of her hair. "I wish I could have been there too. To see you in action."

"Well, I guess...I guess I could have invited you." Victor was dizzy, a lightheadedness that was pleasurable but laced with frustration—he had grown accustomed and addicted to controlling his relationships, and was scared by how quickly things could revert to the old ways. "I will do that next time, if you like."

Barbara kissed his cheek, letting her lips linger. "I do like."

"Oh boy," said Victor.

"I've been thinking," said Barbara, as her soft kisses covered his cheek and padded jaw. "We should try to make things work, like a marriage. I don't even think we need to date each other, since we live together. You think? We can skip a couple steps."

She laid her chest across his, some skin, some satin. Her hair draped either side of his face as she continued to kiss him, everywhere but his mouth. Victor put his hand on her back, tracing the border of nightgown and skin.

And now her mouth was on his. Victor did his best to keep his fangs sheathed, like kissing with braces when he was fourteen and Sara McKlounky had been willing, the inside of his lips mashed and bleeding, while blood coursed through his veins at high speed and great volume, the rushing sound mixed with what he could only describe as warning bells going off behind his eyes.

The bells became a teeth-rattling clanging. He shoved Barbara away and sprang out of bed, striding for the closet. "Huh-uh," was all he could say. He pulled on pants over his shorts and raging erection and grabbed a charcoal gray dress shirt off the hanger.

Barbara stood at the threshold, tears in her eyes. "Honey, it's okay. It's fine if you can't...." She tried to smile, mouth quivering. "If it doesn't work right away, if I don't...it's fine. We'll go slowly. You don't have to leave."

"It just didn't feel right," said Victor, a mild way of saying that something, those warning bells, had scared him to death. He gave Barbara's arms a squeeze as he moved her aside. "Please don't..."

He was going to assure her that his inability to continue wasn't her fault, when a decade's flood of hurt and neglect swept over him. Rather than let the late-arriving grudge break loose, and to break the grip that was rapidly tightening on her arms, Victor chose to say nothing more. Seconds later he was in his car and heading downtown.

The following afternoon Victor hit the Longevity Labs like a cyclone. Tripp was loitering at the receptionist's desk, presumably awaiting his arrival. Victor strode past without signing in or waiting to hear whether the research staff was ready for him.

"Whoa, buddy," said Tripp, in pursuit down the hallway that fed the exam rooms.

Victor chose the first open door. He paced to the wall, taking two deep breaths before dropping into the guest chair.

Tripp entered. "It's 'patient's choice' today, how did you know? You also get to pick your procedure, from a limited, prix fixe menu."

"Fine," said Victor.

"Alright," said Tripp. "Stand up and turn around, let's find the burr."

"What?"

Tripp absorbed the sharp tone and continued his

metaphor. "The burr under your saddle. I'll get it out for you, before you bite someone's head off."

"Literally, right?"

Tripp approached and laid a hand on Victor's shoulder. When he felt his friend relax, he gave it a squeeze. "Good to see you. I won't even ask how the day's going. Merger stress, maybe?"

Victor nodded. "Can we get this over with?"

Tripp studied him more closely. "You didn't sleep much last night, did you?"

That could be said for most nights. He was usually out late—last night he had just skipped the part where he tossed and turned in bed, opting instead to prowl the streets, stewing over Barbara and making three unfocused, botched attempts to claim a victim, finally curling up in the darkest corner of the Good Sisters alley to sleep the morning away.

"Are you fishing for all the gory details?"

Tripp winced as he plucked a lab coat off the rack and slipped it on. "Couldn't agree more, let's get this over with. I lied though, you don't get to choose the room. Not for our first phase, anyway. C'mon."

Tripp waited at the door—the energy Victor had displayed entering the Labs was spent like a sugar rush, little remaining to boost him out of the chair. Tripp was impatient. "We need to keep this moving. Dr. Speer will be back from lunch soon." He spoke over his shoulder as they continued down the hall, Victor lagging. "I had you come in early because there's a separate test I want to run, one the Labs wouldn't condone. I'm probably going to get my butt in a sling with Speer, but we need to do it here, in case she has any adverse reaction." At the last room before the rear exit door, Tripp knocked and entered.

Nikki sat on the exam table in her bra.

"Cripes Nikki, you could have left your shirt on," said Tripp, ushering Victor in and closing the door behind him.

Nikki nodded at the sleeveless camouflage shirt hung over the back of the guest chair, words across the front in the shape of a ribbon, *Give it up for our troops! (I do)*. "I'm not going to ruin another one of my favorites." She hooked her thumb under a bra strap and released it with a *thwap*. "So did you hear, Victor's a full-fledged vamp now?"

"How's that?" said Tripp, at the counter readying supplies.

"He sparkles in the sun."

Tripp straightened up to peer at and take a step toward Victor as he settled into a guest chair. "Come again?"

"We all saw it Saturday," said Nikki. "Sparkly skin. It was so cool."

Tripp leaned in, then pulled the exam lamp in closer and directed the beam onto Victor's face. "I'm going to have to get you under the UV lamp, as soon as we're done here. Dude." He loosed a bark of a laugh. "It's happening. You're not getting any older."

"What do you mean?" said Victor.

"The sparkles are actually fluorescence." Tripp paced the room, absorbing and reporting the news simultaneously, inefficiently. "Jellyfish gene. I don't know if it was the angle of the sun, or some sporadic, patchy expression, that made you sparkle instead of glow."

"Makes sense," said Nikki.

"No it doesn't," said Victor, his irritation with Tripp now shared with Nikki. "Why is there a jellyfish gene inside me?"

"It's a marker," said Tripp, having difficulty retarding his racing thoughts long enough to provide Victor with the necessary backstory. "Everyone in the longevity study carries it. It's harmless. A harmless stretch of DNA that we inserted right next to SIRT. That's the gene that controls aging. Indirectly."

Tripp scribbled on his e-pad, glancing up to take

Victor's figurative temperature. He finished the notation and holstered the e-pen. "What SIRT does is switch your cells into repair and maintenance mode. It's called hormesis—your cells think they're starving, so they go into long-haul mode. Happens in the animal kingdom all the time, say during a drought—keeps the animal alive until conditions are favorable again for procreation. We use the marker, the fluorescence, to alert us if SIRT is activated."

"Then why aren't there sparkly people all over Houston?" Victor challenged.

"Because," said Tripp, "you're the first. The first to activate the SIRT gene. From your last round of testing we knew that your body temp, your blood sugar, your insulin levels, they had all dropped. Those are markers of a sort, that tell us that hormesis may be occurring. But this is definitive." He stared at Victor, shaking his head, in a good way. "Speer and Linciome are going to flip."

"So Victor's going to live forever?" said Nikki.

"We'll have to figure out just how strong the effect is," said Tripp. "And how persistent it'll be. But it's safe to say you're going to live longer." He clamped his hand affectionately on Victor's knee and returned to the prep counter, new life in his movements.

Questions peppered Victor, including whether his parents had given the scientists authority to insert jellyfish DNA in his cells, exactly how they had done so, and whether there were any other such surprises awaiting him. Or side effects. Questions that demanded he ask them.

He asked none of them. Victor was tired, ready to make his final contribution to longevity science. And lately he found himself much less concerned about others' ability to impact him. He turned his attention to Nikki. "What are you doing here?"

"Having some blood drawn," she said.

Tripp planted himself on a stool next to Nikki and

tapped the band-aid on her shoulder. "What's this?"

"Rabies vaccine," said Nikki. "Vic's dog attacked a big pussy in our department, so now we all have to get vaccinated. Vic and I both got our first shot yesterday."

Tripp gave Victor a curious look, some mixture of disbelief and hopefulness. "You're going for it?"

"It wasn't optional," said Victor.

Tripp might have been about to respond, but Nikki was talking. "You missed a crazy day at the office, master."

Now Tripp reconsidered Victor's bloodshot eyes, charcoal gray dress shirt wrinkled and poorly tucked, multi-day beard growth. "So you didn't go to work?" His expression soured as he accurately imagined the reason for Victor's apparent late night, and he abandoned the topic of the rabies vaccine.

"Larry was in a terrible mood again," said Nikki. "He cussed out Casey for doing something piss-poor—his words." She paused while Tripp swabbed antiseptic across the site of her first bite. "She cried until one of her eyes bled, so Florence sent her home."

Tripp brusquely unbuttoned Victor's right cuff and rolled up his sleeve. "Before we begin, I want to get pre- and post- samples."

"Pre- and post-what? I have to give blood twice?" Victor glowered at Tripp. "No."

"We need to see if there are any changes." Tripp worked quickly, prepping Victor's arm and deftly slipping in the needle. "To both of you. I already got a pre-bite sample from Nikki a few days ago."

"What do you think, VV?" said Nikki. "Are you one of those three-bite vampires?"

"What the hell are you talking about?" Victor growled.

"Dr. Linciome is very keen to figure out why you were turned with one bite," said Tripp, swapping in a fresh empty vial, "while the Hilton security guard wasn't. Same for everyone else you've bitten." He paused. "Right?"

"As far as I know," said Victor.

"How many have you..." Tripp stopped. "Never mind. We found the Hilton guard and he volunteered to come in for testing too. Doesn't appear to be anything unusual about his blood." He noticed Nikki was shivering. "It is a little chilly in here. I'll get you a blanket."

"I'm not cold," said Nikki. "See?" She pushed out her chest. "No nips. Just nervous about getting bit again."

"I'm not biting you," said Victor.

"I'd really appreciate it if you did," said Tripp. "The three-bite conversion is probably complete bull. But every legend has some basis in reality."

"Why do you care?" Victor grumbled.

"I've been doing a lot of reading," said Tripp. "Looks like vampire origins might be as complex as cancer. Not much hard science out there, but it's pretty obvious there's more than one transmission method. Until we figure out how you caught it, we could be missing something crucial in understanding your aging process. Which is essential if we're going to be able to create a pill that mimics it. And find you a cure."

"The vamp world is a mystical space," said Nikki. "It creates legends, and it grows out of them. For some it takes one bite under a blood-orange moon, others need to get bit over and over until they accept the gift. Sometimes you need to go through a ritual, plus a bite."

"None of that's in the scientific literature," said Tripp, aggravated.

Nikki pointed at Victor. "Did a black cat jump over your heart when you were a baby?"

Victor stared at the overhead fluorescent light, avoiding watching the blood leave his body.

"Were you ever excommunicated? Do you remember drinking any of the vamp's blood? Did you wake up in her casket?"

"Not the kind of thing we can test here," said Tripp testily, capping the second vial.

"There must be fifty ways to be a vampire," said

Nikki. She waved her arms over her head like kelp in the ocean current. "Slip out the back Jack, make a new plan Stan, don't need to be corduroy, cuz there must be fifty ways—"

"Are you high?" Tripp snapped. "This isn't a joke, Nikki." On top of Tripp's vocal power chord—standard sass, layered with rare authoritative—Victor also picked up on a raw, dissonant note. He could *see* it, shimmering in sine waves over Tripp's head; he was drawn to it.

"We're approaching this in a systematic, scientific manner," Tripp lectured defensively, oblivious to Victor's curious gaze. "Would have been great if Vic was coherent when he was bitten, maybe asked Cruella a few questions." He pulled out the needle and taped a cotton swab over the extraction site. "Didn't happen, so we move forward from there. We rule out variables, one by one, starting with the three-bite legend. Step by step, under careful observation—if we see any changes in your bloodwork after the second bite, we stop."

He was talking to himself, methodically packaging the samples and safety-capping the needle. "This isn't one of your alley encounters, and it sure as hell isn't a mystical experience. It's a controlled experiment in a research laboratory."

Tripp punctuated his last remark by chucking the needle in the bio-waste canister. Then his hand fell limp to his side and he sagged in his chair. "Listen to me. I'm freakin' Dr. Frankenstein." He looked at Victor. "You're right. This is insane."

Nikki hopped off the exam table and climbed into Victor's lap. "You can't stop me from making my contribution to science. If I become a vampire...then so be it. You'll probably have a cure soon. If I don't turn into a vamp..." She winked up at Victor. "Oh well."

"Nikki," said Victor.

"Hit me, master," said Nikki. She wrapped her arms around Victor's neck and brought her throat to his chin.

"Good Lord," said Tripp. He locked eyes with Victor,

and nodded.

"This feels really strange," said Victor. He brought his mouth to Nikki's throat. She was trembling. "I don't know if I can."

"You're tickling me," said Nikki, and then screamed a brief sonic burst as Victor sank his fangs into her taut flesh.

Victor vaguely heard Tripp mumbling epithets, over Nikki's rasping breath and the pulsing of her heart, quickly synchronizing with his own.

Tripp tapped his shoulder—getting no immediate response, he pinched Victor's nose and squeezed his windpipe. Victor broke off with a growl, jumping up and reeling to the wall, leaving Tripp to half-catch Nikki and ease her fall to the floor.

"Christ, Vic, have a heart," said Tripp, helping Nikki to stand, finally picking her up and laying her on the table.

"I'm sorry," Victor croaked, as the prior night's tension with Barbara dissolved into a pleasant mist across his eyes.

Tripp smoothed Nikki's fine limp locks away from her pale face. He pulled the blood pressure machine closer and tore open the cuff. "You were so hesitant," he said to Victor, "I wasn't sure you were going to drink enough. Now, I'm hoping you didn't take too much."

Nikki's eyes fluttered open, and she smiled. "Don't sweat it, doc. VV did it juuuuust right."

Not Getting Any Younger in the
Search For Immortality

Longevity gains: Is it the bloodsucking, or is it P90X?
by Gerald Corvallis
(from the *Wall Street Report*)

Houston — Dr. Regnald Speer straightens up from the microscope and pinches the bridge of his nose.

"My eyes are getting too old for this," he says. Dr. Speer, lead researcher at the Rice University Longevity Labs, chuckles and rubs tired eyes. "Maybe I should speed up my research, eh?"

Dr. Speer and his associates run one of the many public, private, and – like the Longevity Labs – hybrid laboratories across the country attempting to unlock the secrets of aging. While ethicists debate the wisdom of extending lifespans on a crowded planet, and many scientists point out that aging should simply be viewed as another phase in the circle of life, you won't find many longevity scientists sharing those views.

"Aging causes suffering, debilitation, and death," says Dr. Winnie Linciome, associate researcher at the Longevity Labs. "Starting at age twenty-five, aging begins to destroy your body. Aging slowly and surely kills you. How can that not be a disease?"

Every lab across the country and around the world seems to have a different focus and a different theory on the causes of aging, which hints at the difficulty in "solving" it. Dr. Linciome came to work with Dr. Speer after his former lab "focused too much on coping mechanisms, like building replacement parts.

They lost faith in the science of the cure."

Dr. Speer's team believes they have zeroed in on at least one of the keys to arresting aging – the process of cellular repair.

"It's not as elegant as telomeres," says Dr. Speer, referring to the ends of the chromosomes that wear down like sands through the hourglass, seemingly acting as a countdown clock on an individual's lifespan. "Of course telomeres didn't turn out to be as elegant or significant as everyone believed. Cellular repair is an unexpected candidate, but we're excited about the potential."

"Excitement" is only apparent in the long view, as most hours, days and weeks are spent at the microscope and gene sequencing apparatus, analyzing samples provided by an impressive assortment of volunteers lined up by the Longer Labs, as they affectionately refer to themselves.

"We're the spin-off of Rice University's gerontology lab," says Dr. Speer. "So we're fortunate to have access to the samples of hundreds of folks who have been participating since birth in Rice's longitudinal study." The group of infants who were enrolled in the study in the 1960's even includes a man who recently became a vampire.

"Extremely valuable data" from the vampire, says Dr. Speer. "Of late we've noted a drastic slowdown in his aging processes, with a concurrent uptick in his cellular repair function."

"He did recently start P90X," Dr. Linciome cautions, an impish gleam in his eye. "But we're going to assume most of the improvement relates to his vampirism."

The biotech industry is eagerly, impatiently watching the progress of labs like Dr. Speer's, although translating laboratory findings into medical treatments and consumer products is another challenge entirely...

VV

Victor Thetherson stopped at the threshold to the accounting floor, on this the effective day of the merger of Texahoma and Oklarkana. Faced with preserving the two legacy companies' characters with a combo name— Texarkana? Oklahoma?—the new marketing department punted and went with Bizco Diversified, with a cowboy hat logo, which Victor wore as a pin on the lapel of his suitcoat.

Forty-four regular, his jacket size. Over the past two weeks Victor—VV as he now asked to be called—had dropped another fifteen pounds from his waist and added half that as muscle in his shoulders and chest. Middle-aged men would take out a third mortgage to achieve these results. The transformation deserved its own 2 a.m. infomercial, except the disclaimer would have to be carefully worded: *Will result in lacerated lips, garlic allergy and loss of tan; requires constant nocturnal submissions.* And unfortunately for the rest of the aging men out there, the product didn't seem to be readily available on the market.

Just out of Nikki's sightline, Victor watched as the door to his old office opened and Larry emerged, head down and moving quickly on his short bow legs to his cube. Sally from HR came next out of the office, saw Victor immediately and approached him, stopping to stand in front of Nikki's admin station, eyes never leaving his.

Darla was last to appear in the accounting manager's

doorway, her doorway now, if possible looking more drawn and pinched than twenty hours earlier when Victor had talked to her at the Integration Transition meeting. She smiled at him, a bit of her fatigue dissolving.

Nikki scooted out of her admin station and launched out of her chair, announcing their ex-boss's arrival with floor coverage rivaling their emergency broadcast loudspeakers.

"VV! You're back! Did you miss us? How's tricks, man?!"

Victor hugged Nikki with one arm, saving the other to shake hands with Kirby, first to arrive after beelining out of David Copperfield's old cube.

"It is sooo good to have you visit us," Kirby gushed. "It's like having a celebrity on the floor. Your hands are freezing. Gosh. So how's things been? Where are you now?"

"Victor has been promoted to run Chleber's integration efforts," said Sally, observing with cool detachment. She referred to the corpulent Westchase exec who had taken a shine to Victor at the company picnic. "Darla can probably attest as a long-time Westchase manager—I've heard Don is a challenging boss."

"He has a reputation," said Darla, bumped further from the center of attention by the arrival of Raj, Monique and Casey.

"I had to talk to him once, when Darla wasn't around," said Monique. "He needed our year-to-date revenue for the civic center project. You could just tell he was used to people jumping when he spoke."

"I think Victor is getting that reputation too," said Sally. No one interfered with her sightline to him; otherwise the circle around Victor was unbroken, with the arrival two more legacy Westchase accountants.

"Speaking of which," said Raj. "Victor, there's something I was hoping to talk to you about. When you have time. It's the Maryhill variance project I've been working on. Would now work?"

"In a minute." Victor locked eyes with Darla. "I came here to see your manager."

"Darla and I should bring you up to date," said Sally. She willed Kirby and Monique to move aside and create a path for Victor to his former office. "It's been an eventful morning."

As they crossed the old quarter-flip arena, Victor saw Larry, Tessa and Quinten watching unhappily from the mouth of Cube City. At his approach Larry moved ever so slightly backward, settling defensively on his heels.

Victor greeted each of them by name. "How are my old charges?"

"Life has been better, VV," said Tessa.

"They're canning us," said Quinten.

"No..." Like in the dream where he found himself sitting in the Texahoma board room in Chicago, with Jay and various senior management arrayed around the table and ready for him to make the presentation he had forgotten to prepare, Victor broke into a cold sweat. How could he have blocked out his staff's impending fate? How many weeks had gone by since he had left Jay a message, asking to discuss his team's situation? He had a plan, he had been planning on telling Jay how hard his team had been working. He was going to use their recent work to demonstrate how much ability they had, to fight for them....

Casey joined them and announced, without the benefit of functional voice-modulation neurons, "They're firing me in two weeks!"

"Why are you whining to Vic?" said Larry. He walked into his cube, plucked out the stickpin from which a mini boar's head had dangled on the cloth wall, and tossed the mount carelessly in a packing box on the floor. "He didn't care before, and he sure as shit don't care now."

"That's not true," said Victor, scowling and

defensive…but already inside his skull repairs were in the works, and this was no metaphor, physical patches were being made to this weak spot in the Wall. "I've been waiting and waiting to hear back from Jay. They wouldn't make this decision without talking to me."

"Oh, so you were in the dark on this?" said Larry, holding a mule deer mount by the ear, dangled between thumb and forefinger, before dropping it in the box. "Then why is your precious Flo the only one keeping her job?"

From Victor's angle, a sliver of Florence's elegant, s-shaped back was visible in her cube, a couple yards away. She scooted forward, now fully out of sight.

"I heard they were keeping two," said Tessa, eyes fixed on their best-dressed coworker, who was conversing with the legacy Westchase accountants while keeping an eye on Victor. "I'm sure it's Raj."

"I don't think so," said Quentin. "When Raj came out of Darla's office, his face was the same color as the ash from one of his clove cigarettes."

"In any case, there's nothing you could have done," said Tessa to her former boss. "It's the execs calling the shots. I guarantee you, they all sat in a room together and divvied up the jobs. Texahoma got Accounts Payable and Tax, Westchase got Payroll and us. Darla didn't have any say either," she added for Larry's benefit. "All that b.s. about using the audits to determine the winner? I'm convinced Jay had it out for us all along."

When Don Chleber brought him over to his Strategic Positioning office, Victor had been pleasantly surprised how easy it was to leave his twenty-eight year career behind. He looked forward to experiencing his first month-end without a general ledger closing process, and to be in blissful ignorance of the next Financial Accounting Standards Board pronouncement, an event that turned accountants' lives upside down and meant absolutely nothing to the rest of the world, including the rest of the company.

And he had his hands full getting up to speed on Bizco Diversified's sales approach, in order to participate in fact-finding meetings with various developers and government agencies. Victor put in the time to ascend this learning curve even though it was largely overkill; it had quickly become apparent that his contribution was not knowledge of, but conviction in, Bizco. When Victor told a client that Bizco would build them a building on time and within budget, they believed him.

Because of this, because vampirism was screening his calls these days, Victor hadn't lost sleep worrying about the fate of his former team. But now he saw Jay orchestrating his team's removal, gloating all the while; and in his chest flared what Victor considered to be a fierce loyalty.

"This is inexcusable," said Victor with a snarl.

"Is there anything you can do?" said Quinten plaintively. "You can convince them to keep us, can't you? Are there any openings in your new department?"

"Quinten," said Tessa. "We're accountants. We're not adaptable."

"You're old," Quinten shot back, desperate. "A lot of you are old. I'm still young, I can change."

"How long have you been here?" Tessa asked him.

"Five years," said Quinten.

She shook her head. "Too long."

"No," said Quinten, refusing to believe.

"I don't learn well," said Casey.

"Let me talk to a few people," said Victor. He leveled his gaze at Darla and Sally talking quietly in front of his old office. "Starting here, starting now."

"Hurray!" said Quinten, forcing Tessa to high-five him. "Go get 'em, VV," said Casey, loudly. She dashed forward and kissed his cheek, then retreated behind Tessa. Larry muttered in his cube, continuing to pack in sloppy fashion.

Two steps into his battle march, Victor turned and

found Florence, now standing along the window before an empty cube formerly occupied by one of the Payroll department's merger casualties. She wore a blue western shirt, with the bolo clasp low on its runners, and slacks, no belt buckle. No belt, period, and she hiked her pants above nonexistent hips as Victor reached her.

"Congratulations, I hear," he said.

"I hear I should be thanking you." Few people established personal space as effectively and in such abundance as Florence. But she was now in his shadow, her metallic twang blunted by his frame. "Everyone's making it sound like you did me a favor." Her voice rose, syllables coming in quick staccato, becoming available to interested ears. "I told them that whatever you did, I hadn't asked you—"

"I had nothing to do with it," said Victor. "I would guess that you were simply Darla's choice."

Florence mashed her lips together to stem the vitriol, blood leaving the area via the surrounding network of radiating creases. She nodded, crossing her arms and using her head to reference his physical whole. "Being a vampire is agreeing with you. Looking at you now brings back memories of that night at the Bayou."

"I remember that night very well," said Victor. "I see you that way all the time."

Florence shook her head, darkness shrouding her eyes. "Did I ever tell you my husband used to make me stay on the horse all night when we were cutting sheep? If I got down, he'd put me in a crowded pen until I passed out. Did I tell you that?"

"You did," said Victor. "And you left him. You came back here, to start over."

Florence laughed derisively, predictably breaking into a wet cough. She studied Victor as her hand lingered at her chest, popping her shirt's highest pearl snap and slipping inside.

Before Victor could protest she pulled out a nicked

dart with a blunted plastic tip, and held it up for his inspection. "I'll bet you don't remember this."

Victor took the dart, flexed the tip, and grasped it with fingertips in throwing position. He could see the dartboard lit up in the corner of Bayou Mama's game room, backlighting Florence and Barbara's forms and faces. "That was a special time." When he looked at Florence there was wistfulness in his eyes. It wouldn't last long. For this brief moment Victor was wondering how life could have been different.

The slightest quiver ran its course at the corner of Florence's puckered lips. "That dart kept me going. If you want to know the truth, it's always on me."

She swayed side to side, kinked, rusty warm-up movements to a long-dormant dance track. Her eyes caressed his lips, seeing through them to his fangs. Nikki too always stared at his teeth, willing them to her throat. Florence's covetousness was different. She seemed to want a pair.

Anticipating being asked to return the dart in their non-traditional fashion, Victor took Florence's hand and wrapped it around the artifact. "Don't give up, Florence. Believe me, things can change."

Florence gave one last phlegm-clearing hack, and another visual sweep of her ex-boss's improved body. "It's the vampirism, right? That's your secret?"

She nodded, answering her own question, and closed the small gap for a hug, raising on tiptoes, turkey neck matched to his cheek. "I want to share that with you, Victor. Just like you, I want to start over."

Sally watched Victor approach. "Aren't you the killer."

"It's always better to be an ex-manager," said Darla, leading them into her office. "We're only loved after we're gone."

"I think you're missing the bigger picture," said Sally. She left not quite enough room for Victor to pass cleanly by her, then closed the door behind him. "Victor is a special case."

Darla sagged into her chair. "I think part of it is being a woman," she said. "It's really hard to be tough and not be a bitch. I admit it."

Sally shook her head at Darla's failure to grasp Victor's impact.

Darla equally misinterpreted Sally's feedback as agreement. "You've missed a terrible day," she told Victor. "We gave two weeks' notice to most of your staff."

"So I heard," said Victor, glowering.

Darla worried when his expression wouldn't soften. "You know I had absolutely no choice, right? I have plenty of work to keep more. We're going to be swamped. It's the budget we were given from Jay."

Victor found so much to like in Darla's face, in the way her mind worked. He liked her posture. "I do understand. Just know that this is not the last word."

"The staffing levels have been locked in and the resulting savings communicated to Cromartie," Sally referred to the Bizco CEO. "You're not going to get Jay to go back now and say, 'Whoops, sorry, I over-committed.'"

Victor stewed on this, losing some steam.

"If this was any other business you could have played the diversity card," said Sally. "Only in the construction industry can you ax a mental deficient, a Latino and an obese lesbian all in the same day." She quickly reached a hand out to Darla. "I'm sorry if that offended you."

"No offense taken." Darla sank lower in her chair. "A lot of people mistake me for a lesbian."

Victor looked at each woman in turn. "I understand you are retaining Florence."

"I was given budget to retain two," said Darla. "I went by seniority. And age, frankly. I didn't want to force out someone in her position, in this economy."

"Then why isn't Larry your other choice?"

"That slot is taken," said Sally. "HR and Legal talked it over with Jay, and decided we'd be exposing ourselves to undue liability if we fire someone who's on a leave of absence because of harassment."

"What do you mean?" said Victor.

Sally pantomimed the flick of a magic wand. "Poof. David Copperfield reappears."

Victor was stunned. "You said you had his harassment charge buried."

"It's not a chance we can take," said Sally.

"No," said Victor, a tremor in his voice. "Not in my department."

"It's not yours anymore, love," said Sally. Her cellphone sprang to life on the edge of Darla's desk. She checked the caller ID and excused herself to take it. At the door she told her caller to hold on. "If I don't see you again before I head back to the Marriott," she said to Victor, "promise you'll track me down the next time you're in Chicago."

Victor barely acknowledged her, leaving Sally less than satisfied as she resumed her call and exited the office. He stood and paced to the porthole window—the light was too bright, forcing him to shy away, infuriating him all the more.

"I knew you weren't going to like that," said Darla. "Sally passed along all my arguments. Our arguments. I tried for a week. We lost."

"I am not going to allow it," said Victor.

"I'm assuming the decision was vetted at a pretty high level," said Darla, "but if you have Chleber's ear.... Right now, I don't even have time to worry about it, that's how busy we are."

Tessa was right, Victor told himself, mergers meant casualties, and where the axe fell was arbitrary. That two had survived was something to celebrate; there was nothing he could have done to save the rest of his team. Contrary to Sally's opinion, however, he would have something to say about who made the cut. "Then allow me," he said.

"Thank you," said Darla. "I hope you don't mind me changing the topic...but thinking about something other than work would be heavenly. Kimberly has been bugging me to go to Six Flags, for months. Would you and Amberly want to join us on Saturday?"

"I would like that."

"Great. I'm so glad. I think our girls hit it off at the picnic, don't you?" A smile tugged the corners of her lips. "I have another surprise for you. Oh, but before I forget, a gentleman was here the other day looking for you. Sorry I keep switching gears. I swear I've got late-onset ADHD. This guy, I don't think he was an employee. And I got the distinct impression he didn't like you."

"Tall and thin, completely nuts?"

"I couldn't say about his sanity."

"Vampire hunter," said Victor. "Eugene has been trying to get to me for some time. He broke in here once before and put a stake on my desk. He even tried to date my daughter."

Darla frowned. "Speaking as a mother, he's too old for her."

"Agreed," said Victor.

"So here's my surprise." The smile crept back onto Darla's face. "Your boss called me today. He received a request from someone in the home office in Germany, to have you attend the big management confab over there. Before he approved it, Don wanted to make sure I wouldn't be uncomfortable having you there. Because of what we just went through."

Victor raised his eyebrows. "And?"

Darla pushed aside a stack of work and leaned on her forearms, fingers splaying and arching, stretching, and then resting comfortably atop Victor's old desk protector. "The thought of being in Germany on my own had me shook up. I wasn't looking forward to it. I think it's all the stress, here and at home. When I got the call from Don, I pictured you there with me, and I instantly relaxed."

When Victor didn't react, nothing more than another bob of the eyebrows, Darla flattened her hands, reaching her fingers further across the desk. "Can you do it? Do you, do you *want* to?"

Victor's thoughts were not in the present. He saw David Copperfield munching a donut in the conference room; he saw Jay Hansen smirking in the chair he currently occupied, with his arm around David, who was eating a donut; he saw Eugene Foreman kissing his daughter's neck, his hands upon her. "Sure. Sure I do."

"I know it's a big trip to get prepared for on short notice," said Darla. "I still have a ton to do, and I've known for three weeks. My ex is playing games, it's got me stressed out.... But I just keep telling myself, when I leave the country, he won't have any choice but to step up and be a father."

The office door opened and Nikki entered. "Master," she said, hands on her hips. "Sorry," she apologized to Darla for the intrusion, putting three fingers in front of Victor's face. "When's number three? I'm ready to finish the trilogy. I heard you're going to Germany. Let's do it before you leave, 'kay?" She wiggled her three fingers at him as she backed out, closing the door behind her.

"She's a unique admin," said Darla. "I'm not sure you completely prepared me for her. But she's very tapped into the company grapevine, which I need. I don't know how she heard you're going to Germany. I also don't know who requested your presence over there. Any idea?"

Victor shrugged. "Probably just general curiosity. Everyone wants to see the vampire."

Twice during Sally's prior stay, Victor had allowed her to see him, prowling the Marriott halls. A glimpse, and no more. Both times he had slaked his thirst on a stranger—an immigrant cleaning woman, an older guest with a tight, graceful neck—and gone home, leaving Sally in anticipation of the bite.

Whether truly by habit or designed to make herself available to him, Sally had now taken a late nightcap all four times he had come to her hotel. This night, with two scotch and sodas in her, Sally left the lounge shortly after twelve-thirty and walked past the vacant front desk and down the empty hall, past the placid swimming pool, to the guest room elevator bank.

The silence was only now complete, and Sally became edgy waiting for the elevator. Once inside, she pushed the button for her floor, then stabbed it again. Eventually the door closed.

Sally's room was right around the corner, first door on the left. She wasn't dexterous with the key card, but the lock did spring, and she slipped inside.

After she unshouldered and dropped her briefcase on the bed, before she could reach the bathroom, there came a knock at the door. She hadn't yet thrown the deadbolt or latched the chain, making it easy to let Victor in.

"Well well well," Sally greeted him. She leaned past him and looked both ways down the hallway. "How much time do we have? When does your ex show up?"

Victor had warmed to his new mental state, a curious partnership of serenity and extreme thirst. It made it easy to skip questions he couldn't answer. "May I come in?"

"Aren't you the regular vampire now," said Sally. She stood aside. "Please." She closed the door after him and twisted the deadbolt and followed him to the window, overlooking a dark warehouse receiving dock and an adjoining strip club with one small backlit sign, open for business. "So," said Sally. "I had dinner with Darla tonight. She mentioned that you two have a date this weekend. The amusement park, huh? I just have to say, yes she is a sweet thing, but she's clueless. Have you ever given her a good look at your teeth? I just can't see you on the roller coaster at Six Flags. Make sure she takes pictures."

Victor waited for her to finish. He realized serenity wasn't the obvious name for thirst's partner. There were no longer twenty different nagging concerns active in his mind, jostling for his attention and never resolved, each brought to the forefront and contemplated for a few moments before returning to the swirl, immediately replaced by another nagging issue.

He now focused on one goal at a time. He pictured that goal as an adversary standing before him, to be wrestled to the ground. Beyond that adversary stretched acres of tranquil open space, no other worries in sight. That was serenity.

"Do you know why I am here?" Victor asked Sally.

"You know what?" said Sally. "After all this time? I am not even going to speculate."

"Can you connect to the company network?"

Sally's smirk lingered. "See, that was not what I expected you to say."

"You have something I need."

"That was closer."

"An address," said Victor.

VV, WUNDERBAR

Don Chleber arranged for Victor to fly first class to Amsterdam, and again on the short hop to Dresden. Victor's seatmate on the first leg was a man in his mid-fifties with a ballcap, blue Dickies workshirt and pants that pooched in front for lack of a butt in back.

"Well hello there," Victor greeted him as they settled in. He gave the man something short of a smile, with a lot of teeth.

The man nodded in return, and began to fidget.

"I do not sleep on these all-night flights," Victor made conversation. "Something like restless leg syndrome. Are you a heavy sleeper by any chance?"

The man replied with a few polite words unrelated to the question, while coughing into his fist. On their ponytailed attendant's next pass he reached out and stayed her, and they engaged in quiet conversation. She straightened with furrowed brow and looked into coach. The man twisted in his seat and did the same.

"I know someone in 17B that would love to sit up here," said Victor. "Of course it is a middle seat...."

Moments later Darla dropped into the wide leather seat beside him. "How in the world did you accomplish that?"

Victor regarded her with a smile. "Sally was right."

"About what?"

"You are very committed to whatever is important to you. To the exclusion of everything else."

"Can you tell I was working already?" Darla nodded

at the messy file stuffed at an angle in the satchel at her feet. "I have a lot to do, to prepare for my meeting with Kurt."

"Bleckmeier, Verrstagg's head of financial reporting? Already on a first-name basis," Victor complimented her.

"Well Kurt has been…yes, I guess I am picking things up. Have to. There are so many questions I need to ask—I have notes to myself and web articles I've printed out, that I need to read through and organize and compile into a coherent list."

"And you're comfortable your staff will be able to handle things while you are gone?"

Darla thought about this and sighed. "I hope so. Larry and the others have a definite case of short-timer's disease. I was really hoping they'd do the right thing and help the rest of my staff with the transition. But I can't blame them for being in a funk. Thank goodness for Florence—she's been in a terrible mood, but she is helping my guys figure out their additional responsibilities. And believe it or not—I'm sure you do—there's been no sign of or word from David. First week back, and he's already pushing it."

The ponytailed attendant was taking drink orders from the rows in front of them, keeping a worried eye on Darla all the while. Now she turned around and disappeared into the nook outside the cockpit.

"Maybe David decided it would not be fair to take Larry's job after all," said Victor. He replayed the events from three nights prior—driving to David's townhome, parking on the narrow street, shutting off the Subaru's engine and waiting for its headlights to wink out.…

A tanned male attendant emerged from the stewards' nook and approached them. "Hi," he said. "Everything okay here?" He addressed Darla, trying not to look at Victor.

"I could use a drink," said Darla.

"Ma'am," said the attendant, "if you would be more comfortable, we do have a seat in coach, in the exit row, with ample leg room."

Darla gave him a goofy, quizzical look. "Are drinks free in coach?"

"Not ordinarily, but we would make an exception."

"I'm fine right here," said Darla. She nodded at their fellow first-class passengers. "I'd love to see if you get any takers on that offer. Even for the exit row."

The attendant tightened his mouth. "Just don't hesitate to let me know if anything changes."

"I promise not to bite you on the airplane," Victor told Darla, after the attendant left them alone.

"That's a deal." Darla put out her hand and they shook on it. Her eye was drawn to the blinking light from her Blackberry, already positioned on her leg. "Speak of the devil."

Victor was shown the header of an e-mail from Sally, with David Copperfield's name in the subject line. He had an idea what it might say.

Three nights earlier he had rung David's doorbell. Given what had occurred between them in the past, and that Victor had clearly roused him from slumber, in t-shirt and boxers with his wavy, stylish hair flat on one side, David had been remarkably happy to see him. "VV! Vic, I mean. What the heck, what are you doing here? Oh no," he pretended concern, "don't tell me we had a project due tomorrow?"

"Hello David. You can call me VV now. I was talking to Darla and Sally today." Victor had walked in without an invite, suffering no other consequence than having to brush against David's thinly-clad body.

"Good gal, Sally-Sally," said David. "She's the one who pulled the strings to get me my job back."

"Interesting." Victor had processed this for a moment. "Of course that is why I am here, David. To discuss your employment."

Darla put her hand on Victor's forearm, summarizing for him as she scrolled through the e-mail. "Sounds like David had an accident. He's been in the hospital." She lowered the Blackberry to her lap. "That's why he didn't come in. Or call."

"Ah," said Victor. "What happened?"

"She doesn't say." The wide-bodied jet taxied through a one-hundred-eighty degree turn to access the departure runway.

"She has a thing for you, do you know that? Sally I mean. I don't know if you could tell. She talks about you a lot." Darla pressed her fingers to his forearm again, leaving pink heat lines against his pale skin. "She told me the story about the first time you met. How you reenacted your incident with David. I swear I think she wishes you would have bitten..."

Darla's words were scrambled to white noise by the thrust and the roar of the engines' acceleration.

In this bubble of sound and gravity, Victor returned to the scene in David's townhome living room, a short flight up from his front door. "I would appreciate you putting on more clothing," Victor had said.

David put his hands on his hips and affected a lisp. "Well that's a switch, huh?" He faked a punch to Victor's gut. "Just kidding, big guy. We gotta be able to joke about it, right? I'll be right back." He kept talking en route to the bedroom. "So I heard Darla beat you out for the manager job."

"She did," said Victor.

"Bummer, dude," David called out. "So I'm surprised..." He returned to the living room in sweat shorts, tugging a light pajama pullover past his head. "You said you're here to discuss my employment. I've got that dialed in with Sally and Darla. So unless you're here to offer up some more developmental gems..." David winked.

With a quick move Victor stepped forward and patted David's sculpted cheek, generating a look of surprise and unease on the young accountant's face. "Darla is a great manager, and a great person. I'm here to ensure she has a great team."

David's expression cycled rapidly from smiling to uncertainty. "You know I'll treat her right, VV. VV's okay now, you said?"

"VV is perfect. Do you live alone, David?"

"Yeah, I had a roomie, but about a month ago we had a knock-down throw-down fracas about—"

Victor backhanded David. The younger man's avoidance reaction was quick but late, leaving his face to absorb most of the short powerful stroke before his feet carried him stumbling sideways, the false support of an end table prolonging his awkward recovery. The table's lamp teetered before settling back in place.

"VV! No!" David pointed at him, jabbed his finger with each emphatic syllable, could have been scolding his dog.

Victor advanced. "I have rewritten and replayed a number of our encounters over the past year. They always start like that."

David stood his ground, and seized Victor's hand as it reached for him. "Stop it! What the...stop it!"

Victor's other hand grabbed a handful of David's pajama shirt. "No!" said David, grabbing that hand too and trying to pry it off. Victor levered in closer as David struggled to prevent it, intent on disconnecting from Victor's hands and creating separation, loosing a stream of angry objections. "No-no-sonofa...VV-no, stop it, damn it..."

Victor bared his fangs with a guttural hiss that bathed David's face in feral humidity. His protests trailed to a whimper. Victor punched him in the face, and again, this time a straight right hand with everything he had, sending David crashing against his dining room table and face down on the floor. Victor slugged him in the kidney, then with David clutching at his back, knelt over him and lifted his head by the hair.

"In case you are confused, David," said Victor, "this is not a come-on." He wrenched David's head to the side and plowed his fangs into David's flesh. A violent rush of rage and revulsion had Victor screaming deep in his throat as he drank.

The pilot cut back on the 767's thrusters. Darla picked her head off the back of her seat and the Blackberry from her lap. "Sounds pretty bad," she said in reference to the e-mail on the little screen.

The male flight attendant caught her eye from his jump seat. He shook head and finger and motioned for her to put the device away. Darla complied, telling Victor as she did, "Sounds like David lost a lot of blood."

The drive south to the home office of the Texahoma— now Bizco Diversified—parent company, Verrstagg GmbH, removed them quickly from the Dresden metro area.

Verrstagg had arranged for shuttle buses. After loitering at the shuttle pick-up point for an hour-plus, they and five other Houston-based employees left the busy airport just before ten a.m. local time.

The road they traveled wasn't the autobahn, but provided a smooth ride that had Victor's head lolling and then canted at an extreme angle over the top of the bench seat he shared with Darla. Only Darla had slept on the plane—the other five had been crammed into coach, while she had decompressed soon after take-off, work stack sliding off her lap to the floor, head nestled against Victor's shoulder. Only Victor slept on the shuttle bus, the others kept awake by his open-mouthed snoring and exposed fangs drying in the bus's aged-diesel air.

Outside the administrative office building resembling the von Trapp family manor, a Verrstagg representative awaited them. Victor was last to shake hands with Dieter Josch, a man with hair that appeared to have been sawed to its present length with a blunt knife.

"Hello. Welcome to Germany."

"It is good to see you again, Dieter."

Dieter's mouth made a big 'O' at the sight of Victor's

fangs. "So I was overruled! But welcome, of course."
Dieter reached for a second handshake; when Victor
hesitated, Dieter nodded eagerly, and was rewarded
with Victor's hand. "It is cold, isn't it?" He brought his
other hand in for confirmation. "Look at you—you're
Victor, Victor..."

"Thetherson."

"I remember you, very well. Funny when you say your
name, with your tongue darting between those teeth."
Dieter knuckled his own teeth and wiggled a finger like
a protruding worm. "I heard Giselda had invited the
vampire. I became quite upset. You're not what I had
imagined! Of course if I had only recalled that night at
the hotel, I would not have worried. I'm not very good at
putting two and two together—that's better left for you
accountants!"

Darla and the others had made it inside, while Victor
believed Dieter was intentionally keeping him in the
sun. The glare off the broad white front of the manor
watered his eyes despite the wraparound sunglasses.
The direct sunlight was scorching the skin around his
widow's peak, which had taken root to his scalp like a
creeping vine, allowing him to cut it short. A boil was
about to form, reinvigorating the burn bubble from
Saturday at Six Flags, risen in spite of a greasy coating
of sunscreen, mercifully deflated before Amberly could
be a stinker and pop it.

"I am no longer an accountant."

"Where? Where have they put you?"

"Special projects."

"Perfect!" Dieter clapped his hands, then couldn't wait
to put them on Victor again. "*Perfect* for the vampire.
Victor Thetherson, the roly-poly vampire."

Victor had anticipated being something of a spectacle,
but not like this. "If you don't mind, I'd really like to go
inside."

Dieter cocked his head. "Your accent is both local and
from the American South all at once," he marveled. "You

were German, at some point?"

"By blood only."

Dieter cackled. "You are hilarious! You are a fun vampire! This is going to be so much fun! Come in…"

Darla motioned him over to one end of the two-story foyer. "This is so German," she said, eyeing the massively framed paintings of Verrstagg's executives and their BMWs, under pikes and swords mounted between sturdy vertical beams of square-cut timber.

"Everything but the cuckoo clocks, am I right?" said Dieter, pointing their group down the hall beyond the receptionist's massive desk. The receptionist, separated from their passage by two yards of scarred mahogany, glanced up with a "Guten Tag"; and then for Victor, a second look, one that erased Dieter's outdated, first-impression-frozen-in-time perception of him. Her hand fingered the links of the black gold choker across her throat as she returned to making notation in a broad ledger book.

"We have been starting everyone off with a quick tour and then an escort to the guest houses for a nap," said Dieter as they passed a sitting room, the last of the classically appointed rooms before entering an American-style stretch of cubicles and offices.

"We shouldn't nap," said Darla. "If we put in a full day today, we'll sleep well tonight and be acclimated to your schedule in the morning."

"We strongly recommend a nap," said Dieter. "Of course I am sure this group is hardier than the average. But we've seen too many American zombies on their first day here. Very few of his kind, though," he referred to Victor, drawing uneasy chuckles from the other Americans who had shared his shuttle.

"Zombie here," said one of them, a middle-aged man clutching a periwinkle blue Westchase ballcap that he had doffed upon entering the manor. "I didn't sleep a wink on the big bird—and then of course I fell asleep ten minutes before we landed in Dresden. I got a cross-eyed buzz like I've been drinking all night and all morning too."

Four others seconded the sensation.

"For this visit," said Dieter, "having you fresh for the evening might be more important than having you present in the daytime."

"I'm not much of a night person," said Darla with a fresh-face and a chuckle. "A couple hours after the sun goes down, and I'm fighting to stay awake."

"When in Rome, Ms. Kieler," said Dieter. "You are here to help celebrate Verrstagg's one hundred-fiftieth anniversary. Not many companies have lived so long. Especially not through what we in the East have endured. We are very proud of this accomplishment. Most everyone is already over at the beer garden, preparing themselves for the festivities. You are welcome to go there too; but please, a nap first. These celebrations always run late."

"'Always'?" said the middle-aged zombie. "How often do you have a beer garden set up?"

"Most weekends," said Dieter. "We only turn one hundred and fifty once. But there is always a reason to celebrate."

Down the aisle a group from Chicago was talking to two local executives. Jay Hansen saw them and walked over. "Welcome to Germany, Darla."

"This is unbelievable," said Darla. "I was hesitant to come, but now I'm glad I'm here. I've never been overseas, I have to confess. I knew it would be different, but this is kind of..." She looked at Victor and blushed. "It's kind of magical."

"The time zone change is a challenge," said Jay. "I flew into London two days ago to avoid the all-night flight hangover. I wanted to be clear-headed for my meetings here."

"I had a great nap on the plane," said Darla. "Victor got me moved up to first class. Thank goodness, because I need to be fresh for my meeting this afternoon with

Kurt."

"Why are you meeting with Bleckmeier?" Jay wanted to know.

"He just wanted to meet with me," said Darla, somewhat evasive.

Jay nodded without comprehension. "Well you might want to catch him quick. I was just down at the beer tent, and he was halfway through a glass of beer bigger than my head." Now he finally gave Victor a greeting, of sorts. "Chleber has you flying first class, huh? That's kind of a waste of money, right? Since you probably don't sleep much. Not at night anyway, right?"

Victor savored his first time not having to answer one of Jay's non-questions.

"You seem right at home here," said Jay. "I'm always ready to leave as soon as I touch down." He checked for Germans within earshot. "But you fit in here. Don't you think?" he asked Darla. "Maybe you'll feel so at home, you won't want to go back."

"Don't say that," said Darla. "We need Victor stateside."

"Not sure about that," said Jay. For Darla's benefit he smiled, as if it had been good-natured ribbing. "But Chleber's sure, so..." He crossed his arms and broadened his stance, stabilized for a thorough evaluation. "Something has changed. You're working out? Rogaine, or whatever?"

"I think we've all lost weight from merger stress," said Darla. "It's probably not healthy, but I have to say I'm not unhappy about it. A couple more mergers and I'll be right where I want to be."

Victor slid next to Jay and put an arm around his shoulder, whispering in his ear, "I think your wife would be eager to see how I've changed." He nodded to Darla. "Shoot a few seconds of video with your cellphone and send it to Jay."

"Blackberry," said Darla, holding up the device. "I don't have a clue whether I can take video." She frowned

at it. "Ten more e-mails. I wish I hadn't brought this
with me."

Dieter joined them. "It's good to see close relations
between our American associates. Hopefully we will
have some of that between us before you leave. You want
a picture? We have someone who will be taking photos
and film of our gathering, but unfortunately I believe
she is already at the beer garden."

Jay was stiff under Victor's arm, making a subtle
attempt to escape.

"Give Dieter your cellphone," Victor told Jay. "I know
it has video capability."

"Let's skip the picture," said Jay, now struggling. "You
need to let go, Vic."

"Of course." Victor squeezed the junction of Jay's
shoulder and neck before relinquishing his hold. "We
wouldn't want your wife to worry."

Jay brusquely excused himself. "So," said Dieter. "I
should have mentioned about Giselda. I'm afraid she is
on an extended absence. But she sent word that she
would very much like to see you. I was asked to urge you
to come visit her. Tonight. She said you will have a lot to
talk about."

"Tonight?" said Darla, heavy with disapproval. "At
her house?" Her eyebrows shot up. "Tell me she isn't the
one who invited you here?" She looked to Dieter, who
gave an elaborate shrug that ruined his attempted
discretion.

"Giselda and I have unfinished business," said Victor.
"But I can assure you that it is all business." He waited
for Darla to look into his eyes a moment longer. "And I
am thankful it brought me here."

Darla's eyes sparkled. She remembered Dieter and
struggled to adopt the unenthusiastic, no-nonsense
career woman persona Victor had come to know. "Jay
tells me that Kurt Bleckmeier is already at the beer
garden. I was really hoping to discuss some accounting
issues with him."

"I'm afraid the rumor is true," said Dieter. "Perhaps it would be best for me to take you over there now, as time is likely of the essence. We can drop the others at the guest house, and then the two of us can continue to the party."

Darla considered this while looking at Victor. In an instant her professional demeanor was gone, unable to assert itself on a face that couldn't stop glowing. "You know, I could do with a little freshening up. Maybe even a nap. There's always tomorrow to talk business."

"No promises," said Dieter.

The guest house backed up to a dense forest that climbed up and out of sight over a gentle rise. Before dropping them off and promising to return in three hours, Dieter informed them that their quarters were a converted East German military barracks in turn converted from a milking parlor. Victor's room was still nearly as Spartan as it might have been for the milkmaids and the soldiers. The knock at his door carried crisply across the tile floor.

Darla did not pause in slipping inside. "Hi." She put her hand to her mouth. "Everything echoes. I'm afraid someone will hear me."

"Is that bad?"

"That's true, they could assume we're talking accounting." Darla's gaze was at the floor as she gathered her thoughts. "I was all gung-ho to get a lot of work done. But something about being here is changing my mindset."

"There is something in the air."

"It's romantic," said Darla. She searched Victor's eyes, which were bloodshot from lack of sleep and an excess of daylight. "It's probably pretty clear how much I think of you. I'm really glad you're here. I'm sorry for barging in here, but I really just wanted to spend a little more time with you. I can't completely explain it, but I'm definitely drawn to you."

A wave of warm emotion rose unexpectedly within Victor Thetherson and broke across his face as a smile. Then he remembered who he now was, and eliminated the smile for a wider-eyed gaze. "I too have been waiting for the opportunity to get you alone, Darla Kieler. Come to me now."

Victor leaned in and so did Darla. He moved past her face and dropped his mouth upon her neck. She gasped with momentary pleasure.

And then shrieked when he bit her. Darla spasmed away from him and Victor's fangs ripped dual gashes across her throat. "What are you doing?! Victor!" She looked wildly around for something to staunch the bleeding. "God...you bit me. God!"

"I...I didn't, I didn't know what, I mean—"

"You thought I wanted to be *bit?*" Darla pressed her palm tight to her neck, leaning forward, staring incredulously at him. "Give me something."

"Sorry." Victor sprang to action, hustling into the bathroom and returning with an off-white towel. He expected Darla to slap his hand away, but she allowed him to tend to her. Tears spilled down her cheeks as he held the towel to her neck and met her gaze. "I am truly sorry. I was.... I was stupid."

"Why would you think that?"

"Because, because every woman...no. I am simply sorry." Victor pulled the towel away. "It's not too bad." Fresh blood seeped into the gashes. He covered the wound again, and waited for the image, and the taste of her blood in his mouth, to fade. "I need to go. I need to go find you a bandage."

Darla nodded. She pointed at his mouth. "Can you wipe my blood off your lips?"

Victor swiped the backs of his hands across his lips, then pulled up a tail of his black dress shirt and scrubbed off the rest.

"Better." Darla wiped her cheeks. She wore no mascara to smudge. "I like you, you know. Not because of your vampirism. Despite it." She raised on tiptoes and softly kissed his lips. "That's what I wanted," she said.

Victor's chest constricted, muscles twisting his ribcage in a most pleasurable way.

What he felt in his chest was written all over his face. Darla saw it and beamed, releasing more tears. "I really like you," she said, laughing and sobbing. "I really like you, Victor."

In foreign territory—being liked, being liked as a vampire—Victor could only nod.

It was enough for Darla. "Should I be jealous of you going to see this woman?"

"It is not that kind of visit."

"You better go get me that bandage first."

He nodded. "I am so sorry."

"Hey, it happens. You're a vampire, right?"

Victor grinned. "I am a vampire."

Walking the gradual incline to the manor, croaking insects signaling the transition to evening, Victor laid eyes upon a gangly man in a black felt gaucho hat, cut-off chaps, and sandals, approaching and waving to him, all American and no cowboy.

"Tripp...?! Why are you here?"

"Because you should know better, that's why," said Tripp. They met alongside a pond covered in lily pads. "You knew I wanted to come with you to Germany. Where was my invite?"

"I didn't know you could," said Victor. "You're a broke college student whose only income is a volunteer job at the blood bank."

"Where there's a will there's a way," said Tripp. "By the way, did I just see you merrily whistling up this path? I don't think I've ever seen merry or whistling from you. What gives?"

"It is just good to see you," said Victor. "Honestly, you're here to vacation with me?"

"I'm here for you." said Tripp. "Let's put it that way."

"I am flattered. I was just on my way to the administrative offices." They walked together. "I hate to ask what this cost you. And my return flight is in two days. Not nearly enough time to get your money's worth."

"The beautiful thing?" said Tripp. "It's not my money. So the return on my investment was guaranteed positive the second I got off the plane and grabbed a great big stein of beer for the road."

"I don't believe drinking and driving is acceptable even in Germany."

"Beer sales are two-thirds of their economy," said Tripp. "Of course it's okay."

"How did you find me?"

"I had the Labs' administrator do a little sleuthing. Whether Jimbo is tracking down research publications on chromosomal telomere maintenance or hunting vampires across the Pond, he's gold. Longer Labs actually paid for my flight."

"Why?"

"So I could deliver some news." Tripp made eye contact while holding the manor's back door for Victor. "We figured it out. We know how your vampirism was transmitted."

"Duh," said Victor.

"No duh," said Tripp. "It's not what you think."

Victor froze in the doorway. "So?"

Tripp looked around. "It's delicate. I'd rather not tell you here." He flipped up the collar of his plaid short-sleeve button shirt. "Can you leave campus?"

Victor nodded. He left Tripp outside, and returned minutes later with a bandage in his pocket. They walked the path back down to the guesthouse. "And I have another mission," said Tripp. "In exchange for this ticket, I promised to get a blood sample from your biter. Is she here?"

"You can kill two missions with one stone," said Victor. "I'm meeting Giselda tonight. At her house."

Tripp brought his hands together with a pop. "Wunderbar."

Victor gave him a sideways look. "Giselda will likely have the same mission, you know. Maybe she will agree to provide a blood sample only on condition of reciprocity."

"Then you better damn well protect me," said Tripp. "Oh jeez, before I forget—God help me, guess who was on my flight?"

Victor winced and hung his head. "Barbara."

Tripp laughed, and then laughed again, a big robust *har*. "Eugene. From the Bank. Eugene, the vampire hunter."

Victor darkened. "This is too much..." He reconsidered his first impulse; decided it was the right one. "He is truly intent on destroying me. I'm going to have to kill him."

"I've never been in a conversation that involved murdering someone," said Tripp. "My intuition tells me that my response should be something like, 'Hey, let's call the cops instead.' But like I said, I'm a novice. Eugene said he was here to visit some old Army buddies."

"That strains the bounds of credulity on two counts," said Victor. "Army service, and friends."

"You've gotten a lot funnier since you started biting folks, I'll tell you that."

"Darla has seen him lurking around my old office, too."

"Who's Darla?"

"Darla was from Westchase, our merger partner. She took over my old department."

"Your *old* department? You got a new job?"

"I haven't kept you in the loop, have I?"

"I'd say not," said Tripp. "So this Darla is here?"

"In my room," said Victor as they approached the barracks. He held up the bandage. "I accidentally bit her."

"Accidentally my ass," said Tripp.

"I thought she was like all the others." Victor peeked in the window and saw Darla sitting on the bed, staring at the wall. "It turns out she likes me, Tripp."

"Well what do you know." Tripp clapped Victor on the shoulder. "And?"

"Yeah," said Victor. "I like her."

"Then stop biting her."

"I know, Tripp."

Tripp's face suddenly elongated, eyebrows up and jaw hanging slack. "Vic, did you...tell me you didn't nail her. Nail her in the passionate, love-filled way, I mean."

Victor snorted dismissively. "After all these years? I am not sure I could, even if she wanted to."

Darla's bleeding had stopped. With Victor looking everywhere but at her throat, Tripp cleaned her neck and applied the bandage, trimmed to a relatively unobtrusive size. When Darla emerged from the bathroom wearing one of the high-frocked blouses she was partial to, the effect of the attack was barely noticeable.

"So you're still going to the beer garden?" Tripp marveled. "Vic, you've got yourself a trooper. And a cute one at that."

"I'm fine with just being a trooper," said Darla, somewhere between good-natured and a weary acceptance of her station in life. "The woman you're going to see," she said to Victor. "She's the one who bit you, isn't she."

"Yes."

She looked at Tripp. "I think you're the trooper here."

"Anything for science, ma'am." Tripp gave Victor a friendly backhand to the chest. "But a couple steins for the road would go a long way toward maintaining my trooper mentality."

The GPS in Tripp's rental car took them into the

forest. The road was in premature shadow, a thin dark artery through tall trees and dense undergrowth.

"Tell me what your testing showed," said Victor, after Tripp showed no inclination to take the initiative, possibly pouting over Victor's refusal to agree to a couple traveling beers.

"Tell me what you remember from that night," said Tripp.

"Not a lot. Drinking with the Germans, falling in lust with Giselda, getting it on with her. Waking up, bit."

"So you do remember having sex with her?"

"Vaguely," said Victor. "I've actually been having flashbacks...whoa, look at that—was that a bat?"

"I didn't see it."

"A big bat or a drunk hawk," said Victor.

"Cruella hurrying home," said Tripp. "So you're not sure whether you were in the saddle for the full eight seconds?"

"That night is really blurry. You know what, I'll tell you something." Victor soured from the memory. "My worst fear is that I repressed what actually happened, because maybe nothing happened. I've been...I have an issue, with...that process." He paused, hoping for a fraternal response from Tripp, who stared at the road, showing no recognition or compassion. Their age gap yawned in the tight Euro-vehicle space between them. "It's an issue a lot of guys get when they get a little older, with work pressures and all. It's normal—"

"What is erectile dysfunction, Alex," said Tripp. "You confessed it to me a long time ago. I figured that was just with Barbara. Wholly understandable."

Victor squirmed. "Maybe, but...I haven't had a, uh, ejaculation in four years. Not even on my own time, if you know what I mean."

"Again, I would attribute that to the Barbara Factor," said Tripp. "That woman's aura is like watching a sex ed video on gonorrhea."

"That probably isn't fair," said Victor. "I think I share

a lot of the blame."

"No you don't."

"I was a complete disappointment to her."

"All the more reason for her to pretend like you're not," Tripp argued. "Men are a basket of insecurities. That's a woman's job, to lie to us to whatever extent necessary. Women fantasize all the time—there's no excuse for her not to have made you into a fantasy man, too. At least once a week."

Two tight turns slowed them before the trees ended and the land fell away. The paved road necessarily made a sharp eastern turn and skirted the cliff, becoming dirt. Below, the cliff transitioned to valley, trees resuming where they had left off, interrupted again in the far distance by the river Elbe, Amazonian in its path through thick forest.

They arrived at a gate with a sign in bold red letters. The gate was open. The sign was in German. They drove on through.

"So you may or may not have had carnal relations with Ms. deVil."

"Does it really matter?"

"Makes all the difference," said Tripp.

The road plunged back into the trees and took them through a series of sharp turns with clearance for passing sedans, perhaps a Euro-van, but no more.

"After one hundred meters turn left onto Schwarzflock Lane," said the GPS man in a barely recognizable sequence of poorly-spaced English phonemes.

"Tell me what the lab found out," said Victor. He pointed at a path up ahead that the forest was busy reclaiming. "There."

"It hasn't been a hundred meters," said Tripp. "Okay, here's the verdict: Your vampirism was sexually transmitted."

Victor's jaw dropped. "What? Seriously? So we did, we must have.... So *that's* good, anyway." He slumped back in the seat, gazing back in time. "It explains why I haven't given it to anyone."

"You almost gave it to Darla, sounds like."

"Oh my God," said Victor. "So you're saying I can't...? I can *bite* women, but I can't.... Oh come on." He cradled his face in his hand, and then pointed at the next nearly invisible opening in the woods. "There."

"Herr GPS says no," said Tripp. "Sorry, by the way."

Victor shook his head for awhile, through Tripp's selection of the succeeding left, onto the remnant of a Renaissance-era cart trail. "That is really, really unfair."

"Tell it to Cruella," said Tripp. He stole glances at Victor, who was pounding his door with increasing intensity, while wrestling the car over rocks, ruts and roots that promised to jounce them against encroaching boulders if they traveled any faster than a crawl. "Stay cool, Viccy. Knowing the *how* is going to make all the difference in the long run for our research. We have a name for that kind of news: far from good, but good from afar. Stick that in your pipe and ponder it."

Victor did not ponder, he brooded, but he did stop abusing the rental, and moments later they were in the clear again, on a loop driveway paved with small river-rubbed stones and pebbles.

"Cruella lives in style," said Tripp. The house was two-and-a-half stories, of jagged irregular stones that gave character to an architecturally flat front. A hen and a cat strolled up to their car. "You know we could be walking into a den of vampires here."

"And you were warned, by Darla and me."

"I'm just saying, the road beer would have been nice." Tripp looked worried. "This might be the stupidest thing I've done in a long time."

"As long as you don't become aroused, you'll be fine," Victor said with some bitterness. He stepped out and the hen pecked his foot. He nudged it away and the bird stepped back in and pecked his foot again.

"That's how Mildred says hello," said the woman now

in the doorway of the house. Giselda Munsch, aka Cruella deVil. "She won't stop until you pick her up."

With some hesitation Victor crouched and picked up the orange-hued chicken, which drew head and feet into its body and relaxed in his hands.

There was a yowl and a yelp from the driver's side.

"Not the cat," said Giselda.

Tripp shook his hand, then with wide eyes held it up for Victor to see the stripe of blood.

Victor licked his lips and winked. "Thank you for inviting me," he said to Giselda as he approached the house. "This is my friend Tripp. He works for an anti-aging lab in Houston that has been studying me. Tripp is hoping to interview you."

"As you wish," said Giselda.

Victor stopped in front of her. "I hope you are feeling better."

"My ailment is of the mind, not the body," said Giselda, "and therefore difficult to cure." She hadn't aged a day, tall and thin with prominent features, captivating Arabesque eyes and a dark streak along her swept back platinum-blonde hair. Her English was nearly accent-free. Her canines were short and pointed. "But not impossible. Please come in."

Tripp spotted a pump in the direction of a low-slung stable built with stones more rounded than those that studded the house. "I've got a little, uh, some red stuff going here, which I don't want getting all over, so give me a second to freshen up a bit." He jogged to the pump and began working the lever.

"I am excited you agreed to visit me," said Giselda, examining Victor. "I assumed you might be interested to hear more about that night."

"That fateful night," said Victor, enjoying echoing Tripp.

"Indeed," said Giselda. "Obviously much has transpired since then. You are a different man." She gave him a strange look. "We miscalculated."

"What do you mean?"

"Seeing as how you are clearly biting people," said Giselda, "and still alive."

Victor locked his eyes upon her as he struggled to make sense of it. Giselda held his gaze, eagerly. "Who's 'we'? You say that 'we' miscalculated."

Tripp trotted up, cat-scratched hand stuffed out of sight in his pocket. He looked at the two of them, then panned up the front of the house past the overhanging eaves to a sky going purple in the dusk. He took a deep breath. "Okay. I'm ready."

Giselda stood aside. "Please."

Three options were presented once inside the entryway: a staircase before them, a dining room to their left, and Giselda's recommendation, a parlor to their right, where couches awaited them on either side of a coffee table. Loaded bookshelves occasionally parted to display dense paintings, of foxhunts and landscapes, possibly of the Elbe valley below. The house was lit with candles and the soft glow of periodic sconces on the walls, two of them marking a diminutive door in the corner.

"I gave up alcohol some time ago," said Giselda. "All I can offer you is tea."

"I can relate," said Victor. "Alcohol does not treat me well any more either."

"You can't relate," said Giselda. "But I know what you're referring to. Please sit." She did so on the far sofa. Victor and Tripp selected the near one, closer to the exit. "I have wondered how much you were able to discover on your own," she said to Victor. "Very little, it appears."

"How about that tea?" said Tripp, squirming, rocking, arms tightly crossed. Victor thought his friend's teeth might start to chatter.

"In a minute," said Giselda. "Victor, I did not bite you. Contrary to popular belief, I am not a vampire."

"Come on lady," said Tripp. "Yes you are."

Giselda fixed a stare upon him. "Only in your dreams, young man."

"Then who bit me?" Victor demanded.

"Surely you recall Agnes, our traveling secretary?"

"The older lady?" said Victor. "The old, really old lady, all wrinkled up with the uh, the..." He pointed thumbs over his shoulder.

"Hunchback," said Giselda.

"Yes. Yes, but...huh?" Victor scooted and leaned forward. "No. Her...her, bit me?"

"Agnes bit you," Giselda confirmed.

"But she..." Victor was struggling to comprehend. "She had normal teeth."

"Those were dentures," said Giselda. "Agnes had already lost her natural teeth to gum disease before she became a vampire. She had two sets of dentures, one with fangs. She would just swap them out at the right moment."

"No." Victor's mind raced back in time. "That doesn't make sense, because then that would mean..." He stood up at a sudden vivid memory of the sight of the smell of lavender, turbulent in the air around him, with Agnes's face mercifully foggy in the middle of it all. "Oh no."

"Holy Mr. Crowly!" Tripp slapped his thighs, arriving at the same realization. "You did the old broad!"

Giselda reclined on the sofa, admiring Tripp. "So you have done your homework? You know how the vampirism is transmitted? To be clear, Victor, Agnes did *you*, not the other way around. There can be no doubt who was in the driver's seat that night. As her vampirism progressed, Agnes had become very strong, and very aggressive."

"The personality change sounds familiar," said Tripp, hooking a thumb at Victor for Giselda's benefit.

"I don't like what's happening here," said Victor.

"And I'm just getting into it," said Tripp. "Honestly," he said to Giselda, "no alcohol? Because you've got to tell us the story of Agnes the vampire. And that story demands a Lowenbrau."

"You are a man of refined tastes, I see," said Giselda. She checked her watch. "I will tell you Agnes's story. With tea." She left the room.

Victor remained on his feet. "We need to leave."

"Come on now, what's the rush?"

"You're thinking you're going to get laid, aren't you?"

"Nooo," said Tripp unconvincingly. "If anything does go down, though, check on us periodically, okay? She may not be a vampire, but she is German, and I need to be in some condition to fly home on Monday."

"This woman does not have our best interests at heart," said Victor.

"That's not a prerequisite," said Tripp.

Victor stewed. Giselda returned with tea on a tray. "Help yourself," she told them. She sat back into the couch and crossed her legs. "Agnes. Until five years ago, she was a normal woman. Too old to still be working, but Klaus Bielman, our CEO, kept her on. She has ties to the company's original founders. And she did a fine job." Giselda nodded at Tripp as he poured hot water through the silver tea cage, offering to prepare a cup for her. "Please."

Tripp walked around the table to deliver the cup to her, sitting next to her, instantly preoccupied with prepping a cup for himself.

Giselda smiled and returned to her story. "And then Agnes met a man. A vampire. I warned her, of course. I knew Agnes for many, many years. She was something of a mother for me. I told her nothing good could come of this relationship. But she seemed to fall in love. And I believe he did love her, too. I willed myself to be happy for her, not to interfere with her chance at happiness. Agnes was not rich by any means, and she was not, if I may be forgiven, much to look at."

"For us dudes, it's what's on the inside that counts, huh Vic?" Tripp needled him, receiving a dark glance.

"If you think she was homely when you met her,"

Giselda said to Victor, "you should have seen her before she became a vampire. Again, forgive me," she said, touching her chest and glancing heavenward. "But that factored into my happiness for her. He was a gentleman, always treating her very well. I was worried he would bite her of course. He never did. Then one night, after months of courtship, it happened. She became a vampire. Of course I never expected that it would happen through sex."

"We've isolated the exact process in our lab," said Tripp. He reclined and slung an arm across the back of the couch behind Giselda. "It's pretty fascinating. I have some schematics our lead scientist drew up. I'll show them to you, a little later."

Giselda paused. "My guess is that you only understand half of the process. Soon after Agnes was changed, her vampire lover Magnus died. Agnes was distraught."

"Magnus and Agnes," said Tripp. "That's the title of a story that demands a happy ending."

"A happy ending is our goal." Giselda settled in closer to him. "For many months Agnes did nothing. I would help her obtain blood from the blood repository."

"You're the German Tripp!" said Tripp. "That's my role."

Giselda sipped her tea. "I should have remained in that role. I took her to a club—right or wrong, I wanted her to find someone, to help her forget Magnus. She did meet someone, and bit him. Agnes claimed to be repentant. But very soon after, she bit someone else. And again. Eventually, fairly quickly, I lost track of her, as her feeding accelerated."

"Oh the parallels," said Tripp. He dropped his arm to give Giselda a squeeze of camaraderie, clucking at Victor.

"And then one day, very close to when we were to leave for the United States, Agnes came to me. Right here, very late at night. She was covered in blood."

"Vic," said Tripp, encouraging him to pay close attention.

"She had just attacked someone. Agnes had gone too far, she had drunk too much. He was dead. It was horrible. She was weeping and babbling. I could not console her. Later I realized she was mourning the loss of two lives: the man she had killed, and her own."

Victor stood for a second time. "This is nothing we need to hear." He had a somewhat inexplicable but ever mounting hatred for Giselda that was more than matched by the loathing for him that flowed from her pores. "Tripp, we need to leave."

"You wanted to understand your origin, did you not?" said Giselda, fixing him with a malignant stare. "I believe you should also understand your fate."

"That's a teaser we shouldn't resist, buddy," said Tripp. "Have some tea."

"It is most likely drugged," said Victor.

"That would be wholly unnecessary," said Giselda.

Tripp looked at her. "Okay, that creeped me out a little."

"That night," said Giselda, ignoring him, "Agnes became committed to ensuring she would never hurt anyone again. I obviously had the same goal. We planned together. We began searching for the perfect candidate to pass the vampirism to."

"Translation error," said Tripp. "To 'pass' something in English means transferring ownership. 'Share' would be more exact. That's when you give it and still keep it. 'Infect' would work."

"I am German," said Giselda. "I am nothing if not exact."

"That's not the way vampirism works," said Tripp, "but go on. I promise not to gloat when it becomes apparent I'm right."

"Likewise." Giselda forced a smile. "It was difficult for Agnes and me to contemplate *passing* the vampire's curse to someone we knew. We also knew we had to be incredibly selective. We wanted no more bloodshed. We wanted the curse to end forever. Whoever we chose had to be extremely unlikely to bite someone. Or to pass it along to someone who would."

Tripp looked at Victor. "Ouch, man."

Victor saw nothing but Giselda's calm, haughty face, and his eyes were filled with hate. The only thing keeping him from pouncing on her was the greater impulse to run. "You should understand," he told her, "that I am no longer unlikely to bite someone."

"And I see you are now fully capable of exerting your will," said Giselda. "You have developed yourself admirably. As I said, Agnes and I erred. During our interactions with you in the Houston office, prior to that fateful night..."

Tripp mouthed *fateful night*, but Victor ignored him.

"...we saw the lack of respect you received from your peers and your staff," Giselda continued. "And your lack of respect for yourself. We were convinced that you were the right choice."

"I have respect," Victor gave emphasis to each word.

"Cool your engines, Viccy," said Tripp.

"It is fear," said Giselda. "They fear you. If this is not apparent to you yet, it will be soon."

Victor bowed his head, eyes squeezed shut.

"That night was the saddest of my life," he heard Giselda continue her tale. "As the party wore on and you became more and more inebriated, it became apparent our crime was going to work. You were too drunk to even realize I was weeping as I kissed you goodbye."

"Shut up," Victor growled.

"As Agnes went to take my place, I attempted to stop her. She had to remind me again that she was giving her life to save an untold number of innocents."

"I don't think I like this story any more either," said Tripp. He retrieved his arm and leaned away from Giselda. The sofa was deep and enveloping, requiring additional effort to fully separate from her.

"You were born in the sexual death throes of the vampire Agnes," said Giselda. "Do you understand, Victor?"

"Are you saying she committed suicide?" Tripp demanded, now on his feet and joining Victor halfway to the parlor entrance.

"In a manner of speaking," said Giselda, rising too as she set her teacup on the table. "A suicide that is unique to this type of vampire. Agnes was special in making her choice so soon, before she had become exhausted from causing misery and death for a hundred years or more. Perhaps most people would never choose to end it. We expected you to do so unwittingly."

"Godammit lady, spit it out," said Tripp, voice cracking, taking a step back and trying to pull Victor with him.

"Ejaculate and die," said Giselda, her face suffused with loathing. "It's as simple as that. We estimated you would die within the week, alone in a bathroom with a Playboy magazine on your lap."

Victor stomped his feet and clutched the sides of his head, a brilliant rendition of the outwitted Rumplestiltskin before he went through the floor.

"Holy shit!" said Tripp. "Your erectile dysfunction saved your life!"

"Under other circumstances I would not have told you this." Giselda moved around the couch, heading for the small door. "Because you would surely attempt to avoid death by choosing celibacy, continuing to make victims of those around you. Thankfully, I have made an acquaintance, an elderly gentleman, a throwback to a more savage time, who has committed—"

The two men whirled at the *whump* of something slamming into the parlor's tall multi-paned window.

"Thankfully," Giselda restarted her sentence, striding for the window, keeping the sofas and then a small dining table between them, "this gentleman has a young man willing and able to take all choice away from you.

Someone who dreams of the same happy ending for you." As her hand reached for the window clasp, a gunstock crashed through a pane at eye level, followed by a knee and most of a leg three panes lower. Giselda recoiled with glass in her face as a foot and a gloved hand crashed through two more panes.

With each limb immobilized through minor impalement on the shards, the man in the window tried to head-butt the pane in front of his face, dislodging his Zorro mask but failing to crack the glass. He stared at them goggle-eyed.

Tripp gaped. "Eugene!"

Giselda screamed—Victor was upon her at the small door she had intended as her escape. Tripp leaped sofa and hurdled coffee table, clipping it with his heel and stumbling into a jolting tackle, crashing with Victor into the corner china cabinet. Both rolled away as tumbling glassware and ceramics beat open the glass door and smashed to the floor. Only three ornate beer steins remained on display.

"I'm going to bite her," Victor snarled. He pitched Tripp aside—both of them for the moment marveling at how easy this was. Then he prevented Giselda's second attempt to flee, pinning her against a bookcase, pressing his forehead against hers. "I am on the brink of insanity with how much I hate you," he hissed, voice husky and quavering. "You chose me, expecting me to die. Do you see the poetic justice right now?"

"Kill yourself," Giselda whispered, sobs coming on fast like hiccups.

"Shall I make love to you instead?" Victor hissed.

"That *would* be more poetic," said Tripp, back on his feet, approaching more carefully this time. "But I think neither is correct. We can figure this out, Vic. Come on, buddy. Dr. Speer can figure it out." Wheeling at the sharp snap of beveled glass and a shriek of pain, Tripp caught a glimpse of Eugene dislodged, falling back out of the window.

Victor maintained his focus on Giselda. "Leave us, Tripp."

"Go wait in the car? That sort of thing? Vic, you know I can't let you do this."

Victor looked at him through white and black wisps of Giselda's hair. "I don't need your permission."

"Vic, don't you see? This is exactly what she was seeing with Agnes—"

Victor roared back, "This is me not getting pushed around anymore!" He slammed Giselda into the door, a thick plank of delicately carved oak, topping out barely an inch above her head. He gripped her throat and brought her face to face again, before shoving her once more, propelling himself away, cursing. "Take her if you want her!"

"No wanting here," said Tripp. "Chick's a black widow. Let's just hightail it and—"

"Not yet," said Victor, marching out of the parlor. "Someone is going to pay."

"Not Eugene," said Tripp, in pursuit. "He's harmless."

A crossbow bolt smashed through a formerly intact pane of glass high up the window and drove deep into a ceiling beam high above.

"That really doesn't disprove my point," said Tripp. He spoke to himself, as Giselda had finally made it through the short door, and Victor was already outside.

Eugene had parked his minivan in the flowerbed in front of the house, the launching pad for his attempted grand entrance. Now he sat amongst wilted violets, propped against the rear tire, bleeding, with Mildred pecking him in the foot. Eugene was attempting to re-arm his crossbow.

Victor hurdled a low hedge and ran at him. "Ahg!" Eugene gurgled. He swung and scored pathetically with the stock of the crossbow and then tried to stab Victor with the bolt. Victor wrenched the bolt from Eugene's grasp and flung it aside. He grabbed the vampire killer by belt and throat and yanked him aloft while Mildred squawked in protest. Carrying Eugene at hip level, legs dangling, arms flailing, head bobbing and curses strangled, Victor marched past the minivan and around the corner of the house.

The backyard was asymmetrically bounded by an eight-foot hedgerow that Victor suspected followed the cliff. Upon using Eugene as a ram to burst through the tangled foliage, he was proved right.

A whispering updraft and the smattering of twinkling lights along the distant Elbe gave measure to the inky drop-off.

Victor swung Eugene back, causing a sharp hedgerow branch to gouge the young man's pimpled forehead, then pitched him screaming out and over the edge of the cliff.

After fighting his way back through the hedgerow, Victor came face to face with Tripp.

"You didn't."

"I will wait for you in the car."

"Jesus, Vic." Tripp protected his face and dove into the hedgerow, struggling yelping and cursing through the twined brambles. Behind him, Victor tried the back door of Giselda's house.

Five minutes later Tripp dropped into the little sedan's driver's seat, breathing heavily. "I couldn't see a thing. I called to him and didn't hear anything. I didn't dare try to get to him. I have no idea how high that cliff is."

"Pretty high," said Victor. His hands were shaking. "I shouldn't have done it. You don't have to say anything." He ran both hands over his firmly-anchored widow's peak. "I couldn't stop, I couldn't even think it through." After a deep breath he nodded with resolution. "I need to bring that under control."

"That is a ridiculous understatement." Tripp slammed his palms on the steering wheel. "What am I supposed to do?" He looked at the house and back to Victor. "You didn't go back in there, did you?"

"The door was locked," said Victor. He didn't clarify

that it was the little parlor door that had been locked—locked, and sturdy enough to resist his attempts to kick it in. The energy he had expended had drained him of anger, if not bloodlust.

Tripp drove them out of the loop driveway. He tapped the docked cellphone that had come with the rental. "You call the police. You tell them whatever you want, but you get them out here to start searching for Eugene."

"I am certain Giselda has already made that call."

"I don't care." Tripp glanced and then made it a double-take. "Vic, you do it!" He pounded the steering wheel and the sedan lurched and scraped tree branches on Victor's side. "There is no debate," Tripp continued to yell and pound, now more safely on the ceiling. "You do the right thing."

"You're right." Victor removed the phone from its docking station. "Tripp, you don't need to worry. Over the past two months, I have learned to control many things in my life. I can control this too."

Tripp shook his head vehemently, lips sucked tight over his teeth and mashed together. "That's not good enough. I saw you, Vic. I witnessed it. That was the scariest thing I've ever seen."

"I understand." With long curved thumbnail Victor searched the cellphone's English menu. "Until I can master my emotions, it's a good thing I am quickly running out of enemies."

"Not funny." Tripp continued to shake his head, now turning them onto the arterial dirt road. "You know...no, never mind. I was going to say you could be in a crapload of trouble—but who cares about you? What about Eugene? Holy hell."

"Would you rather he kill me?" Victor snapped at him, stabbing the entry for *Emergency*.

A woman answered with something unintelligible. "I am reporting an accident," said Victor. The woman began to respond, but he talked over her. "Please go to the residence of Giselda Munsch and investigate. Auf Wiedersehen." He disconnected the call.

Tripp grimaced. "Not exactly what I had in mind."

Victor sat in silence, replaying the scene in Giselda's parlor and growing increasingly agitated as they drove through the gate and turned onto the forest road. "Is this what *I* had in mind?" he finally barked. "Did you hear what she told me? My vampirism is a death sentence! If I have sex—if I ejaculate—if I have a wet stinking dream—I *die*."

"Do you really want to live as a vampire?" Tripp countered with the same intensity.

"What? What," Victor spluttered, "what are you saying? Kill myself? Let Eugene pound a stake—"

"I'm *saying*," Tripp interrupted, "your whole focus should be on getting *cured*. On getting home and walking into our lab, and not walking out until you're cured."

"Sure," Victor scoffed. "I'm sure that's going to happen. Like no one has tried before."

"Maybe they have and maybe they haven't. How do you know? Maybe nobody had developed a vaccine for smallpox before Jenner did. Oh yeah, that's right, no one had."

"Bah," said Victor.

"Bah-bah," said Tripp.

At the entrance to Verrstagg's headquarters they saw the glow and heard the music from the beer tent on the other side of the manor.

"A beer has never sounded better," said Victor. "At least not since I was bitten."

Tripp was incredulous. "You're seriously going to the beer garden?"

"You are too. We are going to hash through this."

"I'm not hashing through anything." Tripp stopped them in front of the manor, windows ablaze but with no movement apparent inside. "You need to get out of

Dodge. You need to leave the country."

"The emergency call came from a phone registered to you. Maybe you better get out of Dodge."

Tripp stared at him. He gripped the steering wheel and nodded. "Okay. I'm going to the hostel for a few hours' sleep, if I can. Then I'm going to be back here early tomorrow morning to pick you up, and we're going to go to the airport together. Okay?"

Victor nodded while considering it. "Fine. Yes."

"You're not yourself, Vic. Do you get that? I have to keep reminding myself, so that I don't just turn you in, or walk away for good."

"Don't forget," said Victor as he got out of the car. "You didn't like the old me either."

Tripp leaned over to power down the passenger window and keep Victor's face in view. "That's flat-out wrong. I liked you a lot. You were my buddy. *Are*," Tripp corrected himself. "You still are. And that's why I'm not giving up. Alright?"

Victor stared at the manor, gazing through it toward his stereotyped imagination of all the action taking place at the beer garden. He looked down at Tripp. Victor loved having Tripp for a buddy. "Alright. I will see you tomorrow morning. Thank you."

Looking morose but satisfied with the sincerity he saw in Victor's face, Tripp put the car in gear.

"Hey," said Victor, pausing his departure. "Do you want me to get you a stein for the road?"

"No Vic, I don't," said Tripp.

He drove ten yards down the driveway and stopped. "Alright," he called back, causing Victor to turn around. "Get me one. For the road."

Victor smiled. "Coming up."

"Hey," Tripp called again, now standing beside his open car door, holding up two fingers. "And one for the hostel."

"Deal, buddy," said Victor.

Jay Hansen was gliding as if on rollers across the

outskirts of the beer garden, a beer in each hand, when he saw Victor approaching. He intercepted his former subordinate short of the gathering and set the steins down on the cinder path. He took an aggressive stance, agitated and clearly struggling with his bravado.

"I know what you did to David Copperfield."

Victor only stared.

"He's going to live," said Jay. "If that disappoints you."

Victor shrugged. "I only hope he chooses not to return to the department. It would not be good for morale."

Jay nodded. "Sure. Right? You made sure of that. Look at you, taking charge. What a great manager you are."

"Yes I am," said Victor, bristling at the sarcasm. "In case my development has escaped you, I am not the same person you pushed around for years."

"Your entire staff was canned, Victor, save for one or two. Is that a good manager in your book?"

"You orchestrated it!" Victor took a step forward and Jay stiffened. "Are you going to claim now that you hadn't made up your mind the day the merger was consecrated?"

"A good manager wouldn't have let that stop him from fighting for his staff."

"I did fight!"

"If you really believe that, you're lying to yourself." Jay was braced as if against the gale, speaking louder and faster, expecting the storm to worsen. "I never heard a *peep* from you."

"I e-mailed you," Victor seethed. "I called you."

"Way too late," said Jay. "I'm talking a month or two ago, as the process was actually being decided. Let me fill you in on something. You and Darla each had a staff of seven. In the original staffing budget we had projected that the post-merger Accounting department would be eleven. You could have saved two more."

Victor gaped. When he spread his arms, Jay flinched.

"You didn't tell me?"

"That's not my job," Jay retorted. "Jennifer Prestlake bitched non-stop about how her Accounts Payable department was going to be understaffed. She sent a different analysis every week showing how the volume was going to be bigger than we thought. Meanwhile you seemed fine with your situation. So she got your two headcount."

A constant high-pitched keening in the air was attracting Victor and driving him mad all at once, as he paced back and forth, faltering, fighting to process what Jay was telling him. Had he quit battling for his team? No, he reminded himself, no, he had urged his staff to greater heights as Darla's team had audited them. Jay was twisting history for his own benefit, recasting his abuse as a managerial technique, pretending that the ridicule, the head games, the deceit, had only been doing his job.

Still Victor agonized. Had he let his staff down? Who had let whom down?

For years my staff had every opportunity to shine, and they chose to coast. I sheltered and carried them. They should be thankful I postponed the inevitable.

"You screw your staff and end up sitting pretty," said Jay, shaking his head. He trembled with righteous anger. "I was so sure you'd be nailed to the wall for what you did to David."

The sharp thin wail—it was emanating from Jay. Victor had heard something similar in Tripp's voice too, and realized now it wasn't a *sound* but a sort of *picture* in his mind, of chemicals flooding the air. He was smelling fear.

With relaxing eyes, face, mind, Victor suddenly saw Jay Hansen, twenty-five years younger. "That was you," said Victor, pointing back toward the United States, toward the armory on the University of Houston campus. "At Interview Day. You were with Arthur Andersen. You interviewed me. With the vampire."

Jay breathed through his nose, lips white against his teeth. "How the hell would I remember something like that?"

"Fear has a way of fixing a memory," said Victor.

"I got that disgusting creature fired, did you know that?" said Jay, shook up, face losing its consistency, his expressions misaligning with his words. "I'd have done the same to you by now.... Sally's making it clear to anyone who will listen that what you did to David was personal between the two of you, nothing more than a long-running personal feud. She's got Chleber's ear. He informed senior management that it won't be a Company matter, that if David wants to press charges, so be it.... But David won't, will he?"

Victor bared his teeth with a slight lift of his head, to give Jay a better look. He was calmed by his former boss's fear. Physical fear; but what Jay seemed most afraid of was what Victor could do to him within the company. "All part of living with the vampire."

Jay lost color but stood his ground. "I'm next then, right? On your list? Maybe we should just do it here, and get it over with." He provoked Victor with a shove to the chest, delivered impotently by arms made short and tight with second thoughts.

Victor bent down and picked up Jay's beers. "I am in no rush whatsoever." Jay reached for the steins. Victor backed away, further yet from the light. "I will take your beers, though."

An inch or so of the steins' contents were sloshed to the thirsty path leading back up to the manor house parking lot, where Victor proudly informed Tripp that he had already passed his first test.

His good cheer was short-lived, although not from lack of effort from the partygoers at the beer garden, which was all it should be, men clashing together steins in ribald toasts, barmaids in frilled corsets and silk-and-petticoat skirts, wandering accordionists and polka music blaring from speakers. Victor Thetherson was only now coming to grips with Giselda's news, of what it truly meant to be Victor.

He waded into the party and was received with stares of open amazement and very soon with toasts, to the Company Vampire.

"To VV!" Dieter Josch cried out. "An American with the blood of the Old World coursing through his veins!" Steins clunked and beer suds rose and fell.

"To the vampire!" bellowed Kurt Bleckmeier, chief of financial reporting. "May he only take what he needs, and leave us enough to absorb more beer!"

With every backslap and cheer and call for him to bare his fangs and pretend to bite a barmaid, Victor's tension mounted. He saw Jay's hatred dancing in everyone's eyes, and recognized in every leering face an accomplice to Giselda's plot and an agreement with Giselda's opinion that his life, of all those who could have been chosen, was disposable.

The Westchase man with the powder blue ballcap was no longer of the zombies. He grabbed Victor around the shoulders and proclaimed, "This is how we grow 'em in Texas, boys! Big and full of *bite*!" This was worth another clash of steins and slosh of beer, down throats and fronts.

Even Darla was soaked, in all senses of the word. The high collar of her blouse sagged from the humidity and the spilled beer, exposing the bandage on her throat. She threw her arms around Victor and forced him into a clumsy jig, then pulled him away from the center of everyone's attention, beyond the direct exposure from the overhead klieg lights.

"I'm so glad to see you. Everyone here has been so great. Kurt Bleckmeier is great," Darla babbled. An outbuilding between them and the beer tent dulled the sharpest of the sounds of revelry. "How did it go with what's her name?"

Victor contemplated his response. "It was a learning

experience."

"I'd like to share a learning experience with you." Darla slurred the words and planted a kiss on Victor's mouth.

He recoiled, chest constricting, leaving him short of breath and panicked. Now he understood the warning bells when Barbara had tried to seduce him. Some part of him was aware of the threat, and eager to keep him alive. "Did I ask for that?"

Darla seemed to instantly sober. "Victor, no, I'm sorry." Her face filled with unhappiness. "I didn't mean to do anything wrong. I wasn't.... I just wanted to tell you I think you're wonderful." She reached for him again.

Victor knocked her hand away. "I don't want that from you, do you understand? Can't you see that? Do you have any concern for me?"

"Of course I do..."

"Don't, don't touch me." Victor breathed hard, on the verge of hyperventilating. "If you cared about me, about who I am, you would ask. You would ask me what I need."

Darla's voice dropped to a husky whisper. "What happened tonight?"

"What happened," said Victor, "is that I took care of your staffing issue with David, so now you can keep Larry, and that's it, that is enough. I don't owe you, I don't owe my ungrateful team, I don't owe anyone, anything, anymore!" At her gentle challenge, another reservoir had broken open and emptied, the last of a cascading flood of pent-up sorrow. "You have my job, isn't that enough? I know your need—I sense it, I *see* it. You *need* me." He had her by the arms. "You need me now, but it's too late. It's too late! Where were you when *I* needed *you*?"

"Victor, you're hurting me," said Darla, eyes brimming with tears.

He reached behind her back, clenching and grasping

for the hair that would have been there, if it was as long as Barbara's. The confusion was embarrassing, and worse was the shame of what his hand would have done.

"Stay away from me," he said, a guttural snarl that was hard for Darla to decipher but easy to comprehend. As Victor stalked away she sank to her knees, the aura of exotic fantasy gone from around her face, the misery suffusing her body suggesting that home sounded no better than the foreign land she suddenly found herself in.

Victor on the other hand knew exactly where he belonged, as he flagged down a passing barmaid. Barbara had created his perfect home, sterile and safe. The lifelong struggle to reveal his true nature was over. *Who* he was no longer mattered; many, many women were attracted by *what* he was. A vampire could make a comfortable living.

The barmaid smiled and propped her tray on cocked hip. "What can I get you?"

The same was true at work. His salary had jumped by half, with bonuses and profit sharing on the way. Barbara and Amberly would be well supported, for as long as they cared to stay with him. And they too seemed much happier to be with VV than they had ever been with Victor Thetherson.

"Let us begin with a beer," said Victor. "But I cannot promise it will satisfy my thirst."

VV, VAMPIRE IN THE HOUSE

Three weeks back from Germany, Victor stopped at the doctor's office after work for his final rabies shot, arriving home at half past four in the afternoon. He heard the garage door rise while he undressed in the bedroom, and seconds later the sound of Barbara entering the house. He was under the covers with his eyes closed when she came into the bedroom, but he could hear her face fall.

"Oh...you're in bed already."

"By the time I get home from work, I have been up all night and all day," Victor reminded her. "I am tired."

"I know. I know," Barbara repeated, softer and losing what little energy she had brought into the room. "I was just hoping we could talk. We never get to talk, anymore. It's okay."

Through slitted eyes he watched her take off the Wal-Mart shirt. Normally she would have taken the time to change at the store, to avoid advertising the identity of her employer on the drive home. Victor guessed she had skipped this step in order to hurry home, before he was asleep.

"Amberly will be here later," Barbara informed him. "She's going to study here, and probably spend the night. There are so many distractions at the dorm, she thinks she'll get a lot more done here."

"I know," said Victor.

"I was just going to say, she was hoping to spend more time with you too."

"Mm. She knows my schedule—"

"No, I know. That's fine." Barbara accelerated her pace in getting dressed. "I just thought you might want to know."

"I had years of availability," Victor retorted. "Years." He forced himself to calm down, before he lost the sleepy feeling. "Funny how you both want to spend time with me only when it's impossible for my schedule."

"Yes, well, I regret that," said Barbara, plucking a t-shirt from the dresser and slamming the drawer shut.

"I will say good night to her when I get up," Victor said as Barbara left the room.

These confrontations were a regular occurrence, as Barbara was slow to adapt to the change. Of course Victor would contend that in fact nothing had changed— they were divorced and living lovelessly as roommates, both free to pursue relationships to fit their own needs and style. Their roles had simply reversed, with Victor now setting their 'civil boundaries'.

Victor was content to be patient while Barbara settled back into routine. He drifted to sleep congratulating himself for keeping his blood pressure in check, marveling at how much better life was, to be the one in control.

The house was quiet and dark when Victor awoke at eleven. He saw Barbara on the couch and continued upstairs, the hall light guiding him to Amberly's bedside. He bent to kiss his daughter's forehead, and scratch Porkie her Morkie behind his limp ear.

"Hi," said Amberly, whisper soft, before opening her eyes.

Victor kissed her sweet skin again, his heart melting, resisting the urge to hug her with everything he had. "I'm going out, wanted to say hi."

"You're going out to bite someone?" Amberly looked for confirmation.

"That is the plan, but you never know," said Victor.

This was an outdated response. Uncertainty no longer accompanied him into the night. Regardless whether the women Nikki lined up had second thoughts, and despite the sometimes energetic resistance from the women he selected himself, Victor would no longer be denied.

"It feels strange..." Amberly had clearly been putting some thought into this. She scooped up Porkie and cuddled him under her chin, her brow smoothing ever so slightly at the sound of his sleepy groaning. "I just never believed you were the type of person to bite someone."

"I know." Victor pushed her hair away from her still angelic face. How long since he had tucked her goodnight, sat on his daughter's bed and gazed upon her against the stenciled choo-choo train border? He recalled—and had to double-check the memory for authenticity—that the train motif hadn't been his idea, but Amberly's, when she was seven. His throat constricted with the sweet nostalgia.

"I guess I was sort of embarrassed that you weren't that kind of vampire."

"You no longer have to be embarrassed, honey."

Amberly frowned. "I think you bit my friend Bertie's mom."

"Oh really? Did she enjoy..." Victor decided to rephrase. "What did she have to say?"

"She's kind of freaked out. Bertie is, definitely, she's really freaked out. Her dad wants to kick your ass."

Victor smiled and scratched Porkie the Morkie's belly. "There is nothing for you to worry about. Your father can take care of himself. Is it the dad who took you to the father-daughter dinner, by any chance?"

Amberly shook her head.

"Too bad. That reminds me, maybe I need to pay his wife a visit."

"I wish you wouldn't," said Amberly.

Victor gave her a wink. "I will behave myself." He rose and backed away. "Time to go. You have a great day at school tomorrow. I would love to see you here tomorrow night, too."

"Okay." Amberly hugged Porkie and watched her father until he was about to close her door. "Dad? I love you."

"I love you too, baby," said Victor, quickly closing the door so she wouldn't see him choking up.

"Dad?" came Amberly's voice through the door.

Victor took a calming breath and poked his head back in.

"Do you think you could leave out my window?" said Amberly.

"The window?"

"It would really be cool to see you go out the window," said Amberly. "Like a vampire."

Victor cleared his throat while picturing the short steep roof outside her window. His palms got slick as he tried to remember how far it was to the ground, and whether there might be a bush to cushion his fall. "Certainly," he said, crossing the room, spreading the curtains and hiking up the window. He stuck one leg through and paused, looking at his daughter. "Until we meet again, sweet young Amberly."

His gut was smaller but still an impediment to the contortion necessary to pass through the window. Feet scraping the shingles, Victor kept a firm grip on the sill as he reached with the other hand, feeling in the dark for something to grab.

"Dad?" Amberly called from her bed. "You okay?"

Victor leaned toward the window. "Shhh, sleep now, young Amberly. Sleep...sleep...." In a state of agitation just shy of panic he let go of the sill and pressed his body flat on the roof, toes settled into the gutter. After a few moments the window closed above him. Victor was reluctant to pick his cheek off the shingle, still bearing heat from the day. Spread-eagled to maximize body-to-shingle contact, he utilized a collection of non-traditional muscles to propel himself across the roof. Fifteen minutes later drenched in sweat he crawled through the spare bedroom window.

"You can have the bed now," he called to Barbara as he hurried past the living room en route to the garage.

Nikki had lined up an encounter with a friend from her health club, also named Nikki if he remembered correctly. His Nikki had bragged up her Nikki's fitness level, "veins popping out all over". The thought made Victor salivate.

They were to meet outside a bar called The Post, downtown. Nikki was under orders to avoid bookings in metro Houston's outlying, am-I-a-restaurant-or-am-I-a-bar?-Yes! establishments. Victor had become a snob, refusing to let a suburban chain ambiance diminish the experience for him or his victim. Even the Village, including the Opposite-Striped Zebra, was no longer on the preferred list, its regulars perfectly cast for the role of blood donors but increasingly protective of their own. Victor's actions blended much better into the downtown scene, where club-hoppers seemed to treat every night like a Vegas getaway.

He also no longer liked to waste time inside the bar, where he and his date would be forced to simulate the desire for a relationship. More time in the bar meant more alcohol in her blood, which fractured its satiny texture and occasionally caused heartburn. Plus, the self-imposed two-pint per victim maximum meant he still needed to find a second donor, to fill his belly with enough nutrients to tide him over to the following night. This made for a tight schedule, because pickings slimmed after one a.m.

The Subaru wagon had been replaced by a Dodge Charger. The cobalt blue box of muscle was parked under the lamppost at the far end of the pay lot, Victor's preferred spot. If things got dicey—cops, bouncers, boyfriends, burly Good Samaritans—he could slip into the back alley behind the club strip, jump into the adjoining viaduct ditch, and make hidden passage back to his car.

Victor used the viaduct now, walking fifty yards and then up the steep side, hopping a single-strand wire fence at the top and stepping into the red-tinged glow of Houston's club scene.

He rounded the corner of Playa da Gama, two doors down from The Post, and came face to face with Tripp.

"My friend. This is a surprise."

"Not for me," said Tripp. "You're too predictable, Vic. You're making it too easy for your enemies. The ones I'm sure you've made by now."

Victor looked past Tripp's shoulder. Thanks to the time spent hugging his roof, he was running late, and didn't want to have Nikki's friend Nikki giving up and going home. He was made irritable and antsy by the fact that any number of girls exiting the clubs and strolling the sidewalk could fit Nikki's description.

"I have been true to my word in Germany," said Victor. "My emotions are under control. No more violence. No more enemies. My life has settled into routine. Predictability is my goal."

"Do you realize you've become my quirky friend who talks funny?" said Tripp. "I'll bring you up in conversation and the other person will say, 'Who? Oh, the one who sounds like a smart Forest Gump, yeah, I know the one you mean.'"

"Be honest," said Victor with a sly grin. "Is my speech pattern really the first characteristic people use to identify me?"

"Can't you talk normal?" said Tripp. "Or at least the way you used to?"

"I will strive to do my best, for you."

Tripp shook his head.

"So you expected to see me here," said Victor. "Nikki must have told you I have a date. So you know I'm being truthful when I say, I need to keep moving."

"Nikki's not coming," said Tripp.

"Which?"

"The one you planned on sucking the blood from."

"Thanks to you," Victor surmised, receiving a nod from Tripp. He paused to take a calming breath. "Why would you do that?"

"You know the blood bank is always—"

"Because you know I'll just go select my own," Victor talked over him. "Now I'm going to need to pick two. Maybe I'll take them together. Hold one down while I bite the other," he contemplated, doing his best to horrify Tripp. "Maybe I'll tie them together, back to back, and try to get my fangs in both of them simultaneously. Congratulations on your humanitarian good deed."

Tripp nodded throughout, as Victor now continued past him. "If nothing else," said Tripp, "at least your speech pattern returned to normal there for a second."

Victor stopped and slowly pivoted, jaw clenched. "Why are you mocking me? Do you really want to push me like this? When I'm thirsty?"

Tripp stared down on Victor, noses six inches apart, most of the distance vertical. He evaluated his friend for some time. "You're not really under control, are you? You're whiter than you were, Vic. Your eyes have a funky luminescence that has nothing to do with the jellyfish gene. Changes are happening inside you, do you realize that?"

"Changes? Really?" Victor was at once sarcastic and incredulous. "How do you think I'm not aware of what's happening? Huge changes, Tripp. And you know what, I like them. How are *you* not aware of *that*? You always prided yourself on knowing me, knowing everything about me. And yet now listen to you..."

Tripp turned away in disgust. Victor pursued, intent on getting in the last word, moving into the path of a rowdy band of young men cruising the sidewalk. One of them drilled Victor with a brawny shoulder.

Victor wheeled on him, lips drawn back. The bar-hopper was ready for a confrontation, but quickly recalculated and continued on with nothing more than a "Geez, dude."

Victor pointed at Tripp to freeze the snide comment on his lips. "So I don't have it perfectly under control. It's a process, Tripp, but I'm getting it. Do you think I want to do something stupid and ruin what I have? I'm not stupid."

"I'm not saying that at all," said Tripp, taking a conciliatory step forward. "I'm saying pretty soon, you're not going to be able to help it."

Victor stood nodding, the anger refusing to abate, leaving him unable to rationally evaluate what his friend was saying. "Well why don't you just get me another chew-doll, and everything will be right as rain."

Tripp further closed the gap between them. "I'm just worried about you, Vic. That's why I'm here. I don't think it fully hit me until a few days ago, how traumatic Germany was for you. I wanted to tell you that I'm sorry for a lot of things that happened there."

The apology only sunk in so far, but Victor was softened enough to nod.

"And the doll was stupid," said Tripp, "you don't have to remind me. I find her at my desk in a different compromised position every time I show up at the Bank. Perry can't get enough of her. The only way I'm going to get it to stop is to make an honest woman out of her."

Victor grudgingly played along. "What would Nikki say?"

"She's all for it, which freaks me out a little," said Tripp, bringing a careful smile to Victor's face. "Like any roommate dynamic, the key will be making sure everyone pulls their weight."

They both enjoyed the semblance of their former relationship. "I'm glad I found you, Vic. Here's what I came to say: We want you to come in full-time to the Longer Labs. A live-in situation. The timing is perfect. With the insight I brought back from Germany, we're making big strides. Let us attack this thing full-on." At

Victor's immediate negative reaction, Tripp sweetened the offer. "We've had a breakthrough. Something you need to understand."

"What?"

"I can't say anything for certain," said Tripp. "I don't want to speculate, in case I'm wrong. Let us run more tests—"

"No. I've had enough, I told you that. You have enough data to do whatever you need to do."

"It isn't like that," said Tripp. "We need real-time tests. We're getting a machine that will allow us to watch real-time changes in your gene expressions. It's incredible, and it's going to give us outrageous insights into the aging process in general, and your affliction in particular."

"No. I won't do it."

"Why?" Tripp demanded.

"Because I don't trust you," Victor hurled it as a damning accusation. "I used to think you cared about me."

"I do."

"It's obvious you don't."

"Vic, God..." Tripp grabbed his own hair and yanked his head down in self-abusing incredulity. "Why would I have traveled to Germany? Why would I be here right now if I didn't care?"

"Because I'm a research subject," Victor had the quick answer, while spotting a great candidate walking alone along the sidewalk, debating whether to enter Playa da Gama. "I'm a ticket to your research and fortune."

"You're a fucking idiot," said Tripp. He turned to stalk away, then continued in full circle, fist thrust to his forehead. "No. I'm sorry. I lost my temper. You're not an idiot, you're ill. You have a disease, and you need to find a cure."

"I don't see it that way," said Victor, withdrawn, stung. "I don't have a disease. I have a blessing. It has its risks, I understand. But it is a blessing. I learned that from you, didn't I? 'You gotta own it, wrap it around yourself like a blanket'," he mimicked Tripp. "You were right. Now it's just up to me to learn to control it."

"That's my point," said Tripp plaintively. "You're not going to be able to. Very soon, you're not going to be able to control it. I'm afraid, buddy." Tripp's eyes registered the extent of his anguish. "I'm afraid you're not going to want to."

With a great sigh Victor joined the tail end of a group of revelers heading toward The Post. He turned to Tripp, walking backward. "Rest assured that whatever I do, it will be *exactly* what I want. For a change. Buddy."

After a lethargic but relatively successful night downtown and then a similarly uninspired early morning workout at the club, Victor decided he must have a mild flu as he drove to his old building, ordered forth from his office in the former Westchase headquarters. His mission today was to get the two legacy companies' sales managers in a room together to end the infighting that had started a buzz in the market and was, in the eyes of Chleber and the execs on the construction side, ruining Bizco's chances to land contracts.

Victor made the familiar turn in front of the city-locked pasture and its smattering of bobbing oil rigs when his Blackberry called out three times in quick succession—an e-mail and a text from Jay's secretary, and a call from Darla.

"Your timing is excellent," he answered. "I will be in your neighborhood shortly."

"I'm glad I caught you," said Darla. "No one's at the office. You remember Bane Lake Park?"

"Where we had the company picnic."

"Jay asked us to meet here," said Darla. "Everyone's here. Even the staff we let go." Darla lowered her voice. "I don't want to get my hopes up, but I have a good feeling about this. Raj knows something, he's all worked up, pacing around and greeting everyone. Jay just arrived," she now whispered. "Raj said Jay invited you too. It was all last-second this morning."

Victor pictured Jay desperate to placate him and avoid a midnight social call, and jumped to a conclusion. "You think they're going to hire everyone back?"

"That's exactly what I'm hoping," Darla hissed happily. "Can you make it?"

"I would not miss it."

Storm clouds were parked over Bane Lake, a merciful sun shield that Victor took for a good omen. Sunny faces greeted him inside the rec center, Darla, Kirby and Florence all hurrying to the door in anticipation of his arrival.

"It's VV," Kirby crowed. "I think the last time I saw you might have been right here—no, wait, you were back in the office once—speaking of which," Kirby exclaimed, "we have something for you. Something you left behind." He looked apologetically at Darla. "It seems that Darla was going to throw it, but I'm sure it was an oversight."

"The can of hairspray?" said Darla. "You pulled it out of the garbage?"

"It's mousse and it was half-full," said Kirby.

"How would you know that?" said Darla.

"Mousse is foamy, and hairspray—"

"The mousse is all yours," Victor told Kirby. "I thought it was magic for awhile. I have no need of it anymore."

"I may just try mousse," said Kirby, picking at his lackluster perma-'fro. He rose on tiptoes to assess Victor's sleek trimmed hair. "You're a gel man now, I'm guessing. I love your new look."

There were fourteen accountants in the room. Darla's team stood as a motley knot outside the hall to the restrooms. Tessa, Quentin and Casey seemed pinned against the far wall, in shorts and summer shirts and collectively uncomfortable, marooned by the power duo in the room's center, Jay and Raj, the epitome of corporate businessmen, impatient in starched white dress shirts. Larry was unattached. Everyone took in Victor's deep blue silk shirt, cuffs rolled twice, black slacks, Italian loafers, Ray-Ban shades.

"The construction industry dresses differently outside the Accounting department," said Victor, having difficulty remaining nonchalant under Florence's particularly immodest appraisal.

"It's you," Florence purred, then broke into a barking baritone cough, hacking through what sounded like a plug of wet wax stoppering her trachea. While sending the rubble back down the pipe she straightened her denim vest and evened the weighted ends of her bolo tie, and winked at Victor. "You've changed, Victor. That's the way it works."

"It's you," said Kirby, already at home with and oblivious to Florence's demons, gazing upon Victor and shaking his head in slow motion. "It's you," he cooed. "So we were just talking—"

"VV," Raj interrupted as he joined them. "It's awfully nice you could join us on short notice. Can I get you something?" He was upstaging Darla just as he had done to Victor many times before. "No? Let's get started then."

Victor ignored him as he ignored Jay while passing within striking distance, seeking out the discarded element of his former team.

"What's happening, VV?" said Tessa quietly.

"Yeah, wassup, V?" said Quentin, in danger of popping his accounting shoulder out of its socket in a sudden attack of hip-hop.

"No," said Tessa, "I meant, what's going on here? Why did Jay call us here?" With years of training her hand was over Casey's mouth in time to garble her shouted contribution.

Casey wrapped up her sentence at normal volume

when Tessa removed her hand. "...eating dog food."

"It's only been a couple weeks and we're still on severance," said Tessa. "So we're not at that point yet. But it would be great to get our jobs back."

"I'm going to work super-hard this time," said Quentin.

"Super double," said Casey.

"VV?" said Raj with syrupy deference. He waited for Victor to turn around. "Shall we?"

"Raj," Victor replied. "By all means."

Jay stepped forward. "Let me kick this off." He realized 'forward' was meaningless in the theater-in-the-round created by the dispersed accountants, and stepped back, briefly tromping Raj's toes under his heel. "I'll get right to why we're here. I would imagine there was a lot of anger when we canned some of you. We're the construction industry, right? We don't need to deal in euphemisms. Your jobs weren't 'displaced'; you were canned."

"Jay," Darla gently protested, her face knit with empathy, "I think you could be a little gentler."

"More respectful is the term I was looking for," said Victor. He advanced two steps on Jay, eager to gauge his reaction. Aggression wasn't coming easy, for some reason; it was an effort to straighten his spine, twist his hands into claws, and menace with his eyes. "But we're construction, so let's skip the euphemism. You should be less of an ass."

"You tell him, VV!" Quentin cheered.

Tessa turned on him. "Shh! Jay's our boss's boss and deserves a respectful audience," she manufactured deference with tools Victor didn't know she possessed. "Let Jay talk."

It was impossible to say whether Jay was avoiding looking at Victor out of fear or the postponement of gratification. He regarded Tessa with an open face and number-crunching eyes. "I'll be really surprised if you still feel that way in a few minutes."

"Jay, if I could." Raj's voice was Reason itself, putting a human echo on Jay's words and short-circuiting the emotional charge building on Tessa's face. "What Jay is referring to is a project I've been working on, for the past two months. The result...how should I put this?" He propped elbow on wrist, chin atop loose fist. "It showed a lack of oversight and control. It still remains to be seen whether that lack of proper controls allowed something truly unfortunate to occur. Like fraud."

"No," Darla blurted, a moan with conviction. "We looked at everything very closely during the audit. If there was something like that going on, we would have found it. There was nothing like that," she said with finality, a defense that stretched from her team to Victor's, allowing him to hold his tongue.

"You're wrong," said Jay. "And that's why we're going to need to revisit the decisions we made about the go-forward staffing for the accounting department."

A silent distress call was emitted from the wide-eyed accountants. Kirby's hands flopped around his wrists as he worked up his nerve. "I've known Darla a long time," he said, "and I'm not an expert, except maybe in certain aspects of the accounting process—a lot of the things Victor has written articles about, which were great, we've been doing for quite a few years—"

"Kirby," Darla appealed. "Get to it."

"Well, I'm already there," said Kirby. "Darla's good at what she does. If she says there's no problem with the controls, then there isn't."

"Great," said Raj. "Testimonials can be informational. Maybe inspirational is a better description. But I think we'd all have to agree that nothing talks like the cold hard facts. So if you'll allow me..." In the spotlight Victor knew Raj had always yearned for, he pondered, knuckles to his lips. "I'm considering the best place to start...let's go to the beginning. I've been gathering data in order to conduct extensive modeling of our construction costs. The intent is to do a better job of estimating our costs, versus the outdated, inefficient method of relying on communications from our construction team."

"I never asked you to do that," said Victor. Was every invite a trap? *Go*, he told himself. *They can't hurt you. You have no obligation to listen to this.* "Our control and communication process works fine."

Jay made a grand gesture of considering his surroundings, taking a few steps to look out the big windows overlooking Bane Lake and the playing fields. "Wasn't this the place where you wowed everyone with your potato sack racing? Maybe you should just stare out the window for awhile and dwell on that day. I'm guessing it was your last victory with this company."

Victor faltered, less confident in his ability to walk out without repercussions. He snarled, and Quentin, Tessa and Casey rallied to it. But it was defensive, not the battle cry before an attack. "You know I knew my stuff."

Jay shook his head in disappointment. "I would have to say now that I *thought* I did."

"To continue," said Raj, "and this is important: I gathered every bit of cost data for our construction projects over the last thirty-one years. I built a sophisticated stochastic model and ran ten thousand simulations, and then fit the resulting data to the appropriate statistical curve."

"Instead of doing your job." Victor's accusation contained a hint of savagery, driven by panic deep in his core. He had flourished as the vampirism had stabilized his mind, calming his intrinsic doubt and allowing his talent to shine through. But the foundation for this success was his talent, not the vampirism. And Victor could feel something giving way as that foundation was found to be weak. "Maybe our competition with Westchase would have gone differently if you had been doing your job."

"Maybe," said Raj, pausing just this long to savor his

position, "the problem all along has been you telling us to do the job wrong."

"That's preposterous!" Darla exploded, maneuvering to establish a clean communication line to Jay, without Raj between them. "Raj is describing something that doesn't exist. You're making a big mistake listening to him."

Victor was mounting his own fevered defense. He addressed his former team while pointing at Jay. "He's the one who wouldn't let you know that it was a merger competition, not an acquisition. I wanted to tell you; but Jay said he'd can us all if I did."

"You know how and why you lost," said Jay, addressing Victor like a psychologist to an agitated, delusional patient.

"Let me get to the crux," said Raj, "and then the debate will be moot."

"It's mute," Casey piped up. She giggled. "You said 'moot'."

"Oh Casey," said Raj. "We should have taken better care of you. But yes, in a manner of speaking, you're right. It may be mute."

"Don't patronize me," said Casey.

Raj frowned before picking up his demonstration in the same professorial tone he had left off. "Through the modeling process, I noticed one incredibly strong correlation that just leapt out of my spreadsheets. The time our machinery spends in operation is a perfect predictor of the ultimate cost of the job."

"Duh," said Larry, his first word, drawn out by his drawl.

"Duh, yes," Raj countered with a touch of irritation and a whole lot of condescension. "Except for one job: Maryhill. You and Victor caught heat for the job being over budget. But it turns out you got off easy. Using the machinery run-time as a gauge, that job actually cost double what your accounting records say it did. Duh, right Larry?"

Larry shrugged.

"With such an elementary connection," Raj continued, "it's really hard to believe you could have missed the fact that twenty-eight million was spent but not accounted for. But you did miss it—because our control system was obviously flawed—and so nobody even knows that our company lost twenty-eight million dollars. Of course maybe it's not lost." Raj looked squarely at Victor. "Maybe it's in somebody's pocket..."

Jay moved past him to address the others, still hugging the periphery. "And now you understand why we needed to test you." He was looking at the three ex-employees, with pointed glances at Larry and Florence. "And why you failed." Jay glanced at Darla before addressing her team. "It also explains why I'm going to have to make another change."

Larry harrumphed. He nodded at his three ex-associates. "Are you saying that's why they were fired?"

Jay widened his stance and crossed his arms. "Don't you think twenty-eight million dollars is sufficient cause?"

"I know where your twenty-eight million dollars is." Larry made for the front door, didn't stop, left the building.

There was a widespread exchange of glances, and a billow of humidity from the breach. Darla mumbled something unintelligible and went after Larry. The building emptied, with increasing urgency lest the twenty-eight million be gone before they got a look. Jay and Raj were the last to follow, shaking their heads, neither of them displaying curiosity as to what lay outside, each man's focus obviously on what the department and their own careers would look like after the upcoming housecleaning.

Larry waited, refusing entreaties to show them the money, until Jay and Raj appeared. Then he pointed, at a newly erected office building in the distance, the top two floors visible over the treetops. "I thought that's why you called us here, Jay. To announce that our department is moving to Bizco's new headquarters."

"What are you talking about?" Jay demanded.

"That building right there," said Larry. On cue lightning flashed in the overhanging storm clouds, causing the new building's blue glass façade to glow. "We built it as a joint venture with Westchase. It was hush-hush, but I knew about it from the construction guys. They've been working their asses off, double time for the past six months. That's why they were over budget on Maryhill. Doing two projects bit into their efficiency."

"What?" Jay was having a hard time coming to grips with the company's ownership of a building he knew nothing about. "How do you know this?"

"Because Larry spends a lot of time at the job sites," said Victor. "Doing qualitative accounting research." He gave Larry a wink; and through a crack in the sullenness that lately enveloped Larry, received a wink in return.

"That's impossible," said Raj. "Jay would have known."

"Obviously I didn't," Jay snapped at him.

"*You* would have known it, Raj," said Larry, "if you spent more time talking to people and less time...what did you call it? Modeling?"

"That's what this is all about?" said Darla. "Raj, you should have told me you were seeing problems. I could have told you where that machinery time was being spent. I've been working on the home office project for months."

Jay seethed. "You knew and didn't tell me?"

Darla was a little cowed. "I was told not to. I've been reporting directly to Bleckmeier at Verrstagg."

"That's why you were meeting with him in Dresden?! Why didn't you tell me?"

"They're moving the American headquarters here," said Darla. "They didn't want anyone in Chicago to know, in case it affected morale during the merger process."

"This means a shadow company was operating under Accounting's noses," Raj asserted gravely. "This is worse than I thought. Jay, I think I need to—"

"Shut up," said Jay, livid, suddenly and completely out of love with Raj. "There's no shadow company. Don't you think Verrstagg can do whatever it damn well pleases? It's private, Raj, it can put its costs wherever it wants. And that includes a secret joint venture, right? God damn it..."

Victor laughed, head back and hearty, in absolute relief that Raj's accusations were baseless, and at Jay's expense. "How ironic is this? Let me ask you, Jay: Wouldn't it have been nice to know the truth? Just think what you might have done differently."

Jay was closing on him as he spoke. He thunked his finger into Victor's sternum. "Nothing. I wouldn't have done a god-damn thing differently."

"I don't think Chleber will see it that way," said Victor, inching closer, forcing his chest into Jay's finger. "Not when I tell him you fired my team under false pretenses."

"That's bullshit."

Larry started to protest. Victor gave him the stop sign. "You just admitted to it, Jay. And believe me, I will not need any witnesses for Chleber to believe it. All he will need to hear is that Darla needs a full team."

Darla waited; Jay couldn't help himself, he looked at her. "I do," she said.

Jay trembled as he squared up with Victor. "I can't begin to convey how much I hate you."

"Maybe you would like to strike me," said Victor, lips parting for a toothy smile.

"Okay," said Jay. His punch was quick and strong, an inside left hook to the cheek with a tight follow-through that left him able to link it with an uppercut to Victor's jaw.

Victor was out on his feet, momentarily, long enough

to drop him on his butt. His lights came back on and he was standing again before Darla could reach him, as Florence and Larry led a cacophony of calls for Victor to drink jay's blood.

Which was exactly what Victor was going to do. He took quick steps toward Jay, who backpedaled, his energy spent in one adrenaline burst, further drained by the near-unanimous rage against him by the throng of accountants, bloodthirstier than one might expect.

For the past two weeks Victor had experienced nausea during his late night "dating", increasingly so. Last night was the worst, to the point where he might not have drunk if his partner hadn't been so submissive. And here it came again, perfectly timed against the moment of the bite. He was a threat to puke if he sank his fangs in Jay's thick neck.

Victor forced himself to attack, leaving the ground to strike Jay high on the shoulders and drive him to the lawn. With his spit peppering his ex-boss's face, Victor imagined his jaws protruding wolf-like, lips stretched back and fangs glistening.

"Your blood will taste oh-so-sweet, Jay Hansen." He did his best to speak without losing his wolf face. "But it will be at a time of my choosing." Victor snapped his jaws shut and pushed off Jay to propel himself to his feet. "Consider yourself on the list."

Jay laid there with his eyes closed, legs drawn up in fetal protection. And Victor realized he had won. The years of suffering were over. Vampirism had delivered him from insignificance and shame. He turned his face to the gray satin sky and screamed.

When Victor turned around, the burden of celibacy that accompanied his vampirism was acceptable. He was rushed, hugged, kissed (by Casey).

"You saved our bacon, VV," said Tessa.

"And I don't even like bacon," Casey shouted. "But I'll eat as much as you tell me to!"

The cheers, the congratulations, it was night and day

compared to the Verrstagg beer garden. There, the vampire in him was the attraction, a freak show for the pleasure of the audience. Here they celebrated him, who he was, and what he had accomplished. They were in awe of VV, but they were grateful for Victor Thetherson.

"You're incredible, VV," said Kirby.

"Please call me Victor sometimes too."

"Victor, do we have to give back our severance?" said Quentin.

Raj had hung back, eyes darting from Victor to Jay, who was striding for the parking lot. Victor separated from the adoring crowd and approached him, causing Raj to shake his head in apology. "Victor, I'm sorry. That was a misguided attempt to help the department, I recognize. I—"

"I want Darla to hire you back," said Victor, loud enough for Darla's benefit as she took in the scene.

Raj nodded, solemn. "Thank you."

"And then on your first day of re-employment, I want you to submit your resignation, so Darla can fill your position with someone she can trust."

Raj wilted under Victor's glare. His chin sank, and he nodded. Victor winked at Darla, her eyes sparkling, and headed for his car.

Larry on bandy legs caught him at the car door. He was distracted briefly in admiration of Victor's new wheels, then offered his hand. "Thank you."

"Nice job yourself." Victor enjoyed their handshake and the cool impact of the few big raindrops beginning to splat about them.

"I'm not going to say I was wrong about you," said Larry, hood-eyed as the only way he could stand Victor's stare and the occasional plump raindrop. "But there's something I need to confess."

"Save it," said Victor. "I'm late for a meeting, and to tell you the truth, I'm not feeling well." A giddy sense of familiarity and hometown camaraderie sprang from his victory and Larry's gesture. "It's not something a vampire should confess to, but lately the prospect of biting someone has made me sick to my stomach."

Larry sighed, but nothing seemed to escape his mouth, his breath and his tension trapped inside.

Victor now stood inside the open car door. He looked up into what had the makings of a downpour. "Get in."

Larry seemed to picture sharing the confined space. "I'd rather not."

Victor waited.

"Your pug's head didn't get lost in the mail," said Larry, shaking his head as he talked. "I lied to you to get you to take the rabies shots."

Further explanation was unnecessary, as Victor was instantly recalling a prior conversation. He bowed his head in preparation for a terrible roar.

"I had the department's best interests in mind—"

"Enough." Victor thrust his face into Larry's. To his credit, Larry, smaller, human, did not recoil. "Get out of my face, and just be thankful I don't demand your resignation with Raj's."

Larry's continuing apology was nipped by the soundproof solidity of the Charger's seal. Victor was dialing Tripp as he accelerated out of the rec center lot. He got voicemail.

"You knew what the rabies vaccine could do to me, and you said nothing. That proves what I said last night." Victor's chest tightened and his throat twisted in sadness. He cursed himself as still too weak, still allowing input from his old insecurities. Although, he acknowledged, his emotional reaction could be at least partially due to the softening effects of the rabies vaccine. Which was also Tripp's fault.

"We were never friends. And my time as your lab rat has ended. Goodbye Tripp."

The only thing stopping the sadness was the satisfaction in how much his message would hurt Tripp. With a little introspection, the inconsistency between that thought and his accusation would have been apparent. This did not occur, as introspection was a casualty of the changes at work within him.

"Vic, wake up. Victor, I need you to wake up."

Barbara stood over him, giving his shoulder a shake, letting go, repeating both her verbal and physical efforts more insistently.

"What time is it?" Victor asked groggily. Even before opening his eyes, he knew, from the intense fog across the front of his brain, the sun had not yet set.

"The appraiser is here," said Barbara as she moved away from his side, retreating to the bedroom door. "He needs to meet with both of us. I can't answer all his questions."

"What?" Victor struggled to make sense of her words before he would contemplate trying to rise. "Why is there an appraiser here?"

"Because I want to sell the house," said Barbara.

The flatness of her voice cleared Victor's cobwebs. For Barbara, a lack of emotion meant she had already traveled the long road through sadness and beyond, drained from an extended time in pain. "What are you talking about?" Victor swung his feet to the floor. "Since when?"

"Since...since Germany," Barbara said, barely audible. "Maybe before."

"No," said Victor. "Tell him to go. We need to talk about this."

Barbara shook her head. "We're way beyond that. You've been saying it, every day. You say it in the way you treat me."

"The way I treat you?" Victor exclaimed. "What, being your roommate? Cutting costs by sharing the house? Refusing to consider anything beyond that?" His anger mounted as Barbara forced him to unearth the memories. "Does that sound familiar? Doesn't that sound *exactly* the way you treated me? Exactly?"

Barbara bit her lip. "Yep," she said, without looking

at him. "I'm sure I did. I'm sorry. But I can't take it anymore. It doesn't matter. Neither of us want to be with each other."

"That is not, I am just..." Victor couldn't decide how to finish the sentence, and it didn't matter, because Barbara was out of the room.

And then she was back, just long enough to tell him, "Nikki's here, with some other woman from your office."

Every few days Nikki stopped by to drop off an updated itinerary for the "dates" she lined up for him. If he was asleep when she arrived, Victor would sometimes find her curled up on the floor beside his bed, his bath towel or discarded work shirt for a blanket.

In skivvies and t-shirt, Victor pulled on sweatpants—Houston was hot in September, but Victor was cold—and left the bedroom. The house was still, voices coming from outside. Dully he shuffled to the kitchen to grab sunglasses from the counter, and trudged out the front door.

"VV!" Nikki ran to him as he took stock of his visitors. "So sorry to wake you."

From the length of the shadow Darla cast across his lawn, he had only been asleep an hour or so. She remained rooted next to her car door, raising her hand to wave. Victor abbreviated the hug with Nikki and crossed the lawn, intercepted by Barbara, who had in tow a tall man with a clipboard.

"Victor, this is Bob," said Barbara. "Bob is here to appraise our house."

"Thanks but no thanks," said Victor, stepping around them.

"Victor, he's going to appraise our house," said Barbara forcefully. "I'm paying for it. It doesn't matter if you like it or not."

"I just have a few questions on a short checklist, and I'll be out of your hair," said Bob the appraiser, nudging his yellow Total Valuation Services cap higher up his forehead and readying the papers on his clipboard. He had noticed Victor's teeth and now kept his eyes averted. "The square footage we have as twenty-two forty. Does that sound right?"

Victor turned his back on him and stood before Darla. "Why are you here?"

"When Nikki said she was visiting you..." Darla's eyes kept moving over Victor's shoulder, distracted by Barbara. "After the way our conversation ended in Dresden.... I wanted to finish it. Or keep it going, really."

"I'm sorry ladies," Barbara's voice was sharp. "Victor needs to attend to our business."

Victor turned on her, ignoring Bob the appraiser standing uncertainly alongside. "We are not selling this house. Therefore we are not going to talk to an appraiser. End of story."

Barbara's mouth trembled, but she exerted enough control to stop the tears and keep her voice steady. "Fine. We won't sell. We'll use the appraised value in our divorce settlement. I can answer any questions you have," she said to Bob as she marched up the front steps.

Bob stood there, looking from Barbara to Victor. "I'd like your permission to be able to enter the house, sir."

"Fine," said Victor, fists clenched.

Nikki rubbed his shoulders. "Take a chill pill, VV. It's no big deal. She's probably just trying to get your attention. She loves you, man. Let her blow off some steam, bring her some flowers, and in a couple days everything will be back to normal."

Darla gave the tiniest of whimpers and stared off down the street.

Nikki looked at her, belated comprehension dawning on her face. "Or, you could just kick her ass out."

Darla's eyes came back to rest on Victor's.

"Why don't you give us a moment," Victor said to Nikki.

"Certainly, boss," said Nikki. "Is your computer up?

I'll go update your calendar."

At Victor's nod, Nikki scampered inside the house. He looked at Darla. "I'm surprised you came here to see me. I would imagine it was a difficult decision."

Darla shuffled closer. "I planned to talk to you earlier today, but obviously things got a little crazy. I'd rather have you see me like this anyway, after I've had a chance to change out of my work clothes. When I'm in the office, I feel so…butch."

Victor snorted. Darla had a way of opening him up. "That is not accurate."

"You're all man, and so am I," said Darla. "Hello Victor," she adopted a low robust tone, "I sure think you're swell. How about you and I go get a six-pack and watch an Astros baseball game. And cuddle."

Victor smiled in spite of himself. "Stop it. You are very feminine."

"I don't feel that way," Darla pouted. "I'm glad you see me differently."

"I do," said Victor. "I am glad you're here. I wanted to apologize to you, for how I treated you in Dresden."

Darla looked up from under her eyebrows. "I thought you might want to."

"Things were changing rapidly that day. I was having a hard time adjusting."

"When things change, sometimes the biggest strength and love can come from the stability of the people around you," said Darla, intensely animated. She took Victor's hand in hers. "Just because things change, doesn't mean we have to."

"But that is the problem," said Victor. "I have changed."

"Not in ways that are important," Darla insisted. "I still see the same gentle soul I saw the first day we met."

Victor's lips tightened. "From my wife to my staff to my best friend, my soul was nearly destroyed by everyone it came in contact with. I am doing my best to harden it."

"Please don't do that." Pain and tension returned to Darla's brow. She held onto his hand. "Nothing good can come from that."

"I understand how it looks from your vantage point." Victor squeezed her hand and disengaged. "I never would have chosen to become a vampire, believe me. But I owe everything to it."

Even now the oncoming night was strengthening him, overwhelming the rabies vaccine's attempt to disable him. He was ready to leap from rooftop to rooftop, swoop down to the street and carry his donor back to loftier heights, where she would experience his special gift under the velvet Houston sky. Victor was glad to be up early. "It is all good, Darla. I have finally unleashed my true self."

"But who you are *has* to include love," Darla countered. She nodded at the house. "It's obvious you're not getting that here."

"Trust me when I tell you, love is the last thing I need."

A girl screamed as Victor spoke. The scream ended abruptly with his last utterance. He started toward the house, trying to place the sound and decide exactly what he had heard. At the pounding of feet inside the house Victor broke into a run.

Barbara was hurrying up the stairs, calling Amberly's name. Victor dashed after her, caught and passed her in the upstairs hall, and burst into Amberly's room.

Bob the appraiser had Amberly in his arms. Her arms dangled, lifeless. The appraiser turned at their approach, lifting his mouth from Amberly's throat, his front four teeth missing. The first teeth he possessed were fangs, dripping with Amberly's blood.

Victor's body shut down. Be it the rabies vaccine or trauma from the horror before him, in that split second he saw himself in Bob's position, rising satiated from his daughter's throat, and was incapacitated. He stumbled and dropped with a thud to his knees, a terrible moan ejected from his twisting gut.

In the corner Yorkie the Morkie whimpered, and in the doorway Barbara screamed. Bob the appraiser vampire dropped Amberly, sending her crumpled to the floor. Barbara dove to her side, dragging her daughter into the small space between the bed and her pink and yellow dresser. A curled cupcake sticker from the bottom drawer clung to Amberly's sleeve as her mother cradled her.

Bob the appraiser vampire tossed his Total Valuation Services cap onto Amberly's unmade bed and stood before Victor, who struggled to his feet, grunting to overcome the paralytic shock.

"That's him," said Darla. She stood in the doorway, talking through her hands as they gripped her mouth. "He's the one who came to the office looking for you."

"I've been leaving my calling card everywhere," said the vampire, mush-mouthed without front teeth. "But you never saw this coming, did you? I can't tell you how worried I was to have my territory invaded by an East German vamp." He looked Victor up and down. "What a joke."

Victor lurched forward on rubbery legs. Bob the appraiser vampire easily slapped down the attack and drove his head into Victor's nose, the crunch loud in Victor's head, bringing a delayed spurt of blood.

"You bastard!" Nikki screamed. She hurtled past Darla and threw herself at the appraiser vampire, who caught her and pulled her close, inspecting Victor's fang tracks before snarling in rage and flinging the bony girl in the same direction as his yellow cap. She hit the headboard on the fly and lay on the bed.

Victor got up off his knees and the vampire slugged him, driving him back down, full out on the floor, unable to make his legs work or understand which direction was up.

"You're not the same, do you understand that?" Bob

the appraiser vampire stood over Victor and lisped down upon him. "You don't belong here. I'm ready to puke every time I see one of your marks. Which has been way, way too often. You bit my freaking mother, do you know that?" said Bob, voice cracking. "God I hate you. Your time here is through." He brought Victor to his feet and hauled him out of the room.

"No-no-no," Darla protested, forced to vacate the doorway as the vampire accelerated toward the low wall safeguarding the stairwell. "Don't do this, don't do this..."

Nikki came alive and flew into the hallway and leaped on Bob's back, hurling insults and clawing at his eyes. The vampire didn't alter his course or intent, picking Victor up and sending him over the wall.

Victor twisted in order to come down on his feet, thwarted by the handrail in the tight quarters of the closed staircase, jolted and flipped so that he landed on his hip on the unadorned wood stairs. Early in his ensuing tumble Nikki landed on him, and together they went bouncing to the bottom.

Darla yearned to win the race to Victor's sprawled body, but Bob the vampire threw her aside and hurried down the stairs.

Tripp walked through the open front door. "Knock-knock. Holy crap."

"Get out," Bob the appraiser vampire commanded, showing his fangs.

Tripp looked left and right, and back to the left, settling on the pair of pewter candlestick holders on the formal dining table. He swished them through the air like nunchucks to demonstrate his prowess. "Vic man, get up. Up, Vic."

Through the sickening pain blossoming from his hip, Victor willed himself to his knees. The appraiser vampire viciously kicked him back down.

"What's your deal?" Tripp demanded, feinting an attack to gauge the reaction.

The vampire did not flinch. He knelt beside Victor. "I'm here to kill this foreigner."

"I gotta call you on that one," said Tripp. "Ol' Vic here is as Houston as they come. But the bigger question is, do you all talk funny?" Tripp chattered while working up the courage to charge. "Am I right, Vic? Chicks might dig your accent, but there is no way they go for a lisp."

"But I dig the chicks," said the vampire with a leer. "That's all that matters." He was fingering Victor's throat as if searching for the jugular. "Have you ever seen one vampire kill another?"

Tripp suddenly realized Bob was drawing blood with his fingernail. "No!" He charged as Nikki was resurrected a second time, diving on the vampire. Tripp redirected the candlestick to avoid Nikki, delivering a harmless blow to Bob's shoulder. He belatedly converted his strike to a tackle, receiving a slug in the face but grabbing enough of Bob's shirt to wrench the vampire off Victor.

With Nikki sandwiched between them, Tripp quickly lost the battle. The vampire tore out of his grasp—and then was slammed to the floor as Victor attacked.

Victor's jaws snapped shut as tried to take a bite out of the vampire's neck. Bob tossed him through the air and he came down butt-first on the edge of the coffee table—it snapped to attention, standing up on end, and Victor hit the floor, the impact rejiggering mental circuits that hadn't yet fully come back online. The table fell back onto all four legs, the glass top cracking lengthwise. Victor sat slumped with the dazed look of KO'd prizefighter.

Before Bob the appraiser vampire could press his advantage, Nikki kicked him in the face. With a roar he reached for her, blocked by Tripp and then staggered by Darla, using a plant stand as a battering ram. The vampire shoved back, driving the stand into Darla's chest and knocking her to the floor.

From the stairway Barbara emerged, wielding

Amberly's karaoke microphone stand like an axe. "The police are on the way," she said, her voice quavering. "Now get out of my house."

Tripp and Nikki were on their feet, Victor and Darla struggling to do likewise. Bob assessed the fight in those arrayed against him, and slowly backed away. "You're doomed, one way or the other," he said to Victor. "You stick out like a rotten tooth. If I don't get you, someone else will." He brought the chiseled, bloodstained fingernail that had been in Victor's throat to his mouth, and sucked on it. "But I will get you."

"Oh yuck," said Tripp.

Bob the appraiser vampire pulled a set of dentures from his pocket and wiggled them at Barbara before putting them in his mouth, filling in his missing teeth and masking his fangs. "Let me know when you're ready to sell. After his funeral." He turned to leave and bumped his shin on the footrest of a circa-1950's wheelchair blocking the open doorway. The man in the chair had his arm in a misshapen plaster cast and his head swathed in gauze, at an angle across one eye and matted with sweat, with a Zorro mask on top.

"Uh-oh, reinforcements are here," said Bob, smirking at everyone.

"Die, you vampire scum!" said Eugene Foreman, vampire slayer. A golden stake popped out of a groove in the underside of his cast.

With his heel Bob the appraiser vampire drove Eugene's arm into the doorjamb, snapping the golden stake in a puff of plaster. He leaned forward and hissed, while Eugene clawed at a switch box that had been duct-taped to the arm of his wheelchair.

In a nifty display of vampire power, Bob sailed over Eugene, ducking the doorframe and drawing his legs up tight beneath him, just as Eugene triggered the release of the spring-loaded shotgun on the back of the chair. The mouth of the barrel popped Bob in the crotch and dropped him face-first onto the front porch. The shotgun dropped into Eugene's lap. He fumbled to bring it to bear—for a moment, his Vienna sausage fingers poking out of the cast were on the trigger and the barrel was under his chin, and those in the house cringed.

Bob the appraiser vampire loomed behind Eugene. He grabbed the slayer's hair and yanked his head back for the bite. The shotgun discharged, and Bob's head was blasted to bits. His slobbery dentures flew intact through the air with a vampire-like hiss, thirty feet to the street.

Eugene sat before the stunned onlookers, his mouth agape and his mask askew. He straightened the Zorro mask until his eye was again visible. He stared at the shotgun in his lap and the body on the porch.

"Eugene," said Tripp, as everyone cautiously converged. "You did it. You killed him."

Eugene blinked through the mask's eye hole. "He was a vampire, right?"

"For sure," said Tripp.

Eugene stiffened. "How do we know he's truly dead?"

"Because his brain is gone?" Tripp suggested.

Eugene nodded. "Finally," he said, overcome with emotion. "All of the Confederate general's training paid off." A tear trickled out from under the gauze and he waved his cast hand at the sky. "That's for you, great-great-great grandpa."

Tripp patted Eugene's shoulder and took the shotgun. "You saved the day, my friend."

"My mask got crooked," said Eugene. He looked at Victor and scowled. "I thought he was you."

"What?" Victor honked through a crooked nose and a split, fattening lip. He hobbled forward, favoring his damaged left hip, vividly imagining Eugene pointing the gun at him, hearing the crack of the gunshot, feeling his brain ringing in death. "You were going to shoot me?" He punched Eugene in the mouth, sending the Slayer toppling over backward onto the remains of Bob the appraiser vampire.

Tripp pulled Victor away and handed him over to Barbara. He righted Eugene's rickety wheelchair and pushed him into the house. "Victor," said Barbara, shrill as she contemplated the dead vampire on her porch. "You didn't have to do that."

"Yes he did," Eugene mumbled, gingerly touching his lips and removing his mask, which had again twisted out of position. "Because I'm never going to stop. You can punch me, you can impale me, you can have Renfield over there ambush me," he said, looking at Nikki.

"Hey now," she protested.

"You can throw me off a cliff," Eugene continued, glaring at Victor. "It won't stop me. I'll just keep coming back. You might as well turn me into a vampire, because that's the only way you're going to stop me."

"I'm not doing that, trust me," said Victor.

"Do it," Nikki urged.

"Nikki," Victor admonished.

"You're going to have to," said Eugene.

"Well I'm not going to," said Victor.

"Do it, I dare you," said Eugene.

"Do it!" said Nikki.

"Right here, right now!" said Eugene.

"Both of you, please stop saying that," said Tripp.

"Oh my God," said Victor, rushing for the stairs. "Amberly..."

Barbara kept hold of him and was towed a few paces. "She's okay. Victor, hold on.... Amberly's okay. I bandaged her and called for an ambulance. She's disoriented..." She touched Victor's lips, which were retracted in a perpetual snarl. His mouth relaxed under her fingertips, and covered his fangs. "Let's give her a moment. She doesn't need to see this."

Distress again weakened Victor's knees so that Barbara needed to support him, guiding him back to the dining area.

"Come sit," said Darla, pulling out a chair from the dining table.

Barbara steered Victor in the other direction, ignoring Darla and looking fondly at Tripp. "I'm so glad you were here. How did you know?"

"We owe that to Eugene too," said Tripp. "He wheeled into the Bank today, looking like hell—but not bad for a guy who was tossed off a cliff."

"Like I said," Eugene started.

"Huh-uh," Tripp cut him off. "So I'm following him around while he's gathering needles and syringes. When he told me he was coming over here, I tried to call, and then came right over. I knew you were gunning for Vic," he said to Eugene. "But I didn't know you actually had a gun."

"What were the needles for?" Victor demanded.

"None of your beeswax," said Eugene. He stood up and grabbed the plastic pouch of needles and syringes he had been sitting on, and stuffed it into his pants.

"You can walk," said Tripp.

"The paralysis was psychosomatic, as it turned out," said Eugene. "But I already had the wheelchair outfitted for battle. Darling!" he exclaimed and hurried forward as Amberly unsteadily emerged from the stairwell, carrying Porkie the Morkie.

Victor, limping and holding his back, still beat Eugene to his daughter. He started to cry as he hugged her. "I am so sorry," he whispered. Barbara joined the embrace as Amberly wept and clung to them, while Porkie whimpered and struggled to paw his way to the top of the clutch.

Eugene hovered, patting Amberly's back, cooing, "There there." His eyes fixed on the blood that had seeped through her neck bandage. "Hey now, tell me you didn't..." He reached in and peeled the bandage down to expose the twin punctures. "You did! Your own daughter!"

Victor put himself between Eugene and Amberly, and reapplied her bandage. "That was the other vampire, numbnuts."

As Amberly cried afresh, Barbara silently asked Victor, *What's going to happen to her?*

He had no answer. How was Bob's vampirism contracted and transmitted? The same as his? Victor had never felt worse as he met Barbara's desperate plea for reassurance with one of his own, looking at Tripp, who gave an extended shoulder shrug with an apologetic question-mark face.

Sirens sounded in the distance, quickly growing louder. Tripp soft-shoed to the dining table and set down the shotgun before joining Victor, Nikki and Darla on the porch. Neighbors had gathered on the edge of the Thetherson property, with more of the curious coming down the sidewalks. An ambulance rounded the corner and accelerated up the street, skidding to a stop in front of the house, crushing Bob the appraiser vampire's dentures with a little *pop*.

Two paramedics jumped out and came together at the foot of the walk, assessing the situation. Tripp looked down at the headless corpse with a grimace. "This would have been a lot cleaner if he had just turned to dust."

VICTOR

Victor Thetherson pulled into the McNulty Preparatory drop-off zone and put the sedan in park. From the passenger seat his daughter Amberly watched students interacting and meandering into the school building. After a bit she leaned over and kissed her father on his pale cheek.

"You sure you're ready for this?" said Victor.

"I am," said Amberly. "I'm going to miss you and Mom." She gave him a small, devilish smile. "Just not as much as Porkie."

Victor made a minor adjustment to her scarf, ensuring her bite mark was fully covered. "It won't be forever," he said.

Amberly blinked and carefully removed a tear threatening to run her eyeliner. "I gotta go." She got out of the car. "Bye Dad," she said, and hurried to join her classmates.

This was her first day back to school, almost two weeks after the attack. She had spent most of her time in her room, reading and working on the assignments Barbara retrieved each day from her teachers. Victor checked on her frequently, bringing her snacks, magazines and hugs, circumspectly inspecting her teeth. After some reflection, Tripp had wagered that even if Bob's curse was passed through the bite, the rabies vaccine in Amberly would save her. When she had gone a week of working on her tan and eating well-done meats, it was decided she was ready to return to school.

Likewise Victor had delayed returning to work. The night of the attack he had retreated to the basement to pace the floor until Barbara returned from the hospital with Amberly, after which he paced the basement floor for a few hours more. At daybreak he had taken a file to his fangs, grinding them to nubs while doing a fair amount of collateral damage to his lips and gums.

He could feel the repair begin immediately. By the following morning his fangs were again serviceable if jagged. Five days later, fangs, lips, gums, hip and nose were fully healed.

Meanwhile Victor's psyche had only deteriorated. He was haunted by the vision of the vampire attached to his daughter, an awful, revolting, parasitic sight. Every one of his bites—except the one on David Copperfield—was recast in his mind; he played them over and over, from a distance, watching alongside his victims' mothers, husbands, children and fathers, feeling their helplessness and listening to their wails of anguish.

Even so, each night a greater urge raged within him: to return to the Houston clubs and alleys to slake his thirst. No amount of Bank blood delivered by Tripp could satisfy the craving.

Last night, Chleber's secretary had come to the house to drop off files for him to review. Barbara and Amberly were shopping. Victor had sat with her at the dining room table walking through the documents, and then he had bit her.

Momentary sanity had returned quickly and Victor ended the embrace after less than a pint. The woman was shaken, but able to drive. She was not angry or particularly horrified, but Victor was. He had called Tripp immediately and set up his check-in for this morning.

Without a doubt the Rice University campus would be beautiful in the early fall sunlight. Enough humidity had left the air that the buildings would be glowing in vivid relief against the surrounding foliage and distant downtown skyscrapers, rather than swimming in near-aquatic summer swelter. Victor wouldn't know—he cursed the sun as he hurried head down and squinting from the parking lot, into the Longevity Labs.

"Mr. Victor," he was greeted by the Labs' secretary, new to Victor, cherub face with bleach-blonde hair parted far to one side so that it encroached on her face. He willed himself not to look at her throat. "Right on time. Go on to Room A. They're expecting you."

"Thank you." Victor knew the layout, knew to veer left, away from the exam rooms, into the research wing. Room A was a conference room where long, long ago young Victor Thetherson and his mother listened along with twelve other longitudinal study participants as the lead scientist explained the years of testing to come.

Dr. Regnald Speer sat on the edge of the very same table at nearly the same spot that Victor remembered Speer's predecessor perching, forty-some years ago.

"Victor," said Speer, tall and primly erect, suit and tie, close-cropped hair the color of his steely charcoal gray eyes. "Welcome. Tripp called us late last night with your decision."

Tripp stepped forward to squeeze Victor's arm, then retreated, ceding the floor back to Speer.

"We're all very pleased with your choice," said Speer.

"Won-the-lottery ecstatic," said Dr. Winnie Linciome, the only one sitting, forty-something and wearing a bowling shirt open two buttons, full good-natured face under a stylishly disheveled and tinted mop. His feet were up on the adjoining chair, creating a stable lap table for his e-pad. "When Tripp told us what you learned in Germany? Blew our minds. We've tested a few vamps—not all of them as willingly as you, you know, some bad boys and girls out there. If we can locate them, the correctional officials will usually let us talk to them and extract samples to our hearts' content. And so we can tell you that sexual transmission is *not* the way it's supposed to work. Not to mention the screw-and-you-die feature."

"We're getting a little ahead of ourselves," said Speer.

"Just to say that your case got us looking in a whole different direction," said Linciome. "One that could be groundbreaking. You seem to be one of a kind, Big V."

"I'll vouch for that," said Tripp.

Speer pointed in reserved fashion at Victor's suitcase. "I see you're planning to be with us awhile."

"However long it takes," said Victor. Chleber and Bizco had granted him a paid leave of absence. They understood the treatment was related to his vampirism; he didn't mention the intent, to end it. "I'm committed to helping you find a cure."

Speer's brow furrowed. He clasped his hands at his waist. "On that topic.... We are not a treatment center. We are a research institution. Our charter is very clear, and our investors are *very* clear in their expectations. We are here to advance our knowledge of the aging process, knowledge that in turn can be used to increase lifespan. We are not here to cure vampires."

"But we're going to do everything we can," said Tripp. Then he stopped talking, silenced by the backside of Speer's raised finger.

"That having been said," said Speer, picking up where he, not Tripp, had left off, "we view you as a special case. You have been part of the Labs' longevity study since you were an infant. That is a contribution we don't take lightly."

"You're super stellar," Linciome piped in, glancing up and smiling with the smallest of pauses in his typing rhythm on the e-pad. "That's a star, baby."

"We have a strong hunch that unlocking your mystery," said Speer, head bobbing, "unlocks ours."

"I am glad this works for both of us," said Victor. "It's come to the point where I'm a danger to everyone around me. I realize now—"

"That is an issue, frankly," said Speer. He bowed his head in contemplation. This was Victor's longest exposure to Speer. Tripp had described the researcher as a man who sought no one's counsel but his own, adding that a less charitable soul would have labeled Speer a pompous ass. "We're going to need to take steps to ensure our staff is not at risk."

"I will vow to you right now—"

"Your promises are irrelevant," said Speer. "Make all the vows you like, all well and good. We're going to rely on medicine. We're going to hook you up to a portable IV with a nutrient solution containing those elements of the blood that seem to be essential to the vampire's metabolism. We're also going to have you on a constant mild sedative that targets and blocks the portion of your brain that triggers your cravings."

"You'll be familiar with the feeling," said Tripp. "We took our lead from the rabies vaccine."

"We know what makes a vampire tick," said Linciome. "We'll also do our best to limit your contact with any of our particularly comely employees and grad students. Which Reggie has been threatening to do to me as well," he added, looking over his tortoise shell reading glasses at Speer.

"To soften the deprivation," said Tripp, "I'll let you have the pin-up poster of the medical training doll from the Bank. Perry made it for me."

"He didn't," said Linciome, slapping the table and grinning at Tripp, who nodded, sparking a guffaw from Linciome. "I gotta see that."

"The upshot," said Speer impatiently, "is that we will be controlling your physiological and psychological state to the best of our abilities. But should there come a point we can no longer control you, you will be ordered to leave. Do you understand?"

"Yes," said Victor. "You won't have to worry about me."

"Correct, we won't. Campus and Houston police are a phone call away." Speer turned to Linciome and Tripp. "Anything else?"

"Just welcome to the family," said Linciome. "I feel

like we just got a steal of a deal on a top-of-the-line, oversized research monkey."

Tripp hiked a thumb at the far door. "I'll show you to your quarters, big fella."

Victor extended his hand and received a quick limp shake from Speer. "Thank you for everything," said Victor. "This means so much to me."

"Mm-hm," said Speer. He moved past Victor, pausing at the door to give Linciome an order. "Get him hooked up to the IV and under sedation immediately."

"Sure Reggie." Linciome winked at Victor. "Tripp, you heard the man. Get Big Chimp on the sauce and mindbenders." He shook Victor's hand and held it, gripping it warmly in both of his, until Speer was gone. "Don't read too much into Reggie's Gestapo act. We'll make sure this is more than tolerable for you. This is going to be a great experience. I'm very glad you decided to take us up on our offer."

Victor nodded. "Thank you."

"Show me those fangs one more time."

Victor peeled his lip back.

Linciome whistled. He let go of Victor and looked at Tripp. "I keep waiting for Reggie to grow a pair."

"I'm afraid his bite would be just as bad as his bark," said Tripp.

With the unsnapping of the collapsible closet's canvas door, Tripp finished the brief tour of Victor's home away from home. "We didn't bust the budget on the furnishings, did we?" said Tripp, in reaction to Victor's sour expression as he sat on the cot contemplating the tube television set on the surgical cart in the corner. "But we did corral all the experimental rats that were running wild and free in here."

"Thanks," said Victor.

"That's a bigger selling point than you might think. For awhile, growth hormone was all the rage in the longevity industry." Tripp hunched his shoulders and showed his two front teeth and stomped about Godzilla-like, making the sounds of crunching buildings and exploding power stations. "Dr. Linciome recommended walling off this section of the building and letting the mongo-rats have it."

Victor smiled with his eyes. "So growth hormone is no longer the ticket to immortality?"

"Worse, it turns out extra growth hormone might kill you early. Gives you a lot of confidence in us, huh?"

"Lucky for you, I'm more of a research rat than a patient," said Victor. "No expectations. A workout wheel would be nice, though."

"Seriously, we didn't have much time to prep for you. I'll be upgrading the amenities over the next couple days, I promise. Including the human equivalent of the hamster wheel." Tripp gave him a wink. "Man I'm glad you're here. When that vamp was busting up your living room, I have to admit I was really keen to see you go ballistic and beat him to ashes. But in retrospect, seeing how well things turned out, that would have been the wrong direction."

"I wish I could say I'm sure this is the right direction," said Victor.

"First day at camp is always tough on the new kid," said Tripp. "By the end of your time here, we'll have to kick you out."

"Nikki seemed let down by my performance," said Victor, deflated by the memory of his beat down at the hands of Bob the appraiser vampire. "She's probably looking to join a new team as we speak."

"I'm not sure you two had the healthiest relationship in the world anyway," said Tripp. He witnessed Victor's skeptical reaction. "Who am I to talk? Is that what you're thinking? You're probably wondering whether I've considered my parents' horror if they were ever to pop in unannounced and find me in a nurse's uniform and clown makeup." He nodded at Victor. "Yeah, she's turned on by clown nurses."

A nurse in a blue smock knocked on the open door and entered, pulling an IV cart along with her. "Okay time?" she said.

Tripp arched an eyebrow at Victor and received his approval. "Hook him up, Marcella."

"Don't mind me," said Nurse Marcella, donning gloves. "Continue your conversation."

"Please don't make us," said Victor.

"Suit yourself," said Marcella. She swabbed the crook of Victor's elbow, looking at him under her eyebrows. "You're not the type to give up a vein easily, are you? That's okay, I like a challenge."

"Allow me to take your mind off all the probing and rooting around that Marcella is about to undertake," said Tripp. "I wanted to pass along a little info, before the sedation kicks in. It's only supposed to take the edge off, but depending on your tolerance, the first couple doses might hit you pretty hard."

"Mom always said I was susceptible," said Victor. "When I had headaches, she used to cut my baby aspirin in half. She wouldn't go to a full baby aspirin until I reached puberty."

"This isn't a psychiatrist's office, Vic."

Marcella clucked. "I'll start at the low end of the dosage, honey."

Victor pistoned his thumb, encouraging her to open the spigot. "La-la land sounds okay for awhile."

Tripp's thumb mimicked Victor's, seconding the motion. "So Darla stopped by."

"Really?" The news was a feather duster tickling the inside of Victor's stomach and chest. He hadn't seen or heard from Darla since the vampire attack. The tickle left when Marcella buried the needle in his arm. Victor patted a drum beat on the cot as an alternative to whimpering. "How come?"

"To threaten me," said Tripp. "Not in so many words. She wanted me to know that she'd be watching, and that we better not screw anything up. She seems to like you, with or without fangs."

"Sorry she got tough with you," said Victor. "I've seen her steely side."

"Sounds like a good woman," said Marcella as she taped the needle to Victor's arm.

"Marcella, you promised we wouldn't know you were here," said Tripp.

"No, I said talk freely," said Marcella. "I love listening in to juicy love gossip."

"Is it love, Viccy?"

Victor shook his head. "How would I know? I have no idea how to categorize my relationships anymore. It's too confusing."

"No confusion for Darla," said Tripp. "I couldn't say whether she *loves* you, but she definitely *likes* you. She likes you like a woman likes a man."

"Good for you, honey," said Marcella.

"Trouble is," said Tripp, "I'm just as certain your Barbara-doll feels the same way."

"Barb has been unbelievably good to me, considering," said Victor. "She's jealous of Darla. It's bringing back memories of when we first started dating. I have to say, I never thought I would have this problem."

"What can you do," said Marcella, adjusting the IV drip on the two hanging bags. "Vampires are sexy."

Tripp covered his eyes with one hand and pointed at the door with the other. "Looks like someone needs to take Dr. Speer's vampire treatment orientation session."

"A lot of girls see a vampire and think, 'Bite me, baby'," said Marcella.

"Out," said Tripp, continuing to point at the door. "But maybe you should ramp up that sedative before you go."

"No need," said Victor, looking to lie down. "I can already feel it taking effect."

Alone on the cot, Victor tried to focus on the television screen where Drew Carey hosted the Showcase

Showdown, the big spinning wheel warped by the impotence of the set's rabbit ears and the power of the drugs flowing into his vein. His eyes drifted to the ceiling, where the unbroken pearl-gray expanse allowed his vision to comfortably blur.

Darla's face was there, crystal clear against the fuzzy gray background. She was gazing lovingly at him—but which of his two images was reflected in those doe eyes? And now Barbara appeared, not floating angelic on the ceiling but poised on hands and knees atop him, her eyes hungry to make up for all the lost time. Only with a cure could Victor receive the gift Barbara offered. That in itself made the decision a no-brainer, he told himself.

But Barbara never had an appetite until his vampirism kicked in, and Darla hadn't witnessed him otherwise; she wouldn't *recognize* him otherwise. Fangs and a willingness to use them were the only reason he now enjoyed their affections. It was the only reason he was in Chleber's highly compensated employ.

Maybe best of all, Amberly now wanted to be his daughter. Everything positive in his life had come in the past two months, and all this good fortune was due solely to being a vampire.

Now Nikki's face appeared on the ceiling, making him jump. She was licking her lips and leering in a way Victor wasn't comfortable with. He looked back at the television, and had a similar reaction to Drew Carey.

As the drugs passed the blood-brain barrier and began to run interference with vampirism's synaptic activity, Victor Thetherson felt his newfound, beloved personality slip away. Fear gripped him, fear of the dull, ignored, irrelevant man in his future.

"Knock-knock," said Nurse Marcella as she entered the room. She had changed out of her formless blue smock, into a tight stretch top and flower print skirt. Her hair was loose. Marcella crossed the room and laid her hand on Victor's arm. "Just checking on you one more time before I head home." She eyeballed the drip-

drip of the hanging bags and had him show his IV entrance point, clucking at the slight bruising.

"I'm fine," said Victor, forcing a smile and focusing on the ceiling.

"Alicia's on duty now, right down the hall, so if this gives you trouble, or if you need anything, just holler."

"Will do."

Marcella's gaze lingered on the lips that had for just a moment exposed the vampire's fangs. "And I don't usually do this, but I'm going to swing by later this evening to check on you one more time. Just in case." She gave his widow's peak a motherly tousle. "Would you like me to bring you back something to drink?"

Victor turned his head on the pillow, bringing both eyes to bear. He held her gaze, before speaking. "Yes, Marcella. That would be wonderful. I do get thirsty at night."

THE VAMPIRE VIC TRILOGY CONTINUES WITH
VV²: MORBIUS REBORN...

ABOUT THE AUTHORS

Harris Gray finish their third pint and mull over their next writing project, simultaneously deciding on a vampire book. Because the women in their lives eat up every vampire story on the shelves. And for the gratuitous T&A. But hunky, smoldering vampires are beyond their grasp; and dammit, T&A should mean something. Deciding to write what they know, Harris Gray return to their wheelhouse: An aging, uncomfortable man, not so happy with his lot in life. A man bitten by a vampire, unsure what to do with his new...*skillset*. Vampire Vic – VV – is born. Perfect.

The website: harrisgray.com
The marketplace: amazon.com/Harris-Gray
The tweets: twitter.com/harrisandgray
The posts: facebook.com/HarrisGrayAuthor
The sharing:
plus.google.com/u/3/102066651638902173967
The community: www.goodreads.com/harrisgray